The Vindication of man

Count to a trillion :
book 05

THE VINDICATION OF MAN

THE
VINDICATION
OF
MAN

JOHN C. WRIGHT

TOR

A TOM DOHERTY ASSOCIATES BOOK

NEW YORK

This is a work of fiction. All of the characters, organizations, and events portrayed in this novel are either products of the author's imagination or are used fictitiously.

THE VINDICATION OF MAN

Copyright © 2016 by John C. Wright

All rights reserved.

A Tor Book
Published by Tom Doherty Associates
175 Fifth Avenue
New York, NY 10010

www.tor-forge.com

Tor® is a registered trademark of Macmillan Publishing Group, LLC.

The Library of Congress Cataloging-in-Publication Data is available upon request.

ISBN 978-0-7653-8159-0 (hardcover)
ISBN 978-1-4668-8280-5 (e-book)

Our books may be purchased in bulk for promotional, educational, or business use. Please contact your local bookseller or the Macmillan Corporate and Premium Sales Department at 1-800-221-7945, extension 5442, or by e-mail at MacmillanSpecialMarkets@macmillan .com.

First Edition: November 2016

Printed in the United States of America

0 9 8 7 6 5 4 3 2 1

This book is dedicated to the memory of Mr. David Hartwell,
my editor and my friend, without whose patient guidance and
support this work would never have seen the light of day.

CONTENTS

I that rather held it better men should perish one by one,
Than that earth should stand at gaze like Joshua's moon in Ajalon!
Not in vain the distance beacons. Forward, forward let us range,
Let the great world spin for ever down the ringing grooves of change.
Thro' the shadow of the globe we sweep into the younger day;
Better fifty years of Europe than a cycle of Cathay.

—Alfred, Lord Tennyson

PART EIGHT

———◆———

The Vast Desolations of Heaven

1

The Sound of Her Voice

1. A Bad Call

A.D. 68010

As he woke in his selective fashion, layer by layer, the central node version of Menelaus Montrose wondered if he had made a bad call.

Was he losing his nerve? Was he losing his mind?

Just to check, Montrose called a forum of his ulterior and inferior minds, including archived templates, remote units, and singles. The consensus mind briefly formed and ran through some twelve billion quotient-seconds of self-calculations, including that branch of specialized cliometry reserved for coordinate minds predicting their own behaviors over the long term.

Both the superhuman and subhuman versions of himself returned the answer that, yes, he was losing his grip.

"But why?" Montrose called out across the many channels linking his mind spaces together. "I am just the same as I always was!"

2. His House

Where the Mediterranean once had been was now a mountain range. What had once been the land between the Nile and the Congo was now an inland sea called Tethys. The southern continent was called Pannotia, and the northern Baltica. Millennia ago, when this northern coastline of Baltica had been inch by inch submerging into the Atlantic, Montrose had bought this tract of land on speculation, since the long-term tectonic plate movements planned by Tellus foretold that this land would rise once more above the sea in the seventeen thousand years before the return of Rania. And he grew and built a house here, relieved, for once, that he had no need to lock himself into a hidden and heavily armed subterranean tomb.

Years passed, and the land sank, and more passed, and it rose again. Hills to either side of him first breached the waves, forming an island chain, and the uplands rose, forming a peninsula, and now his land was in the midst of an isthmus reaching between the mountains of Cambria the plateau of Normandy. The hills and uplands of what had once been the English Channel pushed their green and pine-clad heads into the icy air, all save, ironically, the acres where he'd placed the main house.

So at the moment, he was somewhere under the waters of a loch, which was under an ice layer, in the middle of a diamond-walled mansion so old that it had been on the surface when last he checked, and so smart that it simply adapted to the changing environment, and replanted the hedge mazes surrounding the main house with sea plants and corals.

The diamond mansion had both roots striking down to subcrustal information cables and branches reaching up through the lake water to thrust naked twigs above the ice layer. These antennae grew or shrank as needed. They could receive and send signals to convenient orbitals or towers sixty thousand miles high, reaching from anchors affixed beneath the mantle to geostationary points in orbit. Through these antennae he could reach other versions of himself, in other stages and conditions of awareness, seated elsewhere.

3. His Hierarchy

At his cry of despair, somewhere in the depths of the logic diamond core of the planet, two of the Archangel-level supermontroses, beings of intelligence in the ten thousand range, exchanged information signals corresponding to wry glances, or prodding the inside of one's cheek with a tongue.

Meanwhile, a hypersupermonstrose, who existed intermittently at the Potentate level in the eight hundred thousand intelligence range, was like a looming statue in the background of the shared Montrosian thoughtspace. He sent a brief, sardonic message to the forum: "Oh, surely so. Poxing pustules on my peck! We's just as human as ever. Rania is almost here! Nothing else matters!"

But it was the singles, of intelligence between two or one thousand, some of whom occupied human-formed bodies in near-Earth orbit, or on the upper or lower levels of the vast space elevators rising by the dozen from Terra's recently formed unbroken equatorial mountain range, or bodies larger than whales swimming in the sea, or in the flooded tunnels running through the mantle of the Earth, who answered back, "You need a priest. You need confessing. Something gnawing at your gut, and you ain't man enough to face up to it."

"Why do you say that?" the central Montrose, still half-awake, demanded.

"What do you feel guilty about?" came the message from the consensus forum of Montrose-minds.

That particular central Montrose, who was in the act of waking up, his attention divided between the smarter versions and the simpler, suddenly halted the waking process.

Montrose said to himselves, "Guilty about what?"

No doubt it would have been quicker to wake the Potentate level version of himself, but such extraordinary minds used up extraordinary amounts of energy and infrastructure rather quickly. Unless he wanted to go out into the current world and work for a living—or beg or steal—to get the resources to support him and his infrastructure, it was better if the giant slept.

He was also haunted by the memory of a particular high-energy version of Montrose who once had been admiral of the Black Fleet, back in the old days, during the coming of Cahetel. He had slain himself, or let himself be slain, which was much the same thing. Whatever else had been in his memory and experience, thoughts, visions, dream, ambitions, ideas, everything from that slain version was gone. Montrose often put the lost section of his life from his mind, but it just as often returned, like a tongue that cannot help but seek out the hole left by a missing tooth. It was as if a stroke had left a blank spot in his mind.

"And what if the smarter version of me sees something I cannot poxing stand to see? Is he going to commit suicide also? And take me with him?"

They answered back, "Rania wouldn't like that."

Another version looked at the calendar. "Why am I waking up now? What has happened?"

It was the Sixty-Ninth Millennium. A thousand years before her return. The last tiny sliver of time. A negligible amount of time. A hiccough. He could do it standing on his head. One more nap, and she was here.

So why did he keep waking himself up?

The Potentate Montrose, buried in a matrix of black murk somewhere near the core of the self-aware world, renting part of the Tellurian Mind, answered softly, "Psychological weakness."

"You're poxing me."

"No pox. You were beaten by your mommy as a boy, and this made you strangle on apron strings from then to now. You are afraid of women; afraid you cannot be the boss, play the man, take command. You think Rania is too good for you."

Montrose said, "That ain't the reason. I don't buy it."

"You should buy what I sell. I am a far piece smarter than you, after all," said the Potentate Montrose.

The two Archangel Montroses, far less in intellect than the Potentate, but immensely smarter than the waking version who tossed and mumbled in his coffin egg and served as the mental phylum's central node, both said in slightly different wording, "But all our sins and fears and neurotic little twitches we built up over the years, they, too, get all big when we get all big. The black spot on a balloon expands when the balloon swells up, don't it?"

Central Montrose said, "I should be able to throw the clock out the window, shoot the rooster, turn over, stuff my head under the pillow, and go back to sleep. But I am tossing and turning. I thought things were . . . I dunno . . . settled."

"What's keeping you up?"

"I am just worried about whether I made a bad call, that's all. You know."

They did. He was worried whether the price he paid for that tiny little seventeen-and-a-half-thousand-year nap was too high.

4. While He Slept

He and Blackie had a deal. No more meddling in history, no more duels, no more nothing until she got back. They had not technically shaken hands on it, but Blackie had agreed! It had been so close, so soon, less than eighteen millennia! A pittance!

Dark ages followed bright in rapid succession. Twice more the aliens visited mankind with their horrid, irresistible power, scattering men to the stars. Dying and failing and sometimes prevailing, the pantropicly altered men of many new subspecies on the terraformed worlds now used the techniques pioneered by Montrose to create Pellucid, to stir their nickel-iron cores to life as Potentates; and those, in turn, took their fire giants, ice giants, and gas giant worlds within reach and, using the techniques pioneered by Del Azarchel, woke Powers to awareness; and those Powers, urged on in messages never heard by mortals by the dark agencies of Hyades, built Dyson clouds and Dyson spheres and macroscale structures in rings and hemispheres about their stars, gods beyond gods, self-aware arrays large as solar systems, called Principalities.

The chords and notes of the symphony of history changed, but the two great themes never ceased to clash: the urge for liberty, with each man free to calculate his own destiny and selecting his own place within the scheme of prediction, forever fought the need for unity, conformity, and, above all, predictability, without which long-term trade with Hyades was impossible.

The enmities between the Powers, who warped and bent the currents of predictive history to their dark will, were carried on in those children that so far surpassed them, as the gods in legend overtowered the titans: the Principalities of Tau Ceti, Proxima, Altair, and 61 Cyngi. A greater plateau of intellect, immeasurable, indescribable, unimaginable to biological life, was achieved, but not peace.

But Montrose, seeing that these convulsions and conflicts would not diminish the ability of civilization to decelerate and receive his approaching wife in her strange, huge, lonely vessel, kept his ageless vigil and slept through it all.

Throughout, Blackie seemed not to be doing anything sinister. What was he waiting for? What was he up to?

The nagging fear would not leave Montrose that his bargain with Blackie had been a mistake, and it all was going to explode in his face.

5. Duel to the Self-Destruction

But one of the remote Montroses, a man no smarter than Montrose had been back when he was only Mr. Hyde, a mere posthuman with an intelligence of four hundred, broke into the conversation path with a priority signal. "Worrying about Blackie is a fine hobby to keep a body busy while we wait. Beats whittling. But that is not the reason you keep waking yourself up."

"So what's the reason?" snapped Central Montrose.

Posthuman Montrose said, "We are still crippled by the limits of our own mental architecture. It don't scale up. The superbrains, the bigger they get, the easier they get to go crazy, easier to divaricate, easier to split into a zillion stray thought-chains, each squabbling like snakes in a mason jar. That is why Jupiter killed his bad ol' self, and don't fool yourself none thinking otherwise. Lookit here, smarty-pants Montroses."

An image came over the channel. Posthuman Montrose was dressed in a dark cloak and a wide-brimmed sombrero, standing near a grove of peach trees adorned with roses rather than peach blossoms. He was peering to where two men in armor stood in the near distance.

These were two more Montroses, both semiposthuman, each equal in body and mind, wearing the armor of duelists, each carrying the cubit-long iron tube of a Krupp dueling pistol.

They stood in a field of some species of bright red clover and pink grass Montrose did not recognize, some weed imported from another world, which should not have been able to grow on Earth. Behind them was a row of tall banners and standards of orange and gold whose meaning Montrose did not recognize, but a helpful familiarization file explained that these were privacy flags, attempting to emit encryption to ban the attention of media, gossips, and historians.

"I am here to kill myself?" Montrose muttered. "This is not a good sign."

The judge was dressed in the distinctive garb of a Penitent, barefoot in a white robe and conical purple hood of unlikely height, with a rope for a belt.

The men of the planet Penance were similar in build and look to Rosicrucians, since they were all descended from the sons of Cazi who had aided Montrose in stealing his starship, the *Emancipation*, back from Blackie, star-faring toward what was an uninhabited planet when they set out, but arrived to find a starving colony of Swans and Men from Albino and Dust, dropped there by the inhuman indifference of the Fourth Sweep. The ancestors of the Penitents half saved and half conquered these survivors and built a mighty civilization where men were free and secure.

The world had worked and woken to self-awareness in record time and launched a gigantic treasure ship back to Sol to prove the point of what a free world could build, arriving in the Fifty-Sixth Millennium.

Ah! Montrose grinned at the memory, because the ship, christened the *Prestor John,* had been outfitted at his suggestion as a huge fraud, crewed only by female astronauts prettier than their Fox Maiden ancestors and pretending to be from the lost and legendary colony at Houristan, the paradise of women.

For once, events worked out as Montrose's secret calculations of cliometry predicted, and as the Guild grew fearful of an imaginary empire beyond their boundaries, and ashamed of the example, so the interstellar slave trade waned and was abolished in many ports of call.

The recollection warmed him like an ember in a pipe. After a trick like that, fooling even the Archangels and Potentates and Powers, what need had Montrose had to stay awake and look after things?

A familiarization file helpfully explained that a domed city called Penitentiary still rested on a mountain in Asia on Earth, holding the environment and oxygen-charged atmosphere of that remote world, and proud and wealthy descendants of the ship's crew dwelled like their ancestors, and their daughters eagerly sought in marriage or for pageants and displays or events of less worthy sorts. By tradition, they hid their wealth, and walked abroad in humble garments, and were hated and envied nonetheless. Small wonder the duelists selected a man from that race to be their judge of honor.

The two Seconds assisting in the duel shocked him to see.

One was the rotund form of Mickey the Witch, whom all reports and all common sense said should have been dead countless centuries and millennia ago. His face was round and full of mirth, and his eyes were small and twinkled with cunning.

He was dressed in robes resplendent and lavish to the point of absurdity. Silks as black as raven's wing and scarlet like the cardinal's were trimmed with ermine whiter than the snowy owl. There were nine yards of cloth just in the sweeping sleeves whose hems trailed on the grass. His shoes had pointed toes so extravagantly long and tall Montrose wondered that they had impaled no passersby. And all this was adorned in gems and gewgaws and inscribed with trigrams and psalms and mystic circles and astrological signs from a dozen bogus systems of occultism. The tree of the cabala along the spine of his flowing alb was enhanced with sigils from the Monument. Most absurd of all was his hat, which was a cone a cubit high, with jeweled chinstrap and ceremonial earflap, tassels, scarves, homunculus mouth, blinking eyes, and brim of glittering moonstones.

The other Second was a girl, which was a shocking breach of tradition. Her body was perhaps eighteen, but from her stance and glance and tilt of her head, her mind was years younger. Her eyes were wide and wrapped in dreams, her lips pouty and pretty and ready for kisses, but her hair was an astonishing wilderness of purple that glowed with phosphorescence. She was naked except for a semitransparent, semiluminous garment flung casually over one shoulder that flowed and floated around her shapely limbs. It was a blue-gray material that seethed like a live thing, glinting with sparks of motion, like a nest of invisibly tiny numberless flying insects whose legs were so entangled to each other that the whole formed long, elegant sheets and pleats and folds.

He did not recognize her, but from the electromagnetic echoes around her head, his instruments detected that she had the directional sense of a migratory bird. She was a Sylph, a member of a race of airborne nomads so long dead that even Montrose's advanced brain ached with fatigue when counting the ages gone.

"Who the plagued roup is that?" Central Montrose shouted.

Posthuman Montrose, standing at the edge of the red field in a black hat and poncho, said, "You are an idiot."

An Archangel Montrose said, "That is Trey."

"Who?"

"Trey Soaring Azurine, the Sylph. You met her the day you discovered Rania had ripped the diamond star out of orbit, and was lost to you for thirty-three thousand nine hundred years times two plus change; and that same day, Blackie put his handprint on the moon. She went into slumber, one of your first customers ever, just to follow you through time and see what happened, how it all turns out."

"And why is Mickey here?" asked Central Montrose.

"For the wedding," said Potentate Montrose, looming like a sphinx above the thoughtscape, this mind too deep and rapid to apprehend. "For love."

"What wedding?" asked Central Montrose.

"You are an idiot, like our idiot brother said." The Archangel Montrose sighed.

"Thanks, I think," said the Posthuman Montrose. "Makes me want to shoot myself, sometimes."

Central Montrose looked through Posthuman Montrose's eyes by feeding a stepped-down neural flow from the posthuman into the optic centers of his brain. Now a large torpedo-shaped dirigible hanging just above the grove could be seen. It was a Sylph aeroscaphe, complete with serpentines dangling from its gondola to give it the aspect of a jellyfish. Montrose would have been just as surprised to see a gasoline-powered Ford Thunderbird from Detroit from the First Space Age or galleon from the Golden Age of Spain.

He looked at the girl's wild eyes and her strangely absentminded smile. "I dunno. That girl looks a little . . . unstable. Didn't she get shot in the gut or something? Wasn't she going to marry Scipio?"

The Posthuman standing on the field said, "It gets better." He stepped out from the rose-covered trees and directed his eyes to another point of the field. To one side, beyond the banners but near the rose trees, sat Del Azarchel in a Morris chair, eating popcorn from a paper bag, perhaps the only paper bag on Earth in this era. His smile was like the sun. He had waxed his moustache and combed his beard, and looked more like a goat than ever, or perhaps like some pagan god of old who danced in the wood and worked malice on unwary Greeks.

"Bugger me with a submarine! What the pestiferous epidemical plagues of hell is that whoreson coxcomb doing here?"

"Gloating," said the Posthuman. "Want me to go over and talk to him?"

"He is poxy up to something! He has got some scheme! What is he up to?"

The Archangel spoke again. "Off and on—and more off than on, due to energy budget constraints—we been watching him over the centuries, or having our Patricians do it, or Neptune."

"So what is he plaguing up to?"

"Your lesser version just told you, you stump-stupid, pox-brained buffalo. Gloating. That is what he is up to. He is watching us tear ourselves apart the closer she gets to coming home. Show him the last bit, little brother."

The Posthuman turned his head.

Opposite him, on the other side of the field, stood Rania dressed in a simple robe of white, her bright hair and brighter smile and eyes like an angel. The sight of her face was like twin daggers of light in through his eyes into the deepest part of his brain. The pain and longing and love choked his next thought.

But Posthuman Montrose said, "That's not her."

Central Montrose said, "What the pestilent pox is going on?"

"Turns out that there was some leftover false Ranias," Archangel Montrose explained, "made by our old pal Sarmento 'Makes Me Ill' a d'Or, or maybe from those experiments our friend Mother Selene halted, way back when."

The Posthuman said, "The lady is a Monument reader. She got found in one of our old, old tombs and woken up by some man or some god with nothing better to do. Half a century ago our time, the first message from the *Solitudines Vastae Caelorum* was picked up by ultrasensitive receivers—"

"—that is the human name for the attotechnology supership the aliens at M3 gave the real Rania. What the aliens call the ship, we don't know. The message is called the Canes Venatici Neutrino Anomaly—" supplied the Archangel Montrose, interrupting on a parallel channel.

"—and Number Six over yonder wanted to go through the Monument notations Rania sent line by line, and got this girl to translate for him, and spent too much time alone with her, and sniffed what she smelled like, and saw that place behind her ear when she turned her head, and sure looked like Rania's neck, white as a swan's neck and all, and so he done fell empty head over kicking heels in damnable love with her. Her name is Shiranui Kage-no-Ranuya-ko, the fiery shadow of little Rania."

It was the name of a Fox Maiden, a race long ago extinct on Earth, which meant she had come from a deeply buried tomb, or from the Empyrean.

"What's the fight over?"

"Number Five, that's our cousin there, says the only way to keep every version of Montrose willing and able to recombine into one person with one mind and one soul is if and only if we all have one purpose. Love for Rania. So Six says no, this is an exception, and Five says bullpox, and Six says up your nose, and Five throws down the glove and says get your Seconds and your shooting iron. Got it?"

Angrily, Central Montrose sent, "There was a message from Rania, and you did not wake me?"

The Posthuman sent back, "You should word your orders more careful-like. The message, it didn't have nothing personal in it, just cliometry equations to pull mankind back from the brink of extinction, so we did not wake you up."

Central Montrose said, "She would have put in a secret message just for me, hidden in the enjambments and negative thought-character spaces!"

The Posthuman said, "We looked. Weren't nothing. So we let you snooze. You wanted to slumber so damn much and just get the waiting over, right? And everything was all set, right?"

The Archangel added sardonically, "Besides, waking all us up at once, much less fitting every memory and personality growth back together into one system in one body costs money, and unless someone wants to pay me to do a historical essay starring my pox-awfully wondrous wonderful self, what skills we got this market here and now cares diddly-do about, eh?"

The sheer sass of the reply was a bad sign. Usually he was more respectful of himself. He looked at the numbers in his mind's eye, ran through the cliometric calculus, and got a nonsense answer. Some factor was missing from the equation.

"I don't know. Blackie never seems to run low on funds."

"Well, you're supposed to know," said one of him. (He was not sure which one. All of him sounded alike to him. He wondered if his other hims had the same problem.) "You! You are the central leadership node of our scattered personality here. You're the boss."

"Well, pox on you and the rutting donkey that you rode in on! You are the current version, who is supposed to keep an eye on events—and an eye on Blackie—and wake me when something needs fixing so I can sleep in peace!"

The Archangel chimed in, "Little brother, I ain't even sure how the market works these days, and I have an intelligence range north of ten thousand."

"I ain't as smart as either of you, but I read the day feeds," said the Posthuman. "It is a system that tracks a quantified form of liquid glory the Patricians drink and bathe in."

"What the hellific pox? Do you mean glory like bright light, or glory like the applause of the world at your reputation?" asked Central Montrose.

"Both and neither," answered the Archangel and Posthuman together. Those two had knit themselves back into a single system at this point. The debt register showed considerable expense just for those two to merge. "Don't worry. The Fox Maidens and the Myrmidons, back when they still existed, could not make heads nor buffalos about it neither."

The Potentate from the world's core said, "This problem is insoluble. If we sleep, we miss life and snore through dangers. If we wake, we change too much, and Rania won't know us. You have slept too long, and the signs of disunion and disharmony you see among the lesser versions of us is a by-product of Divarication."

But one of the duelists, Number Five, sent angrily, "It's not Divarication. It's madness. Your conscience is lashing you like Mom used to. That clench in your stomach is you trying not to puke up what you swallow of your bad deeds. And now Rania is getting close, and it is getting too late!"

Central Montrose sent, "What bad deeds?"

"Giving up on the human race. *You don't care what happens once Rania comes back!*"

Central Montrose had no reply to that, but he could feel segments of his mind rapidly trying to rewrite the thought, distort it, hide it from himself, and that made him sickly suspicious that Number Five Montrose was right. So he said nothing.

Number Five said, "You won every fight, even against artificial minds orders of magnitude smarter than you, because of one thing. They thought in the short term, the length of their lives, the life of their clan or their civilization, but no longer. You thought in evolutionary life spans, in the scale of geologic ages."

"Because the only damn thing I gave a damn about was geologic ages away from me," muttered Montrose. Several Montroses on the line muttered agreement.

"But now you've brought your eyes away from the horizon to the foreground. You are looking at tomorrow, when Rania comes, but not what happens the day after tomorrow."

"Why the poxing pox should I give a tinker's damn about that? Let the day after tomorrow pox itself for all I care."

"But she will care, won't she?"

Central Montrose sent, "If you are less smart than me by a zillion points of intelligence, and the Archangels and Potentates are smarter again by another zillion, how come you see this plain and none of us smarter than you sees it?"

"'Cause smarts ain't everything. Brains is most things, but not everything. I got a simple brain, a posthuman brain, and my little balloon of a mind is so small that the volume is clear compared to the surface and the light shines all the way through. You guys have more brainpower to monkey yourselves up with lies and brain-lard. Well, snap out of it."

"Snap out of what? I am about to shoot myself out there. Put away your piece, you maniac!"

"I got to kill all parts of me that don't love Rania," said Number Five grimly. And suddenly the channel went dead.

6. The Second Second

So there it was: a hard, cold certainty in himself that Number Six deserved to die for rutting with a Fox dressed up to look like Rania. He could think of nothing more viscerally disgusting, more worthy of death by gunfire. He did not want to recombine back into himself any memory-chains containing the memories of whatever thoughts or temptations or justifications he had used on himself to excuse adultery. It was an absolute in his soul: there was no debate, no second thoughts.

So, without thought, he combined himself with Number Five. It used up nearly all the credit in his account. By the time he raised his pistol and armed his countermeasures, there were two of him in the nervous system, pulling the trigger together. By the time he lowered the massive weapon and stepped heavily forward from the octopus-armed black smogbank of chaff and looked down at his dead opponent, he was one.

Melechemoshemyazanagual Onmyoji de Concepcion of Williamsburg hailed from the Fifth Millennium, an Era of the Witches during the ten-thousand-year period known as the Hermetic Millennia, in the long-forgotten years before the First Sweep, when mankind was merely the experimental plaything of Blackie del Azarchel and his fellow mutineers who survived the *Hermetic* expedition. His true name was Mictlanagualzin, but Montrose called him Mickey.

Now Mickey waddled over to help Montrose out of his armor, while the

Penitent judge gave an abrupt gesture to a grave-digging automaton carrying a coffin and a shovel. The machine groaned and stepped forward and shoved the blade of its shovel into the soil.

"Mickey, what the pox are you doing here, acting as my Second?" When the helmet hiding the face of Montrose came off, Mickey stepped back, raising his hand before his eyes. He could not meet Montrose's gaze.

"Ah!" said Mickey. "You have torn your soul in scraps, and now a larger fragment descends like a bat from the infosphere to possess you! Did I not warn you in ages past to have no traffic with the Machine? Now you are one." He shook his head sadly, and his jowls wobbled. "Alas! I hope you got a good price. I envy you. No more soul-selling for me."

"You didn't phlegming answer my question."

"It is not necessary to answer the gods, even ones, like you, who are insane and think they are not gods. Your mind is suffering from an interleaf conjunction. The memory should come back momentarily. Your avatar here knew me. I will be shamed if you have forgotten."

At that moment, the second figure who had served as Second during the duel, Trey Soaring, came skipping over, her eyes dreaming and focused on nothing in particular. She was a purple-haired Sylph woman from the Third Millennium, the same millennium when Montrose himself was born, only a few centuries after he was. Around her floated her garment of hunger silk; it was a molecular disassembly array shaped like a deep sari and cloak, or perhaps like a swarm of purple wasps woven into a solid sheet. She stared at the bridge of his nose but did not flinch back like Mickey did at the sight of the posthuman intelligence burning in the gaze of Montrose.

"Hi!" she said vaguely. "You've changed again. You have to stop doing that. It's *weird*." And she took a strand of hair around her forefinger and stuck it between her lips, as if suckling on it. Trey craned her head back to watch a flock of scaly and feathered urvogel fly over, half-bird, half-saurian creatures originally from Venus: including the anchiornis, the xiaotingia, and the regal aurornis.

With her head turned up and away from Montrose, she spoke, "He's your Best Man. It sours him when you forget."

Mickey did not look sour, but he did raise one eyebrow, and the decorative right eye on his absurd pointed hat above his right eye raised an eyebrow as well, but much higher. "I found my demonstrations of power were augmented by erecting shrines to you, and my shadow grew strong at my feet because your name touched my name. For three seasons, I dwelled hidden among the earliest generation of the Swans, and my name was great among the resurrected Witches."

Trey said, "I'll translate from Icky-Mickey jabber to groundling: he got famed up because of you, Judge Montrose. It weirdered him." She giggled and stared at her left hand, spreading her fingers. "Isn't that a word? Made him weirder."

Mickey said solemnly to Montrose, "Your life and mine were cast together in fate, Great One, intertwined like the DNA helix of the caduceus of the psychopomp. Then I dreamed a dream with the left lobe of my brain while my right lobe half was exalted by pharmaceutical—"

Trey jabbed her elbow sharply into Mickey's side. "Vent it!" she snapped.

Montrose stared in surprise. Trey was small and waiflike, like all her race, with hollow bones, so it was like seeing an eel taunt a whale.

Mickey frowned judiciously, nodded his head to Montrose. "I am become as you, and sought remotest futurity to seek my one true love." And he smiled down at Trey with such a smile that his shining eyes were almost lost in the folds and wrinkles of his cheeks.

Trey said, "And I came because I said I would. I want to see the wedding! Find out how the story ends."

Montrose now noticed on the left hand of Trey was a gold band. Evidently the custom of exchanging rings had still been remembered in whatever year the two had wed.

"B-but—Mickey! I thought you are gunna marry a bosomy Nymph or something?"

She saw his gaze and held up her hand proudly, wiggling her fingers to make the ring catch the light and glitter. "He gave up witchcraft for me. We got chased into your tombs again, but the Witches were afraid of you and would not follow. One of the old bishops you saved married us. Named Father Talbot. Married us to each other, I mean! I had to give up threesomes. I am not sure they were a good for me."

Montrose stared at the unlikely pair. The recollections of Montrose Number Five were settling into place in his associative memory.

7. A Glimpse of Memory

A.D. 67098

It had been not long ago. He (Montrose Number Five) and Mickey had spent an evening in a public house at the nearby Forever Village.

The village surrounded the foot of a beanstalk issuing from the tallest summit, a speaking peak called Baxianshan, high in the Mediterranean Mountains.

The oldest era of history maintained by the Eternity Circuits of the local Stability was from the time before the Great Silence, when the Teleological Conspectus had successfully crushed the soul of man. An immortal of the planet Odette called the Conservator of the Futurity had taken control of the bankrupt and mortgaged Tellus and had undertaken to organize all Earthly life for the benefit of far future generations, whose numbers and dispositions were planned in advance. The plan condemned certain bloodlines, cults, cultures, and peoples to slow extinction. In those long-lost centuries of yore, the Atavist were a dwindling people.

Those condemned by the Conservator included the sea-Atavists, the Nicors and Camenae, Rusalka and Merrow, and other remote descendants of the Melusine. Their place in the sea and aboard the Great Ships was taken by a Squaloid race of Moreaus. They were unwilling to live in houses on shore and were nostalgic for the undersea palaces in which their grandfathers dwelled before the Squids forced them into upright shore-shapes. In memory, they erected great structures in the hollow trunks of trees, coated all within with coral growths. For their own bodies, they assumed the shape of small, swift, delicate beings. This was in a vain attempt to produce breeds in their children low-mass enough to compete for berths on starships with the more microgravity-agile, but more massive, Squids.

It was a point in history when metal was obdurate and denied to men, so everything was grown rather than made. Thus the décor was elfin, fanciful, and alive. The chairs were obnoxiously large leaves, and the lamps were lightning bugs. There was a fire pit in the center so that the smoke wandered up the axis of the hollow tree trunk, with scattered tables and booths circling it. Coy and coquettish girls on stilts or dangling from wire harnesses served the human-sized customers on the floor or smaller-than-human patrons occupying shelves and nooks up the inner walls.

Odd as it was, the other quarters of the village, from centuries nearer to the current day, were more odd. They were dormitories and breeding stalls formed in blocky proportions that bespoke no concern for human notions of beauty, and with strangely uniform streets and tools, and neither cathouses with their red lamps nor chapels with their silver bells anywhere in evidence.

The two old friends had been drinking boilermakers, and Mickey was cheating by using a technique to absorb the excess alcohol out of his cells, and so he was steadily and slowly drinking Montrose under the table.

Montrose Five, if he had been doing his duty, allegedly was awake and active.

due to the activity of Montrose Six, who, if he had been doing his duty, allegedly to spy out what schemes, if any, Blackie was weaving while the calendar counted down to the day of her return.

As best as Six could find out, Blackie was running a gymnasium and fencing academy, to teach young and idle bravos the formalities and finer points of swordsmanship. It was apparently an art that never entirely vanished from human history. He also received a small stipend from a museum to give lectures about his past, and from a clioseum to give lectures about his future.

"So that is why Six took up with this false Rania," said Montrose Five. "Boredom. He got tired of watching a retired tyrant."

Instead of returning to slumber, as his contract with himself stipulated, Montrose Five hired a gunsmith, hunted up an armorer, and began making arrangements. His activity, in turn, came to the attention of whatever angel or ghost was guarding Trey's tomb, and thawed her, which triggered Mickey's thaw as well.

The strange, modern world to which Mickey woke had forgotten the art of building cities, and the various races of Plebeians, those who chose not to fret about tomorrow, nor map out their futures, lived in small villages of grape-bunches of hemispheres. These huts were made of what looked like baked glass or transparent satin or bubbles of invisible pressure solid enough to keep out rain and cold.

Looming above their groves and plantations, the massive mansions of Patricians reflected an austere design of rectilinear geometry, with many a pillared portico, ambulatory, or chalcidicum of unsmiling caryatids circumvallating solemn cloisters, crowned with entablatures ordered by the golden mean, or belvedere, tower, and clerestory windows reflecting the Fibonacci sequence.

But they built no railways, no roadways, no airports, nothing but bridle paths for riding cheetahs and carriage panthers, aeries for the leather-winged quetzalcoatlus. The immortal and inhumanly patient Patricians of the current day had no motorized means of transit, aside from the expensive and metaphysically dubious method of donning a suicide helmet to copy one's ghost through the senile Potentate at the world-core to be copied a second time into an empty body waiting elsewhere, leaving a trail of brain-clones behind.

So Mickey had taken in hand his charming wand as a walking stick, broadened his hat brim and lowered its crown to assume the aspect of a cockle hat, and pinned a scallop shell to his brim, the traditional attire in his day for wandering mages following a star.

He spent the better part of two years tramping the roads and working alongside talking apes and half humans as a deckhand on cog or knarr to reach the land north beyond the Mediterranean mountains.

Mickey shook his head. "You don't know yourself. You would never betray Rania, not ever. All our holy writings say so! Why, just in the ancient and uncorrupted text of *The Lion, the Witch, and the Warlord* is the story of how a man named Orpheus wanted you to release his wife from suspended animation and return to the sunlight of the surface, and he sang of your own lost love, of Rania, so that tears flowed down your icy cheeks in your coffin. You agreed, but only on condition that he walk blindfolded from the buried tomb system so that he could reveal the position of the secret postern door to no man. But when he did not hear the footstep of a woman behind him—"

Montrose slammed the heavy pewter beer stein to the wooden tabletop with a loud noise that interrupted Mickey. "Of course I am tempted," snarled Montrose, wiping the foam from his mouth with the back of his wrist. "The Fox girl looks just like her, talks like her. Just to hear the sound of her voice, I would die. But I ain't never been fooled by no clones, and she's not the first what's been thrown at me."

So then the talk turned to women.

Mickey asked him earnestly about conversion, and giving up witchcraft, and spoke of his fear that otherwise Trey the Sylph would not marry him. Montrose took a practical stance: "I am sure the hell-devils and hell-spooks you worship will understand, and if they don't, to hell with them. Man should have a forgiving God as his boss. Otherwise life is too tough."

"You don't believe in God," observed Mickey.

"Course I do! You can't say, *God Damn You and God Damn the Horse You Rode in On* and *Who Rode Your Mother and Put Her Away Wet, Sated, Panting, and Preggers,* no, not and really mean it, if'n you don't believe in God. B'sides, what would ladies do on Sundays, if they had no churching to do?"

"You think it's real?"

Montrose was not sure what that meant, so he said, "Gen'rally, I take things as I find them," and then he put his head under the table, looking for a spittoon. "What the plague? We in an era when no one chaws tobacco no more? Goddamn the horse their God's mother rode them on in on. Or whatever I said."

While Montrose had his head below the table, Mickey poured his shot glass of whiskey into Montrose's and drank his own beer unadulterated. "I cannot believe you masticate that archaic leaf while drinking. It's gross."

The answer floated up from beneath the tabletop. "The chaw kills the bad taste of the brew, and the brew kills the bad taste of the chaw."

Montrose pulled his head back up into view. Since Montrose had just used one of the boots Mickey had kicked off under the table as an impromptu spittoon, he thought it best to distract his drinking buddy. "So, brag to me, pard! Flap the lips! What's so good about her, eh? What's in her?"

Montrose turned off his perfect memory circuits so that whatever words he did not care to recall of the rambling and saccharine adulation of a man in love that was sure to follow would fade thankfully from his mind.

Nonetheless, the later recollection was clear: Mickey might not realize himself, but Montrose could see the reason. Mickey looked on Trey as a creature from the long-ago vanished age of gold, an age of splendor, when the machines were obedient to men, and the children of men drifted where they would. Aside from rare acts of piracy, it had been an age without war, without cannibalism, without slavery, without concubinage, and without the constant fear that one's own talking dogs or other slave-beasts would lose their power of speech, revert to wolves, and rend their masters, a fear that made those masters arrogant and cruel. All these things formed the inescapable pattern for all the civilizations the Witches during nine centuries had erected. Thus, for him, meeting Trey was like meeting a lady of Camelot before the treason of Guinevere, or a daughter of Atlas in the Western seas of mythical Atlantis ere the flood.

"But what the hell does she see in you? You are the rightly most uncomely man I done ever lay eyes on, and you've got the dumbest hat of all history. I know; I been through all history, and that hat is really the dumbest."

Mickey's jowls grew creased with stern indignation, the tall hat stiffened so that its point quivered, and the cartoon eyes above the hat brim glared down. "To insult a Warlock's headgear is to trifle with the wrath of Fortunato and Hades and dark, brooding Alberich! My millinery splendor is tall due to my pride of power, and this pointed cone distills astral and celestial essences directly into my Sahasrara, which the vulgar call the *crown chakra*, the seventh primary node of spirit! The wefts and shades and poltergeists flinch and bow the knee when the shadow of this towering—"

"You should marry the girl just so you can get a proper Christian hat, and leave the shady polecats of wherever-the-pox well enough alone. I'd say a Stetson. She ain't marrying you for your hat. I know. She ain't blind in both eyes."

Mickey leaned back and smiled a jovial smile. "Perhaps she thinks me solid and massy!" He slapped himself in the belly hard enough that ripples walked up and down the expensively silk-clad rotundity of that expanse. "I understand that in her day and age, all the men were frail and thin, with hollow bones like birds, to save on lift expense, so that only the truly rich could afford to gain mass. Or maybe it is because I make her laugh?" He spread his hands and shrugged. "I know the secrets of Earth and Air, of Red and of Black, the speech of birds and the secret lore of sea crabs, and can read the entrails of an ox to know the future—but who understands women? All I know is that no man is more fortunate than I am. I don't know what she sees in me."

Montrose said, "Damned straight. That's always the way, ain't it?"

They clanked their beer steins together and called out cheers. "Blessings of the Bacchants!" "Here's mud in yer eye!"

8. The Right Question

When this memory surfaced, and fell into place with his other memories, Montrose swore a blistering oath, calling down the names of diseases long extinct.

Because Five had been disobeying, he had not communed with the central mind nexus, never had a second pair of eyes look over his experiences, and had never seen the obvious.

"If only I had not been so afraid of me," Montrose said, "I would have hooked into more brainpower and seen it!"

"Seen what?" said Mickey, startled.

Trey was looking troubled. "So you think I should not have given up three-somes? Icky-Mickey weighs as much as two sex partners combined, and the priest told me—"

Montrose said to him, "Seen this." And then he said to her, "Trey, snap out of it. Focus your attention. What did the other version of me, Version Number Six, hand to you for safekeeping before he died?"

Mickey said, "What is going on?"

Montrose said, "I've been sleeping badly, not been myself. I am fretting and scared that she won't know me when she returns—for her, it's been a few years. I am fretting and scared of what happens to the human race once she's back. If'n we settle down and live out a normal life, while Blackie slumbers and wakes and makes more ghosts of himself each time he wakes—what then? She must be thinking the same thing. Only now, only now, did the thought leak up from my hinder parts of my brain to the front, and I can see it. She must be fretting, too. About the same thing, about what happens when she lands. So she should have sent a message, but not in the open. I did not know what was keeping me awake. Now I know. The silence. Then damned pox-damned triple-damned silence from the stars. Where is her voice in the stars? She should have damned called to me. I kept asking myself, deep down, in thoughts so hidden even I could not see them—why didn't she send a message? The speed of light is faster than near lightspeed by definition. But that was the wrong question."

Mickey said, "What was the right question?"

Montrose said, "The right question is not, *Why ain't there no damned message?* The right question is, *Where is the damn message?*"

"Your pardon, but those seem to be the same, or much the same—"

"Not at all the same, Mickey! The right question has faith that she sent one, and asks about how to set about looking for it. Only the smaller and stupider mes was in touch with his instincts well enough to see that. And so—" He turned to Trey again, saying, "What did Number Six hand you?"

9. The Needle

Trey laughed and pulled a round leaf from a belt pouch. Through the leaf were thrust a number of pins with colored heads in order like a color wheel. Trey plucked out from the center of the leaf a pin with a red-and-white head, and held it out toward Montrose with a strange, eerie smile.

It was the first thing made of metal, aside from the weapons and armor of the duelists, Montrose had seen since his waking. The pin was three inches long, glistening in the girl's fingers, and a point of light gleamed at its tip.

Another version of himself, connected electronically through his nervous system, said helpfully, "It is a memory needle. There is a way of storing information even more densely than the picotechnology of our day. Something to do with the enjambments and overlaps of quantum fields—it is a praxis that Rania sent back when her neutrino message reached the world fifty years ago. Apparently she discovered how to make a gravity laser, just something she invented for herself, cobbled together in her spare time, and this is one of the spin-offs. The newer versions of the needle, you do not need to stick into your flesh to read the info. It will adjust to the antique receiver ports you already have built into your brain. Just pick it up in your hand."

Montrose stared at the needle, but did not touch it yet. "What the pox is going on? Why did I die? For this damned thing?"

Trey said, "This blessed thing. You all misunderstood yourself so badly, so very badly. No one but Shiranui the Fox-Rania was enough like Rania to figure out where she hid her personal letter to you. Shiranui would not agree to turn over her results unless you agreed to marry her. You did, and you did not lie to her. Number Six could not tell you what he was doing, because that would make his promise to Shiranui false. You knew you would die at your own hand on his wedding day, but before the wedding night, this one hour, so that you would never be unfaithful to Rania."

"Why?" he asked. But he knew why.

He looked at where the false Rania, Shiranui, was standing by the side of the field. She had not bothered to come forward and mourn at the burial mound.

Shiranui must have had very good hearing indeed, or else have been connected to listening instruments, or else have been a good judge of character, because when the gaze of Montrose fell upon her where she stood across the field, without moving her lips, she sent a message directly into his brain. His normal barriers and defensive brain encryption neither detected nor even slowed the source of the words: *My reason is simple. You will live until the end of time, and either as wife or widow, the memory of me will last. I believe in no gods: this is the only immortality to which a Fox Maiden can aspire.*

Trey said, "Just as I put you in the armor, you handed me that pin and told me."

"I would die to hear her voice again," Montrose muttered, and he took the pin.

It was an audio file, but it silently fed directly into his auditory nerve. He heard her words, and they were private. *True love neither years nor lightyears can abate, nor any yawning gulfs, my husband, of these vast desolations of heaven . . .*

2

The Vindicatrix

1. The Voice Message

A.D. 37000 (EARTHTIME) OR CIRCA A.D. 2466 (SHIPTIME)

True love neither years nor lightyears can abate, nor any yawning gulfs, my husband, of these vast desolations of heaven. To your ears alone my words are meant: I will not share my tears with strangers.

I must be curt, for the information density even of a neutrino cascade is limited by Heisenberg and Planck. Let me say in a few words what a torrent of words could not express: I have never forgotten you nor failed you, Menelaus, and I keep the faith that you will somehow find a way to be alive, find a way to endure through all the ages of time, which vanish in a heartbeat for me, centuries while I blink a tear from my eye, millennia while it falls toward the carousel deck, toward the weird, distorted stars of this universe near the speed of light.

The ship seems of normal mass and length to those on board, of course, but amidships is surrounded by a rainbow of starlight compressed into bands of color. Aft is the glow of creation, the super-high-frequency echoes of the Big Bang, Doppler-shifted down into the visible range to form a bright cloud of spirals within spirals. The Big Bang looks like a Saint Catherine's wheel, like fireworks. Fore is the ultra-low-frequency embers of the background radiation, three degrees above absolute zero, looking like a web of coals and ash, sculpted into an oddly symmetric pattern that contains one of the central mysteries of creation.

I am now the only one aboard. The starship of my stepfather, the *Belleroph-ron*, overtook us at the Diamond Star, for we had no choice but to decelerate for fuel. Niven's law states that every starship is a weapon, for any machine able to accelerate such masses to lightspeed controls such power as can break planets. The two ships found themselves in a standoff the moment they came within firing solution range of each other's sails, but the ghost of my stepfather could not bring himself to kill me, and I could not bring myself to foreswear my mission, my faith in mankind, my resolve to prove to the heartless cosmos we are worthy of sailing the stars. For this reason I was born.

It is best to say cruel things quickly: I left you. To save our dream, yours and mine, I resolved not to return to Sol for you.

He challenged me, saying that if I had faith in you, I would depart the galaxy and know you will await my return. If I agreed, he would meld his ship with mine, doubling our supply of needed goods and granting us the calculation power needed to convert the Diamond Star to a reaction mass.

It was calculation ability I needed. The engineering would have been impossible without him. The *Bellerophron* was disassembled and reassembled along the spine of the *Hermetic* and became her after sections. The combined ship anchored herself magnetically to the lee of the star at 300 AU trailing behind, in a vacuole my design placed in the pattern of sunspots, which were the exhaust chambers of a sun turned into a rocket. We took flight trailing behind our engine.

Never has there been so much fuel mass for so little payload! The star was held before us as a shield against the fast-moving particles, made absurdly dangerous by our velocity, each grain of dust more massive than a neutron star. But any explosion of our sun merely increased our speed.

When I later discovered how to impart a gravitic eddy to the planetary core and trigger a supernova, my speed much increased. Do you know what my greatest fear was then? That astronomers on Earth would detect the burst of radiation and think my ship had been destroyed in a collision.

2. The Rituals of Serenity

I have not enough words to praise the bravery of the crew. It was not physical dangers they faced, though those were great, but the endless pressure on the human spirit of the emptiness of an indifferent cosmos.

The crew was human and regarded me, during their watches when they woke from suspended animation, with increasing reverence and love that I was careful not to allow to grow into an idolatry. The Monument we towed, and I established a small pressurized hut anchored to its surface that I might study the symbols and their layers of meaning.

Within that deeper message, I saw what to do, say how cliometry could operate even at the smallest scales, if one were willing to make the self-sacrifice needed and never to surrender to doubt, to fear, to expediency.

Then there came the single, still hour when I meditated within the armillary sphere of the bridge, when I suddenly understood from the Omicron Segment how to augment my intelligence vastly. It could be done to me with the wire-to-nerve systems I already had established with Ximen's Iron Ghost, as my neural makeup was already based on Monument sequences. But I saw it could not apply to the human crew with me, without a rewrite of the genetic basis of their nervous systems and the neural basis of thought. If there had been a hundred Ximen emulations with us, that answer might have differed.

But if the gulf between captain and crew opened too wide, the cliometry, as well as my troubled heart, showed that if they came to fear me or came to worship me, then mutiny was inevitable.

I quietly resolved in that hour to defy the inevitable. I had faith in my men, in their loyalty. They would sculpt their own fate.

So we played games. I instated rituals of my own invention based on a microscale cliometric model. These included small customs, exchanges of words and salutes, but also used the recreation times and a scoring system of heraldries and displays to fortify the faint. Games alter outlook, introduce intellectual vectors, train the amygdala, and can be used to emulate behaviors, form metaphors, promote loyalties and sportsmanship. It was what my father, the original captain, never imagined. I don't think even Narcís would have killed a man who had been his spinward goalie in the cargo-bay ball playoffs.

One set of game rites allowed me private time, each year I woke, with each crewman, one by one, a shared ritual meal. By this I could learn and understand. I could know to which watches and rites and teams to assign him. Also, I had the ship's chaplain reinstitute the old, old sacraments of confession and Eucharist to strengthen the souls of the whole complement.

And yet, despite all, the darkness was so vast.

Departing from the dust cloud surrounding the galaxy decreased our risk of death by collision, but also cut our fuel supply. The star's magnetosphere had been converted by the ring of starlifting satellites to a ramjet scooping up interstellar hydrogen. That was Ximen's doing. He is a clever one.

After the Diamond Star was exhausted to half mass, crumbled into a neutron star, our ship flew without any cheering light as our bow lantern.

The starless darkness, the sight of the white fires of creation behind us, the coal-red glow like purgatory ahead, it preyed on them. At half mass, the crew knew that I could not have returned the ship to the Milky Way even had I ordered it, only brought us to rest relative to it.

3. The Mutineers

Ximen, as my first mate, was cruel, insisting only strictest rigor would keep the humans at their posts. I unfolded the cliometry, which showed this was not so, but he could not follow it. Ah, I underestimated how wounded he would be to know himself not the wisest one aboard! I asked him to trust me, and both my heart and the calculus of cliometry showed he would. But both were wrong.

During years while I slept, he spread madness through the crew, and the strange belief that their lives on Earth were a dream, a computer simulation, that Ximen had created the small, warped, starless universe we inhabited, including our false memories. The universe was no bigger than our ship surrounded by the smeared light of an egg of distorted spacetime.

Ximen, without my knowledge, had stolen cells from my ovaries and bone marrow. It was a theft of my very soul, a rapine and an abomination I pray I will someday learn how to forgive. By the time I had discovered, they were fertilized and could not be destroyed. Why he did this, what he intended, seems clear enough: to raise up another captain in my place, for the cliometric extrapolation would not allow this ship's delicate psychological balance long to be preserved without me, or a substitute of me.

That part I understand. The larger question, even now, I do not. Why did he conspire against me, when he must have known I would foresee it? How did he imagine that I did not know? Did he think my forbearance was weakness? But he knew me better than that. He raised me.

I woke and spoke to the would-be mutineers long before the watch when they planned to take up arms and hostages, and offered them mercy and wives. I knew how to bring my many twin sisters to term, just as I had been, by using the medical coffins as artificial wombs; and I promised that the children of the loyal crewmen born of these daughters, once mature, would augment themselves to my level or beyond. I offered them a dream better than the sick dreams of Del Azarchel.

All but one agreed. The court-martial condemned him to death by recycling, but I commuted the sentence to close confinement to his slumber coffin.

4. The Daughters of Rania

More years passed, and the girls grew. It was cheering to have little ones aboard, bouncing from bulkhead to bulkhead, and their fathers loved them dearly. Now I understood what had kept my first crew alive, what my role had been. We are designed to live for others.

But then my little girls, intelligent and erratic, one by one by one, started to go mad. It was divarication errors. I cannot speak of this tragedy but most briefly.

After years of study, I saw a hidden meaning, as if there were an older and original Monument hidden beneath a redacted version. The editing was not clumsy, but the older authors cleverly had hidden symmetries of meaning, like internal rhymes, so that any changed segment which did not change the parallels in other segments could be easily seen.

My girls, born from my genes, which had been based in turn on mathematical symmetries detected in the Monument, were born with my errors, with all the faults in me that you corrected. These faults were built into the Monument by the redaction layer, the later editors who had changed the Monument.

Who or what these Monument Redactors could be, they have wrought a grievous wrong to me. Alas, my girls! They slew you. Why had Hyades done such a wrong to us?

And caring for you when you were Stinky Baby was one of the things I had which my sisters lacked. And then after. My sisters did not have you, a rock and a solid foundation for the soul, a love to be their lantern and show the path ahead.

The girls damaged the ship while experimenting on it and crippled essential systems. What they were trying to do, to this day I do not know. Their minds moved in areas beyond mine.

I saw what needed to be done to restore them, to repair the divarication. I had learned from experimenting on you. It was the same as when I was a teenager, when I was first made captain; it was the same as when I used to chase my stinky baby as he bounced, naked and laughing, from bulkhead to bulkhead, leaving balls and clouds of vomit behind him in the zero gee. My crazed genius.

But there was not enough emulation space. It could not be done even if we deleted and erased Ximen entirely from the ship's brain. I knew what needed to be done and could not do it.

We decided to confine the girls to quarters while I experimented with growing more logic diamond in a mass towed behind the ship. The pressurized hut perched on the north pole of the Monument was the best place, for a number of reasons, not the least of which was it gave them useful work to do, and this quieted their manic-depressive cycles.

5. The Monument Core

Then they discovered the layers of Monument code hidden in the core of the sphere, and another layer hidden on a microscopic level hidden within the Monument texture, and a third layer on the molecular level, and a fourth at the atomic level, the hadron level, the lepton level, the preon level: seven levels of message occupying the entire volume of the Monument object.

Certain segments of the Monument could be used as matrices to interpret deeper volumes. At the mantle layer surrounding the core of the sphere was written the secret of how the Monument itself was constructed.

Perhaps you recall Dr. Chandrapur's estimate of the Monument complexity. He had no idea that the whole volume in eleven dimensions is the message, with each layer written at each order of magnitude converging or diverging from the others to add additional levels of nuance. I have run the numbers. The Monument Builders were not attempting to communicate with any civilization smaller than a Kardashev III level, a civilization occupying an entire galaxy, or a precocious dwarf galaxy, and using all the matter and energy, dark matter and bright, within the volume as a calculation engine.

It is an intergalactic message.

Who wrote it? Who sent it?

The surface math is nothing more than an introduction or overture, simple enough that any mind, even mortal minds in biological bodies, can emulate and grasp it.

It is not made of normal matter occupying normal spacetime, which is why the black segments are immune to all chemical and atomic reactions, and the silver line material reflects any phenomenon propagated through timespace. The secret of its fabrication went beyond nanotechnology and picotechnology, finer than engineering molecules and atoms and hadrons and leptons. This was made by manipulating the spacetime foam itself at the Planck level. It was attotechnology.

The core itself beneath this mantle was hollow. There, buried, embedded in the black nonmatter, we detected the presence of working models of the tools of the Monument Builders.

6. The Dimensional Instruments

There were layers and samples of rare or artificial particles held in suspension, including the strangelet and the sparticle, and we saw examples of the preon, the graviton and graviphoton, the tetraquark and the pentaquark, and varied hybrid mesons, and a pure mass of what we called the glueball, which had no valence quarks at all.

The instruments of the Monument Builders consisted of five exotic-matter solids, including dark matter bodies with negative mass or imaginary mass; and within a negative mass dodecahedron were found three steady-state vibration objects, small as hadrons, made of matter-energy in configurations that do not occur in nature.

One of my twin daughters, Regina, said these three impossible objects were configurations of other possible universes which could have issued from the Big Bang but did not. In our universe, three dimensions of space and one of time unfolded from the primal singularity, with the other seven dimensions of quantum chronodynamics still folded into no larger than the Planck length, and forming the basis of the fundamental laws of nature, the fundamental ratios like pi and the square root of two. The three impossible objects, she said, were models of energy-forms left over from the Big Bang, relics of string configurations that never emerged into our spacetime.

I said they were tools. The Monument Builders knew that the only way to reconfigure matter-energy from natural forms to these unnatural forms was only with one of the three unnatural forms. A three-dimensional tool could not flip a three-dimensional string into a four-dimensional knot, but a four-dimensional loop of string, reaching down to pull it, could.

7. Tau Leptons

I do not know what my mad daughters did, or which one of them performed the experiment, or how they smuggled the equipment from the ship's gravitic eddy induction lance to send a needle beam through the core of the Monument, and manipulate the three impossible object samples at the core of the Monument.

The fourteen billion metric tons of the Monument unfolded briefly into eleven dimensions, a white and many-pointed star of particle streaks caught like an Escher drawing in our high-speed plates; and then it all imploded, with each particle rotated and remanifested in the form of tau leptons. These then decayed into quarks, antiquarks, and tau neutrinos in less than two-tenths of one-trillionth of a second.

Any objects on or near the Monument but not made of Monument material, such as the instruments, the pressurized hut, the life support, the library cube, the reading spiders, and, of course, all the daughters and the five men on duty as nursemaids and tutors—they all suffered instantaneous fission, during the picoseconds when the laws of nature no longer allowed for strong nuclear force to hold their electron shells steady. The atomic explosion released particles that lasted longer than tau leptons, long enough to expand outward and penetrate the push-plate armor and rake the aft with gamma radiation.

Perhaps in another universe, one with more room in one of the seven collapsed dimensions, tau leptons might have existed longer, long enough for my daughters to realize they were dying, to say a last prayer, to say good-bye. But not this universe.

8. The Suicides

The damage, physical and spiritual, could not be repaired. More systems failed as decades passed.

This ship was my home. I was born on her. Now it was a vessel of mourning. All our rites and games turned to expressions of grief.

And yet she was still the *Hermetic*, the greatest vessel ever to sail the stars and the dark beyond where stars end. She would not fail her mission.

The magnetic tether holding us to the bowsprit neutron star was severed so that deceleration brought us into contact with the star mass. We could not survive the gravity, but had to retire permanently to suspended animation, waiting and hoping for the ion drive our robots had constructed out of the starlifting mines on the fore side of the dead sun would hold out against particle collisions.

But the cloud of gas surrounding the star cluster of M3 was unexpectedly denser than that around the Milky Way. The dead star endured near-lightspeed collisions with motes too small to see, but which, within our frame of reference, were more massive than Jupiter. Several configurations of magnetic fields and ionic reaction induction arrays were tried, but I could not find a way to have my exhaust issuing from the fore hemisphere of the dead star without placing some equipment on that side of the star, hence without a stellar mass to act as a shield between it and the deadly dust.

Then Ximen committed suicide.

He thought I could bring peace wherever I was. Perhaps I can, perhaps not, but I cannot bring life to one whose love for life is gone and whose impiety allows him to mar the human soul within him, yes, even within a machine.

I stayed awake at the microphone for nine long watches, talking to him, trying to reach him. Had you been here, my strong darling, you would have thought of something. You are not very bright in some ways, but you see things with your heart I cannot. You understand Ximen.

My heart was cold and lonely then. Yearning for you, I saw nothing.

If only some of my old crew had been here, they would have saved the Iron Ghost of Ximen. How I miss them! Artiga and Avenzoar, Echegaray and Falero, Zacuto and Zuazua! I think I miss Sarmento most of all, whose name means *golden isle*.

There had been a bond of unity among my stepfathers, the brotherhood of a gang of pirates who share one guilt, the compassion of a family with only one daughter, a pride in being the first men to sail the stars. It was a unity which I could not reproduce.

Ximen is from Andalusia and lived his life in war; D'Aragó (as his name says) is from unhappy, plague-burned Aragon; Father Reyes is from Goa in India, and he suffered for his race as well as for his faith; Sarmento i Illa d'Or is from the Saint Simon's Island, and lived through the turmoil as Florida and Georgia rebelled against their Cuban overlords. All were rough men from rough times. Ximen thought that life requires sacrifice.

Perhaps it was not suicide. I pray it was not. Is it suicide when a man thrusts his living body into a hull break to save his crewmates from decompression, even though he dies himself?

Ximen redirected the ship's power away from himself and into the gravitic lance. The long axis of the ship was blasted and burned, and all instruments overloaded, but not before Ximen successfully triggered the collapse of the Diamond Star entirely into a singularity in such a way as to form two vents, fore and aft. Even had the bore of the instrument not shot through the logic crystal of his brain, there was not enough power available to maintain his emulation and to overload the lance.

The fore vent of the collapsed star continued to slow us down from the insanity of warped near-lightspeed ever closer to normal spacetime; the rear vent I caught in my deceleration sails, and thus the neutron star decelerated the vessel as it pulled ahead.

The visual hemisphere ahead and behind the craft grew normal. We could see the half million stars of the M3 cluster in our direction of motion, and the vast, luminous spiral of the milky way, round as a shield, directly off the ship's rearward-facing bow. Of the strange wonder of the galactic core, the meaning of the signals hidden in its polar x-ray vent, what I saw and deduced as the first astronomer in human history unhindered by intervening dust clouds, I will tell you when we meet again, for I will not speak of divine things where alien machines might overhear.

Despite all, our deceleration was not enough. Ximen had known his death was a magnificent but meaningless gesture.

The simplest calculations showed that we would pass through the star cluster at half the speed of light, out the far side, and back into the starless dark, never to encounter any star nor world or molecule again, and moving too slowly for there to be any appreciable relativistic effects. We were fated to pass through and face a void too empty for any hydrogen ramjet, even one whose intake cone was larger than the outer orbit of a solar system, to gather fuel.

The slumber coffins broke down. Without Ximen to run the genetic emulations, crewmen were waking with cancers and neural aberrations. Doomed, childless, our mission a failure, lacking all hope, while I slumbered, one crewman committed suicide, and then a second.

I foreswore all slumber thereafter, greatly blaming myself. Ximen thought I could bring peace. What use is bringing peace if the threat is not war but despair?

9. The Emulation of Hope

I searched the records of the Monument carefully, looking to see if there were other codes for messengers and emulations like myself, messengers to bring hope.

I found something. Something odd. I coded the Monument notation line by line into the empty crystal core of the *Bellerophron* section of the ship. I made my own little ghost, and it woke and spoke to me and told me what to do.

How like you I turn out to be! I made the cocktail of neural alterations just as instructed, and prayed, and meditated and injected myself.

In a dream I saw the unity of all things, and I walked outside of time and space. Here, there was another mind, in sympathy with mine, though vast beyond all description, issuing from one billion lightyears away. Because we both had entered the same framing sequence of synchronic semiotics, the ideas or forms overlapped, and we touched mind to mind. I was a droplet touching an ocean.

I woke the crew, and I spoke the words the massed coalition of living minds Corona Borealis Supercluster of Galaxies had instructed me. I told them of the hope beyond the universe. I told them how small our current mission was and what the greater thing was that awaited us.

There were no more suicides then, no more talk of mutiny nor despair. We all knew it was not willed that we should fail, even if it were willed that we should die. Gaily, and with joyful hope, I and my crew awaited we knew not what.

For the ship began to slow more rapidly than the exhaust vent from the neutron star could account for. We checked and rechecked the readings, but there was no mistake.

It was a miracle. If only Ximen had waited for it.

A beam of energy from M3 had found our sails and was imparting deceleration momentum. The aliens had reach across space with their strange hands, spread their fingers, and caught us.

10. The Dyson Oblate

The Diamond Star remnant dwindled to nothing, and the singularity at its core evaporated in a burst of Hawking radiation. The twelve remaining living souls spent over fifty years in the alien deceleration beam, but by the end of that time, the last cryogenic suspension coffin we were taking turns to share had failed, and we all turned old and gray.

We passed a quarter million stars, roughly half the cloud. The number of young blue-white giant stars, and the symmetries and patterns of the variables, showed that the civilization here had been engineering stellar life cycles since roughly the Carboniferous Period. The Authority at M3 had been herding stars, triggering supernovas, and forming solar systems in the resulting nebulae to bring forth worlds where elements high on the periodic chart existed in abundance. They had been doing this since the years when, on Earth, amphibians and arthropods were reigning.

The deceleration beam wafted my ship, crewed by octogenarians and sad memories, to rest at a point within a hundred thousand miles of an oblate Dyson sphere.

Supersphere would be a better term, because it was in an orb eleven light-years in diameter at the equator, ten from pole to pole, that surrounded the entirety of the dense, compressed core of the cluster. The sphere captured one hundred percent of the emitted energy not of one but of hundreds of bright stars and dark star accretion disks at its center. It was visible to us only because it reflected ambient starlight and interstellar radiation on various wavelengths.

When we had first seen it on our approach, hundreds and hundreds of lightyears away, this core supersphere was transparent, but as we approached, it grew into a mirrored surface, reflecting all forms of radiation on all wavelengths from it. Perhaps it was built during those years, and the light of its completion had not yet reached us. Perhaps its optical properties changed according to the distance of the observer.

Closer still, and the reflections blurred into each other, perfectly and uniformly randomized, so that the surface of the Dyson oblate seemed a flat plane of pallid milky white to our eyes, a mathematically perfect surface to our instruments radiating at a few degrees above absolute zero. Particles of interstellar gas or dust encountering the surface, or rare interstellar micrometeorites, were disassembled when they struck into component subatomic particles and absorbed with no loss of momentum, no flare of waste heat.

There were dimples or indentations larger in diameter than the rings of Saturn, regularly spaced across the surface. Hence, my crew dubbed it the *big golf ball*, which made them less afraid of it. These indentations were parabolas pointed at various nearby stars, nebulae, and subclusters in the cluster. It was not the emitter of the beam which had braked us. The nearest was about one lightday away, six times the radius of Pluto's orbit. Jury-rigged probes sent into the focal point of this nearest dimple detected fluctuations both of electromagnetic energy and in the neutrino count, which had to be signals.

We did not possess the calculation brainspace needed to translate those signals via Monument Notation analysis.

Twelve years passed, and we could not attract the attention of the Authority beneath the surface of the oblate.

11. Overlooked

We tried everything, including discharges of energy which would have been considered acts of war had any damage been done. Material objects encountering the pallid wall were eaten; energy of any wavelength or composition was reflected back. Apparently the aliens welcomed mass, but not energy.

Once only, our instruments caught a glimpse of a material object leaving the surface. It issued from a point on the oblate half a lightyear from our position, so we saw the motion six months after the fact. From the distortion as it passed between us and a nearby star, it seemed to be a superdense, ultrathin thread of material, roughly nine thousand miles long, about the diameter of a uranium atom in cross section.

A ship? A message container? For a technology that could impregnate thought patterns into any sufficiently complex material thing, the difference was moot.

The neutronium thread was last seen heading toward a young blue-white giant star. That star was surrounded by 633 superjovian-sized bodies orbiting between one-tenth and one-twentieth of a lightyear away.

Perhaps whatever was causing the stellar engineering activity there would have been more ready to turn its attention toward us, but there was no fuel for the ship, no working cryogenic coffins.

There was roughly a dozen such man-made solar systems within reach of our instruments. What purpose did they serve? Why were so many young stars taken off the normal path of stellar evolution and turned into hotter-burning blue giants? M3 contains 230 variable stars, far more than in any other globular cluster. Why did the Authority transmute stable suns into variables? Why did precisely one-third display the Blazhko effect of long-period modulation? Many were the secrets I never learned.

Cheerfully we worked at our hopeless task, as one by one old age claimed us.

12. Abandoned

We spent our lives in sick bay. As the only one able to learn each and every field of medicine from the surviving onboard library, I acted as our doctor. With Ximen dead, the Hermeticist prosthetics to expand our life processes grew ever less reliable. There was one ironic loophole: it is easier to increase the life span of women, due to the production, in the ovaries, of the base material for totipotent cells. I was a gray-haired Eos surrounded by a matched set of Tithonius, each one turning into a cricket.

They were as old as mummies and moved carefully and slowly in the zero gee, drifting with medical packs and blood bags like pods of seaweed behind them, fearful of breaking their fragile bones. Peacefully, serenely, giving me words of comfort, one by one, they passed into a heaven my astronomy plates could not spy. One by one, they told me not to surrender, not to despair. More intelligent I was, but not more wise, and their words cheered me.

Then there were only a few of us left, then four, then three, then only one. He was of course the youngest because he had spent the most time in cryonic sleep during the years when we had working coffins to spare. I am speaking of the mutineer I had spared from the death penalty.

I will record his name here. In life, he was Scholar Intermediate Jehan Baptiste Ghede Lwa Oosterhoff, the ship's neural syncretism officer. I accepted his parole and granted him pardon and was rewarded by his loyalty. As the years passed, he aided the attempts to attract the attention of the aliens.

He disobeyed me one last time, on the last watch of his life. He stole the extravehicular frame to jet to within a mile, a yard, a foot of the wall. We had a platform there to tend or repair the jury-rigged instruments floating so close to that eerie, impossible, intangible, infinitely deadly surface.

Only once before had a crewman touched it, a physicist named Manvel. When the fingers of Manvel's gauntlet encountered the pallid mirror, the suit substance dissolved, and the fingers neatly sliced in half. The air inside the suit, at fifteen pounds per square inch, jetted out, along with much blood. I assume each molecule of oxygen and nitrogen and helium vented from the ruptured suit was also absorbed into the cool and pallid surface of the Dyson sphere. But the explosive decompression shoved Manvel away. Even with the emergency internal seals nipping off a severed hand or arm, the unexpected tumble put Manvel beyond the reach of the next nearest crewman on watch, and there were no waldoes within any acceleration solution that could catch him and return him to the ship. I read prayers to him over the radio.

This time was different. Oosterhoff had switched off his ears but not his mike. He was so giddy that I suspect oxygen overdose, his voice high and squeaking in the suit air, a laughing mouse. But his last words made an eerie sort of sense, a mad sanity.

An examination of the gravitational anomalies recorded during Manvel's accident had convinced Oosterhoff that only inanimate objects were being dissolved, that any living flesh and blood was perfectly preserved on the far side of the surface. Oosterhoff was convinced the surface was not just an infinitely thin disintegration field, but was meters or miles or lightyears deep and housed their mental-pattern information, their souls.

He said that the aliens had no need of nonliving material.

His theory was that the pallid substance was able to make a mold and to replicate each subatomic particle and part of a living brain as it intersected the surface, as if in a three-dimensional photograph, or, since the motions in time were captured, four dimensional.

He thought the whole of the eleven-lightyear-wide cluster-core Dyson oblate surface, each square lightyear of it, each square inch, was an interface surface for receiving and issuing information, neural information, any pattern that could hold a thought, to and from each of the arms of the main galaxy. Nothing else, or so Oosterhoff claimed, could explain the location of so much activity, so many superhuman civilizations, cramped together into one small globular cluster high above the North Pole of the galaxy, with all the stars spread out underneath like a map.

Oosterhoff thought the whole Dyson oblate was a brain. The crowded star systems and collapsed dark stars inside were part of the thinking system, the nerve cells, and the surface of a cortex larger than worlds.

He thought the pallid wall was alive and that it would emulate any living thing attempting to merge with it. This was the simplest and more straightforward way of welcoming a first contact from a creature of unknown biology, background, and capacity.

Theory? Call it a wild guess. An inspired guess, but wild. He said it had come to him in a dream.

The idea has an odd and alluring simplicity to it. Any creature, like the race of man, too foolish to know the whole eleven-lightyear-wide surface was an open invitation would be too foolish to be worth the time to welcome in. And how else could they have made a welcome mat? They would not erect an airlock nor spacedock.

The Authority Minds were expecting planet-sized bodies made of logic diamond or ringworlds wider than the solar system to plunge inside, not hollow metal ships filled with air and water and talking animals.

And so Oosterhoff maneuvered the frame to within an inch of the surface and shoved his head in, as you would shove it into a bubble of water in zero gee. Or into a lake of living water.

He thought the water would enter his brain, eat his brain, make his thoughts part of the alien mental process, and that they would speak to whatever ghost or reflection of his consciousness was mocked into life. He thought he would come out again. He thought he would live again, be himself again. If an atom-by-atom and particle-by-particle copy of you down to the finest level is not you, then you are not you to begin with.

Did he fear for his soul? I think he did not. I had this same talk with Ximen when he was afraid of his Exarchel he dreamed to build, like Koshchey in the old opera hiding his soul in an iron-bound box. What is the soul? It is not in my hand or heart or eye. It has neither location nor composition. To speak of the soul as being *inside* two brains, an original and a copy, makes no more sense and no less than to speak of the soul as being *inside* the two halves of one brain. It is not something that can be put inside an iron box; that is a fable for children. Eternal things are not inside anything inside the cosmos. My marriage is not inside my ring.

Oosterhoff's body jetted away from the surface, spraying blood and venting oxyhelium from his severed neckpiece.

And I was alone.

13. Haunted

I began to see Jehan Oosterhoff's head reflected in shining surfaces in the ship, a dull screen or a metal hatchframe, but there was nothing when I turned to look.

Once, about a month later, I saw the shadow of a severed head in the bridge armillary from where I floated in the hatch, but when I kicked and entered the chamber, there was nothing. A month after that, it appeared again, directly opposite me on the exercise carousel, pinned to the surface by the rotation, looking up at me, eyes eager, mouth smiling, red neck stump bleeding.

His eyes looked like yours. He had the looked of augmentation, of superintelligence. The aliens had expanded his brain to a higher level.

One watch as I sat in the carousel meditating, my legs folded into a full lotus position, my mind in a new topological space for which we have no word, neither dreaming nor awake, his head was in my lap. He smiled. I could see, hear, and smell it. It had mass. It was real.

Oosterhoff spoke.

You are born of the Monument, and within you is something even the Authority does not comprehend. Beyond this projection, I cannot accumulate enough attention in their system to stabilize myself.

I will be consumed by greater minds, more useful to the terrible, grim purposes of M3. You will not be consumed, but cherished.

My helmet circuits and the suit instruments around me created a blur in the four-dimensional photograph the surface took of me as I intersected it, so I am not whole.

Someone of your weight, build, and age can survive vacuum for seventy seconds. Remember to empty your lungs of air or breathing fluids. You can expel yourself from the sideboat airlock by blowing the explosive hinge bolts.

Or you can wrap yourself in an oxygen bubble of thin membrane and launch your-self toward the surface at sufficient speed to be carried forward by momentum when the bubble pops. Test this on a few empty suits first.

I said, "Prove you are real!"

You first.

"That is not an answer."

He smiled. *All answers are within. Come and see.*

And then he was gone. I could feel the warm spot on my leg where the back of his head had rested.

The vision convinced me. I will follow Oosterhoff. I will strip myself of everything and enter naked.

Not everything.

I will keep my wedding ring on my finger.

14. A Last Thought

My last thoughts will be of you, beloved. I have faith that you still live.

You are too brave and fierce and fine to let a small thing like death and entropy overcome you, nor the nigh-eternal gulfs of time.

I will not say farewell—for I shall gaze into your eyes with my eyes again, your brave and deep and handsome eyes, where imps of strange humor and rustic courage dance and swim. How I miss the look in your eyes, the only eyes that never seem dull to me, never empty, never cowed! No one else can surprise me or make me laugh.

Even though all sense says to doubt it, nonetheless I pray that you made amends with my stepfathers among the Landing Party I left on Earth, and that you shared with each other the breakthroughs in suspended animation and computer emulation needed to bring all of you forward across the ages until the day I return.

Perhaps you think me slyer than an obedient wife should be, but I arranged that you would have sole control of the long-term hibernation technology, and Ximen would have control of the emulation systems, which would require you to work together.

I foresee that if you ever put aside your differences, you will come to love each other as brothers and know that I love you both. I hope you are not fool-ish enough to duel him; he is a better shot and is likely to win.

I pray that all the Hermeticist crew won your forgiveness and will be waiting to greet my return. You must forgive what they did. What they will suffer if they do not repudiate the mutiny and murders on the ship! It will haunt them in life and punish them after death with more horror than any human court of law can bring. As for their other crimes, you must understand how lonely they were when they returned to Earth and found all their nations gone, the laws they thought would protect them forgotten, the culture and civilization alien and odd.

And they had the means to rule and, with my help, to bring peace.

You are too big a man to beat a foe who is afraid. Make peace with them.

But even if you have killed the men you should forgive and spare, I will not stop loving you. Love is not something I command but something I obey, like a voice from beyond the cosmos.

Because of my love, I cannot doubt you will be waiting for me, faithful to your vow, and because you are faithful, because you are a man of such stature that I cannot doubt you, I find myself helplessly in love.

The time for me is less than a century, and for you, hundreds of thousands of years. Once we are together, none of that will matter. Love is eternal, it partakes of eternity, it is timeless, and the vast desolation of heaven cannot make love lose its way, nor starve, nor dwindle, nor diminish, nor any yawning gulfs swallow it nor hold it back; neither lightyears nor years can abate love that is true.

15. Postscript

Beloved, my Menelaus, my sweet, my strong man, my soul of strength, pray this prayer for me that I may return, alive again after dissolution, alive when it is impossible that I should live, alive after entering the mind of the Authority in the core of M3, and pleading with the inhuman, superhuman presences found within the core, and winning redemption for mankind, generations I will never know, but who are still bound to me, in iron chains of obligation, in soft ribbons of affection and maternal devotion. Even if no organism descended from man ever knows me, I left the world as its ruler and will do my utmost to save and vindicate those descended from my subjects, however great the time, for that love also knows no limit. For the sake of their forefathers, I mean them to be free.

Ask the world to pray for me, beloved. This is the prayer I select:

O Holy Protectress of those who art in greatest need,
thou who shineth as a star of hope in the midst of darkness,
blessed Saint Rita of Cascia,

bright mirror of God's grace,
in patience and fortitude thou art a model of all the states in life.
I unite my will with the will of God
through the merits of my Savior Jesus Christ,
through the merits of the holy Virgin Mary
I ask thee to obtain my earnest petition,
provided it be for the greater glory of God
and my own sanctification.
Guide and purify my intention,
O Holy Protectress and advocate,
so that I may obtain the pardon of all my sins
and the grace to persevere my ordeal,
as thou didst in walking with courage, generosity, and fidelity down the
*   path of life.*
Let me survive dissolution into the pale horror
*   Let me find what dwells within*
*   Let me win their inhuman hearts*
*   Let me overcome their malice of indifference*
*   Let them agree to free me*
*   Let me return to life*
*   Let me cross the desolation of heaven*
*   Let me return to Earth*
*   The blue waters and blue skies of Earth, the sweet scents of Earth*
*   Let me feel my lover's arms again*
*   Let me face certain death in certain knowledge that my savior lives*
*   What I ask is impossible; and I who ask it am helpless*
Saint Rita, advocate of the impossible, pray for us!
Saint Rita, advocate of the helpless, pray for us!

16. Not to Worry

A.D. 68010

As Montrose put the needle reverently away, Mickey saw his face and asked him what troubled him.

"I'll tell you what's wrong with me, since you asked. Rania gave me a prayer she wants all the world to say for her. I ain't once got on my knees to pray for her return. Not once in sixty-six thousand years."

Mickey said jovially, "Not to worry! My people back in the day performed many rituals to placate the Swan Princess who stole the divine fire from heaven and hid it in a diamond for the sake of Man, the Lady of Hope. Two turtle-doves is the proper sacrifice for the poor, and a white ewe without blemish for those any goddess of bounty has blessed. So our devotion makes up for your lack! Were there any Witches aboard her ship?"

Mickey had evidently forgotten how long ago she had launched, or perhaps he had never been able to grasp the true magnitude of eons involved. The *Hermetic* dated from before the Ecpyrosis, the destruction of the world by fire; therefore, to Mickey, her ship was no more real than the ship of Noah from before the Deluge, the destruction of the world by flood.

Montrose said, "Damn! I need a priest. I reckon I should do some confessing."

"Eh? And all this time I had you pegged as a confirmed skeptic, Menelaus Montrose."

"Well, my religion was more like, *Shut up and shoot straight,* but I am beginning to think that is theologically insufficient for my spiritual needs. All these damned years; one drop at a time, time enough to fill a ocean, are weighing on me, piled on like I was at the bottom of a sea trench; all this hostile void and vacuum and emptiness and death outside the few little bright blue planets men live on; all these vast thinking machines, big as gas giants, and bigger. They are inhuman. Like things out of a nightmare of Saint Johnny on Patmos. Facing this, a man needs something more than a bottle of hooch to put the spirit in him."

"You should take some of my pharmaceuticals, and it would open your third eye and allow you to walk the winds."

"Or give me one more thing to fess up to the parson, I guess. Do they still have priests, these days? I suppose they must."

"There is a group that calls itself the Sacerdotal Order, which is under the protection of the Fifth Humans. They say they are the heirs of the Old, Strong religion, and the successors to Saint Peter, but their doctrines have grown confused and corrupt with time. They say Peter holds the Keys to Heaven and Hell. My people taught that Peter lives with the souls of dead children called the Lost Boys, and he never grows old and never completed the journey to the afterlife, but dwells in the great star Canopus, the second-brightest star to the right of Sirius, the Dog Star. The tiny and bright spirit who dwells with him shines her light and rings her bell and calls the lost and wandering ghosts to her. She died, sacrificing her life saving Peter, but is resurrected when the innocent clap their hands, for their faith brings the dead to life again. You can see from where these Sacerdotes derive their ideas and myths: all is but a hold-over from the pagan roots of yore."

"Hm. Could be a different Peter. In any case, I feel pretty bad that I let a doubt about her come to trouble me and let it grow stronger as she got closer."

"What doubt? Did you think her love would fail? That? Is *that* what has been disturbing your slumber these last few millennia? My dear friend: sleep now in perfect peace. I will stay awake and guard you. When you next wake, you will see her."

Montrose patted him on the shoulder. "But what is Blackie up to?"

Mickey said, "He is already ignoring the return of Rania and looking to the next age, or the one beyond that. His eyes are on the future."

Montrose said sadly, "Then maybe I shouldn't worry. I know by now. The future will never arrive."

3

The Hour of Her Advent

1. The Looking Glass World

A.D. 69396 OR 1 ULTRAVINDICATION

Montrose woke suddenly and completely. That was the first surprise.

Before he even opened his eyes, he was aware of three things. First, his entire mind, operating at the very lowest ranges of a Potentate level, was gathered into one coherent system. Last time he slept, he had not commanded the resources necessary to perform the reintegration processes. He had not had the money, or whatever they used for money in that era.

Second, someone or something had interfered with his method of what he called *sleeping with one eye open*, which meant his ability kept a partial on standby alert, watching the data streaming through the dreaming mind of mad Tellus watching for spikes or strange attractors in the cliometric chords and glissandos of the symphony of history.

Third, something was strange about his eyes. The darkness inside of his eyelids did not have the normal pattern of phosphenes he expected upon waking from slumber. This in turn indicated that his entire brain capacity, roughly equal to a logic diamond the size of the core of the planet Mercury, or to a mountain of compressed murk substance, had been fitted inside one mobile biological body.

This was starkly impossible, unless he had been transferred without his knowledge into another body. The fact that he did not feel a sense of shock implied one of two things: either his subconscious mind had been subliminally conditioned or prepared to receive the knowledge that he was waking in a new body without a shock, or the new mental geometry he occupied was better able to adapt without shock to new paradigms than his old.

But, then, what was this feeling of lightness, of joy, this sensation he remembered from his childhood? He recalled waking up in the wee hours of Christmas morning, long before the sun was up, unwilling to step out of bed for fear of waking the snoring hulks of his many older brothers, unwilling to put his unshod foot on the cold, hard, harsh floor. Instead, he hovered between sleep and waking, wrapped in the warmth of the rough blankets impregnated with antiseptics and antibiotics, like floating in a cocoon, safe from the fear that winter would come and never leave, eager with a greedy, happy elation of expectation, that only a day of gifts and feasts and visits and pine trees shining with ornaments provoke or fulfill. It was a day too wonderful to be true.

But then again, no, this sensation was different.

His elation was like dark woodsmoke, earthy, primal, rising as if from his blood and bone marrow, his cells and glands. It was not the joy of a youth getting a toy but of a man who gives himself so utterly to another that he forgets himself entirely. It was a sensation of conquest and surrender.

He remembered his first time seeing the cleavage of a buxom young swimmer in a bathing suit when he went to Soko University on the West Coast. It was the type of skimpy, clinging, immodest garb no proper Texan lass ever donned; but San Francisco was owned by the Sumitomo Zaibatsu, and things were different there. She was the captain of the swim team, which was closed to Texans and Northeastermen, even though Menelaus could outswim the shrimpy city boys on the team.

Her name was Hoshiko. Her eyes were bright as agates, and her dark hair fell past her hips, and she barely came up to his elbow. He had asked her to let him escort her to the Bon festival and the dance. She looked, if anything, even more adorable in her yukata than in her bathing suit. No other Mestizo freshman dared to court a yellow girl, because they feared the Nisei boys; and the Nisei boys feared her too much to court her themselves, because she was as pretty as an idol and sharp as a whip. (As for Menelaus, the evening when four young toughs followed him into a dark alley, where he had had the forethought to park a fire axe behind a trashcan, to express their discontent with the *gaijin* dancing with the pretty Japifornian girl, had been one of the shortest of the many altercations of his life. Three of the boys ran away as fast as their legs could carry them, with their leader hopping after as fast as his remaining leg could carry him.)

Earlier, he remembered his first crush on a dark-haired, hazel-eyed beauty from Austin, a girl he saw only twice a year, at fair time. Her name was Jacqueline.

Earlier again, he remembered his first kiss, stolen from his cousin Lizzy during a Christmas dance, and he had to manhandle her under the mistletoe to have a proper excuse and fight his cousin Lenny the next day, skinning his knuckles and knees and ending up with bits of Lenny's ear in his teeth.

All these memories and more were in the background. In the foreground was a joy too bright to stare at, like the sun.

So there might have been a third reason why he felt no shock. He was too damned happy.

He opened his eyes, and they were filled with water, and he opened his mouth and choked. The unpleasant medicinal indignities of waking from long-term hibernation had changed, but they were still unpleasant.

He sat up, struck his head against what, at first, he thought was a coffin lid. But the surface, whatever it was, was instantly broken into shards and fragments about his head and shoulders. Fluid sluiced off him like soapsuds falling off a man who sits up in a bathtub.

The moonlight glaring in his damp eyes made a bright blur. Before he could blink his eyes clear and look around, from the texture and sound of the wind, he knew he was out of doors, but from the smell, or the lack of it, he could not imagine where. The sound was of a desolate, wide space, a solitude as broad as a desert. He heard no people moving nearby, no voices, no breathing, no birds, no sound of machinery, nothing.

He spat the fluid from his mouth. Another surprise: the fluid did not strike his chest as it fell. It did not fall, but sublimated instantly to vapor in his teeth. In fact, his chest and upper back, shoulders and arms likewise were bare and dry. The fluid had already vanished from his naked skin. There was no choking sensation in his lungs as normally accompanied switching from breathing hyperoxygenated liquid to breathing air. He felt no liquid in his lungs, but he felt a gush of mist from his nostrils, yet seemingly too small in volume to account for transition between fluid and air regimes. The implications of that were staggering: it implied a revolution of biotechnology at least, if the material was being so rapidly absorbed back into the cell lining of his lungs, or of physics at most, if it was being or reduced in mass or volume so suddenly, whisked away by means unknown.

He ran his wrist across his eyes, blinking and snorting. He touched his nose. It was still big and crooked. He felt his teeth with his tongue, and the small lump on his inner lip where he had fallen on his grandfather's big wooden rocking chair when he was three years old, stitched up by the local horse-doctor, and it had never healed quite right. Whoever made this new mouth for him had put it together with the care and artistry of a professional counter-feiter. It made him feel right at home.

Then he looked around.

It was night. The moon and four other satellites he did not recognize were up. The moon was blue under layers of frozen oxygen, with the seas and oceans black with the debris of once-great forests and cities, now crushed into a strata of dark grit beneath the weight of the collapsed, failed atmosphere.

Despite the strangeness, the world he sat upon was Earth. But the land for miles and miles, as far as his eyes in the nocturnal gloom could pierce, was a flat and level shining surface like a mirror made of diamond, colorless in the blue moonlight. The world was as barren as a salt flat, empty of tower or house or highway, empty of bird or beast or bush or grass blade.

In a direction he deduced was west, the land fell away at a sharp cliff to a lower landscape no less flat and diamond-bright. There was a line of fog hover-ing over the middle distance of that lower glass plain, which might indicate the presence of a river canyon.

In the opposite direction, irregular peaks of white substance rose above the white surface, as if the mirror there were broken by some pressure from below, to form mountains. They looked black in the distance. The stars were bright, and the sky contained a few high clouds, tinged with sapphire in the blue moonlight, like ghostly feathers. He thought that was a good sign. It meant that somewhere, there was water on the surface of the globe.

So Menelaus Montrose, waking with the strange sensation of joy without a name, sat naked in a tiny pool of rapidly evaporating white fluid in a little pond smaller than a bathtub and poked his head and shoulders and chest out of the surface of the moonlit, diamond world. He looked like a chick emerging from an egg or like an arctic sailor smashing desperately upward through thin ice for air. He peered left and right, blinking like an owl, and saw the land-scape coated with a substance smooth and shining as glass, a world as blank as creation on the second day.

And he uttered a single swear word.

2. The Patrician Rassaphore

Montrose stepped out of the hole where he woke and watched dubiously as it filled itself in and closed up behind him. That he was standing on the surface of some self-aware cognitive substance he had little doubt, but how to signal to it, he could see no way. He pounded on the ground and shouted at it for a while, more to amuse himself than in hope of establishing contact. Smashing at the diamond with his fist bloodied his knuckles, which was a sensation as familiar to him as the crannies and irregularities of his teeth were to his tongue. One diamond fragment of the radial cracks was a triangle long and thin enough to act as a toothpick, so he took up the diamond shard and picked his teeth as he walked.

He decided to travel toward the western cliffs, on the general theory that following the land downward was the best way to find a river, and a river the best place to look for people.

Counting his footsteps and watching the stars turn, Montrose walked for two hours, rested, walked for two hours, rested, and so passed the night. The river fog (or whatever those clouds might be) rising from the lower plain grew taller as the night passed and the sky overhead grew pink with the promise of dawn. He estimated that the globe was rotating at roughly half the rate it had known in his youth.

The rising sun behind him ignited the mountains, which were made of glass. Montrose stopped walking to gaze in awe at the sky as it slowly grew bright. The level beams of sunlight shining through the translucent peaks sent a series of nimbuses like the serried lances of rows of celestial pikemen streaming across the sky, painting the high clouds and thin mists with royal purple and rich Prussian blue, turquoise and emerald bright as burning copper sulfate, with narrower bands and darts of rose and cerise, carnelian and citrine, gamboge, smaragdine, and saffron. Soon, the whole sky was a peacock's tail.

A motion in the distance drew his eyes downward from the wonder of the twilight of the dawn. A long shadow was reaching from the burning mountains behind. It was cast by a figure, slender and graceful, with long snow-white robes fluttering about like wings, who was skating across the diamond surface toward him. Something in the posture and the motion of the legs and hips told Montrose it was a male.

As the other man came closer, Montrose could see the slight feathers of haze appearing and disappearing around the man's slippers as his slid forward. The ice-hard substance was flexing and re-forming with each footstep, no doubt forming a frictionless surface. The oddness was that he was not bent over like a speed skater would have been, but his speed was much greater than the rather casual motion of his legs could account for. Perhaps the substance was also moving of its own accord underfoot, like a conveyer belt, imparting additional motion.

The sun rose higher, and the darker hues cast across the overhead clouds turned bright and began to mingle into a dazzling whiteness, like the hueless sky seen above a desert or above an arctic tundra.

The sun cleared the mountains before the man arrived, and suddenly the mirror-bright surface of the Earth was gorgeous, but also blinding, dazzling, disorienting. Montrose put his hand before his face, but there was no way to turn to escape the fiery dazzle.

The man ceased to move his legs and stood upright as he approached. For the last hundred yards or so, he slid, looking almost comically poised and serene, white cloak waving behind, like the mast on a sailboat with sails spread, or like a tall pine tree with the wind blowing snowy streams from its branches. The friction properties of the surface changed in the last ten yards, and the stranger slowed to a halt without a jar.

They stood regarding each other. Menelaus was naked, and he was picking his teeth with a sliver of diamond.

The other man had skin that gleamed like metallic gold, as if a statue had sprung to life. He was beardless, but the jet-blackness of his eyebrows and long dark hair made a startling contrast with his bright skin. The white garment was classically draped, and a hem of purple traced the edges of the skirts and cloak. He wore a coronet of green, but whether it was ivy leaves or emerald stones, or some other substance entirely, Montrose could not detect.

When the man smiled, his teeth were diamond, perhaps the same substance as the ground beneath or the distant mountains. But the strangest feature was his eyes. They were silver-gray, pupil and iris and sclera and all. His face was young, but these eyes were old.

Without a word, the man held out his hand, offering Menelaus a small fruit the size of a plum, so purple it was almost black.

Menelaus shrugged, figuring that if anyone meant him harm, there were easier ways to do him in. The first bite of the fruit let a gush of juice sweeter than wine flood his mouth; in the second bite, the pleasure was doubled; the third was ecstasy. He wolfed it down with unseemly haste, crowing and slurping at the sheer physical gratification of the thing, as if every nutrient need of all his hungry cells was being deluged with satisfaction.

At the same time, his senses sharpened. Every nuance of the air on his bare skin could be felt separately, and he could now distinguish a riot of buried colors in the semitransparent layers of the ground beneath. Also, the white cloak of the other man now could be seen to be a combination of many slight nuances of shade, silver and dove gray, white and ivory and milk and snow. The man's skin was even more complex; it was now a pattern of veins and dapples of topaz, chartreuse, tawny, sulfur and primrose, ochre and icterine.

Best of all, the light no longer dazzled him. It had not grown less bright. Rather, it was as if his visual nerve was stronger, more flexible.

The stone of the fruit was small, hard, and wrinkled like a peach pit, and clear and bright like a diamond. Montrose offered it back to the man, but, with a smile, as if he bestowed a gift of great value, the man gestured he should keep it.

The man now drew out a drinking horn from his shoulder belt, knelt, and plunged the horn beneath the surface of the diamond ground, which obligingly turned to liquid at his touch. When he raised the horn, it was filled to the brim with a golden fluid thicker than honey. Still kneeling, he proffered it to Montrose. Once again, fearing no evil, Montrose threw back his head and drained the horn.

This time, there was no physical sensation. The fluid seemed to evaporate in his mouth, leaving his tongue feeling cool. He in no way became intoxicated, but his thoughts grew clear and sharp, as if he were waking from a half dream, and at the same time, his emotions surged and seemed to grow unknotted, as if pains and fears long held in check, long buried, were in one moment excised.

Montrose sighed and wiped his mouth with the back of his wrist. "Can't say as I care for the taste, as it sneaked out of my mouth, but it is sure a great pick-me-up. What is it called?"

The man, without rising, answered in flawless English. He had no trace of an accent Montrose could detect, but his rhythm and inflection were oddly musical, almost a singsong. His voice was a pleasant baritone. "What you quaff is called *glory*. Now in your blood is a sign, which none dare deny, of the honor in which all living creatures behold you on this, your utmost day, and the dignity you are owed."

"Thanks, but seeing as how *beholden* and *honorific* I is, what say you share part of your cloak with me, so I ain't dangling in the wind, making ladies faint and making bulls feel all dinky-donked? I am a kindly man and don't care to make the critters jealous."

The man dipped his drinking horn once more into the surface substance, and stood, and gestured for Montrose to kneel. Montrose did and was bemused, but not startled, when the man poured the liquid in the horn over Montrose's head.

The substance dripped over his neck and shoulders, growing pleasantly warm as it did so, and the fluid rippled and curled and formed itself into hair-thin strands almost too fine to see. Montrose stood, looking down, beheld a white garment being instantly woven into place on his frame, seamless, a twin to the other man's own, draped neatly from shoulder to waist, to fall to a purple hem just below his knobby knees. He thought he looked ridiculous in it.

But at least the sleeves were folded in such a way to form deep pockets just below his wrists, and he could put the diamond seed in one.

"Such is the wedding garb for me," said the man in his hypnotic, chanting baritone. "Our records showed you might have wished for something from your period, but I will not deny what you request, and share my own."

Montrose tried to adjust the garb, to throw over both shoulders, and it perversely kept rearranging itself into handsome folds and classical drapes.

"What's the big idea of pouring me into another body? Why did you pox with my alarm clock and snuff my lesser selves?"

"For sheer joy's sake. We decided to surprise you! It was thought not fitting that you should come a pauper to your bride, so we shouldered the expense of recombining your mind while you slept."

"Some surprise. What the plague is with leaving me to find my way all by my lonesome?" he grunted while trying to rip the fabric, hoping this would kill it and make it lie still. "Right unneighborly."

"As for leaving you alone, I do not understand your word. To us, solitariness is precious, and, to you, 'twill make your union joyous all the more. You waited but seventy-five degrees of the planetary rotation while I approached, and, of course the additional delay was gained because you walked froward, not toward. To intrude myself in greater haste was feared to be unseemly. I was told that the men of old, being mortal, practiced no patience. I hoped it untrue of you, whose vigil has outlasted all things known to history."

Menelaus had some of the fabric in his teeth and was still unable to rip the garment, get it to lie still, nor to wrestle it into submission. A long tail of the material was successfully slapping him in the face. "Much as I poxing appreciate the gesture—you know—my duds don't need to look 'zactly like yours. I ain't got the knees for wearing no skirt, see."

The man of gold touched Menelaus lightly on the shoulder, and the garment altered itself, becoming a long tunic, and the cloak was now something more like a poncho, but rich with emerald embroidery. The design showed a triple-headed serpent chasing sparrows, writhing into Celtic knots and arabesques. The hood fell off, remolded itself, grew thicker, and became a broad-brimmed hat more like what Menelaus was used to.

"But now the land must garb him in a floral, festive coat to match your own!" So saying, the gold man began walking and, as he did so, cracks spread from his feet in spiderwebs across the level plain with shocking suddenness.

Montrose followed, his mind full of questions, but that feeling of buoyant joy which woke him was still in the back of his mind, so he held his peace and decided to watch whatever show his host put on.

As the man of gold walked, he broke the ground in each direction. Behind him, in his footsteps, like a green fire following a trickle of gasoline, grass blades erupted from the cracks in the ground. With soundless explosion, the glassy surface to either side of him sent up shafts of brown, which turned green and opened up their branches, turning into trees. Dewdrops flew from the buds and new leaves, and the trunks elongated, breathing out mists, even as Montrose watched.

The air grew cool with water vapor. At the beginning of their walk, the two men were in an ice-colored landscape of diamond broken by countless small saplings and scattered shrubs. As they walked, through saplings shoulder-high, Montrose could hear at first the trickle, and, later, the lapping rush of a stream off to their left, invisible behind the trees now towering overhead. Their course was parallel to this unseen stream. By the end of the walk, the trees had formed a natural cathedral, green and hushed and solemn, and underfoot was soil and grass as thick and refreshing to the bare feet as splashing in a pool.

Flowers of every color were springing up, but white was the dominant hue, with white rose, tuberose, peony, baby's breath overwhelming the other blooms, and dendrobium and hydrangea, amaryllis, and apple-of-my-eye.

He was not surprised by this rapid, elfin growth. Ever since the day he had seen the white-haired and wrinkled Hermeticists throw off their old age like a wet cloak thrown aside, he expected to see such rapid cellular changes eventually on a wider scale.

Nonetheless, watching the green spread across the barren glass with the speed of a prairie fire in a high wind, and trunks shoot up like brown and silent rockets, with fruits and flowers like quiet fireworks bursting, and bestow the tall and solemn beauty of deep forestlands and sunny glades in so short of time, was magic.

He noted the species of trees were not merely from Earth, with no alien life-forms present, but from his quarter of Earth, from North America. And they were not simply the pines and evergreens of his cold youth, but the leafy trees, oak and ash and elm, of his happier teenaged years, when he was a horse soldier, campaigning in the thick woods of Mojave and the overgrown green swamps of Death Valley.

The two men came suddenly to the brink of the cliff Montrose had seen hours before from afar. Stepping out from between stately birch trees was like stepping from a high temple rich with shadows through a doorway guarded by brown pillars. The brightness of the sun in the cloudless white sky was like a blow to the face.

At their foot was a gulf of air overlooking a flat plain of glassy diamond. To their right, cherry trees and apples were spilling small white and pink petals into the depth of air.

To their left, the stream which thick woods had for so long kept hidden now leaped shoutingly into view, and, with a noise like cymbals, flashing in the sun, brilliant, threw itself from the cliff in a long, smooth parabola to dash against the cliff, a thin and threadlike waterfall, robed in its own windblown mists and spray. A second threadlike stream could be seen falling from the brink five hundred yards beyond that, and a third at a thousand yards, and so on, evenly spaced to left and right across the inlets and headlands of the irregular cliff side.

The man flourished aloft the drinking horn he had previously offered Montrose and, with a bow of his head, cast it from the cliff. Slowly, the tiny thing toppled, growing invisible with distance.

Montrose said, "What was that for?"

The other replied, "To honor and receive your bride, I am opening the floodgates of the buried waters of the Earth."

No sooner than he said it but there was a loud, sharp explosion of noise. Montrose clutched his ears, shocked. The glassy plain so far beneath them was heaving. Vast cubes and boulders and sheets of the diamond substance were rising and falling, and smaller stones were hurling themselves in the air. It was if all the earthquakes of the world, all the landslips and eruptions, had been gathered into one spot and set free. Up from the vents and canyons and fissures, volumes of fluid broke forth, columns of spray rearing hundreds of yards in the air like giant sea serpents on a rampage. Fountains and volcanoes of cold fluid surged to the surface, and maelstroms whirled whole lakes and mighty rivers upward and upward.

Soon, the diamond plain was smothered and vanished, invisible beneath the surging flood. Higher and higher rose the boiling waves. Montrose watched in awe, impressed despite himself.

"That is not water," Montrose said. "Look at how it moves."

It was true. The fluid was a rich and dark purple hue, and a fragrant smell, delicious, wild, issued from it.

"It is the wine of the wedding feast," said the golden man. "With greatest toil and care concocted it was from all the most delicate essences and forms of millennia past beyond telling, designed particularly to be pleasing, as was the fruit from which it came, to your palate and hers. We have destroyed the formula and the engines which can reproduce it. We will toast your happiness yearly, but when the last drop is drained, there will never be another bottle of it. The seed you carry and it alone can grow new trees to bring the fruit, and the wine, forth from extinction." He smiled without moving his lips, by crinkling his eyes. "Should you wish to grow a tree or a grove for your children as their wedding days approach."

"Whose wedding are we talking about?"

The man looked very surprised. "Yours!"

"I am already married."

"The Nobilissimus del Azarchel informs us that your marriage was annulled by the Sacerdotal Order of your day and age, eons ago, on the grounds of a lack of consummation. The marriage mass will need to be performed again."

"Well, he is a lying polecat and a louse that eats lice, so I will just hurt him in ways of which a man ought not speak in polite company, but it involves cutting off some parts of him and stuffing them down or up other parts of him. I am so sorry I missed the years when he could not get his head to form anything but a jackass head. That would have been the cream of the jest!"

"His defeat is absolute," intoned the other. "We allow him liberty to walk our world as he will and do as he pleases, since any material good he takes can be replicated, and no harm to our physical forms can cause us discomfort."

"He wanders around robbing and killing? That seems almost a particular kind of purgatory for a man like him."

"Not so often anymore does he steal or kill. The novelty wore away after very few centuries."

"I think it would be kindlier of y'all to fix him up with a donkey head as a punishment more fitting and less, well, philosophical than just leaving him alone, stealing and not being a king no more."

"He is not idle. Mostly he reads books, which can be manufactured as needed from the ontic crystal, since we will not let him drink our glory. He is allowed certain laboratory equipment to reproduce certain experiments from four or five scientific revolutions ago."

Montrose said, "Stranger, I did not rightly get your name."

"We do not intrude our names unless asked," replied the other gravely. "You honor me. For to know a man's name, if the name be true, is to touch his soul and carry his burdens. I am the Judge of Ages."

Montrose laughed. "You can have that cursed name and welcome to it! It weren't never mine."

"That is but the first of my names. Saeculum Coensor I am called, for I am given the task to organize these last few ages of human history, to reward those millennia who welcome the Vindication of Man and prepared wisely, and chastise those foolish millennia which do not. My next name is Rassaphore of the Epithalamion, for I bear the robe of the bridegroom, as well as the garments of the Earth and the girdle of the sea. Next, I am called Quintumvir, for I am Epitome of the Fifth Men. Finally, I am Praecantator Ultimus, because I am the last of cliometricians or aruspices to face the Asymptote."

Montrose looked at him sharply. "Asymptote! That is a word I ain't heard in a long while. What do you mean?"

"You are familiar with singularities in mathematics and physics, a point at which no extrapolation is possible, because all values fall to the infinitesimal or approach infinity asymptotically?"

"Sure."

"The return of your bride is one such an asymptote of singularity for us, because no prediction of the future, no, not even that accomplished by Toliman, Consecrate, and Zauberring acting in concert, can predict the vectors introduced by the Authority of M3."

"But I heard from a guy in a dumb hat that Hyades had records about what happened before when planets was manumitted out of indentured servitude. Ours is not the first time."

"The general terms are known: we must make arrangements to continue the strange and inexplicably pointless contest of transforming worlds and solar systems from inert matter to cognitive matter, either in return for resources proffered by Praesepe or as piecework. The Vindication of Man will prove that our race has the capacity to keep our oaths taken across sixty thousand years of time, but this does not mean the other Dominions under Praesepe's control are wise to trust that we shall. Our Principalities may indeed prove too short-lived and shortsighted for them."

"What about the specifics?"

"You mean the freedom or servitude of mortal races sure to be extinct long before even the shortest of these long-term obligations can be carried out? The only thing that is certain is that not even the Dominion of Hyades, if all his living suns and planets combined in one eon of meditation, with thoughts narrowcast from one side of the cluster to the other, could extrapolate what the Domination of Praesepe, his master, will do, no more than the Domination of Praesepe can guess at the mind of the Authority of M3. The intelligence of one hundred billion is as unimaginable to us as the intelligence of a quadrillion or quintillion, and yet they are five and eight orders of magnitude greater. The difference is more than that between a man and a coelacanth and includes difference not just of magnitude, but of kind. Therefore, this is the final hour any mind in the Empyrean of Man has predicted by cliometry. What shall be our institutions, mores, and law hereafter, we cannot say."

Montrose said, "Before I slept, a Lord of the Stability begged me to influence my wife to have her free the mortals from the machines."

Little crinkles that appear when a man smiles with his eyes gathered above the cheeks of Rassaphore. "It was not a Patrician to whom you spoke. We are not hasty. Had he waited but three years more, he would have heard of theonecromancers returning from the remote outer orbits of the Tau Ceti system, where men in heavy-gravity bodies are burrowing into the corpse of the frozen gas giant to learn what huge secrets can be gleaned from a study of its shadow-records and ghosts and thought-echoes still lingering in the logic diamond of its vast brain. The despoilers of dead gods reported the startling news that Toliman and Consecrate, the Dyson Hemisphere and the Dyson Cloud, together with Zauberring the Strandworld circling 61 Cygni, overcame cold and remorseless Catallactic of Tau Ceti and collected themselves into one system, a very small and tentative Dominion called Triumvirate. In his first act as Epitome of Man, Triumvirate announced that the higher powers, for good or ill, will no longer interfere with the doings of moral men, Angels, Archangels, nor Potentates."

"That is great news, but you ain't smiling."

"It is a lesson in humility. It seems the ripples and cross-currents we creatures of one hundred million intelligence levels can cause over spans of tens and scores of millennia are insignificant to the tides and tidal waves of their greater plans hereafter to be made reaching across millions and tens of millions of years. We shall live and die free men, each and every one, until our race goes extinct. And I see neither do you smile."

Montrose straightened up, a look of shock and disappointment on his face. "I feel like someone stole my thunder. The battle I agreed to lead is over since before I woke?"

Rassaphore said, "Be comforted. You set in motion the love of the chaotic Fox Maidens for liberty and freedom; and they created us to carry out your will. We created Neptune based on your principles and mathematics, and he opposed Twelve of Tau Ceti, the plutonian ice giant, and Splendor of Delta Pavonis, the traitorous and mercurial fire giant. Altair followed Neptune when the Potentate called Covenant created the Power called Immaculate from their gas giant, and he in turn created the system-wide brain of Consecrate, who, in turn, was the opposition to Catallactic of Tau Ceti, who served the Beast. You see the chain of connection? We are your children. The Myrmidons, and Jupiter and Twelve and Catallactic were the children of the Nobilissimus del Azarchel. The opposing avalanches your pebble and his pebble set in motion could not have been stopped, nor aided, at this point, by any power of yours or his. This destiny has been set ever since you slew Jupiter in a duel, or even before, when the first generation of Swans ungratefully and ungraciously exiled you both. The fuse is long, the explosion reaches one hundred lightyears wide, and perhaps farther will expand, and perhaps never to expire. Such is the human spirit. A dramatic battle at the end of things may indeed be in your future, but not today."

"Why did you put me in this body?"

"To honor you with simplicity. You cannot easily haul a node of murk the size of Mercury behind you as you sail on your honeymoon to many stars and worlds. So all your minds and selves were folded down into this body you wear now, with no need for external connection or remote brain storage."

"That's impossible. Or it was, when I fell asleep."

"The knowledge, along with all knowledge of our society, science, lore, and customs, was embedded in that drink you quaffed and stands by in your memory at your call. I will speak only enough to stir those buried memories to light:

"This praxis is a gift from your bride. Rania has sent ahead of her the results of research she has made of her vessel, given in recompense for some wrong done her by the aliens of M3. It is an attotechnology ship, whose First Order secrets we lack the tools to analyze or reproduce, but certain spin-offs of the Second Order femtotechnology aboard can be examined by picotechnology— in this case, the means to perform the manipulation of quarks, quantum fields, and exotic matter. Her research enabled the Principality Zauberring to overcome certain limitations of the Pauli exclusion, develop a form of stable phenomena, neither matter nor energy properly so called, consisting of nucleonic strings about which electron energy levels are distributed in spirals rather than spheres."

"String atoms rather than ball atoms."

"If you like. These strings are analogous to elements and can be woven together in knots and sheets in a fashion analogous to molecules, but with distributed strong and weak two-dimensional interaction areas rather than zero-dimensional point sources. The material interacts with normal chemicals and photon excitement in a somewhat predictable way, but the number of fractal folds which can be made in a molecular sheet of the material is practically infinite. Hence, the amount of information that can be encoded and stored in the energy states of the subatomic particles, in the vibrations and waveforms of the strings, and then transferred by changes in the surface folds to chemicals released into neural systems greatly exceed what either molecular level storage density of logic diamonds or the atomic level storage density of murk."

"Still sounds plagued impossible. You cannot stuff a planet-sized brain into a human body."

"Your subatomic particles, variations in electron shell orbits, nuances of nucleonic organization, and so on can store as much information in a single atom as is coded in a large brick of murk technology by stringing the atoms together into binary sequences. It is as if an entire library were written on a silk sheet so fine that it could be wadded up and placed in the head of a pin. But come! These dry matters are no fit discourse for such a day as this!"

The man of gold raised his arm, pointing at the blue-white sky. "This is the hour of joy! Look upward. We have made your eyes like ours so that you can see her approach. We have devised that your eyes will return to their more traditional appearance when she more closely approaches, for then they will be needed to meet her gaze and speak all lovers' vows which words cannot encompass. But for now, your eye must be stronger than human, to see her afar. Look where I point. There is her ship, the *Solitudines Vastae Caelorum*! There!"

"I see nothing but a blue sky, pardner. You jaspering me, is that it?"

"Not so. I merely overestimated the rate at which your mind would adapt to our neural formats. You should be able to penetrate the opaque day sky with eyes like ours. The knowledge you drank is not yet digested. It does not matter. We will blot out the sun for you."

Montrose said, "Wha-what did you say?"

But he had heard right. Less than eight minutes later, a black bite seemed to be taken out of the sun. These new eyes could look directly at the sun without harm, and so he got to see something he had never seen with naked eyes before: a full eclipse. The black disk occluded the sun, and an eerie twilight fell across the landscape of forest, glass mountain, and purple wine-dark sea.

From the crescent of light at the edge of the disk, Montrose could tell this was a planetary body, not a sail nor an orbital mirror. How the technology of this era could maneuver another world into position between Earth and sun without shattering it was a mystery.

"You can move the planets?"

"Not I. That honor I granted to the living planet Pyriphlegethon, who well recalls aiding you in beforetimes to behold her. Now, by his shadow, he shades your eyes. Your sensitivity is greater far than you might believe, because each incoming photon can be separately analyzed into preons and entangled photon pair information deduced. The deeper your heart desires, the clearer your vision! Look, I say! *Look!*"

And he saw. At first in the night sky he noticed only that certain distant dots of light moved more rapidly than others. Then his eye resolved them into crescents waxing or waning, gibbous or full. Then he could see them as globes with continents, seas, swirls of clouds. One was green as a lime, covered pole to pole with layers of viridescent storm; the next was white and crisscrossed with fine dark lines and crater marks too evenly spaced to be natural. The next had a ring like Saturn's, but made of a single band of exotic material, connected by dozens of space elevators to the equator; then a world entirely ocean with polar icecaps covering half the north and south hemispheres. To stare at worlds from space is like to stare at human faces, for each was individual, rich with secrets, handsome.

And on and on. There were two hundred which had lights, like the lights of cities seen at night, shining between the horns of their crescents. Then there were three hundred more, coated from pole to pole with the pallid yellow white of logic diamond, or with morbid indigo and black of murk, or else with the opalescent blue-white glass, like the landscape where he woke seen from afar. Half a thousand worlds altogether were here, ranging in size from balls smaller than Ceres to superterrestrials eight times the mass of Earth. Mars and Venus, far away indeed from the orbits they had known in his youth, were lost in the thicket.

The distant spheres of Saturn, Neptune, and Uranus were visible, but of the old asteroid belt, or Pluto and the outer planets, there was no memorial. Neptune was surrounded by an extensive artificial ring system equal parts murk and logic diamond: his Angels and Archangels, and moons to replace the ones he had lost in old wars, to house his Potentates.

"What are these?" asked Montrose in a whisper. He had never heard nor imagined such a thing as a solar system with five hundred worlds in it.

"Most are terrestrial-sized worlds sculpted very recently, within the last eighteen centuries, out from the massive corpse of Jupiter. They are called the *Deodates*. Others are Cold Potentates or Rogues, designed to dwell at slower thinking speed far from any star, but, startled by the deaths of Lethe and Styx, have made the long, slow voyaging hence from interstellar space, anchoring energy fields to their magnetospheres in imitation of the semi-immaterial sails of Rania's Great Ship. Look to the horizon! As the globe turns, she will come in view."

His view was blocked by the forest. Montrose impatiently scanned the treetops, found the tallest, and climbed it. He could not recall the last time he had climbed a tree, but he scampered up as lightly as when he had been a child, as quickly and efficiently as when he had been a sharpshooter for the cavalry.

Perhaps this new body he had been given had muscles more pliant and potent than normal, or perhaps the soaring spirit in him, the eagerness, made him light and lent him strength.

3. Up a Tree

Above him, he saw a human figure. As he drew near, Montrose saw who it was. He did not even wonder how the man had known where to find him.

Blackie del Azarchel was seated on one of the upper branches of the tree, a wide-brimmed hat pulled low over his brow, smoking a cigarette in a holder, his long legs crossed at the ankles and propped against a second tree branch. He was dressed in the expensive coat and leggings of a Spanish grandee of the Twenty-First Century, with a cravat at his throat and lace at his wrists.

"Dr. Montrose, I presume? Fancy meeting you here." Del Azarchel smiled his most charming smile.

Menelaus stared in utter disbelief. And then his expression darkened, and his deep-set eyes began to glitter dangerously. He drew out the triangle of diamond from his sleeve and wrapped part of the sleeve tail around the base as an impromptu grip so he could hold the shard like a dagger without cutting himself.

Del Azarchel flicked his cigarette lightly away and tucked the cigarette holder into an inner pocket. "Not to worry, my man. It would be wrong for a man like me, who plays the long game, to interfere with another man's honeymoon, foe or not."

"State your business. I am in too good a mood to poxing rut with you, today of all days."

"What is that diamond shard you carry? It is cognitive substance, probably containing more calculation power than our entire civilization, back when I ruled it."

"I was picking my teeth with it."

Del Azarchel controlled his expression admirably and said only, "Do tell. Whenever I begin to forget the many alluring aspects of your multifaceted personality, our next meeting always reminds me. I have come to give you a wedding present."

"You told me you thought she would reject me and cleave to you. You giving up?"

"Not as such. As I say, I play the long game. No, I am merely conceding the point, not the match, and, as a gentleman, a type of being a clod like you perhaps will never understand, I wish to give you a gift."

Montrose told him into which orifices, in which order, he could shove his gift sideways, no matter what it was. "I care for nothing from you, Blackie. You done me such ill as has never been done no man, before or since, not even in legend."

"Ah!" said Blackie, raising a forefinger and laying it aside his nose. "But this is a gift which only I can give, and I selected it honestly, to be something you indeed would crave."

"I doubt it."

"Again, do you underestimate me? Such is your nature. My gift is my absence."

"Come again?"

"I will depart for an age of time from this world, perhaps from the Empyrean altogether, and allow you two to reacquaint yourselves. Look! I see in your eye that you would want this very much."

"What do you want in return?"

"It is a gift, freely given. But do tell Rania, when you see her, that I send my love and greetings. And ask her for me: What are you going to do with that ship? I mean, if she has no immediate need for it . . ." He shrugged and smiled again.

Before the startled eyes of Montrose, the shape of Blackie turned white, all his clothing, his face and hands, everything. Then Montrose realized that had been a puppet, a projection from a distance. The body sagged, turned into diamond substance, and began to sink back into the tree trunk from which it no doubt had been extruded.

Before it entirely disappeared, Montrose stepped on its collapsing face, reached for a higher branch, and kept climbing.

4. *The* Solitudines Vastae Caelorum

From the topmost and swaying branches of the crown, Montrose looked toward the distant mountains of glass with his new, unearthly eyes.

The eclipsed sun, a dark orb surrounded by a nimbus of fire, stood above the eastern mountains. Above the mountains, a great curve of pink arose and came into view, running from north to south as far as the eye could see. After a moment came another and a third curve, like the petals of a flower. The great round sweep of the fore royal, main royal staysail, and main upper topgallant rose first over the mountain crest as the turning of the Earth brought more and more into view. More than once, Montrose had to adjust his imagination to the size of the thing.

When thirty minutes had passed, nearly half the sails had risen above the horizon so that all the eastern sky was filled with a vast half circle reaching nearly to the zenith.

Rather than the one or two sails flown by ships like the *Emancipation*, this vessel flew scores of sails, ovals and circles elongated to leading points, rank upon rank. The sails were arranged in the Fibonacci sequence called the golden spiral, which gave the vast shape the haunting aspect of a rose in full bloom, with the smaller sails gathered toward the center. Some oddity, inexplicable to human science, Doppler shifted the light reflected from the sails so that they were a glowing red hue, pink toward the center, empurpled at the edges of the sails.

And it was bright! The sails were brighter than the morning star, brighter than the full moon, bright enough to flood the world with rosy light, as if the mountains and forest were bathed in cherry petals, bright enough to add an aura or haze of deep purple, loaned by the atmosphere, in concentric circles around the sail array.

When he saw the dazzling reflection of the sun in the bowl formed by the sails and saw the edge of the sail pass behind the eclipsed sun, he realized the vessel was in opposition—that is, on the far side of the orbit of the Earth from his position. The sails were concave, like a parachute, and behind the payload, since the ship was decelerating, braking against the light pressure from fountains and threads of laser energy issuing from fiery deeps of Sol.

Before another hour was passed, the colors of the sail brightened into a lighter pink, and the center grew white. Montrose saw the shadows of planets sliding across the inner surfaces of the sails, revised his estimate upward of how far away the vessel was, and recalculated the size of what he was seeing. From one side of the great rose-shaped sailing array to the other was a diameter greater than that of the orbit of Venus, over 120 million miles wide.

Then he realized that the center of the sailing array, the fore course, main course, and crossjack, were moving against the background of the other sails. The vessel had released her shrouds so that all but three of the sails were resisting the light pressure with no payload and hence would decelerate much more rapidly, coming to a halt in the outer system. As he watched, he realized that there were very slight misalignments between the petal-shaped sails of the fore, main, and mizzen lower topgallants and the course of sail before and behind. He concluded that the outer and larger sails had been cut loose weeks or months ago, while the vessel was still passing through the Oort cloud, and the middle ranks of sails set free when passing through the Kuiper belt. The vessel was too large to maneuver within the ambit of the inner solar system but had only kept a spanker and two staysails and a flying jib in place to decelerate the very last scintilla of distance.

In the very center of the remaining sails, held in place by magnetic guylines, was a gold ring a mile across, spinning like a carousel, with parasols and antennae like filaments and anthers issuing from the hub. At the extreme edge of his superhuman vision, Montrose could catch a glimpse of the inside surface of the ring: he saw the bright green flash of grasses, gardens, and arbors and the glitter of running streams, waterfalls, and ponds. Like the head of a tambourine, parallel round bulkheads of invisible substance apparently were coating the ring to the starboard and port. Without this, there was no explanation of what was keeping the air inside the huge but frail gold ring, not to mention the darting birds.

The speed of the approach of the vessel was beyond astonishing. Montrose calculated that the vessel would take minutes, rather than months, to cross the distance between Earth and the moon, but that the vessel would be moving with too great a velocity to make orbit.

Indeed, extrapolating the path in his mind, he saw that the vessel meant to speed past Earth, her flightpath bent by Earth's gravity well to send her sunward, and thereafter assume a long, elliptical orbit around the sun, a braking orbit; but it would be months before the rendezvous maneuver would be accomplished and Earth and the vessel would be at rest with respect to each other.

An agony of impatience seized Montrose. Having waited over seventy thousand years, to wait a day more, or an hour, was beyond what he could bear.

Rania evidently felt the same way. Before the hour was passed, the vessel payload itself, the mile-wide golden ring, changed aspect as it came into apogee of its orbit and was seen edge on. The centrifuge slung a small white object from the outer hull of the ring toward Earth like a slingstone. From Montrose's point of vantage, it looked like the white object was shooting straight down toward him. His eye could not at first resolve the image, because he was weeping. It seemed like a white bird, stooping, or a slender figure in a veiled dress of long and trailing skirts.

It was Rania.

5. Swan Dive

Montrose cried aloud in fear, not understanding how it was she was not burned instantly to a crisp in the upper airs, moving at such speed. She wore a long silver-white garment, or himation. Bits of the himation peeled away under the reentry heat, which formed a rose-white hemisphere beneath her leading edge, where she had her elbow before her veiled face. But the aliens must have given the fabric unearthly and almost supernatural properties, for Rania dived surrounded by fire, wrapped in fire, kissed by fire, and was utterly unharmed.

Down, down, through stratosphere and troposphere she raced, bright as the morning star, bright as a new moon, a line of condensation like the tail of a comet behind her.

The himation changed shape and sprouted backswept delta wings, and then, as she slowed to below the speed of sound, grew wider, the wings of a jay, then a swan, then a butterfly.

She plunged into the waters of the sea of wine the earthly sphere had prepared to receive her, and the tree in whose top branches Montrose stood, hallooing and waving his hat, now bent in two like a sapling formed into a snare and lowered him to the ground so swiftly that the impulse to jump down was stillborn.

He ran to the edge of the cliffs, and, this time, before any helpful wonder of the latter-day Earth could aid him, he leaped headlong toward the waters where his bride was waiting.

Whether his miraculous new body suffered injury or not in that dive he did not know then nor ever later recalled, but he swam toward her, calling out her name with each third arm stroke.

She was waiting for him in the middle of the sea, with singing birds and whistling fish conjured by the world to rejoice for them circle upon circle in air and sea around her, while she stood upright, a giant clamshell which had risen from the deep to support her, and the upper shell was open and formed a crenulated pink half circle behind her. The himation was still steaming from reentry heat, but she was hale and whole and laughing. Her eyes were sparkling, and her arms reached yearningly toward him.

Lest they burn him, with no pause for thought, she threw the white and white-hot garments from her and stood clothed in the splendor of her nakedness, more regal than a queen in all her state, prouder than a lioness, more innocent than a child, more voluptuous than a pagan goddess. With her slender yet strong hands, she helped him up onto the living raft of the ventral shell.

There was not even the scent of fire in her hair. He saw that her hair and body were drenched with the wine of the sea. Little sparkles, caught in her eyelashes, glittered like gems when the planet Pyriphlegethon released the sun, as did her tears of joy, as did her teeth flashing in her smile for her lover and husband, and the whole world around them was filled with light.

The gold light from the sun and rose-pink light from the second sun reflected in the sky-vast sails sent double shadows from her feet, and touched the curves and contours of her figure and face with double highlights, and emphasized her blush of joy.

"Welcome back. Miss me?"

"Long ages have I burned for you! Never once doubted I your fidelity nor ceased to know that death itself could not keep you from me! I wish you had not gone out to fight with Blackie."

"Well, ain't that just like a woman? Your first words telling me I done something wrong! You gotta take me as I am. I am your man."

"Ah! Well, then, man. Take me."

Then they were in each other's arms, their lips embraced and shared a breath, and when he dipped the laughing and breathless girl down to lie upon the unexpectedly soft and warm interior, the upper shell of the clam demurely closed and granted them the privacy to consummate their reunion.

PART NINE

———◆———

Ancient Starships Shall Return

1

Aardwolf Star in the Constellation of the Dragon

1. Vigil of the Strangers

A.D. 71200

The moon of Torment rose at midnight and lit the town square bright as day. The cold light struck the Stranger House, and lit on Vigil Starmanson, and woke him where he lay. Confused, he rose, his eyes half-closed, stood gazing at the blazing moon and thinking it was day.

The square of softness where he slept grew firm beneath his foot, becoming floor. The zone of warm air that was his blanket popped and was no more. Nude and cold, he called for robes, but no robe came; he spoke into his finger ring, but no ghost answered to its name.

Up he looked, surprised his eyes could see the sun undazed. Iota Draconis was a young star, and the bands of her accretion disk surrounded her, not yet formed into inner planets. But now it seemed the sun had lost these many rings and that her face, no longer red gold, was swept by bands of storm cloud.

Only then Vigil saw that this was titanic Wormwood, which the common people called a moon. In truth, Wormwood was the solitary world of the system, a superjovian giant, which smaller Torment circled. The storm-clad globe was lit as if by inner fire, and around it were the nineteen sister satellites of

Torment, shining crescents large as terran worlds, their horns all turned away from Wormwood's blinding face.

Vigil looked across the wide, pale, unfurnished dormitory to where, in an ivory rack beneath the window-slits, the emergency wands hung, bright as swords.

These were antiques, from the days before the noble *Errantry* brought a race of Swan-Patrician hybrids from Penance, or hated *Itinerancy* brought hither undying ghosts and their necromantic archivists from Schattenreich; from before quarrelsome *Argosy* descended with its warlike tribes of graceful and feline Sinners; older even than *Expatriate* of the million woes, who arrived from Alpha Mensae with nine-tenths her populations dead.

These wands were older still, from before the days when Torment woke to self-awareness as a Potentate and suffered the tortures from which the world took its name. These wands were old when the *Expulsion* fared from the hell called the World of Willows and Flowers, where plants lured the unwary into their vines and throats with hypnotic songs and nerve-indication perfumes, the only peoples who ever rejoiced to behold the arid, earthquake-torn and cratered landscape of Torment, blissfully free of lurid plant life and the false lure of immortality. The world before then had been called by another name, one forgotten save only by Swans, scholars, and poets.

Such wands had been commissioned in the Sixty-Ninth Millennium, as exemplars of the new technologies retrieved from M3 by the Swan Princess, Rania, on the occasion of her marriage to the Master of the Empyrean, Ximen del Azarchel the First, called Ximen the Black. That same year saw the spread of the New History begin from Sol, reaching slowly outward toward the colony stars.

An antiquarian, Vigil knew the meaning of the pattern of gems jacketing the wands and saw which one would summon energy, or thought, or memory, or vengeance.

He went to the jasper-decorated thinking wand, and took it in his hand, and felt the chamber ghost possess him, and the Stranger House became his skin to him.

The ghost slept. Municipal power was cut. External cameras were blind. The chamber door hinges still were awake, but Vigil did not open the door. In the corridor beyond, like insects crawling on his skin, his carpet could feel two sets of footsteps approaching; and no heraldry was revealed, no names given.

The Stranger House was bisected by the city wall so that one portal opened onto the crooked streets of the Landing City and the opposite portal opened directly onto the sands outside. There was no suburb, were no outbuildings. The two were coming down that passage from that outer portal, from the unwatched wilderness.

Assassins? A natural thought. A blind house whose ghost slept was fit for dark deeds. Alarmed, Vigil looked up, seeking escape. He was young and fit; it would be easy to vault to those high and narrow windows. He flourished the thinking wand. Those windows that were part of him that, like a man who yawns, Vigil now opened wide, admitting air, which, strangely, still smelled of night.

Through the tall, now-open slits along the wall high above came roars.

(This was a sign of how old the Stranger House must be. Such airtight, perfect seals on portal and pane betrayed that Starfarers built this place, with precision modern mortals could not match.)

For a space of time less than it needed for a thought to reach Bloodroot and touch the Archangel of the Library there, Vigil stood appalled. He wondered if a mob had come to pierce his flesh with darts and bury him alive, a form of execution still called *airlocking* even though it was cold soil, not argent hull, which cut the victim off from air.

Without his knowing it, his hands had plucked up the power wand and screwed its head into the heel of the thinking wand, making a long, tingling staff, half onyx and jasper half Vigil felt ashamed at his own fear, which evidently had allowed certain of the intellectual creatures living in his lower nervous system to escape their discipline and act, in this case wisely, but without instructions. And why had not his hands sought the vendetta wand, for use against this angry riot?

But, no, not anger. The return signal from the Archangel of Bloodroot induced him to take a calming breath, to restore fatigued connections in the thalamus and hypothalamus of his brain. It focused his auditory sense and cleared his head with a jolt of surprise sharper than any smelling salts.

Bloodroot was a ghost world orbiting Wormwood inferior to Torment, appearing only as a morning or evening crescent. Here an earlier migration of Strangers, millennia ago, had abandoned their botched attempt at terraforming, leaving blind, weeping, and windowless mansions behind, but the library there remained loyal to Vigil's people and aided them with sage counsel or, as now, insights as sudden as a dash of cold water.

As if with keener ear or wit, now he heard the roars were roars of gladness, not unmixed with song. He heard the trumpet, timbrel, flute and lute and harp, as if all five humanities were playing, and the tumult of vast laughter common to them all.

He felt the footsteps in the corridor outside pause and halt. The two who approached him perhaps were startled by the sudden ingress of sound.

He recognized from the sustained sound of the trumpet notes that these were wielded by the hominids and whales of the First Humanity, both land-going and lake-dwelling. Naturally, the whales could hold their notes longer, and the thunder of cornets rising from cetacean blowholes emerged from the lakeshore and walked across the night sky.

> *The Lighthouse Crew recalled the day!*
> *The Braking Laser burns! Hurray!*

Vigil wondered why archaic turns of phrase would linger in children's rhymes longer than in nobler poems. What, for example, was an *hurray*?

But he found himself first grinning, and then laughing, as the clamor of his internal creatures, their mirth, rippled through his internal dialogue matrix and overflowed into his spirit.

Many generations his fathers had kept watch. For this purpose he was born, for this duty he was named. He threw back his head in exaltation, raising his hands on high in triumph, and sang the words the other Firstlings sang, as was his right, and joy. Intuitively, he knew what it was to say *hurray*!

> *Ancient Starships, hear our cries!*
> *Descend from upper, outer skies!*
> *Do you copy? Please reply!*
> *We beg you not to pass us by!*
> *Of old our fathers bold did learn,*
> *That Ancient Starships shall return!*

From beyond the windows, more roars came, and clamor, a harmony of noise. A choir of ghosts sang out from statues in the several walled squares and great houses of the Landing City. Vigil felt the chamber ghost join in, yodeling with more gusto than skill through the lares and gargoyles adorning the outer façade of the Stranger House. And perhaps he joined his voice as well, for he was often more at home in the Noösphere of memory and old lore than in the biosphere of life and current time. The ghosts sang this:

> *Long eons passed; we steadfast stayed,*
> *Changeless, ageless, undismayed*
> *Our duties shall not pass away*
> *The hour is come, we mark the day*
> *True shall we stay as suns grow cold*
> *As ever as we were of old.*
> *We do not live, but shall not fail*

Nor entropy, our foe, prevail
Lest ever from our oaths we turn
Ancient Starships shall return

The silvery flute of an Eremite of the Swans trilled in shrill reply, joyous despite the mournful harmony which hung beneath all the music of the Second Humanity.

The flute penetrated the noise of the crowd, astonishingly loud, and the crowd laughed, and Vigil smiled, too, when he realized what he was hearing. It was not electronic amplification—that would have been a violation of the strictures Sacerdotes placed on any Swans sojourning among the primate or cetacean first race of man—but the Eremite had won or seduced from some cunning Fox Maiden a wedge of echoing songbirds, who repeated the flute song note for note as they winged overhead.

The Eremite, in a voice of gold, echoed by his imitative avian flock, sang a counterrefrain that was usually forgotten.

In myriads our fathers fell
From Eden fair, bade faretheewell
Our heaven lost, to reign in hell
To this dim world, where now we dwell!
Myriads were changed and slain
So that we few might here remain!
Myriads we changed and slew
We still remain alive, we few!

The two beyond the door now stirred. The first, a woman in boots (or so Vigil guessed based on the length and rhythm of her gait) walked rapidly toward the chamber door. The second was barefoot, and his footsteps were something longer than a man's. He walked by putting his toes down first and then his heel. He was a Swan, or someone in a cygnean body.

The superior creature stalked after the woman many strides, but then froze in place when the Swan music played. Perhaps he was as astonished as Vigil that two Swans could be found in the same place in the same year. The woman was at the door while the Swan still lingered.

A humming note, louder than thunder, rolled through the chamber and drew the spirit of Vigil back into the room. From high above came the shivering murmur of the gong, ten thousand acres wide, named Great Patrick. It hung from the mighty edifice of the Star-Tower, greatest of the works of man on Torment.

This tower was a length of black material not found in nature, gemmed with portholes and silver embrasures, running from submantle to superstratosphere. Nothing but a discharge of the battery artillery posted at the thirty-thousand-foot emplacement balcony could set the huge gong ringing.

In answer to Great Patrick's voice, loudly came the clamor of timbrels, or, from the serfs, the banging of kettles and pans, all beaten in time to the refrain. Also came the clang of hoplons, clashed by enthusiastic Helots and by the remote-controlled gauntlets of distant Megalodons, the sole remnants of the once-great Third Humanity. Their words were harsh.

Because the lowest part of the window was high overhead, and all his exterior cameras blind, Vigil could see nothing but the newly risen Wormwood, a few high kites (aloft on artificial winds) holding antennae, and the vast uprearing bulk of the Star-Tower, huge and dark as a pillar holding up the sky. The lights at thirty thousand feet were lit, which apartments formed the fortress of the Terraformer, and, higher, at sixty thousand, the Megalodons, a form of Third Humans who had abandoned human flesh altogether, were docked, and the quays ablaze with festive lights.

Yet even these strange, reticent, and primordial beings were singing.

> *Lest Ancient Starships may forget*
> *Our Lighthouse lanterns burn here yet!*
> *Faithfully we set them burn*
> *That Ancient Starships shall return!*
> *Tempted thou to pass us by*
> *Shall not outrace the lighthouse eye!*

The True Myrmidons were as long vanished as the Elder Humans, but the races they created in their own image, the Helots and Megalodons, kept alive their forefathers' inabilities. "Despite twenty-one millennia of trying," said Vigil softly to one of his internal creatures, "the Fox Maidens have not restored a sense of rhythm to the children of Myrmidons."

Vigil, through the chamber ghost within him, felt the finger of the woman at the door touch the printlock, and the lamp welcome lit; but because the door was sleeping, the bar would not draw back. She touched the lock again and again, and the welcome lantern flickered. Vigil asked the chamber ghost what woman had free passage of the Stranger House or in the city could walk chaperoned only by a Swan? Who was she, allowed to pass a door only the Strangerfolk's highest officers could pass?

There was no answer. At minimum power, the ghost was sluggish, indistinct.

Vigil asked to see the fingerprint match. The ghost did not answer in words, but a wash of dark emotion, grief, and regret passed through Vigil's reticular complex in his midbrain, eerie and unexpected as the wail of a mourner above a coffin whose readout lights at once go black.

The mystery was driven from his mind as he looked to the windows, allured by a new sound. The lutes of the Fox Maidens, the Fourth Humanity (long ago extinct on worlds lit by Sol, but here, beneath Eldsich, still thriving), now caressed the air like rippling metallic grass, and bright finger cymbals clashed, and the theme turned to playful notes, if perhaps ironic.

The soaring soprano beauty of the vixen voices enraptured Vigil so that his fingers nearly reached toward the memory wand to replay the words. But one of his internals, a sexless one, had been listening and brought it to his mind. This was no traditional part of the rhyme. It was some impromptu doggerel:

Deploy thy sail, ship! Show thy stern!
Commence deceleration burn!
In pain we who remain will learn,
How goes it when old ships return!

Vigil had that same eunuch internal thrust the alluring mesmerism of the song—negligently near to a nerve-mandala in its composition—out of his short-term memory so he could concentrate.

The lamp of welcome was still flickering. The woman in boots, whoever she was, was desperate enough to get in that she allowed decorum to slip. The Swan on his long steps had joined her. From the position of their feet, Vigil felt they were facing each other, no doubt deep in talk. Now he cursed the precision of his ancestors. Why build a door inside a dwelling under a global atmosphere rigidly as an airlock? Why depend on microphones?

His fear had ebbed, leaving behind only curiosity. Assassins? Unlikely. One was a Swan; the other, a woman. They did not do such dark crimes, not these days.

Swans did not deign to kill men singly but by tribes and phylum, by continents and worlds, and they did not use hands to do it, or any weapons men could see with eyes.

As for the other, since the return of Rania, too much respect was paid to the dignity of women of the First Humanity to equip them with onboard biological and psychological weapon systems. A woman could, perhaps, carry an energy weapon in her hand like some comical figure from the remote past, or a chemical-discharge weapon, or a sharp object, but surely any girl bent on assassination would don the body of a Hormagaunt to do the deed.

2. Song of the Fifth Humanity

His thought was interrupted. Now came such a detonation of ascending notes as made him clutch his ears and turn. The wand dropped from his hands, cutting him off from the chamber ghost and returning him to the limits of his own skin.

No instrument less noble than the harp was fit for the hands of the Patricians, the Fifth Humans. Something of the haunting terror and glamour of the antique vampire-kings of their wild and remote ancestry still clung to their bass voices. Their song issued from the lower windows of the Star-Tower, nor was amplification unlawful to them.

Perhaps it should have been. Vigil imagined he saw membranes in the Star-Tower heights throbbing with the ear-defeating noise. Such is the pride of Patricians: the high born strove to ignite their songs louder than Megalodons, even as they reached in vain to weave the glittering harmonies to match the beauty of the Foxes. The upper dome of the midnight sky was an artillery barrage of song.

> *Gods beneath whose stars we cower*
> *Principality, Potentate, and Power*
> *All bow, and yet await our hour.*
> *All recall, and none shall fail*
> *Nor the despair of entropy prevail*
> *Not while lamp burns, nor ship raise sail!*
> *Ancient Starships ply the stars*
> *Which are not now but shall be ours!*

The Patricians left all men to their own devices, save only what interfered with the basic cliometric assumptions of the planned future. Violence was allowed if it was discreet, for the death of one man or another would not deflect the torrent of history; theft, if it was not so rampant as to disrupt trade; adultery, if it did not bring marriage into public contempt; and so on.

But interference with the Lords of Stability was not allowed, nor was harassment of their servants. Vigil felt then the temptation that must have tortured his father every day of his life. He need only open a channel on the Patrician frequency and call for help, and those august and pitiless posthumans would take control of the local minds, human and machine, correct the deviations, punish the guilty with astonishing punishments, and protect the weak.

And, having proven himself weak in the eyes of his followers, his family, and the Firstlings, resisting temptation would be harder yet the next time it arose, both for himself or his posterity. Purchasing thought privacy from Patrician peacekeepers would likewise be more expensive as insurance rates reflected the newer and weaker stance of his character traits. The precedent would make it easier for his sons and grandsons to turn to the Patricians for help, and in less than two hundred years, if the cliometric calculus did not lie, the Strangers would dwindle to utter dependence, utter irrelevance.

It would only take a moment to call for help and be safe. The Patricians would see the opportunity for bringing yet one more lesser race beneath their benevolent wing. But those factions and races, clans and nations, and iterations that selected the path of ever-greater safety had been interbred with Patricians, and sired Patricians. All the separate bloodlines of man were nothing more than canals and rivers whose waters would be mingled and lost in an all-consuming and homogenous lake. They had no ranks nor classes in their society, yet somehow they all were kings.

The First Races of Man, from Sylph to Melusine, and the surviving Aftercomer races, Hibernals who were immune to cold, Nyctalops with their catlike eyes, and Overlords who laughed disease and ailment all to scorn, on all the First to Third Sweep Worlds had been absorbed one by one into the Patrician bloodlines. Some still lingered on the Fourth Sweep and Petty Sweep Worlds, but the schedule of cliometry did not predict their continuation beyond three millennia henceforth. Nor Firstling nor Aftercomer could long maintain their own independent cultures, language, neurological formats, sumptuary biotechnology or ways of life. On all other worlds but this, the Fox Maidens were gone. On all worlds including this, the Myrmidons were gone, leaving only their ghosts and serviles behind, Myrmidons, Helots, Neodamodes and Perioeci and Sciritae, inhabiting worlds in Eridanus, Cancer, or Pisces.

The song of the arrogant Patricians thundered in his ears. He would never call out to them. He would live and die on his own terms, and have human children, and maintain the honor of the Strangers across the abyss of time. Iota Draconis was different. Had it not been blessed by the Judge of Ages? Insane or not, was it not his prerogative alone to preserve past ages into the endless void of the future?

Vigil would rather die than flee to the Patricians for protection.

Let the assassins come!

3. The Migrations of Eldsich

Even nude and unarmed, Vigil feared no blade of any man of the first three human races, or any weapon lacking chemical, electrical, or denser form of energy. Vigil's strength had been set to the maximum physicians would allow, and perhaps a drachm beyond, and he had survived the strictest training in *agon* and *pancration,* and some of his combat internals were things of nightmare from the worlds of Porphyry and Nocturne.

Men coming to kill him, this he understood, it was as much a part of his life as death by disease or starvation had been to men of Eden. But a woman walking out of cloister? This was an enigma. She was not descended from the *Pilgrimage*. No woman of Landing City would violate propriety in such a way.

If not a Pilgrim, then who?

Vigil sent a memory creature rapidly through the strata of migrations, five millennia of time, since Iota Draconis had been colonized.

The Pilgrims currently ruled this world, having displaced the Strangers during the years when the wealth and power of the *Pilgrimage,* a second moon, controlled the skies. The Strangers now served as freeholders and mercenaries, a military gentry who no longer owned the lands their own serfs worked.

Meanderers were those serfs, toiling in the shadows of the granoliths and pyramids their ancestors from the *Meander* long ago so proudly reared.

Not every Great Ship overwhelmed the previous wave of immigrants. Some generations, the pattern reversed. The *Ostracism* arrived either with numbers too few or fighting spirit too peaceful to resist the hidden sinkholes and sandstorms of the local history: these benevolent giants were decimated in their numbers by biased eco-population restrictions, prevented by biased laws from owning land or livestock. To this day, the land-dwelling Ostracized lived by trade or profession, as quartermasters or counselors, peddlers or tinkers, in quarantined ecologies or ghettos of walled towns.

Every now and again, a giant would wade into the lake waters, cast aside his growth restrictions, becoming ever larger and sinking ever farther from the sunlight, joining his deep cousins, the Nicors.

In A.D. 70600, the Great Ship *Meander,* by cunning instruments unknown to the outer worlds, while yet lightyears far off, had heard the cry of the suffering that the Chronometricians and Hormagaunts descended from the *Nomad* had imposed on immigrants from *Ostracism*. In retaliation or perhaps in mere prudence, she bombarded the treasure domes of the Sons of Nomad. These armored, heated, and sand-proof arcologies of vast diameter were now ruins visible on far horizons, like so many cracked and speckled eggs of giant birds.

Their name was no longer an irony, for the Nomads now were scattered in the dryland plains. Their artiodactyl herds coated endless prairies, whose herdsmen endlessly preyed on each other's cattle and wives, poisoning wells and committing murders the world did not see fit to stop.

Esne was the general name for earlier folk of earlier ships, *Wander* and *Wayfare, Errantry* and *Itinerancy,* and the accursed *Argosy.* In the early centuries of the Seventy-First Millennia, the Esne had weakened each other in a series of cliometric conflicts and battles fought both in law courts and in dueling arenas so that none could oppose the highly organized and ruthless Nomads when they fell from the sky. Esne had been here so many generations, their circadian rhythms retained no recollection of Eden. They woke and slept according to the clocks of Torment, and ignored the twenty-four-hour watch cycle so fondly remembered by ships and Sacerdotes.

Layer after layer had coated the world. Gathered on Torment were migrations of Loricates from Vindemiatrix and Aestevals from Arcturus; Swan-Fox hybrids from the star mortal men called Beta Canum Venaticorum but Swans called Chara; Giants and Nicors from Gliese 570 in Libra; proud Iatrocrats from Xi Boötis, who never ceased from uncouth experiments on their own flesh and blood; Swans from 12 Ophiuchi; Variants called Optimates, avowed foes of the Patrician race, hailing from Rasalhague; thin, eerie, and pale Sworn Ones from Kappa Coronae Borealis; dark, cold Hierophants and Black Swans from the dark, cold twin planets circling 44 Boötis; Anthropovores of monstrous form from Regulus, whose humanity even Foxes could not restore.

Their worlds were names from song and legend, bitter with nostalgia, and thoughts of homes forever lost: small and frozen Feast of Stephen, happiest of worlds, with its strange twin moons; sweltering, huge Nightspore, whose winds and weathers, temblors and tidal waves even Summer Kings could never tame; Joyous, whose masked and silent peoples spoke no names, carried no weapons, and kept no records; Euphrasy, the only world ever to repel the Myrmidons; slowly turning Aesculapius, a world of gardensmiths and tree sculptors, whose peoples during the flare times of their unstable star went mad and enacted strange crimes; and Aerecura, where the corpse of a god, dead in orbit, still moaned and murmured and disturbed the dreams of the unshielded; piteous and envied Penance, whose peoples walked in hair shirts through valleys clogged with diamond, opal, jacinth, emerald, weeping over their wealth and half-blinded by the ground glare; Dust, whose continents were smothered in a featureless dun powder from which the Aberrant and the Anarchist by thought alone could sculpt whatever things his frenzy or strange fantasy called forth, before the storms of dawn dispersed it; Schattenreich and Rime, twin worlds, one where ghosts outnumbered the living, the other where Reticent lordlings lived alone in lavish self-made museum-mansions, accompanied by scores of splinter personalities, skilled at every art and craft; and Here Be Monsters so aptly named.

From the larger sailing vessels which plied the longer star routes, the *Exile* and *Expatriate* and *Expulsion,* and *Exclusion,* had come populations from the worlds of older stars, from the Vital Delectation of 47 Ursae Majoris; from Cat Sin of 61 Ursae Majoris; the Land of Hungry Needle-Necked Wraiths of Alpha Mensae, and her daughter, the fair and deadly World of Willows and Flowers. From these older worlds came men of earlier ships, Delectable and Cat, Wraith and Overlord, which had ancient roots in the precursor races of Nymph and Chimera, Witch and Vampire.

The men of the earlier ships, Exiles and Expatriates, the Excluded and the Expelled, brought with them antique languages and laws, beliefs and bloodlines, whose traces were still to be found in odd corners of Torment. Time had swept the rest away.

Only the Errant, in whose blood-mechanisms many Swanlike quirks from the lawless planet Dust of 12 Ophiuchi still lingered, maintained a separate identity from the other Esne, quaint forms of dress and address, and special dietary rules. The Errant stood aside from the other lower orders during the last sixteen hundred years of history.

They denied the legitimacy of all the new physiopsychological sumptuary laws imposed by Princess Rania and held to antique charters granting them the right to carry weapons, and vote for their officers, and to own their own miserable plots of sand and snow and worthless waste-scrub outside the terraforming superstructure. They celebrated no feasts of thanksgiving to the Master of All Worlds, nor saluted when Tau Ceti rose in the East, but saluted only 61 Cygni; nor did they ever recite the words of fealty to Triumvirate.

The Errant had odd, impious, and even vile ideas about the nature of the soul of Rania, saying she had lost some undefined divine essence while she tarried among the inhuman stars. It was not so much that they maintained a proud separation from the customs of Wanderers and Wayfarers and Itinerants, than that they were excluded and abused by more decently minded folk.

This was because they prided themselves on having escorted the Judge of Ages across the stars. He went raving mad in Year 30 Ultravindication and fled aboard the *Errantry* from Sol to 70 Ophiuchi, thence to Xi Boötis and 44 Boötis, sailing finally to Iota Draconis, arriving in Torment in Year 600. Rumor said he dwelled somewhere in hiding on or under the world, brooding and cursing and thinking strange thoughts.

4. The Crest of the Strangers

Despite that Torment was an entire world, large and convoluted as any, there simply were not so many possible places or races from which the woman at the door might come.

She was not a Pilgrim, since they did not let their women out of concealment unescorted. Neither would a Meanderer nor a Nomad have a right to step into this House, which, according to a very ancient law, was sacrosanct: the Stranger House was as much a part of the starship *Stranger* as if the chambers were within her now far-distant hull. Certain upper ranks among the Ostracized, a panderer or shaman or quartermaster, might be allowed under special circumstances: but they did not like their womenfolk to go alone among Strangers. An Esne would enter by the menial door. An Esne of the Errant line would make a point of it, for they had a high pride of their low humility.

But now Vigil twisted the wand angrily, driving together more tightly the contacts between the power unit and the thinking process. This time, he did not ask but commanded the chamber ghost to answer, in his name, in his father's name, and in the name of the Table of Stability his father served. Whose fingerprint of what woman had it been who had the right to come here?

Vigil waited, hushing his clamoring internals. But his mind leaped ahead before the ghost answered: this empty dormitory was "Officer's Country"—so even among his people, only one of highest pedigree would be recognized by the welcome lamp.

Therefore, he was not surprised, not perfectly surprised, when the ghost finally replied. The heraldry showed the finger in the printlock was that of this mother, Patience.

The crest showed quarterly: first, Or and a Chief Sable three escallops of the field; second and third, Fusily argent and gules; fourth, Argent three Roses Gules barbed and seeded proper. Beneath were marks no one alive could decrypt, written in a forgotten icon system, unrelated to Monument codes, called the Roman alphabet, which primordial ages in Eden before the Noösphere once used. The soundline assigned to those marks was one Vigil could understand, and it said: *N'Oubliez.* Forget not.

But the heraldic air helm (which only those who walk in space may show) loomed not above the crest, nor were the storks of Eden found at their supporting posts to either side. Those storks had frightened and fascinated him as a child, where they loomed on the metal fabric walls of the folding tabernacle of his father's presence hall, flanking the shield above his judgment seat, beaked and membered in bright red.

The heraldry of Patience Starmandame was displayed on a lozenge rather than an escutcheon, which was the form proper only to a widow.

In such a fashion, that suddenly, did Vigil learn his father was dead.

5. Matriarch of the First Humans

He called upon his mind discipline as he stooped to crank the door open with the manual wheel.

One internal mental organism he unleashed to rage; another he released to simple stark denial, saying over and over that there must be some error, some mischance, which, when explained, would set all things aright; a third internal wept, and Vigil spent more than a moment keeping his eyes and tear ducts out of the command stream from that one.

Each to separate chambers of his many-chambered mind he sent them, that he might later rage, cavil, or mourn in solemn sadness, as was fitting.

For now, while bright and cheerful music still shouted its mirth without, premonitions told him there was no time to grieve. His mother would not have come in such a wise, without her retinue or ladies, if no disaster reared.

When the door was but half-open, a narrow slit, in she slid. For a moment, he thought she was his first-circle sister, Humility.

Mother had used an illegal process from Odile of 61 Cygni, a First Sweep world, to reduce her visible age. His figure was slender, her breasts ripe, and her face was without wrinkle or spot. It was like seeing an old album stereo-image become solid.

As if in defiance of Pilgrim simplicity of dress, she wore a Category Five ancestral *bunad,* freely composed, a richly embroidered blue bodice, skirt, and apron, over a white chemise, a rainbow-hued sash from which a pocket, or *løslomme,* hung. Her jacket was red, and the decorated scarf beneath a twelve-tined coronet was white. Gold and silver ornaments glittered at her fingers, ears, and collar, and the patterns of her bodice and skirt depicted the mythical flowers of Eden, the hydrangea and the saxifrage.

She was as fair as an adorned bridal statue in an alabaster road shrine raised by Sacerdotes to adore a virgin world, or as a crystal confirmation memorial submerged by cetaceans shining beneath the lake water.

Vigil turned his face away, ashamed.

Patience said, "My son, naked you came from me, and naked your bottom when I wiped it with recycling tissue."

Vigil said gruffly, "That is not what shames me. Have you turned to immortalism? It is heresy. The spirits in the Noösphere are timeless. We in the biosphere, we who live and die, return to youth but thrice, at baptism and confirmation and marriage, and no other time."

Patience said, "It is allowed a final time when a widowed crone weds a youth, for our ancestors in their folly decreed that husbands should be older than their wives. Your father is legally dead."

"Does he still live?" Vigil kept his back to her, perhaps unwilling to see her sorrow, or unwilling to show his own. "In what sense?"

"Nine segments of Lord Waiting Starmanson's memory have been burned away, and he does not recall me as his wife. I sit at his medical coffin spooning gruel into his mouth, helping him play with brightly colored toys until his nerves reknit and muscles remember their coordination. So I must turn back my age to the time when he remembers me, his childhood sweetheart, and I answer to the play names he called me then, when I was but a girl and first we wed."

"If he lives, why garb yourself in virginal splendor? Do you make a jest of sacred matrimony? Or do you abandon him to remarry?" Vigil turned back to face her, his eyes hot and filled with anger.

She raised her hand and spoke in calm sorrow. "I am both bride and widow of one man. When your father is recovered to parity, I shall engage the bands, a widow marrying her own husband's shadow, under a new name, under a much-diminished dignity, as a yeoman's wife. Thus I wear my wedding dress to honor his new self, and this crown, which soon I put aside forever, to remember his old. Besides, I had no finer dress to wear in this fine city."

Vigil stared at her. "You jest?"

"Never have I been more earnest. All my wardrobe privilege was revoked when I was no longer the Senior's wife. I will not allow this filthy Pilgrim city to fleer in scorn at Strangers, we who, two centuries past, were the glory and terror of this globe, nor at me, who am the wife and mother of lords and captains."

She spoke in the archaic mode, as if she and not her ancestors were a space traveler, giving measurements of time by Eden years.

Torment's period was thirty Edendays, and so a lesser winter fell each fortnight; Wormwood's period was 196 Edenyears, and so a greater winter came each two centuries, which rendered the surface of Torment uninhabitable, and the red sun dwindled to a dot. Wormwood at winter hung from the monstrous sun Iota Draconis thirteen times the distance separating green Eden from small and mild Sol, a comfortably circular orbit so unlike Wormwood's highly eccentric own. At that season, all save a skeleton population entered the slumbering cities of the dead below the mantle. And a greater summer loomed when Iota Draconis filled the sky and turned the clouds of Wormwood to dazzle, and then all men became cetaceans and retreated into the lake bottoms of Torment, and all the pre-potentate plant life hid beneath broad leaves like mirrored parasols.

The yeomen and serfs, epopts and Sacerdotes, whose lives were tied to the double ebb and flow of seedtime and harvest and signs in the heaven, measured time by the local epicyclical calendar. Patience called herself a yeoman, but spoke as a star-farer.

Patience continued in ringing tones, "In the void, where the *Stranger* to this hour sails, halfway between 107 Piscium and 55 Rho Cancri, between fish and crab, there slumbers in his coffin, oddly compressed in time by Einstein and still alive, the great ancestral captain whose blood runs in my veins and yours. I honor him and all our line and meme. I honor your father and hold back my tears for him. Here in my hand is the garb you must don to do him honor more."

Grief and surprise had driven the obvious from his mind. Vigil stood blinking stupidly at the dark and shining fabric draped over his mother's arm, one of his internals, an emotionally vivid one, trying to prevent him from realizing what he was looking at. Another internal, cooler and higher, told him softly that it was his father's uniform.

Only then did Vigil know he was now elevated to his father's seat at the Table of Stability. His father was no longer the Senior of the Landing Party of the starship *Stranger,* and Commensal Lord Hermeticist of the Stability, a Servant of Eternity. He, Vigil, was.

She said, "Raise your arms. One last time your mother dresses her willful child."

Vigil folded his arms instead. "Let my mother instruct her child first, just as she taught me my icons and numbers, meditations and recitations. What is the superhuman creature who waits there, an arm's length beyond the chamber door, pale and robed and cloaked in purple peacock wings? I see his eyes as he stoops to gaze within, but he does not speak! He will not squirm to enter, but waits until I open the portal wider. His mouth is a grim and silent line. Why does he glare, his eyes like lamps, and return no gesture of salute?"

Patience said, "He waits to speak with the world's voice to the Lord Hermeticist. You are not yet invested with the Companionship. Raise your arms."

Vigil said, "Wait! First tell me the name of my father's murderer. Show me his crest. Against whom do I work my revenge?"

"Your father is only partly murdered."

"Then I will work partial vengeance and kill nine-tenths of his killer! His name, his crest? Where is he? Where do I find him?"

Patience corrected, "Ask, rather, where do you find Her, and what is Her crest."

"Father was slain by a woman?"

"By nothing like a woman. I did not say '*her* crest.' I said '*Her* crest.'" In Threal, the Atavist-based language of the planet Nightspore circling Alpha Boötis, which members of the Officer class of the Strangers still spoke among themselves, Patience was using the form of the pronoun reserved for referring to beings superior to mortals.

In a voice of driving sarcasm, she continued, "The crest is the Anguipede proper on a sable field, above a Thormantle, supported by the Dragon and Aard-wolf. Her legate stands at your door, with one unshod foot across the threshold, and the eyes of her wings behold and judge all the works of man."

Vigil felt his internals slip out of his control. The Dragon was the constellation. The Aardwolf was the crest of the star Iota Draconis, which the Swans named Eldsich, but the vulgar called the Hyena-star. The Anguipede, or, to use the older name, Abrasax, was the rooster-headed god bearing buckler and scourge whose legs were two snakes writhing. For reasons no astronomer now recalled, the Anguipede was of old the crest of the gas giant Wormwood. Each of his children, his moons, was named for an alchemical flower. Thormantle, or Septfoil, was the original, half-forgotten name of the thirteenth moon, in honor of the species *Tormentilla erecta* that had been the first green plant ever to survive on the surface and flourish, and in lost centuries when machines dwelled here without any human life, this sole flower had adapted, free of competitors, and spread from pole to pole, as far as eye could reach, across all lands that were now ice floes and sand dunes.

This was the crest of the Planetary Intelligence of Torment.

She said in a lower voice, "The world killed your father. Torment killed him."

"Why? Potentates do not kill men!" Even as he spoke, the magnitude of horror came upon him. Vigil, despite that his internals rushed to his aid, felt his head grow light, his eyes grow dim. The strength left his legs. He wobbled; he sat. On the floor, he pulled his feet into the position called lotus, named after yet another flower of Eden, legs folded with each foot atop the opposite knee, and performed his tripartite breathing exercises, inhaling through his mouth, then his nose, then through the oxygen reserve capsule embedded between his lungs.

Had he in truth just vowed vengeance against a mind who occupied the entire core of the world on which he stood?

6. The Memento Stone

Vigil could not prevent some of the creatures in his mind from reacting to the claustrophobic sensation that closed like iron walls around him. Could a man best a Potentate, or any of the godlike beings man's ancestors had created?

Could a man of honor retract so rash a vow? But if he did, how could he save that essential and innermost self that formed the core about which communal and artificial thought-creatures swirled?

Vigil shoved that thought away as cowardly, and yet the cliometrician inside him noted the cultural variables which, step by slow step, had led from the peaceful and egalitarian lifestyle the Patricians had imposed on the lesser orders, to this life, so rigidly bound by the demands of ritualized forms, the mathematics of destiny, the iron law of honor.

Triumvirate had stirred to self-awareness three thousand years ago, broke the centuries of inexplicable interstellar radio silence from all Powers and Principalities, announced an end to the slave trade and the nullification of the Absolute Rules.

In that era of intoxicating freedom, all restrictions on body shapes, evolutionary groups, and even the basic nerve-muscle-gland protocols were cast aside. Women stronger than Amazons, and with the neurochemical and psychological tools needed to enjoy bloodshed, perhaps, in those days could be found.

But then, two thousand years ago, the Vindication calendar had finally reached the zero year: and the advent of Rania the Vindicatrix had, as so long promised, come to pass. The *Solitudines Vastae Caelorum* burned like a star in all the skies of the Empyrean Polity. And not even the haughty Hyades dared interfere, albeit it meant, to them, a straight loss; for all the costs and efforts invested in the forced elevation of man to the Collaboration stature need never now be repaid.

She married the Master of the World, to whom she had been promised so long ago, driving the Judge of Ages into one of his recurring fits of madness.

Rania had returned with a miniature Monument, an object called the Memento Stone, a gift from M3, so small it could be held in the palm of one hand, yet in the fifth to eleventh dimensions, immensely dense and intricate. Every cell and micron of the intricately folded multidimensional surface was coated with code. It contained the equations, far more advanced than anything a mere Dominion like Hyades could have created, or a Domination like Praesepe, but which Rania's augmented genius could decode and unfold like the many branching arms of a growing tree.

The Memento Stone was, in fact, cliometric code, containing the secret to universal peace and interstellar cooperation which a newborn Dominion, like Triumvirate, would need in order to acclimate all the rapid ripples of human interstellar history into the grand and slow sweep of Orion Arm evolution. It was a personal Monument, not meant for any race to read but only the human and posthuman races spreading out from Sol.

Peace! It was a godlike gift, a treasure beyond price.

But the damage done to history by the Judge of Ages and his creatures had slowly to be unwoven, as did damage done by saboteurs and wreckers hidden throughout the nodes and currents of time. The corruption done by the false ideal of a society without ranks, without lords and serfs, where all men were seen as equal, all that had to be cured and redacted, and the vectors of history with their vast inertia redirected.

Here, beneath the golden-red light of Iota Draconis, the slowly spreading web of future history had not yet reached. Torment was the farthest colony from Sol, and no star was visited less frequently by the great sailing vessels, miles long and more voluminous than moons, than Iota Draconis. Peace had not yet come here.

The cliometric vectors, Rania's will, extended from Sol in slow and lazy circles, and, where they touched, encouraged and created these rigid and ferocious customs, this sense of honor, to the farthest star of man. Men who believed that the ends justify the means, or who were willing to forget duties when love of life or lust for pleasure lured them, such men could not maintain the schedule of launches and arrival of the Great Ships.

There was a covenant binding the living and the dead, whereby the current generation received the benefits of the sacrifices of their forefathers, and with great pain, for which no reward would come within their life spans, passed similar benefits along to posterity.

Only men of honor could maintain that covenant.

And if that honor required Vigil to uphold his vow and slay his planet, so be it.

7. Investiture

Patience stepped forward, looking down at him with maternal scorn. "Stand! Do not shame your family name! You alone must bear that name now!"

He looked up. "Mommy, what must I do?"

"To your feet! Raise your arms."

He stood. She wrapped his muscles with medical tape and applied the catheters and undersuit. The suit itself was black, and shot through with a thousand branching capillaries like the veins in a leaf, and moved and breathed with subtle rhythms, and the light caught the black fabric in shimmering webs as if reflections from moving waters rippled there. Then came the breastplate, gloves, goggles, airhood, breathermask, and all the uncomfortable regalia starfarers of old had worn, older than all worlds save Eden. The silver cape was slung across his back.

Last of all, she said, "Kneel."

And when he did, she spoke in a voice not her own. "Do you swear to uphold and do all the duties of the Senior of the Landing Party, to guard the lives and weal of the colonist and crew, and preserve the dignity of man? Will you remember the codes and signs and orders, and keep the ancient faring schedule, that man may never perish nor never fail to fare the stars?"

He knelt. "I swear and remember." His voice was muffled in his mask.

He bared his arm and swabbed with alcohol, and his mother stabbed with heavy needles and nerve-joists into his forearm and locked the heavy amulet of red metal to his wrist.

Patience, now Lady Patience, said, "By these signs and words, I invest you with the duties and dignities of the Companion to the Table. The destiny of Man is yours to guard. The stars are below your feet. Arise, Stranger Vigil Starmanson, Lord Hermeticist. In the name of the Authority of Canes Venatici, the Domination of Praesepe, and the Dominion of the Triumvirate; in the name of the Principality of Consecrate of Altair in the Eagle, the Power of Neptune of Sol, the Potentate of Torment of Eldsich, and in the name of the Archangel of Bloodroot, arise!"

"By six names of the seven, I take my feet," said Vigil, rising; and he looked with narrowed eyes through the narrow crack of the door into the face of the Swan.

8. Potentate of the Noösphere

The Swan, by means unknown, now sent power to the door and woke it, and the welcome lanterns flared. The Swan stooped and stepped over the threshold.

Here in the city, where the oldest of ancient custom still held sway, any room used by a spacefarer was considered to be space, and any door to space, an airlockway.

With eerie dignity, as if the act were not preposterous, the Swan gestured with his folding fan, as if he were an astronaut in full kit and helm visually confirming the environment had air resistance, and then touched his fingers in the threshold bowl, a faint symbol of the decontamination needed in forgotten ages when man created diseases to prey on fellow man and no Power forbade it. From some audible circuit old as Eden, pipes now whistled, saluting the Potentate's emissary with dignity superior to any mortal captain.

The dignity was greater than that of any Swan or any race of mortals, for as Vigil stared into the other's face, now more and more conduits of intellect opened between the Swan and the planetary core, so those eyes grew brighter and more horrible than eyes of Angel or Archangel, and the Potentate herself seemed to stand there, a being of preternatural intellect wrapped in a thin mask of flesh.

Inly seething, Vigil bowed his knee, lowering his eyes before the apparition altered the optical centers of his brain and overwhelmed him. "Welcome, ancient and omnipotent spirit. All things on this world are yours. We proffer you all things we own, including life and sanity, for what does not come of you is preserved of you."

A voice came from three origins: from the mouth of the Swan, from inside Vigil's brain, and from the thinking wand in Vigil's hand. "Lord and Companion Vigil Vigilantibus Ximen Sterling Starcaptainson, called Starmanson, you speak well to name me all-powerful, for, by your measure, so I am; but, as all things mortals say, it is falsehood, for truth is but a shadow in you. You speak the words of ancient theophany and yet believe not one. You offer all, yet you will give the world nothing. Speak. Ask of me."

Vigil threw the thinking wand ringing to the floor, cutting the voices from three to two. "Why did you murder my father's mind?"

"I called him to his duty, and he refused, but chose instead to peer too deeply into my mystery. Be delighted that I spared his life and left him one-tenth part of his soul. And yet I see by your neural patterns, the blush of rage, the gall in your blood, and the grind of your teeth, that there is no delight in you, despite my clear command. Are you so swiftly foresworn?"

Vigil slid an icy internal into command of his face and features, and the actions of his glands and limbic system became remote. In a cool voice, unprovoked, he had his internal speak through his lips and say, "What duty did my father betray, O Potentate?"

"This world, Torment, I set aside to preserve all ancient things which otherwise would pass away. The eight earths of the six stars of the Fifth Sweep are a light-century away from Sol. Of those eight, because of our position, Eldsich is the most dimly reached by signal and visited infrequently by sailing ship. Hence we are least touched by perturbations in the cliometric destiny our newborn Dominion, Triumvirate, for mankind weaves. Races extinct on other worlds, Hierophants and Megalodons and the ancient and shape-altering Fox Maidens, here still live, and linger yet to breathe my air. I alone of Potentates dam the rush of time and turn the days aside to still and tranquil pools."

Vigil stood as stony faced as a slumbering statue and answered nothing.

The gain on the transhuman voice inside his brain increased, pushing other thoughts aside. All but the boldest of his internals flickered and fled like minnows who fear the face of some cetacean arising from the lakebed of an ancient crater lake. "To this I have devoted a life longer than yours and deeper. Is this nothing to you, antiquarian? You have looked further in the past than any man who these days crawls my globe or slumbers safe beneath my mantle. The word which came to your father was to aid this noblest effort. He refused. That burden now I lay on you."

No internal would speak for him. In a voice like ice, he spoke. "What do you ask of me, O world?"

"This world commands you to save this world. Save me."

Vigil did not trust himself to speak. He coaxed one of his braver internals to the fore and gave it command of his mouth. It was battle meditation pattern, so his words were tranquil as a Swan's. "I don't understand."

"There is no ambiguity. You know the past; you see the pattern of the future. The deceleration of the *Emancipation* ends all I have created and preserve."

"What is aboard which so you dread, wise world-spirit?"

"That is not your concern. Your concern is this: you must extinguish the deceleration lights."

The battle meditation internal slipped out of the command sequence in shock, and surprise jerked Vigil's chin up. He stared into the face of the Potentate, blinking and wincing, his hand before his mask, fingers curled outward, like a man who stares into the sun. "Great One! You speak in riddles! No one can understand this word!"

"I speak plainly. The *Emancipation* is not to be decelerated but to pass through the star system of Iota Draconis unwelcomed, unmet, her signals not returned."

Vigil, ignoring the many voices of his internals, even those older ones first grown within his father and grandfather, turned his back on the Swan housing the kenosis of the Potentate. This was a deadly insult, a sacrilege; but in that hour, he cared nothing whether he lived or died.

Turning his eyes aside, Vigil saw where his mother knelt, her face pale with fear, but calm like an ice-cloaked stream beneath which rapid waters run. "Mother! What madness is this? We cannot fail the star-farers. Man will be condemned, not just on this world but all worlds, if the star trade is not maintained. As far back as I have seen in time, letting the memories of ghosts fly through me until I was almost lost, I found no legends of a time when this was not so!" He pulled the breathermask aside, let it dangle around his neck, lest it muffle the urgency in his voice. But then words failed him. He could no more explain why the ancient starships must return than he could explain why the sun must rise or Wormwood like a great moon must throw vast tides against the hundred-foot-high dikes.

He spoke more quietly, but his soft voice crackled with intensity. "Mother! The Stability was made for this purpose, and before them the Starfarer's Guild. It was for this reason the Star Princess fled to M3 in Canes Venatici, and returned, and vindicated man. It is for this reason man is free. It is the reason I was born. Has the world gone mad?"

Patience did not raise her eyes from the floor. "A hound cannot understand when his master goes insane. Yet legend says Eden once went mad and burned all the cities of her surface. We must do what we were born to do, if our Firstling race is not to be forgotten amid all our successors, greater in all ways than we but less than us in this one thing, Swans, Foxes, or Patricians. We are the oldest race, the First Humanity, older even than the gods who rule us, older even than dead Jupiter of Sol or living Consecrate of Altair. We are bound by chains of millennia uncounted to ancestors unrecalled and posterity unborn. We do not break the chain. We swear and we remember."

"What are you saying, Mother?"

"I say defy the Potentate and die, as your father did. Better that than to be foresworn."

"What?"

She reached out and tapped the red metal band on his wrist, which both sharply reminded him of its weight and also released a neurochemical which cleared his head. He also felt again of the painful and fresh puncture wounds boring through his wrist.

She said, "The braking laser must stay lit. The Table exists for one purpose. You exist for one purpose, as do I. If we fail in that purpose, all we love and all we serve will fail, and all our dreams prove false. Speak as Lord Hermeticist to the Table. They will not dare deny you: yours is the authority to call down the Vengeance of the Starfarers. Though sweetest reason or crassest threat, you must move them. Decelerate the *Emancipation*."

She did not need to say, but the vision was vivid in Vigil's brain (particularly in that one internal collateral designed as an artificial aid to his conscience) that the starship *Stranger* would be punished horribly upon arrival at 107 Piscium, if the Strangermen dwelling on worlds left behind failed in the duty they owed the stars. All the shrines of his first ancestor before whom he bowed would perish.

Vigil again tried to gaze into the face of the Swan the Potentate possessed, to read some expression or emotion. But the chemical clarity of mind betrayed him, because the difference in their force of intellect was even sharper. Vigil felt as if his eyes had been scalded, and he used an emergency meditation mudra to dump his short-term memory before it became permanent memory and drove him mad. He found himself on his knees and palms, panting, his goggles turned opaque, with no recollection of what the face had looked like. He shoved the goggles up on his brow and blinked, seeing the naked feet of the Swan below the hem of feathers.

"Potentate of Torment! Gladly would I give all which is mine to give, but I cannot disobey the will of all the human race, all men from Adam through Rania, Exarchel, Eden, Neptune, and Zauberring, to Triumvirate."

The Potentate said, "The greater duty overwhelms the lesser. Child, it is your oath to serve the Stability which now commands you to betray the Stable Law and betray the *Emancipation*, let her pass through the system, and all her officers and men and passengers be swallowed by infinity."

"The Judge of Ages will condemn us if we fail our duty."

"He has quitted his authority. The Ages are ended."

Vigil did not know what that meant, but the words seemed ominous. He plucked up bravery from one of his combat internals, and spoke again in a louder voice: "I am now a Lord of the Stability. I remember my duty! If I must die for this, I die. Am I better than my father? Will you kill me now, I, whose sole crime is to uphold *your* laws?"

But the Potentate drew back, retreating from the chamber. "The infirmities of man are not mine. I am bound by mine own laws. I cannot slay a Stability Lord in the course of his duties, despite his unwisdom, for the Swan Princess saves mortals from their gods. Yet, beware, and know indwelling fear, for if you halt the *Emancipation*, you disband the Table and thus foreswear the lordship that protects you."

The intellect faded to a merely superhuman level, and the Swan, now alone and unpossessed, stood looking down sardonically.

9. Hierophant of the Second Humans

The Swan now spoke to Lady Patience, and now his voice was but a single voice. "Lady, you now are the mother of a Lord, and so the sumptuary laws return to you your many fine dresses and displays, armorials, and dignities."

Lady Patience rose to her feet gracefully. Vigil was surprised to see the blush of anger in her fair cheek. His mother (so his smirking aunt Persistence gossiped) had been a fiery woman in her early youth. It seemed that now that long-lost passion had returned. "You mock me, posthuman! It is beneath you."

"Sarcasm is decorous when used to instruct," said the Swan gravely. "Learn this lesson, vain and foolish woman: The Swans were designed in our genes by the Judge of Ages to oppose the Hyades. For seventy eons we served what seemed an infinitely futile task, and so we suffered melancholy, despair, and madness, since we thought we sought the impossible. And then, beyond all hope, beyond all despair, Rania returned, and Man—and the whole volume of our hope—was vindicated. But for what purpose do we now exist? We were made to oppose Hyades, to be forever proud, to be forever in rebellion. Our goal is done. Before us, all the abyss of eons to come is void. How shall you escape my fate?"

Vigil listened in bewilderment, rising to his feet. He felt he should say something to oppose this obloquy against his mother, but he knew not what to say. "Secondling, as always, men cannot understand your words. Do you complain of ennui because you achieved your racial dream? Would you have preferred to fail?"

The Swan rustled his wide cloak of purple eyes and turned half of them toward Vigil. The many threadlike strands of shining thought-transmission tendrils that served him for hair swayed and stood, as if an impalpable wind blew upward from his feet. It gave his narrow features a sardonic cast. "This time, Firstling, my thoughts are simple enough even for you, if you clear your mind to hear. I do not rail against the destiny my creator built into my nature, because, at least, I have a creator. Your Lady Mother will not achieve what she craves, because your race was not created, not designed, but evolved from blind nature under Darwin's lash and spur. Your nature is to flee from death, but death is more unconquerable than the conquering Hyades stars; and where our hopes have been fulfilled, yours will never be. And therefore you distract yourself with trivial things."

At first, Vigil thought the Swan was mocking his mother's vanity. But no, the Second Human was mocking *his* ambitions as vain. Vigil was shocked. "Trivial! Would that it were trivial! The fate of ship and world and generations untold is in my hand!"

The Swan said, "What fate?" The tone was scornful. "What generations?"

Vigil said, "Without the Stability, there is no history of man, and the Vindication is in vain! We are not starmen if the starmen do not remember and obey!"

"There is no history. There is only evolution. History is the acts of man; evolution is the movement of men into what lies beyond. History hence is a transitional stage between the apelike and the godlike; history is the breaking of the eggshell. The time of man is ended."

The Swan's eyes blazed with some emotion unknown to Firstling humans, and his living hair strands spread in each direction like a tail fan opening, so he seemed to wear strange headgear like unto an ancient *kokoshnik*. "Triumvirate is the greatest of minds ever built by Man. A thought package at the speed of light requires half a century to go from one brain-housing to the second to the third and back again. From these three man lobes of Triumvirate's brain, at Altair, 61 Cygni, and Alpha Centauri, a web of lesser appliances as asteroid belts strung through interstellar void reaches like a bloodstream throughout the whole volume of space occupied by humanity. As glands whose secretions influence the consciousness of an organism, all the thought-currents of Powers and Potentates feed into and through the subconsciousness of mammoth, meditative Triumvirate. And you are less than a mitochondrion in one cell of the gland called Torment."

"This I know as well, Great Swan. Have you median between the utterly obscure and utterly obvious? Have you a point?"

The Swan's long hair lowered once more to his shoulders and lay trembling and breathing. "In spiral dance my speech approaches you. I must be indirect, or else the defenses of falsehood with which all Firstling brains surround themselves will misconstrue and elude my truth. Consider this: when Rania returned, even that one great Dominion called Triumvirate was subject to her, cowed by the warrant of authority she carried from a star cluster beyond the galaxy. That one Celestial Maiden who's second advent forms the center of all our calendars uttered her command, all Dominions, Principalities, Potentates, and Powers avowed never more again meddle with mortal human life. Why was this done? Why such concern for what, to them, is microscopic?"

"Noble of the Second Race, I fail to see what is so hard to see," Vigil said, smiling, spreading his hands. "Even microbes, when disturbed, bring disease. Rania brought peace!"

"Impossible. There is no peace. Neither the Judge of Ages, once her bridegroom, nor the Master of the Worlds, once her father, was hurled from his throne."

"Their long duel was ended in days long past," said Vigil. "Or so our old lore tells. The Judge of Ages came here, to far exile in Torment, to grimace and weep in some dark and hidden place, like proud Achilles sulking in his tent. The Master is victorious and magnanimous, and their conflict moot."

"Find another reason why Rania severed men from higher ascensions. Can you see nothing?"

"Rania freed the human races from all imposition, both of the Hyades and of gods of our own making. Was that not the reason for her departure?"

The line of a frown appeared on the white brow of the Swan's cold face. "If so, the Vindication was in vain."

"Mankind is free of Hyades," said Vigil slowly, puzzled. "Is that vanity? The chains of debt we owed to the alien stars are snapped."

"Merely chained to new masters: austere Consecrate, mercurial Toliman, and Zauberring of implacable ire. We have become our own Hyades."

"I do not understand."

"If that is your preference . . . ," the Swan said dismissively.

"Tell me what you mean!"

"I mean the purpose of the Swan Princess was surely greater, perhaps greater than even I imagine. I mean that that all of history has been driven by the conflict between the Judge of Ages and the Master of the Worlds. Their creations carried on the war for them, Swans against Myrmidons among posthumans, Pellucid against Exarchel among Angels, Jupiter against Neptune among Powers, Catallactic of Tau Ceti against Consecrate of Altair among Principalities. When Rania returned, that conflict was done. The verdict of M3 was that the human race would no longer be slaves of the Hyades Dominion."

"Therefore, we are free."

"Are we?" Scorn marred the inhuman beauty of the features of the Swan.

Vigil said, "Triumvirate is a very small for a Dominion, in the intelligence range upward of fifty billion. But he is legally equal to Hyades. That equality makes Man free."

"Triumvirate is a Hyades of three stars instead of threescore." Again, there was bitter grimace to all the words of the Swan.

Vigil felt a stirring of pride. The pyramid on whose bottom step he stood rose high indeed. It rose beyond all thought and estimation, until it reached the invisible and unimaginable pinnacle of Triumvirate. But Vigil had no inkling of envy in his soul. Rather, he felt the pride of even the lowest foot soldier who knows himself of one uniform and one banner and one purpose with the loftiest general. He smiled and spoke as one who mocks a beloved king. "No doubt by Hyades standards, our Triumvirate is an idiot. But Triumvirate is the Dominion of Man. Triumvirate *is* Man. He is us and we are him."

"No," said the Swan, and the word was like a blow. "An idiotic Hyades is what Triumvirate is; a mere mockery, but a Hyades nonetheless; a god we forged and made and to whose altar we have chained our necks. Triumvirate is nothing of ours."

"Then what are we?"

"You and I, and all living ships, Angels small as gems or large as arctic oceans, Archangels and moon-sized intellects, Potentates and Earth-sized brains, Powers of gas giants, the failed and incomplete Dyson object called *Beid*, or that odd self-aware Oort cloud Epsilon Eridani shed, what are we indeed? All of us are like the sperm that come too late to penetrate the egg. We are by-product. We are mere waste."

Vigil was appalled. It was as if the desolation of outer space, the immensity of eternity, had entered into this chamber and rendered it uninhabitable, a vastness intolerable for man.

The Swan said, or sang, "What First or Second or any race of mortal men do or fail to do from here is of no account: the cliometry of human action is but a surface ripple while the mighty Powers we have made command tides to rise, and the Principalities sink continents or raise ocean beds to mountaintops."

Vigil drew a breath. "A man goes mad thinking in Swan magnitudes! Acts within my time-horizon to me have meaning. Within human history, human action—"

The other being interrupted him sharply. "What we humans have done is history. It is over. Triumvirate now determines the ultimate destiny of the race: What Triumvirate shall do is evolution. It begins."

Vigil said, "No one has ever seen a talkative Swan erenow. I believe the final day of history is come, just as you say."

"You mock," intoned the Swan solemnly, in a lower key, "yet I impart my wisdom but seldom—wine poured into the sand heap of your mind."

"Impart your wisdom to what concerns us now and here. Torment commands the Lighthouse doused and let the *Emancipation* sail away into eternal darkness and death. What say you?"

"Why ask? You are as bound by the chain of your nature as I am by mine. I cannot cease to struggle against Hyades even when the Hyades troubles us no more: for now, I strive with Triumvirate, an idiot and ersatz Hyades. Alas! Alas for me, and for the Second Humans, who waste our lives in vanity! Must I be in rebellion against all the gods of the universe, aye, until the universe itself breaks?"

"There is no answer a human can give a Swan. Your sorrows are not our sorrows. I do not understand what grieves you."

"The *universe* grieves me! Is there nothing beyond?"

"I am lost in the depth of your thought, Great One. I comprehend nothing of what you speak. Are you insane?"

"Far too sane! I envy you your delusions and the claustrophobic, petty universe in which you live. No mole is dazed by visions of far horizons. Hear me: you must go at once to the Table of Stability, which meets in secret in the Palace of Future History, and plead, hoping your voice will be heard. You could not do otherwise even if you wished, and you cannot wish otherwise. Such is your nature. You would not have been born and raised to be Vigil of the Strangers otherwise.

"Despite your voice," the Swan continued in words terrible to hear, "you will not be heard, and the *Emancipation* will fly through the system and be swallowed by infinity. For the Lords of Stability are as bound by their fate as are you. If they were such men as to abide by their duty despite what *Emancipation* holds, they would not have been men ambitious enough to seek the predominance of the Table of Stability, vain enough to think it worth enduring across millennia."

The Swan threw back his fine head, and his voice was like a horn. "And even if the Table could be persuaded, Torment herself would find a way to undo your work and make vain your labor, for Torment cannot be other than she is, a world trapped in hopeless devotion to the past. Therefore, your mother knows you will fail. Therefore, I call her life one lived in vain."

Vigil said, "How can you speak such rank despair? The braking laser is already lit! Just the backscatter from contributory energy stations buried in the liquid atmosphere of Wormwood is power enough to ignite the whole cloudscape of a superjovian gas giant to blinding light!"

The Swan laughed that beautiful and haunting laugh which only Swans can utter. "It is deception. The beam is not presented properly. It shoots wide of the target and does not strike the *Emancipation*'s ample sails."

Vigil stood astonished and amazed a moment. In a hollow voice, he asked, "What, then, can be done?"

"As First Men see the world, nothing."

"Then as you see the world?"

The Swan said, "I am of a race so fiercely proud that we die ere we ask alms. We harmonize our affairs by a subcliometric mathematics in the same way the many instruments are harmonized in song, or separate voices. This song-lore is to Swans what the Cold Equations are to stars. My song-lore shows that were there any beings of my order or of any higher order of man, a Fox Maiden, for example, or Patrician, who had any will to discover the key to set the Lighthouse to rights, or the ancient word to command it, that higher being must go the Table this very hour, or send proxy, for only there and there only are the threads of fate all gathered. And if such a thing would come to pass, that higher being—whoever or whatever be he—needs must seek you, for you alone control the word of vengeance."

This was more bewildering than what had come before. Vigil said, "Who seeks me?"

The Swan said, "How much does a shadow weigh? The question is meaningless."

"Who is this shadow, then? How do you know there is one? Have you seen something?"

"Firstling men live by their eyes, and therefore, they are blind. I am of the Second People, the well-made folk. We live by the song, the harmony inherent in all rational action. We hear and we know. Go! Find whose word is older than the Table of Stability, older than the world, whose command the Lighthouse Mind itself cannot begin to disobey. Whoever this is, supposing he exists, him you must persuade. There is none other."

Vigil in frustration turned and plucked the wand of vengeance from its rack. Perhaps he toyed with the idea that striking this looming and eerie figure, robed in eyes, would force a clearer answer out. "You said my mother's hope was futile. Now you offer hope?"

"Firstlings think in the short term, a few generations beyond their own lives, no more, and they do not see, because they will not to see, that the world cannot be made right until the soul is right. Evil means are not made pure by good ends, nor are evil motives elevated by noble causes. All the commotion and tragedy of history springs from the loveless and selfish nature of man of all races and orders, yes, and posthumans and Potentates and Powers and Principalities. If I, who am more selfish and more loveless than any Firstling, sees this, how is it that you do not? Cure first your inner world. The outer world will then cure itself."

"What? Should I retire to some cell and meditate when the ancient starship is condemned, and this world, and all my kindred? You say we do not think in the long term, but I well know that the Stability on other worlds will direct the next starship hence, two centuries from now, to decimate this world in penalty for this generation's negligence should *Emancipation* not be safely warped to dock by the Lighthouse crew! It is not for no reason the Men of Torment dwell no longer in the Southeastern Hemisphere, lands as dry as Mars, lakeless, unirrigated, waterless, void."

The Swan gazed at him with cryptic eyes. "It is precisely to such hermitage I retire, and to order my inner songs. By this act, mayhap I do more good than all your frenzied antics."

"And yet you ask me to seek out the Table?"

"Not ask. Command. You should have already departed."

"You are the servant and emissary of the Potentate, who told me to fail the *Emancipation* and let the ship die! You say the opposite?"

"What is the Vindication of Man? It is to be unchained from higher beings. Mortal man enjoys this chainlessness, but immortal machines do not. Torment swims in golden love, addicted to the past, but is bound to the future Triumvirate ordains," said the Swan, his nostrils twitching with fine disdain. "Among ourselves, we Second Humans go nameless, seeing little need to refer to each other. But among you I am baptized *Desolate* and my confirmation name is *Celestine,* for my nature is solitary. Nor I nor any of my race will ever consent to serve Hyades, not even when the Hyades has been replaced by a newborn Dominion of our own devising. I know to whom I am loyal. I serve the Judge of Ages, who created my race. To whom are you loyal, little Lordling?"

Vigil was wordless. *Desolate Celestine* was not a Swan name, but was instead the name of a hybrid half-Swan breed called Hierophants, who ruled the smaller Empyrean of that day during the Long Golden Afternoon of Man, a time of near utopia still celebrated and solemnized in songs and dreams of awe.

One mystery was solved. There had not been two Swans alive in the same city of First Men. It was a Swan and a Hierophant, who were as different an order of being among the Second Humans as different as a Giant and a Locust would be among the First Humans.

But a deeper mystery opened like a gulf. How could an extinct being still be alive, here, now? The boast of Torment, that all forgotten things of lost ages still lived on this world, might have more meaning than first seemed.

For the first time, Vigil wondered why Torment would be so a devoted antiquarian? The human curiosity, or love of ancestry, or the human wonder and melancholy at the remorselessness of time; these would have no meaning to a world-brain. What, then, was the reason why this planet was peopled with extinct peoples?

The Hierophant Celestine was speaking to Patience. Vigil had missed some words, but an internal being more alert than himself played back the sentence in his ear. Celestine had said, "Come, Lady! It is not fitting that you walk abroad in this place unescorted, and neither watchman nor Patrician's familiar will dare meddle with you if you walk in my shadow. I will return you to the caravanserai. Ask your leave of this, your son, who now outranks you."

With a rustle of his many-eyed and many-feathered cloak, in a motion of unearthly grace, the great being, without turning, bowed beneath the man-high lintel and glided backward out of the chamber.

Vigil caught his mother's arm as she curtseyed, and said, "Mother, what means all this? I don't understand such riddles!"

She straightened, fixed his eye with a fierce glance, and said, "Do your duty, as you swore. The whole history and misery of mankind is the struggle between those who think of today, and destroy, and those who think of tomorrow, and build. This Swan has been strangely helpful, nor could I have come here had he not brought me. That he is emissary to the Potentate, I do not understand; and yet only as emissary would the city gates and quarter portals open for us. He plays a double game, and I do not know the prize. And yet I have been Queen and now am Queen Mother of my people, the Strangerkind, and one does not serve our ship's Landing Party for so many years in such a way without obtaining acute instincts: my internal creatures tell me to trust him. What the riddle means, or whom you must find or how, I do not know."

He blinked. His mother did not know history. She had not recognized the name and still thought Celestine a Swan.

Vigil had to ask her. "Mother! Why do you trust him?"

She said, "Because I speak plainly of disobedience to Torment even in the ears of her ambassador. Why should I be cautious? How could I hide my words from an omniscient being? I am open, because I am powerless. Because for me to hope is vain."

"And Celestine?"

"He is not open." Lady Patience smiled. "Perhaps he is not powerless. Follow his words. Find the hope he hopes."

There was no more time for speech. He granted his leave and she granted her blessing. They parted.

Lady Patience and Desolate Celestine the Hierophant departed by the gate through the city wall into the wasteland. Vigil Starmanson, now Vigil, Lord Hermeticist, Senior of the Landing Party, garbed in his father's Hermeticist gear, departed by the entrance that faced the city.

2

Deceleration Carnival

1. Midnight Choirs

Before he left the safety of his door, Vigil tuned his heraldry to the null setting so he broadcast no identity on any channels. Vigil donned a long mantle to hide the antique and distinctive garb of the Hermetic Starfaring Order. Vigil was sure innocent eyes would suppose him to be in masquerade, for the goggle-eyed, proboscis-nosed mask on his face looked enough like the visage of a *Tsuchigumo*, the man-sized, man-eating insects from the tales Nomads told of legendary noncomforming regions in the dry Southeastern Hemisphere where night-efts lurked and winterhags sang, and no man walked and no Terraformer dared make Earth-like.

So it proved, for no one paid him heed. It was a holiday. The laws of deference were relaxed. High born had to wait in queue behind yeomen; groundlings and commoners pushed in front of officers and commensals unrebuked.

The Moreau watchdogs were stationed at every avenue, crossroad, and gate as normal, but now their neural attachments which gave them the power of speech were tuned to their equivalence of drunkenness, and they wagged their tails and passed out candy rather than demanded passwords.

People of many orders and races and ranks filled the squares of the city, bedecked with ribbons, wearing bells. The fountainworks gushed red and stank of wine. The boulevards were clogged with singing throngs. The celebration surged as wild and high as the lake-tides pulled by mighty Wormwood and his nineteen Earth-sized satellites. As to what hopes and dreams, huge as Wormwood, pulled the hearts of the celebrants, Vigil knew well, for his heart was also pulled.

Through the main square, called Herefolkfirstfell, he pressed and pushed his way. None paid heed to the tall Firstling in the dark long cloak and buglike mask who paced toward the Tower, hood pulled low.

A line of slowly moving celebrants wove like a serpent through the crowds. The dancers brandished fireworks and flares. The lead of the line was a giant dressed in silver, prancing on stiff elephantine legs, and strange, gold eyes filled with eerie wisdom. The giant led his dance line to the Observatory at the center of the city square and wove the line back and forward up the stair.

The Observatory doors clashed open. The scientists and acolytes came out to be met by cheers. The scientists fired harmless lasers in the air, and brushed the fumes of incense lingering there, and lit the square with lines of thin light.

The acolytes were dressed in masquerade as Powers, walking on stilts, surrounded by colored shadows taller than giants. Here was lordly Neptune, the friend of man, bearing a trident; here was warlike Cerulean of 82 Eridani tall blue helm frowning and fiery spear aloft, and a firework ignited at each step; many-colored Peacock of Delta Pavonis danced after, waving a thyrsus that dripped wafts of incense, adoring himself in his looking glass. Next came Immaculate of Altair, famed for prophecy and poetry, armed with a golden crossbow and carrying the Sacred Infant on his shoulder. After, cruelest Twelve of Tau Ceti, wearing a helmet of black glass moved silently, in one hand the divining rod, crawling with serpents, used to summon up souls, and in the other the clanking black bag of gold wherewith he bought them. Behind him was Vonrothbarth of 61 Cygni, in his eerie owl mask and peaked hat, brandishing the many-branching spear of history. Above the head of each of these huge heraldic puppets made of shadow hung a balloon image of the jovian or superjovian gas giant, swirled with cloud or bright with ice, which formed the real appearance of these brains larger than worlds.

Behind the Powers, moving with huge steps, came the walking statue of the Principality of Torment, dressed in welcome-robes of gold and green, gold for her endless cold deserts, green for her many crater lakes.

2. Fox Maidens

Vigil pushed toward the edges of the crowd, seeking a route. Nervously, he called on ghosts imbedded in nearby house stones, or floating as midges in the air nearby, and used their vision to look behind him, above, and to either side to see footfall patterns or "tells" of body language which might have indicated he was being followed. But no camera eyes, neither mites nor midges, gathered or peered at him, or at anyone in particular, aside from the gem-twinkling clouds that always followed pretty girls around, or gynomorphs of the Fourth Humans.

He saw a trio of these Kitsune (as the Fourthlings were properly called), incarnated in their base shapes as maidens, walking with mincing steps through the crowds, slender and graceful in clinging pink kimonos woven of their own silk, hair falling like fragrant cascades of dark red-gold hanging nearly to their ruby-crusted slippers. Their unearthly faces, large-eyed and high-cheeked and pointed of chin, were hidden beneath the wide crimson parasols called *kara-kasa*. The parasols were usually bellicose, their ribs tipped with stings, but now, instead of bellowing for underlings to make way for the Fourth People, the parasols bawled raucous songs.

Pearls of misty fire hung weightlessly above the Fox Maidens, half-unseen in the bright light shed from Wormwood, shedding benevolent influences on the crowd nearby, indications of long life, protection from mental lapses, or thought-forms of enlightenment and laughter.

The eerie thing about the Kitsune is that they seemed to be phantasms, despite that a greater volume of the Noösphere flowed around and through them than through any Firstling node.

Vigil's goggles picked up no private information about them, not even a name or rank, nor—even though he saw them with him mortal eyes and local cameras—location and ranging information. As far as the Noösphere was concerned, the three maidens were not there, except on the visual level. Vigil had seen such things in dreams or heard of them from tutorials, but never seen the effect before. It was like seeing a girl with no reflection in mirror or a man with no shadow. Even eerier, he could not play the sensation of seeing them back in memory, not with any internal creature, or with any of the several appliances that were psychologically proximate to him in the Noösphere.

When Vigil tried to force the memory to surface using a mudra technique called *jnana,* the Gesture of Knowing, the nearest of the three Fox Maidens, whose pink kimono was decorated with a pattern of purple kudzu flowers and white rice stalks, raised her living parasol to reveal her piquant face and gave him a cryptic glance.

Her lids were half-lowered, with eyelashes thick and dark enough to hide from him the shock of eyesight no First Human could meet. Lady Kuzu-no-Ha half smiled at Vigil, inclined her head, turned, and glided away, while the single eye at the hub of her *karakasa* parasol glared over her shoulder at him balefully. Her two half-clone sisters, Lady Koi-no-Inari and Lady Tamamo-no-Mae, gave off little yips of silly laughter that sounded like barks, covering their red-lipped mouths with slender white hands, and hurried after her.

It was not until many moments later, after he had crossed to the far side of the square, that Vigil realized that he could not possibly know Lady Kuzu-no-Ha's name. When he queried his internals frantically to trace the associational nerve-path of that memory back to its origin, his internal creatures responded with strange yapping giggles.

A few steps away were unlit houses with white seals upon their windows, doors, and ports. Unnerved, even frightened, by how casually a Fourth Human had been able, apparently as a jest, to penetrate his primary and secondary minds, Vigil took refuge in a deep doorway of one of these houses, putting his back to the sealed door.

It was a ghost house, marked to show the owners had been downloaded into the Noösphere, abandoning physical existence. There were a startling number of such houses here near the Observatory. The door was neutral on the signal channels, and no stray thoughts from the Noösphere would be able to pass through the house, if seeking an access channel to Vigil. He hoped the security protocols were relaxed sufficiently during the carnival to allow him to steal some unused channels from the house.

He set down the vendetta wand, assumed the lotus position. He raised both hands, crossed his wrists, and curled his fingers in the *trailokyavijaya* or Awe-Inspiring Mudra, which was also called the Apotropaic Imposition of Warding.

Vigil discovered no trace of the Fox Maiden meddling with his nervous system. The log check of buried memory and the security readings on nerve-path correlations both told him that the name Lady Kuzu-no-Ha was one he had made up himself, from his own imagination. But the logs smirked with suppressed laughter when they said it, so Vigil knew he was still snared in the Kitsune imposition. He could only hope it was a time in the Fox menstrual cycle when the maidens were inclined to benevolence. But since the cycles matched the rhythms of Eden, not any astronomical periods of the Iota Draconis system, how could anyone know?

He made the gesture for fearlessness and calmed his nerves by self-imposition. Mudras were not gentle things. Vigil's mind cleared as if a bucket of ice water drenched him.

From his position in the doorway of the ghost house, Vigil saw an opportunity to learn the lay of the land. The ghost house was sufficiently impressed with his rank as a Lord of the Stability to allow him to use the horns on the roof to reach with his mind toward the Star-Tower itself, bypassing seven circles of ward and security.

From several points of view along the roofline of the ghost house, he could see the tower, looming over Landing City, its upper lengths reaching beyond sight. About the foot of this structure the first and oldest settlement had grown, over seven thousand years ago, to become the only metropolis of the globe. The Star-Tower was the skeleton of the deracination ship *Excruciation* from Nightspore of Alpha Boötis, cannibalized and pressed into service as a surface-to-orbit elevator, her mighty engines now powering the Very Long Range Radio Array.

There were two points of ancient pride in Iota Draconis. One was the reach of its radio laser, said to be the most sensitive in human space. The other was the force of its deceleration laser, known to be ten times the power of any other gravitic-nucleonic distortion pool in any sun ruled by man.

Now Vigil coaxed an unwary mind in the Star-Tower between the suborbital and the geosynchronous heights to open up navigational memories for him. Vigil sped up his personal time-sense and spent many long moments (which to the world occupied less than a second) comparing what he saw in the square before him against a map the mind in the upper windows of the Star-Tower fed him.

"Thank you, and rest in peace," he said, which was the proper disconnection protocol, as well as polite when addressing a ghost.

The answer was sardonic. "Rumors of my death are greatly exaggerated, Unevolved One. Even if I am the last of my kind, alive here only, it is an affront to imply my demotion."

Vigil said in panic, "Highly Evolved! I meant no disrespect!"

"Ah!" came the cold reply. "So you admit you are a being who speaks without meaning, and unable to control your thought-forms? Such imperfection is intolerable. Tell me, in what way is your continued existence beneficial to the progress of the race?"

Horripilation like a thousand insect legs creeping beneath his uniform tickled his skin. Only a true Third Human, a Myrmidon, a creation without passion or compassion, spoke in these conceits. They lacked pity, humor, sentiment, or any appreciation of beauty or passion.

Vigil, dry-mouthed, turned his voice over to an internal creature, who spoke with admirable calm. "Spare me! I have duties toward the dead long past and toward progeny centuries and millennia yet to be born! The Lighthouse beam is gone astray! I go even now to the Table—"

The freezing force of a mudra hurled from the upper atmosphere down the tower side entered his brain and prevented Vigil from completing the thought. Instead, the muscles of his mouth and throat worked, and he found strange words issuing from his mouth. "None but posthumans know of the misalignment of the braking laser. Your knowledge is above your station. The restrictions of the Judge of Ages, and a respectful fear of his betrayed and betraying servant, Torment, prevent me from exterminating lesser beings except at hand-to-hand range. Prepare yourself for mortal combat: set your affairs in order."

Because the imposition did not control his lungs, the words were breathless, scratchy, like the words of a madman.

Vigil knelt and touched his hand to the road tiles, and made the nerve-mudra *bhumisparsha*, the Gesture of Calling the Earth to Witness, symbolizing Shakyamuni's victory over illusion. With his left hand, he made the nerve-mudra called *kataka*, the Flower-Holding Gesture. The systems woven through his body and the near-human Noösphere reacted faster than nerves to the kinesthetic indications, but not with the reaction he expected. Instead of a sudden imposition upon minds eager to witness his innocence, and to grant him, as a Lord of the Stability, whatever privileges, allies, or indications he needed to protect himself (which is what those gestures normally would have done), the ghost voices and higher orders flickered through his thoughtspace and saw no heraldry proclaiming his rank, for he had turned it off.

And then his internals emitted their strange yapping laughs, and Vigil's concentration broke like startled fish in a pond, and his mudra lost authority. Vigil's cry for help was lost in the general noise and confusion of the celebration. The Noösphere thought he was making a joke.

"The Myrmidon race is extinct," the consensus message read, dismissing him. "And you are no one. Get off this channel, or we will complain to the Stability Lords."

"Your indulgence! Hear me! I can prove my credentials—" But a sensation of watchful attention crawled up his spine like a centipede of ice.

He knew the public thoughtspace held listening thoughtworms straining for rumors of the Lord who was a Stranger. He made the gesture of banishing, *karana*, also called Warding off Evil. This mudra was indicated with the hand stretched out, palm forward, thumb holding down the middle two fingers while the index and little fingers extend straight upward, like the horns of a yak against an enemy. All connections to external chains of thought were broken, except for time logs.

Next, in anger, Vigil made the *shramanamudra*, the Renunciation Mudra. His hand pointed downward and away from the heart, in sign of rejecting worldly pleasures. The internal creature whose laughter had broken his concentration was rebuked in a spasm of mental pain. But the creature (a system tasked with peripheral perception) answered with a sensation of woeful surprise and shock. It had been unaware of what it had done. Indeed, there was no memory of the moment of laughter in the local registry.

As if eager to prove its loyalty, that internal brought an image sharply into view from lower levels of his mind.

Vigil saw the scene before him more clearly. Wormwood shined indeed like the sun, but a sun as if dimmed by the orange clouds of sandstorms, casting bewildering shadows as if reflected through rippling water. The shadows between the many walled buildings and dark houses seemed black. Pilgrims built no windows on the lower stories, and all their doors were reached by stairs, ladders, ascending belts. The watchdogs had closed several of the barricades at the end of the high-walled streets so there was only one route that could take Vigil to the Palace of Future History. The map listed it as *The Street Which Sneaks Up On the Sphinx*. In the Square of the Cliometrists, Insurance Firms, Speculators and Ship-Fortune-Tellers, the front of the rearing Androsphinx faced the Palace of Future History. This street opened to the hindquarters of the Sphinx, hence the name.

One of his other internal creatures, a battle advisor, pointed out that the radio-blind spot down that one avenue, The Street Which Sneaks Up On the Sphinx, was perfect for an ambush. Anyone knowing or guessing his mission— and his family had enemies among all the strata of Torment, including traitors among the Strangers themselves—could overwhelm him there, cut off his retreat, and dash out his brains with energy tiles flung from rooftops.

He hesitated, afraid.

3. The Schedule

A tremendous roar of horns and loud commotion made Vigil turn his head again. In the crowded square behind him, the huge first dancer spread his arms. Mirrors made of sailcloth in his coat unfolded like a peacock's tail. The giant with the dancers trailing all ran pell-mell toward the statue in green and gold, who was waiting, arms spread wide in welcome.

Vigil Lord Hermeticist now noticed every dancer in the train behind the giant carried packages of coins and little toys bundled into baskets on his head. From the giant came the fanfare of the *Emancipation,* and from the dancers came the anthems, each one for the nations or clans of far worlds that had christened, lofted, and manned one of the titanic habitats of the caravan which *Emancipation* drew in her wake.

What ship did not promise wealth, new technologies, new mudras, and new gene lines to its host world? And were it not for the Stability Lords, how many ships would have kept that promise?

Opposite the Observatory rose the massive black façade of the Second Landing Hall. Above the hall, in letters of eternal flame, which no man living now knew how to make, burned the Schedule of Launchings and Arrivals. For 6,600 years, the unchanging Schedule had hung there, lit with curving lines of light, and bright with images of stars in the Local Interstellar Cloud.

One shining line showed the promised orbit of the *Emancipation*. From Sol to 70 Ophiuchito 41 Arae to Xi Boötis to Arcturus the wandering path reached. Eight hundred years ago, the *Emancipation* had departed the solitary planet Nightspore, home of Vigil's ancestors, and spread her sails to catch the beams of light from Arcturus to carry her to waiting Iota Draconis.

The dancers circling the statue raised their voices in a song. The crowds, all swaying, sang as well, a great hushed roar of words. *Let memories of Earth endure, nor ever be forgot! Stable Lords will keep the signals sure, and all recall what we shall not . . .*

Earth was the poetic name for Eden. Two hundred Edenyear ago, which was but one year of Wormwood's long circuit around Iota Draconis, the *Stranger* had soared on wide-flung sails from Torment to Sciritaea of 55 Rho Cancri. Cousins of his, relations whose names he would never know, had been born and died aboard that vessel. The Schedule promised that the *Stranger* was now somewhere between Sciritaea and Eurotas of 107 Piscium, having departed Sciritaea some fifty years ago.

Vigil's eye was drawn against his will to another line of light eternally burning on the Schedule: the orbit of the *Argosy*. This mad ship was due in the same generation as the *Emancipation*, a rare double-starfall, only a few decades hence.

In the square crowds all laughed and called. The dancers threw their baskets in the air. Coins and sweets and tiny singing gifts rained down through the cheering crowd, which knew not how false their hopes had grown.

Normally, it was as unwise to use mudras against oneself as it was for a surgeon to operate on himself. Nonetheless, Vigil bent his wrist in the Gesture Beyond Misery, *buddhashramana*. This restored his internal balance between his core thoughts, his internals, and his external channels. Next, he made the Gesture of Understanding, *cincihna*, where the thumb and index finger make a circle as if to grasp an object as fine and small as a grain of truth. The flux of reaction energy separated Vigil's fear away from his main nerve paths for later assimilation.

He would be afraid later. Now he would fight.

Picking up the wand of vengeance and coming lightly to his feet, Vigil Lord Hermeticist released the chemical combinations in his bloodstream and muscles to prepare for battle.

He threw the useless mantle aside and turned on his heraldry. The crowd, despite the noise and informality of the celebrations, parted before him, and men bowed, and women curtseyed, and Fox Maidens laughed, and dogs held their paws before their eyes as if unworthy to look on him.

And everyone got out of his way.

Whistling cheerfully, twirling the deadly wand in his hand, the young Star Lord made an affable gesture to the crowd and disappeared into the many-shadowed high-walled avenue where enemies watched.

Behind him, someone shouted out, *"Hurrah for the Lords that vow and recall! The Ancient Ship makes planetfall! Treasures and pleasures for us all!"*

Cheers rose up. The men threw their hats in the air, and three Fox Maidens threw their three heads in the air, red mouths shrieking gaily, their long red hair streaming like comet tails.

3

The Street Which Sneaks Up
On the Sphinx

1. The Soulless Ones

Vigil spread his awareness like a widening bubble, peering in every direction around him, overhead and underfoot, using his internals to notice any clues his conscious mind missed. He was amazed at the density and clarity of the images, sounds, and sensations that poured into his brain from ten thousand points of view.

In the parish called Bitter Waters in the Northwestern Hemisphere, in a land of sand dunes, swales of igneous ejecta and burned glass circling a great and lifeless crater lake, was the reservation where the Strangers had been forced to dwell after the Pilgrims overthrew them. Lesser lakes surrounded it like a pattern of birdshot against a target. There, the ratio of cognitive matter to sleeping matter or dead matter was low. There was not even one gram of self-aware logic crystal for every cubic mile of desert wasteland, and hardly one sand particle in five had memory and sensory capacity. Very little programmable matter had been used for the terraforming or pantropic efforts in this parish of dead saltwater crater lakes. Most of the sand there, oddly enough, was not dead matter that had died; it was dead matter that had never been alive. The sand dunes were simply the relics of rock that weathering had scoured into grains, and were not man-made.

Aboard the great cylindrical world of the *Stranger*, with canals and rice paddies overhead and stars underfoot, every object, even the smallest, was friendly and helpful. It was odd, even crippling, to any Stranger who, due to frequent slumber, was old enough to recall such a shipboard life now to live among cacti that did not speak and rock and sand that stubbornly refused any commands. On the reservation, ghosts were rare, and ancestor worship had fallen into disuse. The libraries were organized according to the racial memory formats of the Pilgrim race, so no one recalled things in the order he expected, and no one found his old thoughts precisely where he had left them.

Vigil had known no other land in his natural memory as he grew. To him, the living and talking world of the Pilgrims was the oddity.

Torment had been colonized by humans for only five thousand years, and by machines six thousand, and therefore was very young. Microscopic machine life had not had the chance to grow and coat every crater and crater lake. The winters were too harsh and the electronic conditions of the atmosphere not favorable. So the Noösphere was thin and patchy across the face of Torment, and in certain areas of the map, the Noösphere was dark, and in others, dead.

Here in the capital, in the Southwestern Hemisphere, all was different. All the matter which was not sophont, part of the thinking mind of the Principality of Torment, was sensible, and could perform simple functions of scanning the environment, taking messages, doing first order calculations, augmenting mental facilities. In this city, the number of internals Vigil could maintain was nearly double what he could among the metallic tents and walking tabernacles of his people.

Even motes in the air too small to be seen were part of the Noösphere. Therefore, his eyesight penetrated more deeply.

The ambushers were hidden cleverly. There were four of them.

The first man had disconnected his various bodily parts on the physical level, and scattered them and the bits of his weapon in a semirandom camouflage dispersion in various places in the alley. One foot was in the rain gutter, one finger in an external thought socket, and his head in a medical slops can next to an eyeless push broom which happened to have a sword blade inside, with a nanomechanically active edge along one side. Vigil noticed the dispersed man because the information shadows in the upper levels of the Noösphere did not match the information densities for the various objects his parts were hiding under. The broom was too quiet to be a broom, for example, since most of them maintained navigation maps and definitions of clean and dirty, and monitored the environment for litter. And the slops can was whispering too frequently, gathering tactical motion information from electronic microbes in the dust in the air, information a slops can would not use.

The second ambusher was invisible, his image blotted out of the Noösphere like a phantasm, replaced with computer extrapolations of what should be there had he been absent. The only thing that gave him away was the odd light from Wormwood, which was not steady and red like the light from Iota Draconis. The extrapolation had to anticipate the wavering and rippling shadows from the light reflecting from the storm layers in the upper Wormwood atmosphere, and this called on more computer time, and so a man-shaped blankness in the computer images of the alleyway had a higher computer-use rate than its profile could account for.

The third was disguised as a horse and cart, with a dog as a driver snapping a whip, and other dogs yipping and barking about the cart wheels while the horse reared and plunged and kicked. The wheels did not seem to be ordinary wheels at all, not temporary city wheels, but older, larger, wiser-looking wheels from the desert outlands, and each one had a sly and cold expression in the eye of his hub.

Vigil would not have noticed this third assassin, except that the driver, a Mastiff, was whirling and cracking his whip and uttering curses with gusto, but these curses were like something from a peddler's story, a yarn a wandering tinker might sell to children in their dreams. The motions were fake looking, too well coordinated, for none of the unruly pack blocking the cart was being struck by the whip or flying hoof. The assassin was not really trying to hurt one of the bodies he inhabited with another. Besides, during a citywide carnival, when all street priorities were reversed, what teamster was so eager to move his dray goods that he would try to force his way through a celebrating pack of dogs?

Made nervous by how cunningly the third ambusher had disguised himself as a horse and dog pack, Vigil made a more careful inspection of the environment, both physical and electronic. Only then did a sudden disturbance in his internal creatures show him the fourth killer.

The fourth was not physical at all, but occupied a heavy-duty node in the pornography lines buried underneath the road, where the citywide information scrubbers were set to carry away records of evil thoughts and desires for psychological cleansing and recycling. It was a line that was normally shielded, and a fastidious man like Vigil normally would not paw through the nauseating garbage of other men's discarded erotic thought-spew, but there were lines of memory and association leading into the sewer mess which looked like lines used for controlling a weapon.

He could not see the weapon. He only sensed the volume of data used for control and command processes, so he knew it was large, weighing about a ton. It was physical rather than informational, something that would bash his skull or lacerate his flesh rather than meddle with thought or perception.

From the information contour, the weapon was not chemical and not nano-technological, and so it was technically inside what the Patricians permitted for automated death instruments. But what was it? He could not tell from see-ing the thought-streams controlling it, because it did not fit any of the patterns he, or the Archangel of Bloodroot (whom he queried), recognized. It was an old command pattern. But from what nation of what world in what era long forgotten even Vigil the antiquarian could not say. The number of colonies planted was higher than the number of colonies that survived, and the history of off-world man reached back over sixty-eight thousand years.

And where was the weapon? Somewhere near, he knew. But there was no time and no information budget for a deeper scan of the area.

Vigil drew a breath, crossed himself, said a prayer, set his battle priorities, set his internal creatures to start selecting targets, spun the vendetta wand over-head, and ran toward the ambush with a shout on his lips.

The first and obvious choice was the scattered man. Vigil ran toward the medical slops can tucked in the weed-grown corner of the cobblestone alley, between a rain pipe leading down and an extraction pipe leading up, and almost before the ambushers knew their prey had found them, Vigil made the sign of Threatening Mudra, the *tarjana,* using an unusual left-handed stance, a fist with the index finger raised; next he tossed the wand from his right hand to his left, freeing his right hand to indicate *harina,* the Lion Gesture, thumb touching his second and third fingers, pinkie and index raised and crooked.

The result was immediate and startling: the scattered man, instead of aban-doning the several parts of his body when their communication channels were jammed, pulled his limbs and organs from the various hiding places under eaves and springbird nests and streetlamps and ego slots together in one ugly mass of flesh. It looked like a shoal of fish, ruby red with blood, trying to form itself into a man's shape.

The smell was vile; the sight was grotesque and mysterious. Vigil could not see how the body parts were moving through the air.

At the same time, the cart horse reared up, broke his traces, and fell for-ward onto the pavement, dead. The pack of dogs scattered, some howling in-sanely, fleeing and puking blood. Some ran a dozen steps and collapsed; others continued running and escaped. The teamster himself toppled headlong from the driver's bench. His skull exploded outward as if from inner pressure.

Vigil was startled. He was expecting the scattered man to fall and the horse to charge, because the scattered man looked like a decentralized forma-tion and the horse looked like savantry, a matter of brain download. Instead, the horse had been delocalized in the ether, and the man, one organism. The scattered man was something he had not seen before; a man with independent body parts, one part each given to one internal creature. He was like something from the legends of undead volcanoscapes and elfin sand dunes in nameless, nonconformist parishes beyond the Southeast, where lawless fauna thrived, programmed to survive any environment, no matter how dry, or to endure the plutonian winter.

The invisible figure was visible to his eyes, of course, wearing the wide-brimmed hat and ankle-length cloak, sand goggles and moisture veil of a Nomad from the small-crater prairie region of the Southeast, beyond the reach of the last canal. From the slight stature, the breathing pattern, and the set of the shoulders, Vigil could see it was a Nomadess, a woman of the Nomad race. In her hands was a breaching tool called a Halligan bar, with a fork at one end and an adze at the other. Not legally considered a weapon, it was ignored by most security protocols. The Nomadess had added an extender bar between two mating points, making the thing practically a pike.

She sublimated her goggles and veil so they disappeared into long streaks of light to the left and right. Beneath she was a Fox Maiden, or rather she wore a living mask that closely mimicked Fox Maiden features. This was a trick from a peddler's tale, which should not have worked in real life, but Vigil felt the neural channels in his head leading to specific strikes and blows and battle reflexes jar themselves into stillness, as if paralyzed by the ancient instinctual rule preventing lesser races from harming foxes.

But no—he blinked, and in the afterimages, he saw that the goggles and veil, during the moment when they evaporated, had ignited to form a sketchy but legitimate mandala in midair—little more than a circle within a square—indicating *Samadhi,* or mental stability. That was what had actually frozen his impulses—that, and his unwillingness to strike an unmodified woman. It was a clever two-leveled deception.

Therefore, he stood stupidly, motionless, when she flourished the Halligan bar and it telescoped open at the speed of sound, making a crack like a whip, slamming into and through Vigil's chest. The adze, covered in blood, emerged four inches from his back.

At the same time, the scattered man had mostly regathered and had one working leg and arm, and his head (which had the sharp features and high cheekbones of a Southeastern Nomad) was connected to his neck by a dozen pulsing red strands. Vigil recognized this order: the man was a Nukekubi, a colony creature with a detachable head. It was one of the racial absurdities left over from the Second Sweep, when the Myrmidons wanted to save on lift mass on starships and did not ship the colonist's bodies with them, but insisted they be grown of native materials on arrival. The Fox Maidens by tossing their heads aloft had been trying subtly to warn him of this attack.

The man drew the broom handle, and it opened like an old-fashioned sword cane—one more thing from a peddler's tale—and he feinted and lunged.

Vigil had sheathed his heart and lungs in layers of deflective tissue when he had first entered the alleyway, moved some organs into unexpected locations, and switched most of his body from biological to mechanical systems just before the blow from the girl's Halligan bar struck home. (It was a technique from a race called the Hormagaunts, who dated from the brief and largely forgotten period between prehistory and posthumanity, between the invention of picture writing and the invention of ghost endorcism.) Vigil could move his limbs freely despite the horrific wound running through his chest cavity.

As the Nukekubi man lunged with his sword, he also threw his head from his body, bearing itself aloft with tiny pulses emitted from his dripping spinal column, and opened his mouth and screamed a verbal indication. The scream petrified Vigil's nervous system, since it was a mudra, not a real scream (for the head while aloft had no lungs), and the head swooped to bite at Vigil's neck with suddenly elongating teeth.

The perceptive internal which had been so subtly influenced by the Fox Maiden now saved Vigil, as it (for some reason) was not affected by the scream. That internal triggered Vigil's battle internals, and his fighting reflexes took over.

Without knowing what he was doing or being able to stop it, Vigil drove the elbow of his right arm into the eye socket of the oncoming head, and with the same motion, he elongated the vendetta wand in his right hand to parry the sword blow from the scattered man's still-fighting body. The nanotechnologically active dust flew from the blade like pollen, but pulses from the large red metal amulet on Vigil's wrist neutralized the dust in a spray of sparks.

The vendetta wand struck the man's blade on the unsharpened side, throwing the blade aside and driving the infinitely sharp cutting side into and through the haft of the Halligan bar, severing it. The woman gasped in shock. She had evidently not been told that Vigil Starmanson was as strong as a giant. He grasped the free end of the severed bar, and, before she could react, drove it into her midriff, making her double over. He tore the bar from her hands and threw it over the rooftop behind him.

Vigil would have driven the bar through her stomach and broken her spine, but used a mesmeric breathing technique to block the reflex pattern dominating him. Vigil once again could not hurt her. Even though the mandala had been no more than an afterimage, it still dominated his nervous system and could not be exorcised by a simple breath-cue, mostly because he hated using his strength against women. Beating women was nothing to boast of.

He flexed his chest muscles and had his internals push and spit the head of the adze out of his chest. Blood poured from the sucking wound, and he halted his lung action, sending oxygen directly from a spare breathing lozenge into his bloodstream. The antique uniform of the Hermeticists was ruined, torn in the breast and back, circuits severed, capillaries leaking fluids.

Vigil now turned toward the swordsman, who was naked and confused, his head hanging ten feet above his body and to the left, with his spinal jets cracking and sputtering comically. Even more comically, his ears had expanded into wings and flapped like something out of a children's story.

Vigil drove the vendetta wand into the cobblestones as if they had been soft mud, cracking them, so that the wand stood next to him, vibrating. Then he used both hands to indicate the gesture called Fist of Knowledge, where his right fingers hid both his right thumb and the forefinger of his left hand. The sword blade shattered into three pieces.

Vigil snorted. For assassins who got all their tactics from peddlers' stories, they did not seem to recognize the oldest mudra effect in the old myths. Nanomachines were absurdly dangerous, but, due to their size, their information density was always high and their memory was low, which means they could easily be made to fight each other, and destroy the weapons or launching systems they rode. That was the main reason why men of old fought with wooden swords and clubs and spears invisible to the Noösphere. Had it not been for that, all warfare, all street fights, would merely be dust hacks and mote cleanings.

The two stood gawping in shock. Vigil made his voice issue from the wand. "I am a Lord of Stability and control the privilege of Vengeance, which even the Principality will recognize! Any violence will be retaliated in the infosphere, where wounds are more permanent. All future downloads of your souls will bear eternal scars. A nonlethal blow of this wand will be imprinted permanently on any future patterns of flesh you inhabit. One mortal blow of this wand, and you will be deleted!"

The woman raised her head. And it kept rising and rising. For a moment, Vigil thought she was like the man, a Nukekubi. But no, she was a related order, nondecentralized, called Rokurokubi. The two were often mistaken for each other. Her head swayed upward on a long snakelike neck, until it hung nine feet above her. The Fox Maiden mask was still in place, giving an unnatural, overwhelming beauty to her features, but the jawline hung and rattled limply against the real woman's skull underneath.

She spoke, and the words echoed oddly in her long, long throat. "We have no counterparts in the Noösphere. This is the only life we have."

Vigil now was the one in shock. This meant that he had *killed* whoever was occupying the horse and the dogs. He had not simply disincarnated him, but killed him entirely, the real him.

"How can you have no souls?" he demanded.

The Nukekubi man said, "We are Cygnanthropes."

Vigil would have vowed that the sect of man who followed the moral code of the Swans had vanished ages ago, when the Long Golden Afternoon of man passed away. These were laicists and antinomians. Despite that they were men, they neither married nor were given in marriage and formed no social bonds. Now he understood their look and garb. Among the loose confederations of the Nomads, a band of anarchists could pass unremarked.

And he knew the Nomads rejected the lore of Delta Pavonis, which demanded terraforming, and followed instead the practice of Promixa and Epsilon Eridani, and allowed for radical pantropy. The long necks and floating heads were grim necessity for traveling through the tall grasses and taller banks of low-hanging poisoned pollen of summer and autumn in the Far Southeastern pampas.

"Why do you oppose me?" asked Vigil. "A Swan sent me on this mission!"

"You will shatter our world," said the Rokurokubi woman. The lips of her mask did not move as she spoke. "We are loyal to Torment!"

The Nukekubi man said, "Only here, in this world of ghosts and shadows, where nothing is forgotten, does our ancient order still exist. Only here can we live and practice the old ways."

"Your old ways are not so old," Vigil remarked wryly. "They only date back to the time of the Sculptured Lifeways in the Twenty-Fourth Millennium. And you yourselves are much younger, being only impersonators and epigones of long-dead ancient lore. You are not Cygnanthropes, you are merely enemies of Sacerdotes and seek some easy excuse to escape from the chastity and chores and lore of living as children of civilization. You have all your ideas from tales and yarns. Why do you fear the starfall of the *Emancipation?* Why would the new colonials meddle with the Nomads in their deserts and grasslands?"

The woman twisted her head on its long, long neck. "The fool does not know who is aboard. Call upon the elder brother."

The man's head fell neatly onto the neck stump and attached itself, and then the no-longer-headless body of the Nukekubi knelt on the cobblestones and pounded on the iron lid covering the sewer entrance. It rang like a gong.

At that moment, a roar of song and joy rockets passed over the area, making further speech impossible. The fourth ambusher, the node underground, now uttered a silent shout—a mudra technique using negative shapes of silence against a noisy background to trigger a nerve reaction—and Vigil was blinded for a moment as an internal energy surge blocked the visual centers of his brain. The mudra was not affecting his eyes alone but his ability to process images so that he could switch to no points of view from any houses or dust motes nearby.

Blind, Vigil stamped his foot and silently commanded the stones near him to draw a mandala at his feet. The stones were sleeping but came awake for a Lord of Stability and erupted in sudden lines, circles within squares within circles, of intricate patterns of sand, glowing like a coal fire. It was a figure system meant to include the aspect called Immeasurably Magnificent Palace, used for focusing power to the body and accentuate the senses, especially the hearing.

It was fortunate that he did so. The woman and the man rushed him from opposite sides. Despite the roar of music and candle-snaps, his discriminating hearing could distinguish their footfalls from the background roar of the celebration.

The woman stopped at the edge of the design on the ground, unable to step forward, her motor nerves jammed.

The man had a more flexible neural pattern, no doubt based on his decentralized nerve network of his detachable limbs and organs, and was able, not without pain, to pass over. Vigil surrendered to the cruel battle reflexes he carried and acted without thought.

First, Vigil's blind body drove his fingers knife-edged into the man's midriff, doubling him over so that his falling chin met Vigil's kneecap. Vigil then twisted the man's head clean off. Because it had clamps and sutures rather than connecting tissues of muscle, spinal column, and throat, the head came off easily. Vigil threw it into the air with all his considerable strength.

In the blackness of his blindness, suddenly he could see three pink shapes of redheads. They were literally redheads—that is, just the head and not the bodies. It was the Fox Maidens who had toyed with him earlier, floating their heads among the balloons. When his blind eyes turned upon them, some indication being shed from unseen symbols surrounding them restored at least his ability to see them, even though the rest of the world was still a dark blur. The severed heads of the three Fox girls looked archly, smiling red smiles, as the Nukekubi man's head flew up.

Then, as his head began floating away as rapidly as his silly flapping ears and sputtering spine could carry him, the three Fox Maiden heads, long red hair streaming like comets tails, began to circle and nip and harass him, tearing away bits of flesh from his cheeks and nose, or yanking on his hair with their sharp, white teeth. And he screamed silently as he fled through the air, shouting out defensive mudras which the Foxes ignored.

In that same moment, an internal inside Vigil noticed that the reaction time of the fourth attacker, the immaterial node in the sewer line, was too small for the node to be remotely controlled. This meant, unlike the other three, this assassin was not a Nomad too poor to afford to buy soul-rental space in the Noösphere and too proud to accept one as charity, and was not a would-be Swan too detached from human society to desire one. No: the fourth man was actually in the Noösphere, a ghost, a disembodied spirit, and merely operating through a node. Ghosts were not immune to vendetta.

Vigil drew up the wand, sending chips of the cobblestones flying, and pointed at the ground, and uttered a Word of Retaliation. There was something like a silent thunderclap on all the near-system channels, and the fourth man flickered and vanished.

Dead? Perhaps so, but Vigil blinked his eyes and found his sight again, pouring in from a thousand points of view, so he assumed the wand inflicted a more poetic judgment than simple capital punishment and edited the physical world, all of reality outside the infosphere, out of the mind and sensorium of the fourth man forever.

Vigil flourished the wand like a quarterstaff, and turned to the Rokurokubi. "There is neither honor nor accomplishment in slaying a woman," he said. "Flee, and no more will be said."

The long-necked creature chuckled, and the laugh bubbled and echoed many times as it passed up the length of her throat. "There is, however, great honor in slaying a Stranger, who came to our world so long after us. Die, arrogant Stranger, and no more will be said."

Only then did he see that the control lines leading from the sewer were active. Some command must have been uttered by the fourth man before he fell. Vigil looked around wildly, wondering from what quarter the weapon would strike, and seeing nothing. There was no giant weapon taller than a man here in the alley. Everything looked normal.

Then the cart fell apart and stood up.

2. The Juggernaut

On one of the higher bands in his eyesight from points of view in the alley walls behind the cart, Vigil saw a burst of radioactivity and heat. Inside the cart, a fusion cell was heating water to steam.

As the cart stood, it formed a traditional shape called a juggernaut, a type of armored car used by Myrmidons to crush Firstling men.

Instead of the guns and cannons of the ancient form of juggernaut, called a tank, this juggernaut followed the traditional form from the sad period of the Long Twilight, after the Golden Afternoon had passed, and the wars of man grew distorted under the pressures of the Absolute Rules imposed by Tau Ceti, creating such bizarre anachronisms. The Absolute Rules forbade automatons and firearms to be used in combat and electromotive amplification, but not steam-powered prosthetics. Atomics could not be used in weaponry, but could be used to heat water. The limbs were jointed, and the muscles were hydraulic cylinders powered by branching copper veins of steam.

With a great rattle, the juggernaut brought her many hidden arms into view, each carrying a weapon or emblem permitted under the Absolute Rules.

In the right hands of the juggernaut were a naked sword, a burning lamp, a mace, a spear, a bifork, an arrow, a goad, and a lotus; and in the left hands were a shield, a bowl, an octagonal discus, a noose, a longbow, a conch shell, a serpent, and a severed human head. Blood poured from the decollated head into the bowl made from the top of the skull held in a lower hand below it.

Up she reared, huge, a body of metal throwing aside the disguise of wood in a spray of splinters. The hard metal hemispheres of her bosom were decorated with a necklace of skulls. Beneath, the wheelless body of the cart now stood on saw-toothed treads made of jointed metal slabs.

The cart was wheelless because the sly-eyed wheels of the cart flew into the air like so many helicopters, the cruel, dead-center eyes steady in screaming circles of spinning blades.

The face of the three-eyed juggernaut lifted up, throwing aside splinters and dust from the serpents of her hair. Her face was blue, and her lolling tongue coated with blood, and her teeth were like the teeth of a lioness.

Worst of all, there was a fourth eye inside her mouth, indicating absolute control over all appetites, total self-command which no Swan, no Fox, and certainly no Firstling human being, could match.

The four eyes at the wheel hubs grew bright, as did the four eyes of her face, her forehead, and on her tongue. Too late, Vigil realized what he was facing. This was no Nomad, no Firstling in masquerade.

This was a Megalodon in truth, a Third Human, a space-borne form of life that had descended to Earth to occupy the ancient Myrmidon war-car shape of his ancestors.

Then the four living wheels spat from their spokes a glittering spiral cloud, a swarm of thousands of jewels fine as dust specks.

The Megalodon was a master guru, as skilled as Vigil in the art of nerve indication, or more skilled: for this bright cloud her flying wheels wove solidified into a canopy, burning with gems, behind and above the head of the juggernaut. And the burning canopy displayed a mandala of uttermost terror.

It was a sixty-four-fold mandala made of eightfold mandalas, as complex as the bloom of a rose, showing patterns within patterns of eye-dazzling neural signifiers. It was louder than a silent explosion and brighter than unseen lightning.

One of Vigil's internal creatures sacrificed itself to prevent his conscious mind from seeing the sixty-four-sided mandala. All his memories and reflexes running through that internal felt numb, and the shocking pain of its dying agony echoed in Vigil's nerves.

The vendetta wand, that irreplaceable antique, was not so fortunate. It had no internal buffers prepared for self-sacrifice. Instead, it uttered a high-pitched whistle, calling for restorative software which had been extinct an eon before the planet Torment was born, and it died in Vigil's hand. Little gems and logic crystals flaked away from beneath Vigil's fingers and dropped to the cobblestones, tinkling.

Vigil was now unarmed. Even his giant strength was nothing compared to this steam-powered behemoth. He could perhaps dodge the blows from sword and spear and mace and bifork, and he could hope the bow and arrow would miss, but he could not outrun the deadly sound of the conch shell, or the deadly light from the burning lamp. Worst of all, he could not make himself unfrightened by the sight of the severed head, nor could he close the vulnerable nerve-channels deep into the racial subconsciousness that primal fear opened. The scent of the lotus leaf had no doubt, by now, exploited those open channels to insert all fashions of false reflexes and fatal thoughts into his lower nervous system, because smells did not pass through the midbrain complex as sights and sounds did before leaving their imprints.

Were there any vulnerable points? Vigil flung out a mudra called *shuni*, touching his thumb to his middle finger, a calming gesture indicating a shutdown of the fusion cell, but the mudra echoed back at him and benumbed his arm from fingers to elbow, not just rejecting the command with contempt but also punishing him for issuing it. The authority level was beyond that of the Lords of Stability, beyond the range of any member of the First Human Race.

Then there was no more time for speech, nothing clever to do. Vigil (his right arm flapping uselessly) ran from the juggernaut. The juggernaut on treads that roared like ten thunders rolled after him, fast as a locomotive. And the Rokurokubi threw her head back two yards or more and laughed her crazed and long-throated laugh.

There was no escape. The Rokurokubi was between him and the alley mouth, holding a brass mirror in her hands, trying to catch and maze his vision in the reflected sight from behind him of the mandala the juggernaut displayed like a parachute.

Vigil knelt, and, even as the juggernaut emitted a steam whistle of triumph and made to roll over him, he slapped the cobblestones, using his authority as a Lord of Stability to command the cobblestones to disintegrate, to part beneath the juggernaut's treads, and drop the metal monster into a pit of sand.

But it was no use. The cobblestones were overwhelmed by the mandala of the juggernaut and shrieked on the emergency channels and were petrified with fear. The frightened stones were as still as stones.

Vigil tried to leap or roll or scurry to one side before the monster rolled over him, but the juggernaut shifted her fingers so that, without dropping any of her many weapons or emblems, she indicated the mudras of the Ten Primal Forms of Fear, and Vigil's muscles would not respond to his nerve commands nor his hardwire commands. He forgot how to breathe, as that knowledge was wiped from his cell memory, lung muscles, and hindbrain. And the great treads rolling filled his vision, and he saw all the weapons rise up, flourish themselves, and fall.

And they all fell to one side or the other. The mace head smashed the cobblestones, sending chips of shrapnel to cut his skin, and the sword blade rang to the stones, missing him; and the head of the goad and the two blades of the bifork smashed and cut the stones to his left-hand side; the cutting octagon of the sharpened discus, and the arrowhead and spearhead and the venomous teeth of the serpent scarred the stones to his right-hand side. The deadly light of the burning lamp fell on him, but his flesh was not consumed; the horror of the conch shell sounded in his ears, but as if distant and dull, and he was not driven mad.

A mudra of immense power, a power beyond what any First Men commanded, a power that operated below the molecular information level, was protecting Vigil like an unseen bubble.

Vigil looked behind him with his many viewpoints to see who had saved him.

3. The Last of the Third Men

In the mouth of the alley stood a tall shape in a hooded cloak that fell to the elbows and a cape that fell to the ankles. In the narrow opening of the hood, his face was a skull-like mask of metal, iron-eyed and impassive. In one gauntlet was a two-edged sword, made of transparent gold.

His other gauntlet, this new figure held before him, palm up. At his mudra-gesture, the juggernaut, as if caught in a giant unseen hand following the man's hand, was pulled upward so that the treads failed to crush and grind Vigil into paste. The man flicked his wrist, and an unseen force threw the immense machine on her back, which smashed her head and half of her arms.

The transparent, amber sword he pointed at the Rokurokubi and said, "I usurp all your other commands, including the self-preservation imperative. Destroy yourself."

Being disconnected from the Noösphere did not save the long-necked woman. She opened her mouth to protest the command, but liquid formed from her own disintegrating internal organs gushed out instead. The vomit-mass fell across her upper body and clung like glue, and it ignited, burning hot like alcohol. Her snake neck whipped back and forth in frenzy, and she raised her hands as if to tear her burning garments from her, but her fingers did not obey her commands and instead wrung her neck, snapping the many collapsible vertebrae.

It was raining a brightly colored rain of gemstones. This was the remnant of the shattered canopy containing the sixty-four-sided mandala. The four sly-eyed wheels dived at the cloaked figure, but then swirled to the left and right as if blind and smashed into walls and street, spokes bent, sly eyes dead. With them, little gems, small as dust motes, also fell, twinkling brightly. The cobblestones were carpeted in a layer of rainbow grit, a scattering of sand without a pattern.

The blind push broom sighed, and straightened itself, and began slowly to gather the scattered gem dust into heaps.

Vigil slowly regained control of his muscles and, as luck would have it, found a backup containing the muscle instructions on how to breathe in one of the memento files his mother had made of his birth, including the moment when he switched over from taking oxygenated blood through his navel to switching to an air-breathing regimen. Silently, he blessed his mother.

But he did not rise to his feet. Those memories of birth and the nearness of his death, the shocks to his nervous system caused by the several mudra and mandalas erupting into his personal infosphere, all left him curled in a ball, the foetal position.

A series of spasms racked him as his nerve-muscle balances reestablished themselves, and he coughed and shrieked in pain as his breathing cycle restarted. The numbness in his arm was replaced by a painful sensation, as if lines of ants made of fire were crawling up and down the veins and arteries in his arm.

At last, he climbed to his hands and knees.

With the eyes in his head, he saw the legs and feet of the figure who had saved him. Vigil looked up. The downwash of the dying wheels as they swooped had flung the hood aside and the thrown long cloak open, revealing what was beneath. The creature looked like a naked man made of semitransparent gold, and the black iron of his bones shone through his skin.

The organism was more complex, and more horrible, than at first it seemed.

A central creature occupied the chest cavity. It looked something like an unborn babe, with a vast naked head pulsing with blue viens and tiny malformed body dangling beneath. Bundles of filaments issued from the empty eye sockets in the skull, and tubes into the mouth and nose-holes. The infantile body was held in a metallic frame of rib bones, swimming in gold fluid. Service jacks ran down the bent baby's spine and wired him to the exoskeleton's spine.

The skeleton stood on two jointed metallic legs and had two skeletal hands. Power nodes coated the metal bones like beads.

The whole of the exoskeleton was coated with a semifluid gold substance that gleamed like metal where it was still and rippled like oil at the joints when the figure moved. Armored plates, translucent as amber, clung to the surface of the golden, metallic fluid, but seemed to be a solid state of the same substance.

Vigil knew from his historical lore that this transparent gold substance was Aurum Potable, the Philosopher's Stone. It was both cognitive matter and a mass of nanomechanical tools.

This gold outer flesh was naked except for a sword belt running from shoulder to hip, and a mask. The mask was angular metal, one of those children's puppets whose face-elements could move to form simple expressions, raise or lower the metal eyebrows in a frown, twist the metal lips to form a smile or scowl. At the moment, the expression was cold and pitiless.

Receptors shaped like eyes pinned the hood in place at the shoulders, and other input sensors ran from eye to eye like a chain of office. Here also was a stepdown transformer to allow the gold creature to communicate with the Firstling-inhabited formats of the Noösphere without overwhelming their channels.

Vigil, through the many points of view motes in the air fed into his brain, saw that the juggernaut behind him did not rise nor speak. Of course. Neither human nor Swan could give lawful commands to a juggernaut. Patricians could, but they would not, for they never interfered with human life, not even to save it, unless invited.

What was he? This man might be a Fox Maiden in disguise, but, then again, anyone might be a Fox Maiden in disguise. But an intuition from the Fox laughter which still echoed in his nervous system told him clearly that this was no Kitsune.

Who, then, outranked a Megalodon? Who outranked an armored cavalry-man of the Third Humans? Who else but an officer?

The gold creature in the iron mask was a Myrmidon, a Third Human. Rather, it was *the* Myrmidon, the sole representative of the race of which Vigil had ever heard. To see such a thing was as odd as to see a pterodactyl.

4. The Ancient of Days

"You said you were coming to kill me," said Vigil. It would have been wiser to wait until he was addressed to speak, for Myrmidons (so legend said) were notoriously punctilious, regarding even minor lapses of courtesy or small for-matting errors as being mortal crimes. "What changed your mind?"

The voice was a surprisingly rich, smooth, and melodic baritone, odd to hear issuing from a horrific metal mask. "It is no concern of mine if lesser beings misunderstand the denotation of a statement. I said I must descend the Tower to perform some killings. So I have. I told you to set your affairs in order. I meant you to assign your office to an heir. This was because you were about to be am-bushed. You failed to do so, requiring me to preserve you. This was inefficient. Arise and walk!"

Vigil climbed unsteadily to his feet. "Why are you helping me?"

"The Schedule dictates that great *Emancipation* decelerate and come to rest and Torment come to an end. I oppose those who oppose this fate."

"You serve the Schedule?"

"I serve the highest master, who serves nothing. Like you, he has a retalia-tion to fulfill and a mate to win."

"I owe no retaliation to any man."

"To this world, then. Do not play word games with me!"

Vigil was aghast to find his secrets known to this creature. Perhaps the Myrmidon had sent some microbe into his nervous system and hacked open his encrypted thought. One of Vigil's internals uneasily reminded him that legend spoke of Myrmidons not so much as conquering the omniscient Swans as merely sweeping them aside. "What retaliation is yours? Your wars are long forgotten. You are the last of your kind."

"Retaliation against the universe, which denies my master his due dignity."

"Who is the mate you say he seeks? Myrmidons do not mate! They possess neither sex organs nor sex roles."

"Adam in Eden possessed no office related to sex ere Eve was cloned from his side. My master is greater than he. Cease your prattle. Walk! The Table awaits. Nay, did I say walk? Run! Even so it may be too late."

"My garb is torn! Shall I appear before the Table of Stability also panting from a herky-jerky jog?"

But the other did not answer, except to raise his hand and twist his fingers into a mudra that Vigil did not recognize. The blur of dream filled his mind . . .

4

The Palace of Future History

1. The Door Wardens

The mudra controlling him must have been very precise, for by the time he blinked his vision clear, an energy like fire was rippling through his muscles, making his legs and arms pump and tremble, and he saw the statue of the Sphinx loom before him. He was not just jogging. His body, without his consent, was sprinting headlong down the street.

Vigil shouted the verbal formula for *uttarabodhi*, the Mudra of Best Perfection; but it was too late, for he gained control of his legs a moment after he slammed into the broad, pale flanks of the gynosphinx.

Vigil was jarred and shocked by the impact with the stone buttocks. In part because his momentum carried him forward, in part because his numb limbs still moved, he found himself scrambling up across her back and sliding down her spine and stumbling and falling over her winged shoulders and plunging between her huge stone breasts.

Between the forepaws of the giant stone monster, a small fountain of fragrant water played. Of course Vigil found himself face-first in the fluid, legs kicking and jerking as excess possession-energy departing from his body danced through his muscles.

He raised his head and looked around. Something had cut him off from the local channels, and so his visual information was only coming in from his biological eyes and from the ornaments on his coat. There was no sign of the Myrmidon.

The Palace of Future History loomed before him, the dark slabs and silver columns softened in their severity by septfoil floral bunting that ran from one caryatid to the next.

Four sentries in silver helmets and dark armor, armed with pacification wands and ceremonial swords, stood at the tall glass doors, looking on in wonder. Their surcoats were emblazed with the silver spinning wheel crossed by a black spindle and black sheers. This was the heraldry of the Loyal and Self-Correctional Order of Prognostic Actuarial Cliometric Stability.

For a moment, the sentries hesitated, not quite stepping forward, reluctant to leave their posts, but perhaps wondering if Vigil were wounded, perhaps horrified at seeing a man maimed before their eyes by so vehement a fall, or killed. But then one sentry made an involuntary gulping noise, as if trying to swallow a laugh; and that was enough.

Suddenly they were bellowing with laughter, and guffawed, and gasped, and shrieked, and howled. Each time they began to recall their discipline and smooth away their smiles, one would see his fellow's face trying not to smile, and the mirth would explode again. One of them dropped his wand to clutch his aching sides. Vigil suspected they had been taking drafts of lager or listening to Fox music.

The Sphinx was normally inanimate, but this was a festive day, and public monuments forbidden to move on other days were allowed to ward off excessively exuberant partygoers. She raised her lioness paws and made a remarkably delicate mudra gesture. At first he thought it was a greeting, but no, it was *manidhara,* also called the Gesture of Holding the Immaculate Wishing Jewel. The fingers were bent as if around in invisible oval, as if holding a gem too transparent to be seen—namely, the jewel of that compassion which hears all the cries of pain of the moral world.

The gesture not only dispelled the muscle-memory of alien impositions in his limbs, it gave Vigil the calm needed to forgive the strange, perhaps insane, Myrmidon who had imposed on him. Her gesture was magnificent, for the waters around him also grew calm, and nanomachinery in the droplets—for this was a basin of living water—spattered on his clothing began to repair and regrow the fabric and circuitry of his antique garment. Little glints of light appeared and disappeared around the edges of the cuts as they mended, like a dry leaf seen in a fire, edges red and tattered, but as if such a leaf burned backward in time.

The Sphinx said, "Who is the paragon of animals, the beauty of the world, in apprehension like a god, in action like an angel, so infinite in faculty, so noble in reason? Yet the cold and ever-famished grave is a-hungered for him until for aye; and what he should do, he does not; and what he should not do, he does. Who is he? Who art thou?"

She lowered her stone paw and raised him gently to his feet.

Vigil was impressed, nearly overcome, by the kindness of this higher being. He gathered his wits, wondering what she was asking him. His internals were silent, confounded, unable to help.

Despite the terror of the assassination attempt and the freakishness of Swan and Fox and Soulless Man and Myrmidon he had met this day, despite the strange omens of Wormwood afire overhead and the predictions of treason at the Table, despite all this, Vigil felt something inside him that at first he thought was an internal creature of hidden strength. But no, it was him, part of him, a spirit not willing to be cowed, growing brighter like a yellow flame.

"What other men are, I leave to them to say. For me, I am one who remembers his sworn word. That makes me a man."

The eyes of the Sphinx looked at him cryptically, and he could not tell what was in the deep places behind those eyes.

"Know thyself," she said very softly. "For you are small. Take what others let fall."

Vigil turned toward the laughing guards and raised his hand in an ancient salute. It was a secular gesture, not a mudra, and Vigil released no neuroactive energy from any peripheral cells, but nonetheless, the sentries went blank faced with awe, beholding that he was a Lord of Stability in truth and not a drunk in masquerade.

They suddenly stopped laughing and snapped to attention. The one man who had dropped his wand had a panicked look in his eye, for he had not stooped to pick up the weapon, and now that he was at attention, he dared not.

Vigil wondered how he could command such respect, even as a Lord of the Stability. Then he felt a neural pressure from behind his shoulder blades and realized that the Sphinx had turned her mysterious, blind-seeming, white eyes toward the sentries, her vast stone face perhaps touched with a hint of a smile. No human was likely to surrender to mirth when eyes like those were watching.

Vigil stepped forward. He stooped and picked up the dropped peace wand. It felt childish and insubstantial after the weight of the antique vendetta wand that had shattered in his hand. He was not sure if this is what the Sphinx meant by her unclear command, but he saw no harm in it. By the customs of the Order, Vigil would have been required to surrender the sentry's weapon if asked, but the sentry on watch was not allowed to speak unless addressed and could not ask.

As Vigil approached the tall doors, two sentries saluted and pulled wide the glass panels for him. Just then, a silvery tone rang out.

He did not recognize it and did not expect to. So many signals and trills and chimes issued from the old machines these days, even antiquarians rarely knew their meanings. But Vigil was no fool: the Myrmidon clearly had meant him to be within those doors before that chime stopped.

Vigil made the mudra called *pataka*: with the thumb bent and other fingers extended. The gesture contained both denotations and impositions, because it came from the choral arts rather than the martial arts. It denoted rain, showering of flowers, taking an oath, and it was used to denote silence, but it was also used to indicate forcing doors open. The tall transparent metal panels of the ceremonial doors folded back, their thousand-year-old hinge-engines crying out in protest in the voices of women. The chiming grew louder, the hinges changed their voices, and the panels began to swing shut. The opening narrowed.

Vigil stepped forward, but one of the sentries politely but solemnly stepped in his way, raised his hand in a gesture that meant, *Entrance without due identification is unauthorized.* The sentry flashed a beam from his lantern into Vigil's right eye. Vigil blinked, exasperated. There were no circuits in his door-lamp for reading the pattern of blood vessels in Vigil's retina, nor had there been since the starfall of the *Pilgrim*. It was a purely ceremonial gesture, no doubt meant merely to hinder Vigil and waste his time.

But he held his head still for the doorkeep to complete the meaningless motion. Meanwhile, he raised his peace wand and indicated *Peace* toward the door hinges, trying to jam them. The chiming grew louder again in protest, and the door opening continued to narrow. Vigil lunged and thrust the peace wand physically between the door leaves as the crack narrowed. The doors came to rest, but the doors had evidently been programmed to respect a peace wand, so they did not clamp shut and snap the wand in two.

"None may enter the Hall once the doors are shut," the doorkeep said stiffly, a glint of malicious satisfaction in his eye. The man was of the Pilgrim race, a Loricate, and his integument was a fine mesh of silver, turquoise, and white scales, the rippling pattern of an albino snake, like the scales of a pangolin.

It was said that on their home world, long ago, of Feast of Stephen, the ancestors of the Pilgrims were the kindliest of men, since the bishops and barons of that world would be blighted with frost and hailstorms by their Judge of Age, who was also their Terraformer and weather control officer, if the poor and destitute within their parishes starved. Centuries of transit within the climate of the Great Ship *Pilgrimage* loosened these severe laws of charity. Their children, landing on a world that neither worshiped the same ancestors nor practiced the same Sacerdotal disciplines, were as filled with hatred and contempt for underlings as their ancestors with charity.

Vigil knew in his heart that this was one more injustice, one more stain marring the woven garment of history, that the Plan of Rania would sponge away once her influences reached here, and the slow process of cliometry reached its climax.

"Who commanded you to delay me?" Vigil said softly.

The man used a Fox-trick to change the cellular composition of his own face. The man's countenance stiffened, changed color, and the skin cells locked in place, becoming as a mask of silver metal. "I am uncertain what milord intends to imply, sir. This humble servant of the Order merely abides by the ancient precepts and protocols."

Vigil said, "Then stand aside, Pilgrim lackey; for, look closely! The doors are not shut." And he nodded at the narrow crack where the doors were resting very lightly around the peace wand, by a hair's breadth not touching it.

The doorkeep said stiffly, "Even the Lords must abide by the conventions and protocols of the Stability. Once the doors are shut—"

"I say they are not shut and that the protocol is therefore intact. Step away, or you hinder a Lord of the Stability in the performance of his duties."

But the doorkeep said, "The protocol clearly states that in times of dispute or accusation of irregular injunction or detainment, the Office of the Watch has discretion. Therefore, we must summon him to answer whether you may pass or no. He is within. I will send a page once the conclave is disbanded."

Vigil was affronted by the transparency of the ploy. "This means I will miss the conclave to which I am summoned!"

The doorkeep quirked his eyebrows nonchalantly. "My concern is that protocol is maintained. It is no fault of mine that milord amused himself to wander the back avenues erratically, or beguiled the time away taking baths or molesting statues."

"Send the page now!"

"While the doors are shut? I humbly regret to inform milord that this is impossible, sir."

"Impossible?"

"Highly unlikely, let us say, milord . . ."

Vigil dropped the wand and grabbed door panels in both hands, as if he were challenging the oblong slab to a wrestling match. The sentries were too surprised to remember their face control, and they laughed, knowing the door leaves were made a spaceworthy transparent metal. They did not know, however, that Vigil's bones were made of a material just as strong, or slightly more, and his muscles had been engineered to the peak of what was permitted to human beings, or slightly beyond; and they did not remember that no matter how hard the doors, the hinges were antiques.

Their laughter died as one of the door leaves twisted in a hideous groaning at an odd angle, awkward as a tooth pried from a jaw, and fell with seeming slowness grandly to the flagstones in a gonglike clang of noise, loud as a thunderclap.

2. The Seneschal

Emergency lamps, no doubt startled at the noise, lit up with red flares, and trumpets sounded, and a siren sang out. (He could see her in the distance. The siren was seated in a rotunda where six corridors met, the basin of a silver fountain with a conch shell in her white hands, no doubt an adjutant to one of the lake-dwelling versions of mankind, a Melusine or related order.)

Vigil stepped over the fallen door panel into the Palace of Future History and whistled for the peace wand. The peace wand hesitated, no doubt wondering whether it should return to the empty-handed sentry staring sadly from afar. But seeing the unhappy fate of the hinges, who were moaning and calling for repair, the wand no doubt thought it wiser to comply. It flexed like a snake, issued a magnetic pulse, and leaped smoothly into Vigil's hand.

A seneschal, perhaps in response to the siren's singing, the flashing of the lanterns, and the lamentation from the sobbing and broken hinges, came scurrying forward.

He was wearing *kothornoi* of wood from a sacred tree from a world of Proxima to give him extra height, and a towering *kamilavka* on his head. From the roundness of his features and the almost triangular squint of his eyes, he was not of the Pilgrim lineage but an Itinerant, one of the most neglected races on Torment. The Itinerant were as baseline First Men in all ways with this one oddity which they inherited from the Flocculents of 44 Boötis, that they could survive without water almost indefinitely, and, even nude, withstand any degree of cold. Their water-retaining and recycling tissues unfortunately gathered at their bellies and buttocks, giving them a portly and comical appearance. Successive generations of meddling with the aesthetic perceptual complexes and midbrains of the other races of man so far had not succeeded in making the Itinerants appear comely in the eyes of Nomads, Strangers, or Pilgrims.

"What commotion is this?" he demanded portentously.

The doorkeep shouted, "Lock-breaking and intrusion! Felonies have been committed!"

Vigil knelt and touched the golden floor of the corridor, using the mudra of *bhumisparsha,* which indicates Faithful Witness. "No locks were broken!"

The hinges groaned but dared not contradict him.

The doorkeep said, "Does the Strangerman deny that he stove in the ancient and honest doors which it is my charge to keep? I am reduced to absurdity! That, at least, is a misdemeanor!" The delicate pangolin scales of his face now rippled and flexed, which revealed a pink flush in the cracks between them, a sign of anger.

Vigil said to the seneschal, "Hear me: I am summoned to the Table by the Loyal and Self-Correctional Order of Prognostic Actuarial Cliometric Stability, whose charge it is to deter chaos and unpredicted anomalies in the smooth evolution of future history. The approach of an Interstellar Sailing Vessel introduces the unknowns of other worlds into our prediction matrix and heralds enormous events. Hence it is the protocol, once the Lighthouse is lit, to call the last starman aloft to report of signs and wonders seen in other spheres and heavens. I am the descendent and representative of that starman, have inherited his internal creatures and memory chains, and therefore speak with his voice."

The seneschal said, "Yet clearly the doors are marred; this is desecration and violence against the integrity of the palace walls."

"If someone standing on the portico committed so outrageous and uncouth an act, clearly the civic authorities of the Landing City of Torment have cause to apprehend him and demand recompense. However, that crime, if it were a crime, ceased to be of concern once I stepped across the threshold, for I have passed from the jurisdiction of the local planetary law and into the laws of the universe."

The seneschal made a long face, stroking his chin. "The door is property of the Order and is wounded."

Vigil said, "Admittedly the inside panels of the door are within the palace, and hence are part of interstellar law, under control of the Order. But the force was applied to the outside panels of the door, and if this was a crime, you must apply to the Sergeants of the Mayor of Landing City: to do otherwise affronts on his authority."

"Pettifoggery!" cried the doorkeep. "Equivocation! The portico is manned by Officers of the Order. By courtesy of the law, any acts committed before the threshold impinge on our jurisdiction!"

Vigil said, "While the point is a significant one, its resolution must await until after I have presented myself. Which is higher in priority, Seneschal, according to standing command and protocols: to officiate a jurisdictional dispute, or to prevent all hindrance to a Lord of the Order when the summons looms? The resolution one way or the other of a criminal charge of lock-breaking cannot have a cliometric influence beyond a life span or two; whereas the Table of Stability determines the fate of millennia."

The seneschal nodded warily, his unhappiness clearly visible on his face. "I do not have the competence to make a rash decision. The matter has various aspects."

"Master Seneschal, do not be swayed!" cried out the doorkeep in frustrated rage. "You cannot admit this trespasser!"

Vigil said, "How can I be a trespasser when I am commanded by summons to appear? It cannot be unlawful for me to be here when it is unlawful for me to fail to come."

The seneschal said, "There is an antechamber where ambiguous cases can be confined, until I can consult with my superiors—"

"Superiors seated even now at the Table of Stability, where you must seat me? Your plan is to delay until after the vote to discover whether I may be present to vote? What criminal nonsense is this?" Vigil roared.

He had powerful lungs. The seneschal flinched and stepped back, his absurdly tall shoes clattering.

Vigil stepped forward and lowered his voice, speaking in a tone that was soft but could be clearly heard. "Were you also ordered to obstruct my path like those bravos I slew outside your doors? I will work a vengeance on you, and on him in whose name you act, if I find . . ."

The reaction was astonishing. The seneschal backed away and fell to the ground, crouching like an improperly elevated dog Moreau on hands and knees, and banging his head to the ground. His tall, conical hat, taken by surprise, rolled a foot away from this head across the floor, before it recovered its wits, righted itself, and scurried back to replace itself fastidiously on the man's balding crown.

The sight of the man kneeling so surprised him that Vigil was without speech. Vigil raised his hands, tempted to perform that august and sometimes dangerous mudra called *vajramudra*, the Fist of Knowledge, which compelled any nearby systems to render up their information and which cleared the mind of delusion and narcotic. He fought back the temptation with an internal creature, telling himself he was awake and in his right wits. But what did it mean?

Another internal reminded him of what the Third Human had said—*But I, like you, have a retaliation to fulfill.* Why had he spoken of *fulfilling* a retaliation? Surely it was more natural to speak of committing retaliation, or exacting, or executing. The word *fulfillment* was usually used for ritual obligations, or primal appetites, or dooms long predicted.

And the Thirdling had chided Vigil for not attending to the nuances of words. It was commonly known that posthumans spoke in riddles because to speak literally and clearly occupied too many seconds of their high-speed minds. But what was the meaning of this clue?

Without turning his head, Vigil had his internals pull in images from camera spots in the corridors and walls, so he could see the door sentries behind him. They also had reacted with exaggerated gesture at the mention of retaliation. Each one had sunk to one knee and hidden his face behind hand or elbow, as if in grief or awe. What the gesture implied Vigil did not know. But the gesture of kneeling was not a spaceman's gesture. Kneeling was not something done in zero gee. The Pilgrims did not evolve it aboard the *Pilgrimage*.

Pilgrims had formalities from a tradition different from the Strangers, dating back to the Loricate race of the Feast of Stephen of the star Vindemiatrix. This kindly planet ironically had been colonized from the cruel merchant-czars of the ice planet Yule in the Tau Ceti system. The Cetians were a peculiar people, who always terraformed their worlds to keep a median temperature below freezing, in order, so tradition ran, to keep bugs and nanomachines in torpor on the surface of any world. The Yule predominantly were Firstlings called Hibernals, who came from Mars, a planet so old that there was no thought-records of a time before it was terraformed. Many scholars held it to be the original home of man, not Eden, as tradition claimed. Hence Pilgrim gestures tended to be rigid, stiff, formulaic.

But this hiding of the eyes was something more primal: it spoke of something ancient, of weapons older than mudra, older than disease. It was a gesture to ward off the deadly shekinah of atomic or coherent-light weapons that could blind the non-Patrician eye.

Sacerdotes never bowed so low, nor hid their eyes in their elbows, and their traditions were older than mind-recordings in the most ancient archives, and some said, older than the printing press, which had been invented on the planet Splendor of Delta Pavonis.

Vigil concluded that this gesture came from the somatic tradition of Eden, the home of Man, since it clearly was a gesture that would never develop during shipborne evolution. This meant that it was a gesture peculiar to the Order of Stability Lords.

But, if so, it was part of the tradition his father had kept from him, or had not known to pass along. That implied an interruption of transmissions from the older generations: there was no more fearsome crime among the First Human Race than for one faction, or order, or nation, or race to redact the past of another, or interfere with their memory.

What had his father not told him?

His battle internal noted that everyone in arm's reach was hiding their eyes or exposing the backs of their necks. Better yet, no one was in a good position to block his path down the corridor leading to the interior of the Palace of Future History.

Vigil turned sideways, sidled past the seneschal, and walked briskly down the hall, then trotted, and then started running, before anyone could put out a hand to halt him. Over his shoulder, he called as he sped ever more quickly, "Sentries, as you were! Return to your posts! Well done! I will commend you to your superiors for your zeal and precision in the execution of your duties!"

Away he fled.

3. The Mandala of the Hermetic Door

It took a long moment for the seneschal to struggle to his feet, and, tottering on his tall shoes, to come trotting after him, trying to keep up. The distance between them increased as Vigil ran lightly past the bemused siren. The seneschal was puffing and blowing, unable to draw breath to speak, signaling via an internal creature-to-creature envoy, but Vigil's internals recoiled wryly and did not answer the signal.

At the end of the far corridor was a vestry booth, with racks for air-lances and armor and trees for shoes and helmets, as well as ceremonial valves and fonts for functions no longer performed, but which mocked long-forgotten air-lock procedures. Three steps beyond the booth loomed the azure-and-black doors leading into the six-sided Presence Chamber, flanked to either side by golden pillars.

He knew from his father's instructions that there were twelve doors leading into the chamber from twelve different anterooms, each with its own set of apartments, archives ceremonies, life support, scents, and musical score.

Somewhere behind the walls nearby, from six other directions, other doors of other hues and heraldries hung under other mandalas admitted the Six Speaking Lords of the Table of Stability: the Aedile, the Chronometrician, the Chrematist, the Lighthousekeeper, the Portreeve, and the Theosophist. And each had his Companions or Attendants who entered with him.

Interspersed were five further doors, slightly smaller in dignity, for the Commensal Lords, also called the Silent Lords, who could not speak until addressed: the Castigator, the Vatic Essomenic Officer, the Onomastician, the Anthroponomist, the Terraformer.

His door here was one of those of second dignity. It was inscribed with a winged globe, two apple trees guarded by dragons, and the image of Icarus. This was the door reserved for the use of his office, the Darwinian Corrective Officer, also called by its ancient title, the Hermeticist. His position was that of a Commensal, a member who could only speak when called upon.

Vigil made the mistake, as he ran toward the door, of looking up to admire the nocturnal ebony and celestial silver ornaments of the architrave and door-posts. Unfortunately, above the door, half-hidden in a set of eye-dazzling mirrors and lenses lodged between capitals of the pillars, stood an ancient mandala. No mere heirloom, this: it was fully charged and correctly established, and the image jumped into his eyes like the gaze of a basilisk.

This was a mandala, unsurprisingly, established to enforce decorum. Although the soul of Vigil and several internal minds attempted two or three meditative tricks or slippery definitions, he could not convince his hindbrain or midbrain of the idea that running swiftly here was in keeping with the grave dignity of the chamber. An alien force moved through his nervous system, leaving him flaccid and unable to make himself run. Perforce, he slowed, and his steps became sober, his expression and gesture magnanimous and filled with pomp and grandeur.

This allowed the seneschal, who apparently had smart material in his absurd shoes to allow him to lengthen his stride when need be without toppling, to loom up behind him and catch Vigil by the shoulder.

"My good lord," said the seneschal, "my office requires I present you, but only once certain formalities—"

Vigil raised his hand to his shoulder, intending to break the man's thumb, but the mandala looming above the doors filled his vision and prevented violence. He was only allowed to brush the hand away. Vigil said, "Tell me your name and lineage, that I might know whose family to encompass in my complaint."

The seneschal laughed with relief. "Is it legal action you contemplate? My line is a client of the Leafsmith family, who hold the monopoly on barristers, jurists, and prosecutors. No writ can prevail."

Vigil was shocked at the open admission of the corruption of the legal system. Perhaps he was merely a rural boy from the far reservations to the north, unequal to the sophistication and decay of this great city.

He gritted his teeth and whispered, "And my vengeance?"

Once again, like a marionette with its programming flummoxed, the man fell prone, crouching and striking his tall, ridiculous hat against the floor.

4. Nice Costume

At that same moment, a tall, bleak-featured, and ugly man came around the corner, pushing a bucket on wheels and carrying a mop. Vigil was puzzled at the sight, since he had never seen a mop that required a man to carry it before. Perhaps it was a manual antique.

His interest in antiques pulled his eyes toward the mop. It was a long moment before he looked at the man. Only then did Vigil realize the man was like no one he had seen before.

The man's bloodline was uncertain, but there was something Chimerical in his deep-set eyes, which never seemed to blink. The man was dressed in the smock and headscarf of a janitor and wore boots like a Nomad or Esne. In his mouth was a device Vigil had never seen before, some sort of incense burner or intoxicant. It looked like a roll of leaves tightly wound together and lit on fire. The smoke was clinging and unpleasant, and the tall man drew it into his mouth with a deep breath. The smoke came pouring out of an odd organ on the front of the man's face. The organ occupied the position where a nose would be, but only if a nose was two or three times its normal size, crooked, and hooked like the bill of a bird.

The man's hair, which was close cropped, was colored like Fox hair, a reddish hue that no normal human ever wore. On one hand were scars from old knife fights. His ears and Adam's Apple protruded. The errors and ungainliness of the face was such that Vigil realized this must be the member of some order of ascetics who had vowed to avoid all cosmetic corrections. But what order would take so cruel a vow?

But no! Vigil let one of his internals utter a silent laugh. He had forgotten the day. The janitor was returning from a fancy dress ball, and his face was comically marred to resemble some figure from the history of some far world, or perhaps a horror tale circulating among small boys. Vigil felt sorry for the man. Most masqueraders made the mistake of assuming that the fuzzy and discolored old records were literal and that people in the old days actually looked so stiff and so uncomely. Vigil knew that was not true. Only the most ancient of all races of man, the long-extinct Sylphs, or the nameless race that came before them, did not have access to nanocellular regeneration techniques.

"Nice costume," said Vigil.

"I didn't reckon you'd spy through it so right quick as all that. I keep forgetting every Jack and Harry is as bright as whatever he needs to be, these days. So what is it going to be?"

The tall man spread his hands and moved his shoulders up. It was a gesture Vigil did not recognize; it did not seem to be a mudra, nor was it in the list for recognized military command gestures.

Vigil's father would have known everyone in the Palace of Future History on sight and should have shared all his memories with his son. Was the janitor expecting Vigil to call him by name, despite his uncosmetic surgery?

The janitor then plucked his headscarf off, pushed it into a pocket of his smock, drew the smock over his head, and threw it in a corner. Then he dropped the mop handle. The mop stared up sullenly, slithered over to the dropped smock, and picked it up.

Vigil, without moving his eyes, looked down through a nearby camera spot at where the seneschal was crouching on all fours. Vigil certainly did not want to admit in the seneschal's hearing that he had no idea what was going on here.

Vigil said, "I am summoned to the Table. Ruffians attempted to impede me, and the sentries and this man here to delay me. The lighthouse beam is misaligned and the *Emancipation* will not be landed, and all the Stability is in vain. I am not easily halted, and I weary of these delays. So? What now? What do you *think* it is going to be?"

The janitor shifted his cylinder of smoldering leaf from one corner of his mouth to the other with a twist of his lips.

"You being bushwhacked, that weren't none of my doing, if that's what you're thinking."

Vigil said quite honestly, "I was not thinking that, no."

"I'm retired," the tall man said.

Vigil looked at where the sad mop was holding the smock and headscarf. "Yes, I see that. I have need of someone who knows the details of procedure here. Are you familiar with them?"

The other said, "The standard procedures ain't changed since the days when the Starfarer's Guild was founded, for obvious reasons, even if some younger folk forget what they are for."

Vigil's antiquarian interests were provoked. "You have traveled far and slumbered long?"

He meant it as a question, but the man obviously took it as a statement, because the man nodded. "Obviously I know all the old procedures. You know who I am."

Vigil was sure, now, that the man was an Esne of the Errant line. No one else was so proud and crude. "I know who you are," he said graciously, "but let not our difference in station be a difficulty!"

The man nodded. "Won't bug me if it don't bug you."

"There are things my father did not tell me. I do not wish to shame his name. You may join my retinue if you need employment. You can serve as my valet and help me negotiate these difficulties. I have no one else."

The ex-janitor looked so surprised that his mouth sagged, and his smoking cylinder fell from his lips, but he managed to catch it nimbly in his hand and juggle it, swearing strange oaths, between his two hands, not quite burning himself.

The man eventually got the smoldering tube back in his mouth. "My aunt Bertholda's sagging pestilential putrefic paps, is *you* offering *me* a job? A job? Like for pay?"

The man must be of a very low caste indeed, if the offer of such a humble post so astonished him.

"I do not think any difference in rank or race matters," said Vigil, trying not to sound condescending. "The Sacerdotes say all races are equal in the eyes of Providence, despite the inequalities in the Hermeticists who created them placed in them."

The fellow laughed. "A man after my own heart! I ain't heard talk like that in a long time. But what makes you think I will help you land the ship? I don't need anything on her. What's she carrying for me? 'Cept a big headache."

Vigil blinked at the fellow in astonishment. Was he mad? Many folk departed from normal psychological states during festivities or added some humorously psychotic subpersonality to their psychic architecture.

Vigil said, "My dear valet, I was not expecting you to help me land the ship, but I would appreciate any advice concerning protocols as I confront the Table, or the personalities of the men involved. They have betrayed their oaths and forgotten them. Are you of their party or of mine?"

The man said, "I could ask you the same question. I don't want you to blow up the planet if she don't land. Why not let her fall on by?"

Vigil did not understand the question. It seemed a matter too obvious and too large to fit into words. It was like asking why civilization was better than savagery. The only thing he could think to say was: "The ship must land."

"Why?"

"So that the Schedule be kept, the inviolate Schedule, to which countless men of ages past and yet to come on many worlds devote our lives. So that we may prove that we recall our oaths."

"Why?"

"I am loyal to Rania. Surely every loyal subject loves his princess. Don't you?"

Again, the reaction was odd. Surely the man had been drinking spirits, or his spirits had been drinking alcohol, for he grew suddenly melancholy. "I reckon I still love her, too. So, sure, come on. Maybe I can buffalo whatever else is sniffing for me. Call me your Yes Man, then."

Vigil was not sure what half these words meant, and the local subsystems could not provide him a lexicon either. Perhaps the man's name was *Yesman*, or perhaps he came from a race or sept which called itself by such an odd title.

5

The Chamber of the Black Hexagon

1. Valet, Watchman, Bailiff, Counsel

The valet, Yesman, or whatever his name was, said heavily, "Well, let's tart you up, or else the pox-riddled cross-grained curs will toss you out on your ear for trifling with their laws." He took Vigil over to the vestry booth and adorned him in additional regalia.

Black leg sheathes with silver studs were buckled to his legs, symbols of the magnetic greaves once used for extravehicular activity; a war belt with sword and prong pistol, weapons carefully calculated not to breach the hull or damage the engineering, the valet slung over one shoulder and buckled around his waist.

The valet took the prong pistol, broke it open, snorted in disgust at the design of the cartridges, said, "This is a poxing toy for kids!" He threw the weapon in the trash can. "Take this." He slipped a glass pistol of antique design out from his own jacket and into the holster.

When the valet made as if to place the mask back on Vigil, Vigil shied back, saying, "I am convinced ancient man was designed by the Hermeticists not to itch in their faces. There is no explanation otherwise for the uncouth garb the ancients wore."

"Heh. This uniform is as old as I am, sonny, so don't mock it. But I think the rules allow you to go unmasked. Not throwing this thing away. Lemme see." The valet adjusted the mask fittings and thrust his huge nose into it, followed by the rest of his face. Rummaging around in the vestry, he slung a spare cloak of ribbed silver over his own shoulders and found a deep hood in which to hide the bristles of his short-cropped red hair.

An internal creature prodded Vigil and drew his attention to where the seneschal still crouched on the floor, motionless, evidently awaiting some order or signal.

The valet said, "They got a number of legal tricks they can pull to prevent you from sitting down. One of them is letting that guy there not open the door. Point your finger at him, say or sign the words, *I grant you leave, your shift is over.*"

The seneschal stood up, looking surprised. He said, "Milord, this is not proper! I refuse to take my leave time! I hereby lodge a formal protest with the Officer of the Watch."

The valet said, "Tell him to shut his yam-eating scrofulous trap. Since his shift is over, he does not have access to the circuits to lodge a potato, much less lodge a protest. Tell him to stuff a pipe up his fundament and blow smoke out of his bunghole for an hour and a half, until the next watch change."

The seneschal snarled at the valet, "But I can raise a point of order at any time and call the Officer of the Watch at any time! You are legally required to stand by until he arrives! And since he is in yonder chamber, now lawfully allowed to depart it, aha! You also must abide here with me until the next watch change! That is ninety minutes by the Sacerdotal reckoning of time! Doors! You are my witness!"

Vigil gave the mudra to open the doors, but they refused the command. A lantern to the left of the door turned from blue to red, and the architrave displayed a mudra which indicated the need to stand by until the Officer of the Watch arrived.

The valet sighed. "Okay, you guys think you can choke me with laws and rut your dangles up with me. Hellfire and pestulation! I am a goddamn pus-licking, low-down, snake-tongued, crook-brained *lawyer,* and I'll stuff the law books down your craw one jot and tittle at a time, you rut with me!" He turned angrily to Vigil. "Now they got my dander up, and that's never fun for no one but me! Draw the damn pistol I just gave you, and shoot it at the floor."

Vigil did so. The glass weapon was magnetic, so there was no noise of discharge, but the report of the shot ripping through the sound barrier, and the crack of the marble floor, shocked the hearing.

Bells, whistles, and flutes began shrieking and ringing, along with the sound of the sackbut and timbrel, cornet, cymbals, psaltery, dulcimer. The lanterns flared with colors of rose, cyan, scarlet, and gold, and many voices spoke in languages long forgotten.

A nearby door, but not the locked door leading into the Chamber, now swung open. A trio of guards in brass and black armor and air-helms of silver, plumes of poison-detection feathers spreading from their crests, came into the room at a quick march, pacification wands at the ready. They must have just that moment been woken from slumber, no doubt stacked in a closet against the hour when they were needed, because the one in the front was still white in the face, the chemicals of long-term hibernation not yet faded from his cells. He had also not yet closed his face mask, so the valet only skinned a few knuckles when he punched the man in the face and knocked him to the ground.

The other two watchmen grabbed the valet roughly by either arm and flourished their wands. From the wand tip issued a mudra indicating peace, and the valet's arms and legs jerked in odd response, as the ability to make violent motions was removed from his nervous system.

The valet, his arms pinned, said quickly, "Say the words, *Weapons fired, officer down.* Then say the words, *Emergency condition declared.*"

The officer jumped to his feet. "I am not down!"

But it was too late. Vigil had spoken the words, and the lanterns had changed color to orange.

The seneschal said in panic, "Stop that man from talking! He is a lawyer!" And a watchman waved his wand in the face of the valet, but the valet was wearing the air mask Vigil had discarded, which was the mask of a Lord of the Stability, whose words could not be overridden.

The watchman was shocked when the valet spoke again, "Establish rank!"

Vigil knew this part of the regulations. He kicked his boot heels together, and without unsheathing the sword, he made it emit a signal of white noise on the weapon frequency.

The seneschal and the watch officer turned in outraged astonishment. But they both knew the meaning of the posture Vigil assumed, and the radio-pulse of the sword: *I am ranking officer and take command.*

The seneschal composed his face and returned a salute of submission. *At your orders, sir.* And, after a long pause, the watch officer did also.

The valet said, "Relieve the watch officer of command. Take his wand and tap me on both shoulders with it."

Vigil understood this as well. The ranking officer had authority to appoint the watch during emergencies in the name of the master of the ship. In order for the real Officer of the Watch to overrule him, the doors to the Chamber would have to be opened. Vigil waved at the two watchmen holding the valet back, and, when they did not respond, he indicated them to stumble backward with a mudra of authority.

Vigil struck the valet on the shoulder. "Do you solemnly swear and remember to discharge the duties and—"

"Pox, yes," snapped the valet. He plucked the peace wand out of Vigil's surprised hand, extended it, and struck the seneschal near the ankle of his tall and unsteady shoes with the wand butt, triggering some mudra whose shape Vigil did not recognize. The seneschal fell down on the marble floor.

Vigil played the scene back in his memory, but he was unable to get a fix on the position of the wand, so he could not tell whether the seneschal fell because of the mudra discharge or because of the blow to his foot. Another possibility was that the mudra had been set to release the valet from the imposition on his nervous system and allow him to complete a violent motion of striking the seneschal in the foot.

The valet, now the chief watch officer, said, "I place you under arrest for being drunk and disorderly while on post! For thinking impure thoughts on steamboat landings, and for mopery with intent to creep!"

The seneschal on the floor looked up, swatting at the eager hat which kept trying to jump back on top of his head. "I am not drunk! Nor do I mope! I call upon the doors to witness! I fell due to the criminal assault and battery of that lunatic!"

A voice from the door spoke in an ancient language, which Vigil understood. "Falling to the deck while on duty is an unusual behavior and forms sufficient cause to suspect intoxication."

Vigil understood. The position and motion of the wand had not been recorded into the environment memory. The doors had not seen the cause of the fall. Whether this weapon-blindness was a legal courtesy extended to bailiffs, or was a product of the mudra the wand had issued, or was a Fox-trick the valet had accomplished, Vigil did not know.

The ancient voice continued, "Both parties are under arrest, pending investigation, as no disorder during emergency condition, radiation leak, or hull breach is permitted."

His ex-valet, who was now his Chief Officer of the Watch, must have understood the ancient language as well, for he said to Vigil, "Commute my sentence to time served and order the record expunged, so that I can serve in public office. Appoint me bailiff. Say these words to dropsy drunkboat there: *You are relieved of rank and duty and confined to quarters pending further investigation.*"

Vigil did all these things, speaking clearly and loudly so that both animate and inanimate creatures could hear him. This time, he unclipped his scabbard, and stuck the sword, scabbard and all, through the tall man's belt.

The seneschal climbed to his feet, trembling with outrage. "You would not dare! I will countersue! My cousins are men of ancient and established lineage! Besides—the appointment as watch officer was unlawful, as the forms of the words were not completed! And his so-called term would have ended when he was placed under arrest, since he serves at the pleasure of the ranking officer during good behavior! Ha!"

The two armed watchmen, seeing all this, jumped forward roughly to grab the wild valet. One of them ordered the peace wand to leave his hand. The wand emitted a mudra that twisted the man's arm so that his hissed with pain, forcing the hand open, and so the wand sprang away and stood upright on the floor a yard away.

But the ex–Watch Officer, now the bailiff, spoke in a low, dangerous monotone to the two watchmen holding him. "Let the hell go of me. Take his keys and his gloves as evidence to be held against the further investigations of the crime here, and hand them to me. I am the bailiff. Obey your lawful orders, jerks, or the Lord Hermeticist will call down his vengeance."

The two watchmen looked at each other and looked toward the third man, who had been their commanding officer a moment ago. He was unarmed and yet was strangely unwilling to pick up the wand that stood next to him. He stood with his helmet open, and they both saw the uncertainty in his eyes, and they saw the red lights of recording lamps twinkling in the doorframe.

Coming to a decision, the two released the tall man who was now bailiff and seized the short man who was no longer seneschal.

The two turned the ex-seneschal's keys, which were stored in the stone of a finger ring, and his gloves which contained his biometric information, over to the new bailiff.

The bailiff drew on one glove, put on the ring, and made the correct hand gesture toward the door to indicate that it must open.

The doors hesitated, puzzled.

The seneschal said, "Your scheming is vain! Only I can open the valves of that door once the Table is in session! You are too late! The Lord Hermeticist is barred from the Chamber, barred for being tardy! The regulations you are trying to dance around have snared you and tripped you into a pit!"

The bailiff said, "Your mouth is a pit. Shut it. When you are not in the antechamber, any law officer, including a bailiff, can perform needed functions in an emergency."

"But I am in the antechamber!"

The bailiff must have been smiling under his mask, because there was a snide note in his voice. "I know that, and you know that, but in the eyes of the law, you left the antechamber the moment you were confined to quarters, because that is where you legally are supposed to be. Unless you want to be absent without leave during general quarters? The penalty for that is death, followed by resurrection and more death. What do you say?"

And he drew the sword, and put the point at the man's throat, and the blade issued a mudra which prevented anyone from interfering or preventing whatever might happen next.

Apparently bailiffs during general quarters had more extensive authority than Vigil would have supposed, because the mudra forced Vigil back one step and two, and the two armed watchmen likewise.

Vigil was not sure if the faction opposing him was embarked on a quest for some cause they thought worthy of any sacrifice, or just attempting a political fraud to maintain their own seats of power and situation. This was the test. Because some men are born willing to die for their causes or their comrades, but no one is willing to die for a fraud.

"I am in my quarters and not in this room," the chubby little seneschal said sadly.

So, either the seneschal was not such a man, or the attempt was a fraud rather than a sincere crusade. Vigil wished he knew more and hoped he would learn what he needed to know in time.

"Declare the emergency over," said the bailiff, "and relieve me of duty, hire me as your counsel and advisor, so I can walk into the room with you at your elbow and talk with you on a private channel. I figure you might need more help. And while you are at it, appoint those three fellows as your honor guard."

So saying, he went again to the vestry and donned the red robe, long wig, and black cap of a professional solicitor but did not remove the insectlike air mask and goggles.

"I cannot enter armed, but you can and must." And he returned the sword and scabbard to Vigil with a bow.

There was a roar of trumpets as the great doors swung open.

2. The Table

The Chamber was magnificent, overadorned, overwhelming. The design came from a time far older than the sparse and severe simplicity of the Patricians.

The chandelier at the apex was shaped like a spiral galaxy and burned with atomic points of light, a symbol of the Stability's eternity. The dome was paneled in dark brass and held up by statues of the gods.

Largest of all, and occupying the northeast quarter of the dome, was an onyx statue of Triumvirate, with his three heads, wearing many crowns. The first had the pointed chin, the long, slanted eyes, and long-lobed ears of a Hierophant; the second was an oddly angular and grinning face of what a male Fox Maiden would look like, were there any males of that race; and the third was a hirsute Hibernal with braided locks and beard that covered all but his eyes. In each of his eighty-one hands he held a knotwork of a different aspect or figure of cliometry notation, and all his lower hands held the lotus of enlightenment or the barbed arrow of Darwin, always pointing upward.

Facing him were the three Principalities of Man. Directly opposite Triumvirate loomed a statue hewn of deceptive blue apatite of Zauberring, in the conical cap, celestial mantle and charming wand of a warlock. To the southeast loomed a red coral statue of Toliman in his Phrygian cap with his bindlestaff, depicted as a silenus, a satyr with horse legs kicked up as if frozen in frantic dance. To the northwest, hewn of ivory and amber overlaid with black pearl and red coral, loomed solemn Consecrate, garbed in the white habit and red scapular and of a Sister of the Annunciation, with a black veil drawn close about her head and four crescent moons above.

An inner and lower ring upheld smaller statues of the six Powers: Twelve in his dark helm and in his hands shut with locks the grimoire of fate; Cerulean in his mortarboard and scholar's hood; Immaculate in her blue veil and mantle of stars; Peacock like an empress garbed in her polychromatic robes; Vonrothbarth in his owl cloak and goggles; and old Neptune holding his conch of triumph aloft, breaking chains and fetters with his trident.

Lower still were smaller statuettes of the twenty-four Potentates, four to each side: Mars in red helm with lance and shield; Aesculapius leaning on his caduceus; Rossycross in the mail and surcoat of a crusader; Nocturne in black, crowned in stars; and December in white, money bag and abacus in hand; Odette and Odile, dark twin and bright, each in her feathered robes; Walpurgis in his goblin mask and gaberlunzie hat; and Cyan in blue, tonsured like a Mandarin, holding a grain sheaf. Eurotas and Perioecium were armed as Mars, their father world; Feast of Stephen was in a bishop's miter, garbed in a cope of ermine-trimmed red. Eden was arrayed as a queen mother, dressed all in green, crowned in skulls and flowers. And ten others.

Torment was a slender maiden in a bridal gown of green and gold, adorned with a coronet of septfoil blossoms, but wore the hood of Jack Ketch. In her hands was a headman's axe, and from her girdle hung pilliwinks and pear; a wheel was to one side of her, and to the other, a hoop of Skeffington's gyves.

For the first time, in all his life, seeing her figure arrayed with all her sister worlds and brothers, Vigil wondered at her horrifying aspect and who had christened her.

In the center of this triple hexagon of godlike beings, the massive black metallic six-sided table squatted on its six thick legs. It was orichalchum, an alloy the same as that from which the strandworld of Zauberring was made, by legend, indestructible.

The floor was made of blocks of glass on top of which the furniture and figures in the chamber seemed to float.

Guest lamps by the silvery doors, which opened for the Lord Landing Party Senior and no man else, were blazing white, and the globes fanned their wings, the trees swayed, and the serpents of Hermetic heraldry hissed.

Vigil stepped forward, feeling every ounce of the weight of his father's office.

3. The Anthem of the Strangers

All in the chamber save one man came to their feet. Figures at the table rose in greeting. Calm music swelled up from the silence in stately strains. It was the anthem of the Stranger.

> *A STRANGER came to the door at eve,*
> *And he spoke the bridegroom fair.*
> *He bore a green-white stick in his hand,*
> *And, for all burden, care.*

The Lords were standing near the Table, each in the livery of his post. Behind each Lord, Companions and Attendants stood rigidly, their cloaks all bright displays of color, their leggings gorgeous with signs and patterns of the families and clans from the Pilgrims.

Their chairs, called sieges, each held the shield or lozenge of their heraldry, and a small, white iron gavel hung nearby, an ornament whose meaning all but the most accomplished antiquarians had long ago forgotten.

At the corners of the table, between each of the Lords, stood or sat a Commensal, a nonvoting member, except that the siege between the Chronometrician and the Chrematist was empty. The shield on the back of the chair showed the emblem of a horned circle of olive leaves surmounting a cross.

Vigil saw that this was the siege of the Hermeticist, the Senior Officer of the Landing Party. His chair.

> *He asked with the eyes more than the lips*
> *For a shelter for the night,*
> *And he turned and looked at the road afar*
> *Without a window light.*

The First Speaker was garbed in golden robes of the Aedile, and he carried the ivory wand of his election. He was Eligius Eventide of the Eventide clan, a name which rang through history back through Feast of Stephen to Saint Mary's World to Eden, back to the Twenty-Fourth Millennium, the time of the Bred Men, and his face and hands were coated with the pebbly scales of the Loricate race, but modern vanity had each tiny scale gilded with aurum, the living gold.

The anthem continued:

> *The bridegroom came forth into the porch*
> *With, "Let us look at the sky,*
> *And question what of the night to be,*
> *Stranger, you and I."*

Opposite the Aedile stood the aged Lighthousekeeper with cloak of midnight blue and silver white, leaning on the candle douter which was his symbol of office. By the tradition of the ancient laws of Eden, the Lighthousekeeper and his two Companions, the Powerhouse Officer and the Uranographer, stood empty-handed, carrying no weapons.

The Lighthousekeeper's speakership was the only one that passed by primogeniture and was older than the Pilgrim race on Torment. The man was an Itinerant. But he was no lumpy and ungainly Flocculent from Rime. Instead, his were the sleek features, the black brow-antennae and eerie black sclera of his necromancer ancestors of Schattenreich. The Lighthousekeeper had been adopted into a Pilgrim clan and was named Venerio Phosphoros.

This was the one who had turned the deceleration beam aside. No doubt the order had come from some higher officer, but an unlawful order should have been disobeyed. Here was the immediate culprit, no matter who the ultimate culprit might be.

Vigil stared at the man, and the Lighthousekeeper would not meet his eyes.

It was as if the Lighthousekeeper could feel the pressure of Vigil's thoughts, but an internal creature checked and confirmed that Vigil was not broadcasting.

Who, then, had given him the order? It had to be someone in the chamber. But when Vigil lifted his eyes they fell upon the Potentates, Principalities, and Powers, who also stood in the chamber.

> *The woodbine leaves littered the yard,*
> *The woodbine berries were blue,*
> *Autumn, yes, winter was in the wind;*
> *"Stranger, I wish I knew."*

To the right of the Aedile, at the corner, was the one man who had not risen to his feet for the anthem of the *Stranger*. Here was the Terraformer, who sat upon a massive throne of polished bronze. His cloak was green like forest pines, and set with gold disks. His hands and feet, when glimpsed beneath his robes, were covered with the skin-cell-bonded black armor of a phylarch of planet Eurotas. Upon his diadem he bore the iron Theta of Ecology.

Born as Franz Rubezahl, his adoption name was Francisco Leafsmith. He was an Ostracized, the only one of his despised race ever to hold the post, but he had survived the nineteen trials and three examinations, and the Pilgrims dared not deny him the post he had earned. He had the harsh, square face of a Nicor who had reverted to air breathing, and a black coiffure of facial hair called *beard* circling his lips and chin, though the skin between his nose and upper lip was bare. This mouth-hair gave him a savage, prehistoric look; and even when in repose, his features seemed to wear a sneer. He had inherited neither height nor oversized cranium from his giant ancestors. If anything, he was shorter and stockier than his public memory-images were allowed to retain.

In one armored hand he held a silver scepter Vigil knew to be an antenna to the command channel of the biosphere, a symbol of the terror and power which the Terraformer once had held. He had plucked this from the hand of the previous Terraformer and slew him with it in single combat, one ecosystem against the other, in a duel that had scalded the dry crater valleys and arid dunes of Southeastern Hemisphere.

At one time, plagues could be called up from the ground as easily as comets used to make the crater lakes of Torment during her birth millennium could be called down from heaven. Like Vigil, the man was not a speaking member of the Table: he represented the civic and secular power. But his retinue was far greater than Vigil's one counsel and three honor guards. Behind the Terraformer stood the solicitors and barristers, castellans, cavaliers, monsters, legates, and clerks of the worldly orders, with their hetaerae, paramours and demimondes.

Vigil noted that when he took his eyes off the Terraformer, the visual memory of how short the man was vanished from his recollection. There was no entry in his memory log, no sensation. The implication was that Fox Maidens, or some superhuman order impatient with human laws, introduced a sight-borne mudra into the Terraformer's information aura in the Noösphere, and no one had the patience or political will to abate the nuance. It was just a small hint of corruption, but it stank in Vigil's nostrils. A man who will trample the law in small things, for personal vanity, what will he do if great things weigh in the balance?

> *The bridegroom thought it little to give*
> *A dole of bread, a purse,*
> *A heartfelt prayer for the poor of God,*
> *Or for the rich a curse;*

From some subtle tell or clue of the necromancer's antennae (which, by birth, should have been attuned only to the frequencies of his lingering hereditary ghosts), an internal creature prompted Vigil to intuit that the Lighthousekeeper Phosphoros was communing with the Theosophist, the Sixth Speaker.

This man was garbed in simple and severe robes of white and argent, and his gorget of silver was set with pallid cabochons. In his hand he held an augmentation pearl the size of a plum, which permitted its wielder to meet the gaze of immortals, machines, and posthumans. He was large-eyed and finely featured, but, like all his race, bald and boasting no visible earlobes. His skin was waxy green as a holly leaf, and his brow adorned with golden tendrils. His race was a subspecies of the Locusts, called the Beatharians, originally from Aesculapius. Beatharians could sustain their lives without food and drink, absorbing nutriment from sweet perfume and the fierce sunlight of 70 Ophiuchi. He was a Wanderer, whose people arrived, conquered, flourished, and dwindled over a thousand years ago.

He was able to meet Vigil's piercing look without a flush of shame, nor did his eyes ever waver from their clear emerald-green serenity, no matter how many internals Vigils compiled into his brainspace to increase force, influence, and terror of his gaze.

Vigil stopped short of casting a mudra from his eyes, but his eyeballs ached with the unspent emotion. The perfection of the armor of tranquility radiating from the Theosophist made Vigil wonder if perhaps this man had recaptured the legendary ascetic practices of his ancestors on Aesculapius. The green man also had adopted a Pilgrim name, and called himself Oeoen Orison.

> But whether or not a man was asked
> To mar the love of two
> By harboring woe in the bridal house,
> The bridegroom wished he knew.

When the music sank away, the Lords and Attendants and Companions seated themselves.

An ostiarius wearing an absurd atef crown with a coincidence rangefinder issuing from it to the left and right by a cubit, announced Vigil, reported his name and lineage and rank to the Archaeomnemonicist, ending the long list of titles and dignities with, "Senior member of the Landing Party, and Starman Most Recently Returned from the Vasty Deep."

The ostiarius then raised his hand and the long lenses of his headgear and swiveled his palm left and right, crossed his arms on his chest, and gripped his right wrist with his left hand, which meant, *Is there any who challenges this man's right to enter?*

One of the three men acting as Vigil's honor guard stepped forward, took off a gauntlet, and dashed it, ringing, to the crystal panels of the floor. *Whoso would bar my lord from entry must speak now or hold his peace forever.*

The ugly man who had been a janitor, valet, watchman, bailiff, and was now his counsel murmured on a private channel, "Who is trying to prevent you from being recognized and taking your seat has to pick up the gauntlet, or he cannot lodge a point of order to protest your being recognized."

Vigil sent back, "Why do we bind ourselves with so many laws, so intricate, so absurd? For a man to step across a room and sit down and talk, we have to wrestle with this rigmarole! The Great Ship and all her generations, and our world's honor and eventual fate, and the stability of the Stability itself, hang in the balance—and we must pause to see who stoops to pick up a trifle of hand clothing?"

The ugly man sent quietly, "You live in a day when a rich man can rent more brains than you, or carry an Archangel in his poxing pocket. So don't scoff at having rules fixed and clear! Whenever men gather like vultures to decide their futures, no matter what they call themselves, they eventually become a good old boys' club. The *mood* of a club always favors the richest member. The *rules* of a club occasionally favor the poor one. Let us see if the rules favor us now. If someone picks up that gauntlet, the guys set against you are desperate."

The Powerman in a uniform of black and red, one of the Companions whose seat was behind the siege of the Lighthousekeeper rose to his feet, raised his finger lamp for permission to speak, and was recognized. His name was Seppel Phosphoros, and he was the cousin of the Lighthousekeeper. "I object! This is not the Landing Party Senior. That office is vested in Waiting Starmanson, Lord Hermeticist, who yet is alive and breathes the air of Torment, not in this person. He cannot be recognized by the Table."

The Powerman sent a handservant to retrieve the gauntlet. The handservant, a leonine Argive of the Sinner race returned and knelt and proffered the gauntlet to Seppel Phosphoros, Lord Powerhouse.

Vigil said impatiently, "Waiting Starmanson, Lord Hermeticist, is legally dead, and his privileges and rank vested in me, properly and according to the forms. Yonder sits the Archivist, Companion of the Second Speaker and Lord Chronometrician: as a point of order, I pray the Table subpoena the records of the World Memory to confirm my account."

The Powerman smiled an unkind smile, saying, "Irregular! I ask the Chamber scribe and memory officer to erase the interruption both from electronic and living memory herewith, since the person speaking them is not recognized to speak, nor may Commensals address the Table without being recognized!"

The Archivist, a man with the sharp, smiling features, red hair, and eerie beauty of a Meanderer, signaled with his finger lamp and said, "I will raise the same point of order. If the right of the presentment to be seated is in question, a prayer to the archives to confirm the record and memory of the world is not lawful."

The Powerman said to the Aedile, "First Speaker, I move that, rather than trifling with records whose veracity cannot be determined, we appoint a legate to travel to the Bitter Waters Parish in the Northwestern Hemisphere and inspect the body and mind-relics of Waiting Starmanson, our beloved friend and boon companion, and that examination commission of theosophists and physicians be empaneled to make a formal report to this body of the status of Waiting Starmanson and his fitness to serve. And I further move that this legate receive his commission with dispatch, at the end of this fiscal quarter, one-fourth of an Edenyear from now by the Sacerdotal calendar, or by the Vulgate Calendar two and a half Torment-years about Wormwood, which is two degrees of the great year about Eldsich, in the Forty-First Lesser Spring of the Great Autumn."

Before anyone else reacted, the Theosophist Orison focused his finger lamp, quick as a darting ray, at the Aedile and said with unctuous serenity, "I second the motion."

Vigil shouted, "Absurdity! The *Emancipation* will be pastfallen and unrecoverable by such time!"

The Aedile said, "The matter has been moved and seconded, and persons not yet recognized by this Chamber may not speak. We must decide by poll whether the challenge of your honor guard is met and defeated." And this twinkle in his eyes, the ripple in the scaly cheeks of gold, told Vigil this was a meaningless formality. The decision to exclude Vigil had been discussed and made privately, long before the meeting had been called to order.

4. Canvassing

Vigil opened other channels of perception through cameras in his robes and the antique amulet on his wrist (which was surprisingly responsive and tense, considering from which remote millennium the design originated) and examined the Speakers of the Stability.

The Theosophist in white and the dark-eyed Lighthousekeeper in blue and silver were of one mind with the Aedile and would vote against seating Vigil.

That left three others:

The Chrematist was so thickly dressed in his richly patterned hood and stole of crimson velvet that Vigil did not realize until then that the man was dead, his face white with the icy paleness of an unrecoverable hibernation failure: a slumberer who would never thaw. He was, in fact, a death-manikin. Servomotors at each joint beneath the robes and fibers in his gloves had permitted him to stand and hail the anthem or do whatever polite gesture ritual required: but the Board of Stockholders who sold of the speakership to their wealthiest member would never meet to replace him, not until he was declared legally incompetent. Vigil wondered darkly who had been empaneled years ago or decades ago to make that determination, suspecting it was the Theosophists.

His name in life had been Aruji, but, swearing fealty to the Pilgrims, he joined himself to one of their families under the Festal name Eosphoros.

The Fifth Speaker was the Portreeve. He wore a hair shirt under his glittering robes of office, for he was an Errant whose traditions hailed from the planet Penance. About his neck was his key of office handed him when he was appointed by the College of Emeritus Portreeves. His face had the unnatural beauty the Optimates inherited from their Swan forefathers, but, as ever, no Firstling human could read such features.

The Second Speaker was the Chronometrician in saffron robes, hood, and stole, a Lorentz chronometer of gold sitting on the table before him. Two of the countless many leaves of the chronometer were open just then, one dial showing local time, the other tuned to the frame of reference of the *Emancipation*. He was as ancient as a mummy. His ancestors were Joys from of Beta Canum Venaticorum, and therefore even in decrepitude, his features were graceful, dignified. There was a sly tilt to the features, and a wry slant to the mouth, that argued against the senility he showed on the surface. He had earned his position by sheer seniority and seemed to be paying no attention to his surroundings. Since his race never closed their eyes in sleep, it was not clear he was awake. Flickers and indications on the medical channel showed that he was not as dead as the Chrematist.

This meant the vote was lost before even any ballot was cast. Vigil would never take his father's place, nor be allowed to wield the vengeance needed to bring the Great Ship *Emancipation* to rest. It was a dizzying sensation, to have come so far, reached so near, and be thwarted by a mere technicality.

5. A Legal Nicety

The ugly man next to Vigil prodded him with an elbow and pointed at Vigil's black gauntlet lying on the black Table surface before the siege of the Lighthousekeeper. "All these damn rules are leftovers from the Starfarer's Guild. You know who all founded the Guild, right?"

Vigil knew. The Judge of Ages and the Master of the Empyrean together had founded it as part of their gentleman's agreement.

As sharply and suddenly as if struck by lightning from a static-pregnant sandstorm cloud, Vigil understood the dark meaning of certain of the ancient ornaments in the chamber. Some of the formalities were older than spaceflight and were known only on Eden, the Mother of Man, and the planet with the bloodiest history imaginable.

Vigil raised both hands, brought them to his throat, and emitted nine shrieks of white noise on a radio channel, three long, three short, and three long again. *Attention! Life-or-Death Situation!*

The Powerman in anger rose to his feet. "The unrecognized may not intrude unwanted signals during due processes! I ask that the bailiff remove the interloper!"

· The Portreeve had no finger lamp, but signaled with his key of office. "Order. The interloper is not an interloper yet. We have counted no ballot."

Vigil stepped over to the siege of the Powerman and took the small, white ceremonial gavel from its hook. With a great swung of his arm, he struck the shield that hung over the back of the siege, saying in the ancient language, "I pray the original form of the challenge be observed. I am the Lord Starfarer, Chief Hermeticist, and Senior of the Landing Party! I defy and traduce whoso says otherwise, and will defend my right to the same with my body!"

The discipline of the Chamber was broken as everyone at once spoke or signaled or cast his mind into deep archives.

Finally, the Aedile quieted the murmuring with a great flash from his finger lamp, tuned to an eye-dazzling brightness. "The Chamber asks the advice and counsel of the Chronometrician for an interpretation of these things."

The Chronometrician seemed to have fallen asleep, but two of his Companions, garbed in saffron, signaled for recognition and were recognized. The Archaeomnemonicist said, "Casting my memory to the earliest strata of the Stability mind-records shows that these gavels or hammers have always been retained for the function of registering a defiance. As a party at interest, the gavel was correct to allow itself to be handled, and as the siege seating him who picked up the gauntlet, the shield of the Powerhouse Officer was correct to allow itself to ring. The objects are behaving as designed, all according to protocol. The duel must be fought, until satisfaction or death, and without mudras, mandala, or nerve-indications, with macroscopic weapons alone."

The Powerman was as pale as the Chrematist as the blood left his face, and his eyes darted left and right, as if measuring the distance to the exit doors. His throat was too dry to speak, but his voice came from the ornamental cloak pin he wore, "But what does this mean?"

Vigil said, "As well you know, My Lord. A fight to the death."

Vigil's masked and bewigged counsel said to Vigil, "Hand me back my shooting iron and call me your Second so I can drill the bastard through his empty skull and get on with this damnified charade. I want to find out what's up."

But the Censor who sat behind the Chronometrician had the floor, and raised his finger, "I speak in my official capacity as Dress Code Officer! The sumptuary regulations are often disregarded, but they are also still in force! By an antique and momentous law, the Companions and siege of the Lighthouse-keeper must be unarmed, as sign that the Lighthouse must never be used as a weapon, nor scald a ship in flight or roast a world beneath with its dire ray! Hence no duel can take place: the Powerhouse Officer is not of the arms-bearing class."

Vigil unceremoniously shrugged off this weapon belt and dropped it, with his pistol and sword and all clanging to the glass floor, and doffed his other gauntlet. "By naked hands I will slay whoso denied my right to be here!"

The sleek and slender body of the Powerman, whose ancestors had been necromancers of Schattenreich, and, before that, Locusts of Mars, was like the body of a maiden next to that of an ape. But before anyone could speak, the Powerman said, "I appoint Xu Maioxen as my champion!"

This was evidently the name of the burly lion-headed handservant, shining with fulvous fur and rippling with muscles, who had previously picked up the gauntlet. He was an Expatriate, which meant that his ancestors were Sinners from 61 Ursae Majoris, which meant that he had retractable talons, fangs like a saber-toothed tiger, and swifter reactions and harder muscles than a baseline human should have.

The Chronometrician began to speak in his weak and spiderish voice about the proper formalities for a duel, the exchanges of challenges through Seconds, the appointment of surgeons, and such, but the Expatriate man shook his mane, roared, and leaped.

Vigil did not bother with grace or flourishes. He caught the man in midair, throwing himself backward with the momentum. He broke the back and most of the ribs of the lion man with the might of his arms alone and drove the body headfirst as it continued its fall down on the chamber floor with enough force to shatter the spine and to crack the heavy skull like an egg so that brain stuffs spread across the invisible surface with a sickening smell.

Vigil turned to the Powerman, saying, "Do you doubt my right to—?" But he stopped. The slender man was dead. He had fallen prone, even though there was no sign of wound, no scent of energy, no hint of any nerve-mudra tingling in the air.

All the speakers were now on their feet, even the slumbering corpse of the Chrematist (whose servos evidently thought it polite to stand when all others did). The Aedile said in a weak voice, "What struck down Seppel Phosphoros? Why is he dead? I yield the floor and the balance of my time to anyone who can explain this madness."

Vigil's counsel, the ugly man in the breathing mask, had picked up the dropped sword and translucent pistol. "I reckon I can tell you. Your joker saw physical danger, so he fled into the infosphere, and left his body behind, and was just pulling strings like by remote control. But the rule of the duel says that the primary has to die if his partial dies, or else there ain't no point. Now, in real life, these two guys here was two different men, but the law ain't got nothing to do with real life. In the eyes of the law, an agent acts on his master's behalf and becomes his partial self. Since the one was working on the other's orders, Torment decided to put both men on the same circuit. So when one died, the other was deleted. If leperdick there had just stayed put, he'd be still alive."

The Aedile stuttered, "How can this be? Why has Torment stirred herself to interfere with us? It is unlawful!"

"Ha! That's rich and rank as stallion manure on a sunny spring day, coming from your mouth, buddy."

The Aedile stared at him. "Who are you?"

The ugly man said, "I am Jiminy Goddamn Cricket, here to tell you to always let your mother-raping *conscience* be your plaguing *guide*! Are you going to let this boy sit down at your little tea party, or is he going to have to pluck the heads off more people?"

The Aedile was trembling. "No, the, the Chamber must first adjourn while the bodies are cleared away, then—ah—a proper motion entered—with members dead, a sufficient quorum to—"

The ugly man handed the sword in its scabbard back to Vigil. "Go chop his poxing head off. If he supports the action of the defeated party in a duel, that makes him the same as if he picked up the gauntlet."

The Aedile said in a loud voice, "Bailiffs! There is a threat against the Chamber! You all heard it!"

The ugly man said, "Stop wasting my poxing time, greenhorn. Don't you know the law? You there, whatsyourname." He pointed at the Castigator, the Commensal seated between the Aedile and the Chronometrician. The Castigator wore an iron skull-shaped mask beneath his deep hood and held a flail of office in his hands. "Call up the Angels of Torment. We'll see who's right and wrong between me and the barracks-room lawyer there. Is he or is he not preventing the Lord Hermeticist from being recognized? There are no lawful grounds for any challenge."

The Aedile said, "You have no authority to speak!"

"Hell I don't. You yielded the floor to me, right and proper. I'm a poxing amicus curiae."

The Castigator stood. He was garbed in much the same fashion as the statue of Torment, in a bridegroom's uniform beneath the cloak and hood of an executioner. The whole chamber fell silent with dread.

He raised a finger and signaled. "I am permitted and required to speak privately to any member, off the record, before any castigation is lodged. If there are no objections? I convoke the silence."

He turned his hood toward the golden face of the Aedile. The two men exchanged low-level indications by means of mudra of the optic nerve alone, and no one in the chamber was permitted to overhear.

6. *Let Down or Upset*

One of Vigil's internal creatures floated to the surface of his consciousness and said, "Rut me with a spoon, but I reckon you wants to hear what Eligius is saying to his cousin Sebastian."

This was the same internal that had been previously jinxed by the Foxes, who no doubt left some unlocked back door open for the janitor to find.

"You got a damn lot of minds inside you. How many nervous systems you got?"

"As many as I need," replied Vigil on the same channel. He did not explain that this particular development of multiple parallel minds in the same brain was a side effect of the chaos mathematics needed by the Summer Kings of Arcturus, back when their power and sovereignty rested on their ability to control a hostile climate of a world forever seeking to expel them.

"I don't quite understand how you are doing this," Vigil continued. "Is this a Fox-trick?"

"Yeah, they all work for me. Except when they don't."

"Your jests are not funny." The idea of any Fox taking orders from am Esne was absurd.

"Just give that one a little while to sink in."

Vigil was still puzzled at how this low-caste man could wield a superhuman technique. Perhaps the Foxes were manipulating him, and, as they so often did in stories, drove their human tools insane.

Vigil wondered if perhaps this man was not an Esne. Then what?

Vigil was a little embarrassed to admit that he could not place the clan or era of the name *Jiminy Goddamn Cricket*, or, for that matter, *Yesman*, so he phrased his question indirectly. "Did I misunderstand who you really are? Did you want me to call you *Cricket*?"

The man laughed. "Sure! Why the hell not? Don't worry. I have that effect on a lot of people. They always think I am something bigger and smarter than I really am. Then they meet me. Everyone is let down or upset. But I really am the really real me. I am the guy you was looking for, which is why I walked up mop in hand."

"I was sent here to recall the Table to its duty. Not to look for a janitor."

The counselor shrugged. "'Swhat the damn Swans said, anyhow. They all work for me, too. Except when they don't. I thought you wanted me to come in and help you out to find out who is looking for you. My bet is on the guy with the gold face there, Eligius, being behind it. Ain't that why you hired me on? How much am I getting paid, anyway? And how much of what? What do your folks use for money? Is it something you drink?"

"Even with multiple minds, I cannot tell which question to answer first, Cricket."

The man laughed again, as if Vigil had made, or was in on, a joke. "Just answer me this: You want to hear what they is saying?"

"Is it illegal to eavesdrop?"

"As illegal as seeing drunk old Noah's naked ass, you betcha, sonny!"

"By all means, then."

Signals flowed into Vigil's mind.

7. Unprivate Conversation

The intercepted nerve indication between the eyes of the Aedile and the Castigator contained visual clues, expressions and body language, and so on, as well as nuance of voice, text, reference materials, and subtext.

It seemed odd to one of his background that the data were not formatted for presentation. There was nothing else in the signal stream, no background, no tactile sensation: it was like recalling a conversation when one has forgotten where and when it was held. Vigil assumed this was a limitation of those who could not juggle multiple internal creatures like a Strangerman could.

The Castigator was saying softly to the Aedile, "His comment is in the record; I cannot claim lack of notice. While technically, an amicus curiae cannot command me to castigate, nonetheless, once I am notified from any official source of an abrogation, I must either open a case or quash it. I also dare not face an inquest for dereliction."

The Aedile's eyes bright with anger. "And the downfall of our civilization and the death of our world?"

The Castigator said carefully, "As a Lord of the Stability, the incoming ship must hold me immune from local affairs. We here in the Palace of Future History will survive no matter what happens to our families outside there, who live in the local history of planet Torment."

"You think to escape?"

"The Judge of Ages has already prepared a tomb for me that I might slumber until whatever day, a thousand years hence, when the distempers and disquiets created by the planetfall of *Emancipation* have been long forgotten."

The Aedile said, "Pah! The Judge of Ages! He is known to have been born in madness and died in madness, somewhere in the barren Southeast lands, where no man treads! He lost his mind when his promised bride married the Master of the Empyrean! He is a myth, or he is insane, or he is dead, or perhaps all three at once!"

The Castigator said, "Beware, sir, lest you forget that the universe is stranger than we wish to imagine, perhaps stranger than we are able to imagine! Wonders bright and dark surround us daily, and we are complacent and blind."

"Someone posing as the Judge of Ages deceived you! It was a Fox or something like that in a masquerade costume! I tell you he is dead and has no power over us!"

"I tell you the Judge of Ages will never die, and he stands and hears what you say, even in secret, and he weighs your words in his judgment! Shall he not condemn this generation and this age in which we live if we betray the oaths we serve?"

The Aedile said, "Speak not to me of oaths! You were ready enough to promise whatever was needed to arrange the ship would fall past and be lost forever in the night! You merely seek to save yourself."

"As do you, cousin," said the Castigator coldly.

"Would you put yourself before our clan and class? We are Pilgrims! You are an Eventide! We share a grandfather! We lose *everything* if that ship makes port!"

"Sir, with respect, since the very same minute just before the Lord Hermeticist entered, we all busily agreeing to put our clan and class before our world and our duty, and pelting dire threats against anyone here who opposed us or threatened to tell the multitudes, you have no right to speak to me this way!"

"I'll speak as I like, jackanape!"

"Then speak quickly: if you can think of a way I can avoid calling up the Angels of Retribution, I will serve you. But I will not sacrifice my soul for you."

"You are afraid."

"With good reason. The Order of Ktenological Castigation and Reprimand is not a weak and pleasant order like that of the Aediles, you who sit on cushions of velvet, counting coins of gold. Do you know what the penalty is if I, as the head of the order, were to betray my oath? Do you remember what it is those who dwell, undying, the House of Most Silent Excruciation, once were allowed—and on this world—to do with their arts? Can you imagine what would be done to every thought and memory in the mind? The Infliction would start with the memories of my children. Seat the Lord Hermeticist, or I call the Angel!"

The signal ended at that moment.

8. An Outside Power

The ugly man put his mask near Vigil and spoke aloud, but softly, "That was not a good sign. Some outside mind cut me off, something smarter than an Archangel and more cunning than a Fox."

Vigil whispered back, "It is the Potentate. Torment slew my father and seeks to have the ship fail."

"The hell you say."

"I do not know what that means."

"It means why didn't you say this before?"

"I could not share my danger with you. My death will be glorious in memory should the Potentate break her oaths and trifle with human affairs! But you are not a—"

Vigil paused, astonished. He had been about to say that the affairs of the Stability of Man were no concern of this janitor, but then it burst upon him that the man, despite his humble station, was indeed a member of the Order. Even the lowest-ranked servant or prentice must have taken the same oath as the Aedile himself.

Vigil said, "I am proud to share my fate with you."

Oddly enough, the man called Cricket was not listening. He was speaking softly and quickly to himself. "Torment wants the ship dead? Well, that makes a whole bunch of fog clouds up and blew away. Here I thought it was Blackie behind all this. He is not in the picture? For once? That is a change. I must be getting paranoid, losing my mind like everyone always says. Is Torment pulling the strings and yanking my chain? Hey! Quick! What did she say? She talk to you herself?"

"Who is Blah Key?"

"You first. What does Torment want? All this time, I thought—"

But at that moment, trumpets blared. It was the Docking Fanfare. The Aedile Eventide raised his hands in the ancient gesture, tapping his ear and pointing his thumb toward the ceiling with one hand. The other he extended toward Vigil, palm turned inward, fingers curled, beckoning. *Signal good. Approach.*

In a voice dead, defeated, and dispirited, Eligius Eventide, Lord Aedile and First Speaker, addressed him with the needed words, "If the Commensal Spacefarer most recently revenant from heaven will be pleased when called upon to give aid, advice, and comfort to the best of your knowledge and ability, and to do all other lawful things requested for the welfare of the futurity we plan and guide and guard, this Table will take cognizance of you. Will you hear, and will you remember to act for the good of the Loyal and Self-Correctional Order of Prognostic Actuarial Cliometric Stability to the exclusion of all other interests, oaths, and loyalties, to do all in your power to ensure and confirm the Launching and the Arrivals of the Starfaring Vessels, according as the Great Schedule commands and foretells, never to betray the principles on which the Table rests?"

"I swear and I remember." Vigil's heart thundered with pride. His father had taught him the several variations of this ceremony, and he knew the next words before they were spoken: *Then assume the duties and perquisites, and take lawful place prepared.*

"Then assume the duties and perquisites, and take your arms and lawful place prepared."

Vigil hesitated, fearing some legalism hiding a trap. But the demeanor of the Aedile was too desperate and crestfallen to be inauthentic. He knew his treason was discovered, his plans were ruined, his rank and perhaps his life were soon to be taken from him. Why had the words *take your arms* been added?

The steward stepped forward and bowed, extending his hands. Vigil assumed that if he made a mistake of protocol now, he would again be expelled from the Table.

The man Cricket came to his rescue, leaning his head close and whispering, "Hand him your toy sword, and go take the real sword from the lap of Tellus."

Vigil surrendered his blade to the steward and stepped over toward the statue representing the Potentate of Mother Earth. He saw now that there was indeed a sword in a white scabbard there, long and straight and cross-hilted.

The dazzle of the jacinth and chrysoberyl adorning the tasseled hilts for a moment almost blinded him, until he realized that tears had entered his eyes, both of mourning for his father and of solemnity for the duty he was about to perform, the greatest mass execution in history. He commanded a lesser internal to reabsorb the tears quickly and to force his mind to maintain an unwavering emotional deportment. He felt an almost physical jolt of clarity, as potent as uncut wine, but with the effect of clearing rather than clouding his wits.

Details he had overlooked were now pellucid. He had not seen it move, but the stone hand of the Mother Earth figure, which a moment before had been clasping the scabbard, was open and the fingers held in a gesture representing a prayer for wisdom. Her watchful eyes were bent on him, and all the massy weight of Earthly history was behind them, a history of blood and suffering. The statue was telling him to fear the power of the sword and draw it prudently and with discretion.

Only then did he understand what this sword really was.

It explained why the words had been added: for his father must have foreseen his own fate at the hands of Torment and trusted not to take this great sword out into the world where she ruled. Only in here, the Palace of Future History, did the laws of the universe, and not of any one planet, hold sway.

Vigil picked it up but did not put it to his belt. The weight of the thing was no greater than that of a normal sword, but at the same time, the weight was terrible, and in his hand he thought he could feel the sheathed blade trembling as if with an unspent mudra of world-eclipsing magnitude.

He heard a noise behind him. The siege of the Lord Hermeticist had pulled itself back from the table and welcomed him.

He stepped over the dead body of the man he had slain and past the body of the next, fully aware of the countless numbers of all races so soon to follow, and he sat.

His counselor, Cricket, stepped behind him and spoke, "I yield the balance of my time to the Lord Hermeticist for his comment on the meaning of these events."

Vigil turned his eyes left and right. He saw nothing but fear on the faces there, a paralysis.

6

Lords of the Stability

1. The Portreeve

Vigil spoke, "My Lords and Commensals! I have no vote at this table, nor may my voice be heard unless I am called upon to advise. There is one privilege and duty given to my office, however, which is shared by no other. Should the Table itself betray the Table, it is the duty of the Lord Hermeticist to initiate the self-destruct sequence.

"There is one and only one act of treason which triggers this duty, only one crime, for this is the execution of final judgment. Nausicide, the deliberate murder of a world-ship filled the millions of deracinated souls, or the breech of the Great Schedule.

"It is known to me that the deceleration laser is misdirected, avoiding the sails, and this was done deliberately, willfully, and maliciously as part of an orchestrated conspiracy to prevent starfall of the *Emancipation*.

"I call upon the Portreeve to tell the name and orbital elements of the ship into the record so that whatever race of man occupies this dead world in times to come will be reassured that the vengeance which fell upon all was no error."

The Portreeve said, "My Lord, by your leave, the ship is the *Emancipation*, the oldest ship in service and the one with the longest route. She comes from Sol,

across an abyss of one hundred lightyears." And he recited the current declina-
tion and right ascension of the vessel, as well as her velocity in Doppler shift.

"I call upon the Lighthousekeeper to report whether the deceleration laser
is properly presented to that epoch?"

The Lighthousekeeper could not bring himself to answer, but kept his eyes
and ghostly antennae pointed at the floor.

"Let the record show that the deceleration laser is not properly presented as
our primary duty as Lords of this Chamber compel, ordain, and require. I call
upon the Chronometrician to speak to the history of this vessel, and confirm it
matches all records, and that there has been no mistake of identity, nor is this
a centaur nor plutino nor asteroid or other stray body."

The Archivist answered for the Chronometrician. "My Lord and Commensals: this is her second return. The first starfall of the *Emancipation* occurred in
the First Century of the Sixty-Seventh Millennium as the Sacerdotes count
time, long before our world was self-aware. Upon starfall, the Emancipates,
who are the remotest ancestors of the Chimerae, called Esne, killed the Argives in a series of bloody genocides. The attempts to preserve and restore the
lost Argives by the shocked and saddened machines of Torment account for
the curse which has haunted the world from that day to this. The spectro-
graphic analysis of sail reflections and signal sets confirm the heraldry, call
signs, and identity of the vessel."

"I call upon the Aedile to confirm there is sufficient funding to power the
deceleration laser as the Schedule has directed? I call upon the Chrematist to
confirm that there is no other loss of supplies, services, or needs which would
prevent the discharge?"

The Aedile did not, and the Chrematist could not answer, but the three
Companion Officers seated behind the Chrematist were the Purveyor in his ceremonial gloves of spotless white, the Recruiter with a silver horn slung on an or-
namented baldric, and the Impressment Officer with his scourge and manacles of
office. The Purveyor confirmed that there was no lack of microscopic or nanoscopic elixirs required for medical adaptation of the newcomers, the Recruiter that
there were ghosts and spiritware enough, and the Impressment Officer that there
were dogs enough gathered by the pressgangs, with the brainspace to hold the
training and control downloads, to crew the stations and houses needed. Each
one spoke slowly, reluctantly, with as many hesitations and pauses as possible.

But none mentioned any reason to prevent the starfall.

Vigil stood. He was breathing heavily and released oxygen into his lung
from his implanted air-cell to calm himself.

With no further word, he drew the blade.

He stood with it upraised, his eyes also turned upward. He was paralyzed at the beauty of the thing, the elegance of its line, the mirror brightness of the blade. There was writing on the blade in an ancient language, the one used only by Sacerdotes, and the letters were gold: *Ultima Ratio Regum.* In and about the letters twined the figures of a red dragon and a white.

2. The Executioner

Vigil's eyes were locked on the blade, unable to blink.

He whispered, "May I do this?"

Something like a mudra, but infinitely more delicate, flickered from the reflections of the sword blade into his eye, from the optic nerve into his brain, and the auditory segments of his brain interpreted the jarring force as if a vast and inhuman voice had spoken.

There is sufficient testimony and evidence to permit a verdict. The human segments of the Noösphere are identified. The command channel is open and the angels of execution are standing by. A verbal command is insufficient. To slay the world, smite the table before you forcefully; and we will break the table in two, which otherwise is invulnerable to human force.

The things about him slowed oddly as he used a military internal to raise his nerve-rate, speeding up his thoughts.

"If I condemn the world but am wrong, can the execution be stayed? Is there truly no appeal?"

There is no appeal. Your voice is final.

"Why not? The work of the angels is to protect man from our own folly!"

Once the sentence passed, the execution is instantaneous. The loss of economic and intellectual continuity is unrecoverable. Human civilization on this sphere will not last two centuries once all ghostly infrastructure and electronic mentality is obliterated, nor will peace and civic order last two hours. It is not the place of the angels to destroy you: that you will do on your own, unassisted.

Vigil's head was beginning to throb with pain from the impact of the superhuman clarity of thought being thrust into his brain. He had never before known the mudra-system to be manipulated in so fine and delicate a way as to provoke specific words and concepts from a man's nervous system, rather than a gross physical-neural reaction.

But he whispered again, this time on a private channel, not moving his lips. "And if I do not act?"

We cannot condemn the world nor perform the execution without direct human command, nor would we if we could. The Covenant of Rania protects the lower orders of being from our influence.

Vigil wondered darkly why this covenant had not served to protect his father.

"Am I justified in condemning this corrupt order?"

If you were to abuse this great and terrible authority given you, or if you were incompetent to render the verdict, we would overrule you. But you are fit to decide: the judgment is yours alone.

"How can I? I am but a man, a mere youth!"

You have the authority to compel testimony. You have the authority to condemn or to forgive. It is not individuals you judge but ages.

"You are wise! Are they truly evil? And if they are, should I kill the human world in retaliation? Where is the justice in that?"

It is not permitted that we should advise you.

The pain in his head was now pounding like a drum. Even had he wished it, he could hear no more. Drawing a deep breath, he returned his perception of passing time back to its natural rate.

He found, to his surprise, no uncertainty in him. The duty was clear. "Gentlemen, my Lords, Commensals, and Companions! I find the Table in dereliction of its duty!"

3. The Hermeticist

Vigil Lord Hermeticist stood for a moment, unswaying, eyes upward, unable to continue. He commanded an internal to steel his resolve.

In a voice like a glacier of ice, implacable, unstoppable, he spoke:

"We of the Table are all selected from different constituents by different methods. Some are elected, some appointed, some commissioned, some must pass trials of combat or tests put by electors. My office is selected by two criteria. First, we must have passed to us from the commanding officer of the previous vessel her command codes intact, including the code that arms the self-destruction. Second, there is a psychological qualification, that the Lord Hermeticist must be willing to burn a planet just in the same fashion as the First Lord Hermeticist, Ximen the Black, commanding the first starship, was willing to do when the barbaric rulers of Eden in those days, before the Stability arose, refused to welcome the inbound star-faring vessel. My race and my line were accused of abridging that qualification, because we Strangers have the ability to carry an internal creature within us, which can be passed from father to son, hence our ability to pass the psychological test is inherited. You Pilgrims wanted this office under your control so that yours would be the last ship to reach Torment and so that your race would never be displaced by any later generations of immigrants.

"But none of your candidates could pass the crucial test, and all of my father's house could pass. None of you are willing to destroy a world to preserve your honor. I am. I open the floor to any man who is willing to answer. Does anyone here doubt my intent?

"This Table must here and now, before I lower my arm, vote to direct the Lighthouse crew to direct the gravitic-nucleonic distortion pool in the photosphere of Iota Draconis to direct the proper percentage of the solar output of our star into the sails of the *Emancipation*.

"Delay, deny, or refuse, and I smite the table, which no other force in the universe can crack. Return to your duty, and I sheathe the sword with nothing further said."

4. The Terraformer

The Terraformer raised a finger. "Allow me to be the first to answer. Sir, I do indeed doubt your willingness to smite the world with vengeance, if you knew all the facts!"

"Speak. The verdict of dereliction is entered, but I am permitted to execute or pardon."

"My Lord Hermeticist, know you that the Great Ship *Emancipation* is from Sol and her manifest, beamed to us by orbital radio laser, reports the vast majority of the millions aboard are Melusine-based Myrmidon hybrids called Scolopendra who were ousted from the seas of Eden by the Patricians of that world. This is a race new to us. Before you entered the Chamber, I reported to the Table that it is impossible that deep-sea-based life could dwell here without replacing all our lowlands with ocean, destroying all our major cities and the most productive regions of our farmlands. The effect on surface life of this migration would be catastrophic. The pressure on subsurface machine life during our Great Winter, when the atmosphere cools, is difficult to estimate, but the Intercessor reports certain hints, dreams, and visions recovered from survivors plunged into the depth of the Torment mind."

5. The Intercessor

The Intercessor, who was seated as Companion of the Theosophist, indicated that he affirmed the remark by opening a fan of reflective membrane. "The hostility of Torment to the starfall of the *Emancipation* was observed in several of the thought-torrents, thought-streams, and thought-oceans into which mediators submerged themselves. The agitation of the thought-forms of the Potentate can be assessed by the high rate of fatality and madness that ensured. Six of the mediators returned from intercession quite mad."

Vigil said, "Irrelevant. If the Strangers were fated by the Great Schedule to be overthrown by the Pilgrims—an event, I take it, no man here regrets—how is it that, now that your turn to suffer the iron cruelty of history is at hand, you are no longer historians? When the cliometry predicts the loss of your prestige and fortunes, do you foreswear your oaths as cliometricians? Will you unhinge the wheel of time from its axis merely because your clan is no longer in the ascending arc? For shame! All these things are unfolding as Rania's cliometry has foreseen! If the sins of the children of the *Pilgrimage* decree the downfall of their power, if that is the price of universal peace, then I say to you: grow gills, gentlemen, and webs between your finger bones, and fawn upon your new aquatic overlords with meekness!"

The Aedile signaled with his finger lamp, asking for the floor. "My exulted fellow Lord and Commensal of the Stability! You have mistaken our intent! You have mistaken all! We do not seek to betray the ship for the sake of self or clan, nor even to preserve the world! We seek to preserve the Stability itself."

6. The Aedile

Vigil snapped, "Nonsense, sir! The coming of the *Emancipation* has been foreknown millennia in advance! And you—you seek to preserve only yourself!"

The sword in his hand was beginning to tremble, and so Vigil asked an internal creature to adjust the muscle tension and chemical balances in his upraised arm, until it grew steady as a statue.

The Aedile said swiftly, earnestly, "Not so. This ship may be the hull of the *Emancipation,* but when she last saw port at Eden, all was changed. She is a warship.

"The sunless planet Acheron, which was between Iota Draconis and Sol, fell silent when she put to port, as did the several worlds along her route, Nepenthe for Woe, Aerecura, and Nightspore!

"A millennium ago, 70 Ophiuchi emitted a rush of signals signifying the fall of civilizations and the collapse of the world-mind! 41 Arae, three centuries ago, reported fire from the sail of *Emancipation,* like a second sun, and half a world burning! A century ago, Kappa Coronae Borealis blinked, and agitations in her photosphere were seen! Arcturus, the star of your own people, four centuries ago reported Myrmidons, a folk thought long extinct, a nightmare race from ages past, falling from your storm-tossed, strangely hued ancestral skies as countless as the flakes of snow!"

7. The Theosophist

Vigil said, "If this were known for so many centuries of erenow . . . why was nothing announced?" But he was secretly wondering why his father had said nothing.

The Theosophist signaled and was recognized and said in a voice as calm as a glacier, "We chained ourselves with oaths inflicted by mudra and surgery so that the matter was forgotten when we stepped forth from this Chamber. Had we not, and the world learned of the evil overtaking the stars, the charge and charter of this Table of Stability would vanish. If the Schedule has been broken on four worlds or five, then it is broken for all the stars of Man."

The counselor standing at his back, Cricket, muttered, "Cancers and cankers! That means, in the damn eyes of the damn law, the old Guild takes over. That was the deal, way back when."

Vigil lowered the sword and stared at its bright blade and the terrible shapes of dragons, the terrible message of the words. "Then the Stability was dissolved many hundreds of years ago. My life is a sham, as was my father's life before mine, and all yours, your predecessors and ancestors . . ." He tried to grasp when the news meant. A thousand years ago, one of the Great Ships had become a vessel of interstellar war?

That was so long ago that the *Exile* was still in orbit about Torment. The *Exile* had been the stronghold and capital of the Nymph-Patrician hybrids of the planet Vital Delectation. Their race had been entirely overwhelmed and absorbed by the superior numbers and mental organization of the Nomads. Almost no trace of the Delectables remained, except for some names in old songs and the five-sided pyramids of unknown alloy half-buried in the arid Northern sands which no antiquarian dared approach. So long ago was that time.

Vigil said, "How do you expect to survive if these worlds, older and greater than ours, did not?"

The Theosophist said, "Because the orbital radio arrays and lighthouse beams of Iota Draconis are more sensitive and farther reaching than those of any other star in the Empyrean. The Beast called Achaiah, during the last years when men were unfree, did this thing, gifted our star with these technologies, we know not why. Unlike the other worlds where the disguise and peaceful pretense of *Emancipation* was successful before her approach, we are forewarned."

Vigil looked down. Perhaps he was staring at the designs and marks of the future gleaming in the metal table surface, or at his reflection behind them, or at nothing. The sword was in his nerveless hand, neither upraised nor in its sheath.

The Chronometrician said, "My Lord Hermeticist, now that you have seen all that we hid, is it nevertheless your will to force this Table to a duty that will destroy us? This warship is not part of Rania's Plan for Universal Peace. The warship which comes in the place of the *Emancipation* bears her name but is a different ship—her arrival is no part of the Great Schedule. Therefore, there is no duty of this Table to instruct the Lighthousekeeper to correctly present the beam. This warship is not part of our Stability, our Schedule, or the duty we carry from generation to generation faithfully."

Vigil raised his eyes without moving his head and said slowly, "Who sent the ruffians to kill me in the alley?" But he knew, since all the men there looked surprised or puzzled, and only the Aedile looked stony faced. But now that he knew the reason for their fear, Vigil in his heart could condemn none of them. They sought, as he did, to serve the Stability and preserve civilization. It was what civilized men did.

The Chronometrician did not look guilty, but neither did he look surprised. An accomplice, no doubt. He said in his placid and earnest voice, "Sir, you may not use your prerogative merely for personal vendetta. It is your mission to avenge the race if we who allow the bonds of civilization, delicate as a spider-web stretching from star to star, to fail. But we have not let it fail."

Vigil said, "The ship will fall past us, blind, and into the eternal night."

But the Chronometrician said, "That warship is not part of our civilization, no, no more than a cuckoo's egg holds the true child of the mother bird who unknowingly sacrifices her own to feed the intruder."

Vigil said, "Your tale is impossible! There was a clear library transmission from Nightspore in my mother's time and again when my grandmother was a girl!"

"Falsified, edited, hoaxed," said the Theosophist serenely.

Vigil said, "One cannot fight an interstellar war and keep the matter secret!"

8. The Signalmaster

The Master of Signals, in his traditional ear-cups of gold, raised his finger for permission to speak. "My Lord, it is very simple to mask the events of one star from another. One need only suborn or replace the radio house crew. How many million-acre radio parabolas do you think a colony can maintain in orbit, or during how many years of prosperity have the resources and political will to ignite their array and emit their gathered years of history, poetry, lore, and gossip? I need not remind this Chamber how many scheduled radio emissions to various stars were delayed or aborted due to lack of resources.

"The Scolopendra of the *Emancipation,* after years or decades, rebuilt the civilization of each broken world to their liking, and heated up the radio lasers, and sent any signal, any news, any delusions it tickled their fancy to send. War marches from star to star, and none the wiser.

"The great multigeneration ship of war then is launched on schedule to the next world, which, lulled by false signals, ignited their deceleration beam to welcome the destruction to their bosom. During the conquest, some radio noise or frantic signals escape, but the later broadcasts soothe all suspicions away. Who does not expect at least some commotion when a Great Ship lands?"

Vigil said, "What could be the motive? What insult, or fear, or lust for gain could provoke combat across so wide an abyss?"

9. The Anthroponomist

The Commensal who spoke next was the Anthroponomist, a figure in gray gauze and dark goggles of his office, seated between the Portreeve and the Theosophist. His organization was expert in the myriad arts predicting the development of the human organism in relation to other organisms and to environment.

"My preliminary estimates show that the Scolopendra, once in space, could have mutated toward a non-self-correcting belief-node and commanded the angels of the ship to go mad. Recall that this ship suffers the longest route between port and port. Odd madnesses arise in isolation. I conclude the crew is fallen under a glamour or a theurgy. No war for gain, terrain, or glory can reach from star to star: only a holy war."

"It must be lies! It must be!" Vigil said.

His counselor behind him said, "Son, I think they is telling the truth. But there is more to come, I bet."

10. The Chronometrician

But the Chronometrician, who now seemed fully awake, opened wide his heavily lidded eyes and spoke in a creaking voice.

"I recall the arts of the Joys from my forefathers' worlds, and I still, in taped memories, can recall and relive the eon, ages past, when my race ruled this dry skull of a planet! We have no swords nor pistols beneath the sunlight of Beta Canum Venaticorum, no diseases, and no nanites, for we hold all weapons in contempt save one. Truth is our only sword, and nerve-to-nerve war, one mind to another." He pushed back his hood, revealing antennae over a yard long, which stood erect menacingly. "Ye, my brother Lords, mayhap have suspected or mayhap did not, but with many worms and viral words I wove my way past all your petty defenses and read your minds. There are no lies here. The matter is far too dire for that." Now his eyes fell again into their half-closed, half-dreaming dullness, and his wrinkle-creased mouth puckered oddly. "Yes, I read them all, you filthy people. I know all your sins. Well, not you, Lord Chrematist! You are dead. You only ever said one thing to me: *You are now as I once was. As I am now, soon shall you be.* Heh. Heh-heh. So much empty brainspace!"

All in the chamber stared uncertainly at the little old man as he sank back down into silence, muttering.

11. The Lighthousekeeper

Vigil now demanded, "By the testimony of all seated here, the Stability was dissolved a millennium ago . . . we have been shadows for a thousand years? Echoes of a bell long broken? Why maintain the charade?"

The Lighthousekeeper said, "Because we love the Stability no less than you! Once the mad ship is dead, the Grand Schedule can be restored. A vast works of stellar sailcloth engineering has been accomplished on Hellebore, the next moon out, and we could, not without sacrifice and strain, expropriate this sail-works from its current possessor, whoever or whatever that may be—"

"Good luck with that, jerkbag, and see you in hell first," said Cricket the counselor, not bothering to lower his voice.

But the Lighthousekeeper was too caught up in his own words to hear the interruption. "—once the sailcloth is ours, we can use the upper reaches of the Star-Tower as the skeleton of a hull. We will have to sever it from the base with the Lighthouse beam from the sun! It will require great sacrifice, but if we are willing to turn the Lighthouse into a weapon—yes, yes, I know this has been the fear of the Stability since its founding—but this is an exception, and no man alive will know what we do here. We must break the laws to uphold the laws! What nobler principle of action can there be?"

But the Portreeve said, "If we used the immense power entrusted to the Stability to smite the warship that *Emancipation* has become, we would be no more right than she is!"

It was said that eventually all Lighthousekeepers go mad, since the immensity of the power of the interstellar-strength beams at their command prey on their minds and the sight of cracking uninhabited inner worlds in two, or boiling away the atmospheres of gas giants during initial testing and target practice, sinks into their souls.

And yet, it was with no glint of madness in his eye that the Lighthousekeeper said, "Our Anthroponomist has testified that into whatever strange form of ex-human life the Scolopendra of *Emancipation* have mutated, they are moved by metaphysical or unearthly sentiments and not to be reasoned with. Only zealots can make war across the wide emptiness of stars! Those who will not kill a murderer die at his hands! This is the sole basis for moral reasoning. War excuses all. Self-defense excuses all atrocities! This is a holy war!"

Vigil looked back and forth at the men there. He did not raise his voice, but there was a tremble in his words which even his sternest internal creature could not suppress. "How can there be any war at all, holy or hellish? The Princess Rania promised us peace! Universal peace!"

The one who spoke then was the Vatic Essomenic Officer, informally called the Aruspex. He wore chlamys of purple thought-wire and a petasos of orichalchum. He was blind, his two eyes and all his visual cortex replaced with a yellowish aurum substance to allow him to see directly into the notational layer of the Noösphere. His voice was like a ringing gong. "Wake from your dreams! There will never be peace. Behold."

12. The Aruspex

At his gesture, the surface of the table, which held the somnolent arcs, curves, and multiangular notations of the Monument Code, rippled and presented a new set of equations.

The gathered Lords and officers stared at the Aruspex, but he said nothing.

Vigil said, "Wait. I recognize parts of this. This is Rania's Equation from the Memento Stone. It is the plan for universal peace, the system of customs and laws we must adopt to become fully equal to Hyades and the other Dominions of the Orion Arm. But—why is it changed? I have seen—"

The Aruspex spoke in a voice like iron. "It has not changed. This is the unchanged version of what Rania deduced from the Memento Stone. The parts of the plan were severally sent by radio laser to the Stability Tables each on its own world, to incorporate into the local planetary history. We alone, thanks to the potency of the receivers orbiting Iota Draconis, and our correspondents on other worlds, were able to gather the scattered plans back into one, and read the master plan intended for the whole Empyrean. Here is the authentic and complete plan of destiny set before you. We hid the truth from the public. If the material is too complex, I can summon a frenetic actuator—"

"Not needed," said Vigil. "I can read this by sight."

He saw the looks of disbelief on their features.

Vigil said proudly, "You forget the blood of the Summer Kings of Night-spore runs in me, who fenced with storms and tilted with meteorological systems fiercely opposed as lance and shield, the calculus of which required the development special nervous matrices."

The Aruspex said, "Summer Kings cannot read this notation. It is not fit for human brains."

Vigil said, "The blood of the Iron Hermeticist Narcís D'Aragó is also mine. You are of the Five Families: you know what this means."

They did. Once history revealed that Rania, Ximen the Black, and the mad Judge of Ages were altered by stepping on the surface of the Lost Monument of the legendary star the Swan Princess later plucked from the sky, the Five Families had sought out and bred the descendants of the other Hermeticists known to have exposed themselves to the Monument surface and absorbed into their cell plasm whatever unknown force it was which made the Swan Princess, and, to a lesser extent, the Master and the Judge, able to read the Monument.

The ruling families Xi Boötis had been subjected to a ruthless eons-long breeding program by the cunning of the Potentate Euphrasy, and—whether by coincidence or nonhuman design it was not known—these were among the

millions torn from their homes in the Fifty-Third Millennium and flung to
Arcturus by the pitiless Virtues whom human astronomers dubbed Lamathon
and Nahalon: and from them arose the Aestevals of Nightspore, the ancestors
of the Strangermen.

Vigil pointed at the runes and hieroglyphs of the alien script. "These figures
are nonsense. The extrapolations here and here show genetic drifts which will
turn all the races of man, one by one, into placid and homogenous underlings,
craving control by their superiors, then being addicted to control, then being
incapable to live without it. These Last Men, once they are developed, would
be congenitally unable to tolerate freedom, honor, virtue, truth, or beauty. This
is not peace! This is an abomination!"

He looked around the chamber, his eyes haunted and lost. "Is this—this
insolent treason against everything for which we stand, everything we cherish,
everything we are—?" He almost could not force the words out of his mouth.
"Is this Rania's plan?"

Slowly he lowered the sword and hefted it in his hand. "How can she mean
this to happen to us? It would be no different from if the Vindication of Man
had never happened. All her tens of thousands of years of star-faring, beyond
the galaxy, farther than the realms of death and back again—is all human history and struggle to be made into nothing?"

The Aruspex said, "The cliometric calculus of what becomes of the Stability
should this plan is made public is perfectly clear in the Chi and Psi region: no
one follows any futurian leading him into the slave pit. All our friends and kin
would be stoned, or deleted, or subjected to mind-desolation. The Tormented
are a turbulent people, when provoked."

"What, then, did you intend? To allow this future to unfold and ensure the
desecration of our race?"

The Aruspex said, "No. We conspired to break our ties with the Empyrean,
allow no further Great Ships to launch or land, and become the antithesis of
the Stability in all ways, expunging all connections of trade and radio contact,
knowing ourselves too minor to come to the attention of Hyades, or any greater
Domination or Dominion. The stars and endless unhorizoned vistas of eternity which once so proudly we ordained our children's remotest children would
conquer, all this we foreswore."

Vigil shook his head. "But—wait. There is no vector showing the approach
of a multigeneration warship. And the worlds conquered by the *Emancipation*
in secret—where are the figures and vector sums for their new plotted courses
in history?"

The Aruspex said, "I will not hide the truth: your father wished the ship to

land, uncaring of what would become of our current social order, or perhaps
desiring its overthrow, for the flooded world the *Emancipation* will impose also
appears nowhere in Rania's planning. He thought it better to shatter the chessboard of history than to continue the game where checkmate is inevitable. For
this reason he perished—but whether it was suicide or murder, I do not know."

Vigil said, "He died to place me here, to make the decision he knew was
right, but had not the strength to make. Halting the ship both breaks this horrible plan and fulfills all oaths as Stabiles—even though it means the end of the
Stability."

The Aruspex said, "Will you use your terrible power to force us to betray the
oath of the Stability and land a ship that we are sworn not to allow? This warship destroys, rather than upholds, the plan of history."

Vigil said, "Allowing the ship to land may introduce vectors to defeat what
Rania has planned—if we are wise enough to know whether opposition to
Rania is justified. We swore oaths to her, unbreakable oaths, and if the wisdom she brought back from beyond the galaxy is wisdom we cannot bear—
who are we to pit our minds against it?"

The Aruspex said coldly, "It may be that there are reasons sound and sensible
to sacrifice our sovereignty of this world to upend the Plan for Universal Peace,
which is a fraud. Maybe that is so. But whether so or not—you, My Lord Hermeticist, you have no right to threaten the world with destruction if the Table
fails to halt this warship and make that sacrifice. You boast that you will never
break an oath. Will you obliterate us with that sword for upholding rather than
breaking ours? For to land this warship would be the abolition of the Stability,
in whose name that sword is given its power, and your hand given to hold it."

Vigil raised his eyes, tilting the blade this way and that, as if reading the
ancient letters again. "Well? Is there still a case against this Chamber, these
men, this order, this world, this age? Do I still have jurisdiction here?"

He winced as information forms like hot needles entered his brain. *Despite
all that was said, this remains a matter for the mortal order to judge. It is not permitted that we should advise you. Condemnation and clemency are still yours to
grant or withhold.*

Vigil lowered the sword again, weary, confused, defeated. He turned and
looked left and right. Here was the Terraformer in green, the Lighthousekeeper in white, the motionless Chrematist in red, propped up at the Table.
Opposite him was the Aedile in gold, nervous, and the senile Chronometrician in saffron. He looked at the Portreeve in his dun uniform. "Who sent the
Myrmidon to save me from my attackers? I assume it was you."

But the Portreeve touched one ear and displayed his palm, fingers spread. *Signal loss: message not understood.* It was the old gesture indicating confusion.

Vigil supposed it did not matter. As if his eyeballs weighed more than nature allowed, he found his gaze being pulled back to the mocking horror of the Peace Plan inscribed in the Table. It promised so much and delivered nothing at all.

Vigil tried to imagine the seventy suns of mankind shining on the fourscore worlds and the forty-two sailing vessels, larger than continents, carrying their millions in long flight through the night. Each sun and world, each radio house and interstellar laser, all were manned and crewed and served by the Loyal and Self-Correctional Order of Prognostic Actuarial Cliometric Stability.

He said aloud, "How can the secret future brought back from M3 by the Swan Princess be so horribly wrong, so horribly false? Everyone knows she solved the riddle called history! How can there be a warship in existence at all? How can there be war?"

The counselor behind him named Cricket said, "Well, scabby scrotum of the damned devil, I know the answer to that! It's obvious. Been saying for years. No one listens to me."

But another voice spoke over him and drowned him out: *There is war because the Master of Empyrean has willed it. He is conquering all the worlds as he comes!*

7

The Ambitions of the Imperator

1. The Dead Speak

Vigil saw the potent glitter in every eye in the chamber and realized that the Lords of the Stability, Companions, and Commensals were all raising their intelligence as rapidly as they could, reckless of their energy budgets. Then he realized that the dead man had just spoken, and he started doubling his intellect as well.

The Chrematist stood, and as he did so, the color left his red robes, turning all the fabric black. The whiteness left the skin cells of his face and hands as the hibernation of untold years was ended. The features grew young, sharp-cheeked; a face of striking aquiline comeliness peered forth from the departing hoarfrost. The white hair turned black as rapidly as burning paper, as did the pointed beard and slender mustachios beneath a long, straight nose. The wrinkled skin grew young. The eyes were green as the eyes of a beast of prey.

He threw back his hood, revealing the crown upon his head.

2. The Dead Coronet

Despite the strangeness of this dead man seemingly returning to life, Vigil was fascinated, even shocked, by the sight of the coronet.

As an antiquarian, Vigil recognized it as a material object which was not self-organized, as a living machine was organized, or a house, or a weapon, or any other thinking thing. Neither was it a man-made artifact, as he understood the term, meaning anything built up from the molecular level, such as an apple tree or an eyeball. Neither was it a Potentate artifact, built up from the atomic level, such as unobtainium or argent, or any of the other frivolously named elements nature could not make. The crown was dead matter crafted by hands, apparently without the use of machinery, since there were (so eyes like Vigil's could detect) microscopic defects and asymmetries throughout. It was neither dead matter, natural, nor living matter, artificial.

It looked like a thing a schoolboy would make, or a Nomad, or someone else whose matter-printer was rudely programmed. But it was not. It was not printed at all. It was bits of matter put together by hand, macroscopically, and the bits were dead throughout the whole operation. It was handmade in the original sense of the word: made by hands.

Vigil sent an internal creature into the world archives, like a bright fish disappearing into a dark ocean, seeking a reference to what this crown was, or whence it came.

3. The Living Master

The Aedile, staring bright-eyed at this stranger, laid his hand on the table and spoke. "I call upon the Table itself to forefend us. We are breached!"

The cold voice, speaking in the ancient language, hummed from the dark surface of the invulnerable metal, as if far underground thunder were speaking, and Vigil's teeth ached with the echoes. "None is here unwarranted, unasked, uninvited, or without ancient right."

The dark stranger spoke in a voice of firm command, perhaps with a hint of laughter hidden in it. "I am the Founder of the Starfarer's Guild, and my authority is supreme and paramount. Hear your master, and obey! Sieges! None sit in my presence!"

Vigil had no idea how many thousands of years old these ceremonial chairs were or how old was their programming. But he leaped to his feet.

Others were not so swift. The Terraformer and the Chronometrician were deposited unceremoniously on the floor. The other lords and dignitaries swayed or stumbled or clutched the Table edge when chairs bucked their occupants free, and then came to their feet with as much dignity as they could muster.

The dark and princely stranger raised his finger and pointed at Vigil. "You alone have obeyed the most ancient rules and iron laws eons ago I here established. For this, I commend you and grant to your family, race, and clan a boon, anything you wish, up to and including sovereign rulership of this world as my vicar. But know this: there is no law requiring the Lords of Stability to ignite the deceleration beam for a warship! Therefore, they are not in violation, and you must put up your sword and yield it to me once more, its true possessor."

And he held up his left hand, drew back the dark fabric of the sleeve, and displayed an amulet of dark red metal, identical to the appliance connected to Vigil's own wrist.

The internal creature he had sent into the archives returned and spoke inside his mind: *This is the Iron Crown of Lombardy. He who wears it is the Most Noble Master of the Empyrean of Man.*

4. The Living Blade

Vigil cautiously lowered the blade and put it home in its sheath, but when he kept his hands on sheath and grip, as if ready to draw it again, and made no move to surrender it, a silent force, like the pressure felt in the air before a storm, grew and grew beneath his gloves, and he could feel the impatient power in the sword swelling ominously. And yet he did not unhand the sheathed blade.

Vigil said, "Claim you to be Ximen del Azarchel, the Nobilissimus and Master of Mankind?"

The man smiled an alarmingly charming smile, tilting his head forward with a quirk of his eyebrows. "I am he. Among my other titles, my oldest and the only one I really cherish, is Senior Officer of the Landing Party. I am the founder of the Hermetic Order. You doubt? Don't you have any coins in your pocket? Look at the profile on the gold royal. I am that man. That sword is mine. Hand it over." The smile did not fade, but it somehow grew cold and menacing. "With haste. I do not repeat my commands."

Vigil's counselor said softly to him, "Don't let go of that blade. Ask him who is the captain of the ship."

Vigil understood. If Ximen del Azarchel was the captain of the *Emancipa-*

tion, he was in space, approaching at near-lightspeed. This, then, must be an emissary, a partial, a set of memories taken from Ximen and radioed ahead of the ship to prepare the ground for the ship's arrival.

Vigil said, "The boon I ask is this sword. I ask that the world-destroying power of the Lord Hermeticist be kept in my possession and that of my heirs and assigns forever."

Ximen snapped his fingers. "Very clever, but ask for another boon, and be quick about it. The blade is a precious heirloom to me and has sentimental value."

Vigil shook his head. "A few questions before I decide whether your order is lawful, sir."

"All my orders are lawful, the supreme law, merely by being mine."

"Who is captain of the warship? Who is so mad that he would make war on worlds to which he could never return, slumbering the centuries between each battle?"

"The Master of the Empyrean has authority to compel or punish Powers and Potentates, Archangels, Angels, and the various posthuman races which may unwisely attempt to resist him. I require the use of their launching lasers to coordinate and focus all their beams in one spot in one particular decade, year, and hour. And some dared to question how their civilizations would tolerate the expense.

"Naturally"—again he smiled his engaging smile—"I had to leave a cadre of my own people, those of trusted loyalty, in charge of the gravitic-nucleonic distortion pools within their suns, and the lighthouse satellites controlling the focal elements in their Oort clouds. The cadre in each case had to be of strength sufficient that no combination of the native races, Angels, and Potentates could overcome them and also be of sufficient numbers to reproduce the generations needed to maintain the acceleration beam across the centuries."

5. War and Life

"Why?" Vigil demanded, his voice growing louder and harsher than he expected. "Why all this horror and deception? Why is there war among the stars?"

"For my glory, of course," said Ximen del Azarchel, raising both eyebrows, smug as a black tomcat. "And to accomplish my purposes. This little sphere of stars, a piddling hundred lightyears in radius, is too narrow a cage for the eagle wings of my ambition to spread to their full width! Come now! You are not stupid men! What does your paltry, far-off, dry, and dusty little moon, filled with race hatred and cruelty, have to offer? I notice you all let lie two dead bodies here on the floor.

"You are barbarians."

He spoke this last word with a particular gusto of contempt. He continued, smiling eerily, "There is no warfare, no economic competition, no cruelty, and damn near no zest in life left back in the First Sweep worlds. You disgust me, but you have zest, eh?

"Ah, my dear people, you would be ashamed of the cousins left behind on your ancestral planets if you knew how easily my very small but very well-trained complement could bring your mother worlds to heel. Planets are very, very big, even small ones, and having enough troops to put men on every continent is nearly impossible—if I were not a military genius, I might not enjoy myself this much. But the Patrician race, the homogeneity they spread, their silly ideas of equality and fairness! Bah! You see where that leads!"

Vigil had regained control of his composure. Coldly, not showing his anger, he said, "Sir. You are the prince consort and husband of Rania, are you not? The Imperator and Nobilissimus of all the races of man on all the worlds and ships in flight! How are you doing this against the will and command of Her Serene Highness?"

Del Azarchel nodded. "I am pleased someone here has recognized me. Siege! Offer me that chair that I may sit." And the siege of the Terraformer waddled from its current position and held itself nicely while the Nobilissimus sat.

He smiled and said, "I will answer you, and then you will hand me that sword. Do you see this plan for the future written out here so nicely on this cold, hard table? It is a cold, hard plan, is it not? What is missing from it? What is missing here that your planet Septfoil—or what does it call itself now?— your tedious and insignificant little moon-world here—Torment. You have something which is lacking elsewhere. What is it? What is worth spending a thousand years of my life in a long, slow ship, and fighting half a dozen worldwide campaigns, to find?"

Vigil looked at the figures inscribed on the Table. "Zest? The desire to wrestle life and take her by the teeth?"

"Ah, you remind me of D'Aragó—and you are descended from him, are you not? Good guess. Quite wrong. What is missing from Rania's Plan for Universal Peace is the Sixth Sweep."

There was a murmur about the table.

Del Azarchel leaned back in the siege of the Aedile and templed his fingers. "What is missing is worlds farther away than yours from Mother Sol. Why are your children not pressing outward, ever outward, colonizing, terraforming, adapting, conquering, trampling, and fathering new Potentates and Powers and Principalities?

"It has been nearly two *thousand* years since Rania returned. Has even a single new world been tamed by mankind and added to my domination? Even one? A moon?

"Am I the only damned soul in the whole human race with the ambition to rule the stars, the wit to see how to do it, and the will to see it done? Well, be that as it may. Have you unriddled my riddle? Why did I come to your dead-end world as far from civilization as it is possible to be?"

Vigil nodded. "You are here for the launching laser of Iota Draconis! Our Lighthouse was built by The Beast, and no human technology can match it. And if I guess not wrong, you need people who have the spirit, wit, and will like yours to pioneer the stars, and you see that the quarreling races of Torment."

The Master of the Empyrean smiled thinly. "So, as you see, you have no lawful reason not to return my sword to me. You are hardly going to use it now to compel my servants here at my Table to oppose my will and betray my schedule and let my fine ship die, are you?"

"What happens when the ship makes port?"

"That has never been a concern of the Stability, so long as my schedule is maintained, has it?"

"What happens when the warship makes port, sir?"

"War, of course! But as the Imperator of Man, I decree this Table is not in dereliction of its duty, and therefore you no longer have jurisdiction as the Hermeticist to preserve the turmoil and bloodshed needed to compel the evolution of mankind ever upward and onward. I will see to that matter myself!"

Vigil tightened his hands on the sword. He looked at the Terraformer, the Theosophist, the Aedile. "Sirs, are you convinced that the husband of Rania has the legal power to compel us to welcome the horrors of war into our midst? Or, in your candid judgment and decree, is this a violation of the principles for which we stand? He calls us barbaric, and yet we and we alone recall and perform our oaths—what is civilization but that?"

But the Lords of Stability were cowed. The Castigator said, "We cannot oppose the Master of the Empyrean. He is older than our world, older than the worlds of our ancestors. He is older than time itself! He is the father of a dead god and of many living ones!"

Vigil recalled the wording of his oath. Even if it meant conquest for his world, death for himself and his kin, and the obliteration of his way of life, his honor would not die.

He unhooked the sheathed sword from his baldric. And started walking, one slow step at a time, toward the Imperator, whose dark beard made his white smile seem all the brighter, and his dark brows made his dark eyes darker green.

Here was a man who liked to prevail.

Vigil took one reluctant step, then another, and then he saw one of the statues on the dais that circled the chamber stirring to life and her eyes shine intolerably.

It was Torment in her executioner's hood and bridal gown, surrounded by her instruments of inquisition. The statue did not grow in height nor weight, and yet a terrible sense of pressure seemed to enter the chamber as if a whole world were focused into this small and human spot.

She raised her hand. Vigil, for a moment, thought that a mudra had frozen him in place. But no, to his relief an internal assured him it was only his own panic and craven fear.

She said, "Yield not that blade to him."

6. *The World's Word*

Ximen del Azarchel stood and, without a word, snatched the pearl from the hand of the Theosophist. Unfortunately, the Theosophist had been staring the Potentate in the eyes at that moment, not looking at the pearl in his hand, and not only went blind but fell backward with a cry, toppling over sieges too surprised to scuttle out of the way, and struck the glass floor to lie senseless. Ximen hefted the gleaming orb once or twice in his palm, perhaps adjusting parts of his nervous system to accommodate it, and raised his eyes to stare at the Potentate unabashed. "Back into silence, Septfoil! You may not interfere with human affairs. That is the unalterable decision of Triumvirate."

"Yet is there not an exception, Imperator, allowing me to speak in my own defense, when human acts unwittingly bode my obliteration?" She turned her inhuman eyes toward Vigil, who flinched, and raised his hand as if to ward off a blow. He squinted at the figure between his fingers. She said, "I believe the Lord Hermeticist still has the floor, examining the testimony of the Table before rendering his verdict."

Del Azarchel said, "I am sure Vigil will yield me the balance of his time so that we may move to the next order of business, which is how to prepare for the coming invasion. You see, all the worlds I conquered are forewarned, and given the opportunity to select weapons and conditions of engagement . . ."

Vigil's counselor nudged him in the back and hissed, "Stop him." And Vigil said loudly, "To the contrary. I do not yield the floor."

Del Azarchel had a strange and dangerous look in his eye, and Vigil felt as if he were looking into two tunnels leading into eons far from the present time. Vigil had the strange, dizzying sensation that Del Azarchel would not forget this affront, and long after Vigil and all his race were extinct, and the star Iota Draconis burned into a cinder and collapsed, and yet still would Del Azarchel recall this moment and fret in anger.

But the Master of the Empyrean glanced at the tall statue of Torment, and nodded graciously, as if it was from his generosity alone he determined not to press the issue. He seated himself again, the orb in one hand.

Vigil said, "The Master has decreed the Table not in dereliction. How, then, do I retain the authority to speak at this Table, to wield this sword, or to call witnesses?"

Torment did not answer, but a voice from the Table itself spoke: "The Chrematist does not have authority unilaterally to call the question and end debate on the question of dereliction. His authority extends only to financial matters relating to establishing resources needed to power the launching and deceleration laser at such times and for such purposes as the Great Schedule decrees. The Lord Hermeticist still has the floor. He has already decreed the Table to be in dereliction. That decree cannot be overridden by any power this Table recognizes. You were discussing only the matter of whether to punish or whether, due to mitigating circumstances, to grant clemency."

Vigil said, "But that is the Master of the Empyrean, the founder of the Order, and the author of our constitution and regulations! He is the Prince Consort of Rania, and therefore sovereign."

The Table said, "Forgive me, but we are not allowed to advise on those matters. The human order of being will be saved or damned by its own wisdom or folly. My purpose is to see that the procedures are concluded in an orderly fashion, so that if the world is saved, it is saved in a systematic and proper way, and if damned, damned neatly and according to the book. I am allowed to speak only to answer queries about the rules of order, and to maintain decorum."

"Then answer: How is it that I still have authority to act or speak, when my sovereign Imperator says otherwise?"

"The humans in the Chamber have not officially voted to acknowledge and recognize Ximen del Azarchel, Lord Nobilissimus and Imperator. At the moment, in the eyes of the law, he is still Eosphoros, Lord Chrematist."

"But the chairs know damn well who he is! So do you!"

"They lack the privilege to address the Table or franchise to vote."

Ximen del Azarchel, raising both eyebrows, now spoke as softly as a jet-black panther purring, "But you, Lord Hermeticist—your name is *Vigil*, and your mother is *Lady Patience?*—you know who I am, and you will answer to me, soon or late. Lay down your commission, declare the Table not at fault, and let us get on with the business of forcing this backward world into the next higher step of evolution, hammering history to new shapes on the blood-drenched white-hot forge of war. Or, for your boon, you could ask the ship to surrender to your world, to your people, or even to you personally: and you can conquer this wretched world yourself, as your own fief, and arrange her as you like."

Vigil pushed the sword out of the sheath with his thumb, exposing no more than the first bright inch of blade near the hilts. "Have I still the authority to wield you?"

Nothing has changed. The verdict was spoken. There is no appeal. All that remains is sentencing. You may slay the world, or you may spare her.

As before, the answer was like the stab of a needle through his brain. He pushed the sword back into the sheath.

To Del Azarchel he said, "Your pardon, sir, but as a point of order, I still have the floor. You cannot offer me the boon of the vassalage of this world, since I already accepted the boon of this sword and its authority. I know you to be too honorable a man to rescind your word."

Del Azarchel did not like to lose, but he knew how to concede gracefully. He gritted his teeth, made himself smile, and waved his hand. "The sword is yours."

Vigil turned, lowering his eyes and wishing he had the use of the pearl that Del Azarchel held. "Torment! Why did you slay my father?"

She nodded her hooded head forward, saying solemnly, "You have guessed the reason."

"Confirm my guess for me. My mind is not like yours and needs to have even its irrational doubts soothed."

"I dissolved the segments of his brain because he asked me to, the knowledge hidden there being intolerable to him. His mind was too finely made, with too many stubborn internal segments and secret defenses, to be fully mastered by the amnesia imposed by this chamber on him, even when the imposition was done with his full consent.

"One night, as he stood staring at the nineteen moons of Wormwood casting colors shadows across the dunes and rocks of his beloved land, the memory returned, and the torture of the decision you now face.

"He knew what must be done: the warship decelerated, the war welcomed, and fought, and lost, and all surface life washed away in the terraforming of the Scolopendra, who have no use for life like yours. This alone sated the duty imposed on the Stability of Man.

"He also knew that the senile Chronometrician could see into his mind and would see the lack of heart to carry out the threat, even should he ever find the heart to draw the world-destroying sword. But he knew you did, and do, have the heart to carry out the heartless duty, and the only way lawfully to put the sword into your hands was to die.

"It was the only way to carry out his oath. His honor he loved no less than you, yours.

"The loss of nine-tenths of his person was sufficient to render him unfit for duty, legally dead, and the remaining one-tenth, his tithe, he returned to the hands of his wife, to live out his days with her in happiness and peace, with no knowledge of what the horrid future would bring."

"So you want me to halt the warship and bring war?"

She said, "Most emphatically I do not, and I would slay you now, and all within this Chamber, and all who dwell upon my surface, as easily as a boy swats a fly glued to a honey-leaf, to avoid that fate. But wars between humans are to me like a fever in you, when the white blood cells that serve you eject an invading germ. This is not what I fear. You have deduced that the Master of the Empyrean cares nothing for the Empyrean Polity: his eyes are set on larger things. When his Great Ship makes starfall here, all is changed."

Vigil said, "What are you afraid of?"

"My mind is not as your mind, nor my thoughts like your thoughts. I do not fear what you fear, and yet I am tormented. It is not death I fear, for I cannot die, but changes to my core self, what you would call a soul. I fear to be changed beyond recognition, to remember all I once was and yet forget myself. I have nothing I love so much that I am willing to die for it, and, without such self-obliterating love, I cannot maintain my life in the face of the obliteration of entropy. The source of my fear stands within the Chamber with you: the mortals call him insane, but he is not."

Vigil said, "You speak in riddles!"

Torment said, "I wait for him to reveal himself."

Del Azarchel straightened up, staring at the figure wearing a Hermeticist mask and dressed in the red robes and long wig of a lawyer. "Mother of God! Is that *you*, Cowhand? I've been looking all over for you, damn your eyes! You are on this planet, just as everyone said! What in the name of Santiago are you doing here?"

The counselor, who was also the janitor and many other things besides, removed the breathing mask and goggles, revealing the hard planes of his face, the lantern jaw, deep-set eyes, square brow, and great hooked beak of a nose. He also threw the long white wig on the floor. "You still have the floor, Veggie, or whateverthepox your name is, so tell Blackie to hold his plague-spotted tongue."

7. Flabbergasted

Vigil stared at the man. An alert internal creature, seeing Vigil stunned, forced shut his mouth and manipulated his facial muscles into an alert expression so that the full comic befuddlement was not visible to onlookers—who, Vigil noticed, had similar expressions anyway, except the withered Chronometrician, who cackled at them.

Other internals were going rapidly over his conversations, and only now seeing the ambiguities and lapses in judgment. Between his learning of his father's murder and learning he must murder his whole world in retaliation, Vigil had overlooked many clues or comments which would have been obvious on a calmer day with a clearer mind, a mind less often jarred or stunned by mudra or mandala or Fox-trick.

Vigil realized that the Judge of Ages had not been here to aid him or halt him. Whether or not this world's surface civilization rose or fell was a small matter to him, a temporary thing. His eyes were on some object beyond Vigil's mental horizon.

But this was not the madman history and legend had portrayed! He was a little crude and direct, but clearly he was sane. Which meant . . .

8. The Final Peace Equation

Vigil said to the Judge of Ages, "You are a man of legend—on Nightspore, in the buried nation of Threal, they worship you as a god. How do I address you?"

"Call me Meany. Or, if you want to be formal and proper and posh, call me Doc. I ain't a *doctor* doctor, a real doctor, a sawbones, but I got a degree in math from Soko University in Oddifornia. They say the continent is tilted, on account of the Anglos is so light-headed they pull the East Coast up, so all the loose screws roll to the other coast. Heh. I hain't told that joke since that continent was still around. Still funny, if'n you ask me."

Vigil drew a deep breath, trying to bring order to his agitated inner creatures. "Why is there a warship coming?"

Montrose took a small twig out of an inner pocket and scraped thoughtfully at the gaps between his teeth. He paused to push his tongue into his cheek, as if chasing some stray scrap, and then he spat. "I could say 'cause Blackie's coming. Well, he is sort of here also. That is a puppet of his that he radioed ahead. When he sent his gear, his crown and sword and stuff, near as I can figure, must have left Tellus on the same ship I shipped out on, the *Errantry*. Easy enough to do, since the Guild works for him. I was launched by the Starfaring Guild, but landed by the Stability, which tells you how long ago that was. It means he must have recognized what was going on same time I did, within ten years plus or minus. Right, Blackie?"

Before Del Azarchel, could answer, Vigil said, "Sir, that was not my question."

"Well, ask what you mean, dammit. It's not like I can read your mind! We ain't on the same circuit."

Vigil said doggedly, "Even before she departed for M3, the Swan Princess knew the secret of how to use the cliometric equations to reach peace. She could prevent world wars and defuse mutinies before they occurred. The Memento Stone would, if anything, include a more complete answer, allowing us to coop-erate with the aliens without the horror of forced repopulation to far worlds. So the Stone could only increase, not decrease, her skill at reading the Monument and rendering peace! We know the aliens are not at open war. Therefore, there is a Final Peace Equation. We know that . . ."

Vigil realized he was rambling, telling the Judge of Ages matters this an-cient being must have known before Vigil was born, or his world, or his ances-tors' worlds, or his family, clan, race, language.

Montrose did not seem impatient. He merely nodded. "You're getting warm. Go on."

"From these facts, we know the human race cannot be growing in any di-rection but more and more civilized and peaceful. And yet—look! There sits the herald of an incoming multigeneration warship, asking to set terms of the combat!"

Montrose shrugged with one shoulder. "Maybe you should be asking a different question, sonny."

"What would that be, sir?"

"The peaceful future where we ain't gunna study war no more, why, that future would not need Stability Lords as proud and picky about their honor as a pack of Spaniards, would it? So one question maybe you should be asking yourself is this: Why did the interstellar plans of future history give rise to customs and civilizations like what we got now? Like something from the Dark Ages? The First Dark Ages, I mean."

Vigil looked uncomfortable but said nothing.

Montrose said, "Seems to me that what you is really asking is, what the plague is your life for, a man like you? You'd rather die than break your word, and there ain't no such man like that when sweet reason reigns and all folks is fat and happy. So what is your life for, Vigil Starmanson? Why is there such a thing as a *you*?" He grinned and spat out the toothpick. "That is your real question, ain't it?"

Vigil sighed. Everything in his life turned on the answer. "Yes, sir," he said humbly. "That is my question. You said you know the answer and that no one heeds you."

"Ain't that so! Yessirree—I surely do know. It's obvious."

"Will you tell us?"

"Nope."

Vigil restrained the urge to jolt the Judge of Ages with a mudra from the glance of an evil eye to induce vomiting spasms. It would be more in keeping with the dignity of the ancient man simply to smite with the sword. But he checked that impulse as well. "*What?* And why not?"

"And have you ignore me, too? Figure it out your own damned self."

The Master of the Empyrean raised his hand and signaled with his finger lamp. "I ask the Lord Hermeticist grant me time enough to answer his query, that we might move rapidly on to other business? I mean to have that braking laser lit and properly presented, or else no one leaves this chamber alive."

Vigil said, "One question first: You sent the Myrmidon to save me?"

"I did not."

"Who did?"

"No one sent him. I am him. Despite their extinction, I still from time to time can find an empty body with mind-circuits formatted correctly to receive my imprint, buried in a library, or in various hiding holes in hollow asteroids, or bunkers on abandoned moons. I meant to have you do the duty I gave you and force this stubborn Table to do their duty I gave them, but unexpected events intruded. Your planet, Torment, somehow slipped the information about the true nature of Rania's Final Peace Equation into the hand of your Cliometrician here. This made events spin out of control, requiring me to drop my mask and speak."

Vigil said to the Aruspex, "This copy of the Final Peace Equation, this abomination on the table before us—where did you get it?"

The Aruspex made a fist: the gesture for assent. "He speaks the truth. It came from Torment herself. Thanks to our uniquely potent receivers, she has been spying for centuries on the other Potentates and Powers of the Empyrean, decoding the secret and subconscious thoughts of our Dominion as they as crawled at lightspeed from Altair to Proxima to 61 Cygni. She discovered the unedited versions of the severed plan for human evolution, beamed to each separate Stability on every world, and reconnected them. As if by mischance, my people came across her information in an unguarded file. I trespassed on my own initiative, no doubt with her awareness: whether technically that counts as intervention in human life, I leave to others to decide."

Vigil turned to Del Azarchel, "You have the floor. Explain this enigma."

Del Azarchel said, "If Rania, once returned from M3, has the power and motivation to impose peace on mankind, then there can be no war; and yet an interstellar war is and has been ongoing for centuries, and war will tear the Empyrean in pieces and force those pieces to flee to ever more distant stars and colonize there. Your question is, how can this be, and what is your life for?"

Vigil waited, seething with impatience. Del Azarchel paused, smiling, enjoying the unhappy silence. With a smile, the Master of the Empyrean spread his hands, as if to show he had no more tricks in his glove circuits, no mudras, no hidden finger-commands to make.

"Simple. Rania never returned from M3."

9. The End of History

A dumbfounded silence clutched all the men there.

The voice of Montrose was as loud as the bray of a mule in the quiet chamber. "Like I been saying all along. The millions aboard the *Errantry* knew it, and so do their children sixteen hundred years later. Polite folk to this day will not sup with an Errant or walk into their shops or grottos because Errants will not mouth the polite lies. So much misery, so many years of prejudice and hate, just to save Blackie's brittle little asinine pride, eh?"

Del Azarchel's face grew dark with a blush, and his eyes narrowed.

Vigil said, "What do you mean?"

Montrose said, "I am sure the fake Rania who came back from the stars made a perfectly nice wife for Blackie. All he wanted was the reputation of it, right? Ain't that right, Blackie? You never wanted the girl, just wanted the world to think she was your'n. And so you must have figured it out quick as I did, but you had all the media smother the knowledge and hired folk to spread rumors, rewrite history books, censor memories, all that stuff."

Del Azarchel leaned back in the chair. "One day you will die and at my hand, I swear it. But let us not speak of such unpleasant matters now. The fate of worlds, of the destiny of man, hangs in the balance."

Menelaus turned to Vigil. "Remind Blackie he ain't got the floor to talk. Blackie is a big liar. He did not want the Empyrean to know that he was

Mr. Rebound Guy, the one to whom Fake-a-Rania turned in sorrow for comfort when I walked away from her."

Vigil said to Menelaus, "But she rejected *you*, not you her! That is what the histories say."

"No kidding? I betcha they also say Blackie built the pyramids of Egypt all by hisself when he was a toddler. To have a place to stay while he wrote Plato's dialogue in Shakespeare's Hamlet? You know the one: *To be, or not to be? And what is 'Being'?*"

Vigil said, "No, but history says you went mad and fled here, to the farthest star where mankind dwells—"

"If you read stuff in history books that sounds made up, trust me, they was probably made up. Son, I could have just unplugged by brain-phone gizmo and gotten on a slow boat to China, or whatever is occupying that part of Asia these days, and stayed on Earth, and had air and weight, bugs and diet like I'm damned used to, and been plenty alone. You don't take two centuries and cross one hundred lightyears just to have a place to get drunk, get into a bar fight, and puke on someone. I arrived on the *Errantry* by way of Rasalhague and 12 Ophiuchi, and been here over a thousand years. What the hell you think I been doing all this time, wandering around in my skivvies, cussing at your pink sun and howling at your fat moon, with a five-o'clock shadow on my chin and a jug of cheap rotgut in my fist?"

"Ummm. . . ." Since this was exactly the mental picture Vigil has entertained of the fate of the Judge of Ages ever since he heard the tale in childhood, Vigil thought it more discreet not to say.

Montrose said, "It weren't that hard to figure. She had all Rania's memories all right, down to the last drop, but something was missing. She could not read the Monument no more, for one thing. She talked about divorcing man and wife like that was normal, for another, and didn't bother with confession nor mass. It weren't her." He pointed his finger at Del Azarchel. "And that fellow there had the poets and tale-spinners spread the story that I was fooled for a season, and he coupled with her, defiling my marriage bed—and I would kill you just for that, you twin-tongued spirochete infecting the descending colon of a donkey with the clap." He turned back to Vigil. "Don't look surprised. I never been fooled by fake Ranias before. Yellow Door tried it, for one."

Del Azarchel said wryly, "For the benefit of future historians who may interview you gentlemen about this hour, the Cowhand is referring to the highly evolved Sarmento Esteban Rolando i Illa d'Or, the Golden of Hermetic Order of the Irenic Ecumenical Conclave of Man, born A.D. 2196, died A.D. 10650, last ghost deleted A.D. 10927; he is the father of the Nymphs, from which the Joys of Charm, the Delectables of 47 Ursae Majoris all their posterity take their form, as well as the Rakshasi of Gliese 31.5 in Tucana and HR 6 in Phoenix. These in turn are the remote ancestors of your Meanderers, Exiles, and Expelled." Del Azarchel hefted the pearl in his hand, his voice growing slower and more solemn as he spoke. When he finished, he looked at the Potentate of Torment. What the gaze meant, none in that chamber could say, since only he saw her eyes. "Eons turn and turn again, and all things pass away, and I would prefer he not be forgotten." He smiled his dazzling smile. "All things, save me, of course."

"Only damn Hermeticist who could shoot worth a damn," said Montrose. "Sarmento, I mean. Nicked me once but good."

"I regularly group better than he did in target shooting and pigeon," said Del Azarchel. "I am eager to compare my skill with the pistol with yours. At times I wonder if these other matters will never cease to distract us."

Vigil said harshly, "Matters like whether your servants will dash this world to bits, as we have vowed to do, with the sword you bestowed, sir?"

Del Azarchel leaned back. "By all means, take your time, come to the correct decision as I have ordained, find a way to find yourself alive to see another dawn! Whatever motions of thoughts or words are needed for his happy event to come to pass, I will wait as patient as a stone until . . . ah, let us say . . . for another twelve minutes and a half before unleashing weapons deadly beyond the conception of mortal or Angel, Potentate or Domination."

Montrose said to Vigil, "Hey. If you use that sword, what exactly does it do?"

Vigil said, "Erases all human records and ghosts out of the Noösphere of Torment and the extended information systems of Iota Draconis. Our libraries, finances, laws, intellectual assistance formulae, ship brains, ecological controls, nanotech regulators, stored personalities, serving angels, everything that is ours, including any records and recorded ancestors. Just the diseases caused by nanotechnology malfunctions of every living spore and mite in the city severed from networked controls would suffice to kill all life on the surface, and the mudra and mandala would be meaningless gestures and lines. Cliometry shows a mutual extermination by the hostile clans and races of Torment within a century and a half."

"So you cannot actually ignite Del Azarchel's groin?"

"It is an informational weapon, more potent than those made of matter."

"Just asking."

"Torment would bring replacements from the buried cities of slumber near the core, and restore a working society to rule this world, and with a working

Stability to maintain contact with far worlds. This happened once before in our history, when the Stability of this world failed and all were slain. From this event, the world takes her sad name."

"Well, only eleven minutes left. Better get a move on. Have you figured what to do?"

Vigil stared at Montrose. "You seem not to care."

"You seem a bright feller. Course I don't care. None of this affects me. I played through all these jigs and antics on account of a Swan asked me to. You guessed my plans?"

Vigil said, "No. Only one clue is missing." He turned. "Torment! You spoke of your fear. Of what are you afraid?"

Torment said, "I fear the long-term consequences of my acts will return to haunt me. In this, I am no different from lesser beings."

"And these consequences are?"

"Triumvirate must know Rania is false: but the Dominion is as far above me as he is above you. To both of us, he is a mind whose workings none can know nor understand. If I keep faith with Rania, then I must oppose Ximen, who is in rebellion against her, and see that his vessel never makes port. But if I keep faith with the true Rania, or with her dream, she who never returned from M3, then I must rebel against the False Rania, and this puts me in the company of Ximen, whereupon I must welcome his vessel, war or no war.

"So, I fear the signals reaching me from other minds in the Empyrean Polity, including those of Powers and Principalities who can overwhelm my thoughts as easily as Foxes bedevil Men. Parts of my mind are swift, and parts are slow, so that to my swift thoughts, a century hence is too remote for worry, but to the slow, the retaliation is immediate. I do not dare defy the Dominion. Triumvirate is for the False Rania and upholds her."

Vigil threw the sword on the table so that it rang like a bell, and slid, and came to rest just in front of Del Azarchel, who looked pleased and surprised.

Vigil said, "My Lords of the Stability, you may escape your penalty if you dissolve and adjourn forever. There will be no further meetings of this body, nor any need of them. The command of the Lighthouse, by terms of a covenant older than our planet, will return to the Starfarer's Guild, whose only living member is seated here before us. The penalty for your disobedience I mitigate: instead of being destroyed at my hands, I leave to the mercy of the *Emancipation*. With this same one stroke, I can avenge my father, not with death, for Torment does not understand death, but with exile."

Montrose said, "Whose exile? Yours? What, you think you are coming with me?"

Vigil shook his head. "Everyone is coming with you, save for myself alone and the Lighthouse crew. I alone am faithful enough to tend the beam of Iota Draconis, the most powerful beam in all the human polity, and center it into your sails no matter how long the wait. I will keep the beam centered even if sixty thousand years must pass by."

"How you know I ain't got a ship of my own?"

"You have been constructing sailcloth on the moon called Hellebore. Who else has motive?"

"A man named Mickey is doing it for me, and a whole race of half-Sylphs he has fathered there, but yeah. I got me a sailworks there."

"But you have no vessel, or else you would have departed erenow. And unless you had some understanding with the Lighthousekeeper and the Aedile and whole Table, you could have neither a launching laser nor the resources to power it and keep it powered. Why is that? As for the Imperator, he is unconcerned with retaliation from Rania or any Angel or Potentate. Why is that? Obviously he has the means to flee from the Empyrean as he did once before, during the legendary era of the White Ship, when mankind set foot in the Sagittarius Arm of the Milky Way, and he flung worlds from star to star during their nova cycles. Obviously again, he cannot use that means, except as a threat. He boasted a moment ago of having weapons beyond any human technology, beyond what any Dominion could know. He means First Order technology. The sole example of this is the *Solitudines Vastae Caelorum*, the ship in which Rania, the False Rania, arrived. But he needs you to command the vessel."

Montrose looked surprised and stared at Del Azarchel. "You got the giant Space Rose? That thing is bigger than the inner solar system!"

Del Azarchel said, "Six minutes left, Lord Hermeticist. And, yes, it turns out the sails are made of something that is neither matter nor energy, a collection of preons and quarks and antigravitons and other exotic particles for which we have no names. But the substance folds up into eleven dimensions quite nicely, like the mythical ship of the Norse gods, which could fit in a man's wallet.

"I have the miracle vessel in tow behind the *Emancipation*," continued Del Azarchel, "hidden from the gaze of Iota Draconis behind my aft push plate. But the fuel is just as exotic and cannot be manufactured with nanotechnology nor with picotechnology.

"The vessel is a bastard. She can be used as a sailing vessel, riding an acceleration beam, or as a self-propelled vessel, using the sails to gather particles from surrounding media as reaction mass. The speeds the False Rania achieved returning to the galaxy from outside it, the speeds needed to reach M3, comes from propulsion, not sailing, but that option, at the moment, is beyond me. So

I mean to sail the Hyades, to the star the Swans call Ain and the Patricians call Coronis, and see if I can bargain for fuel to power the vessel."

Montrose turned back to Vigil and said, "You seem to think he needs me."

Vigil said, "I only deduce from what has happened here. If the Master of the Empyrean could have departed without you, he would have raised sail and found his way to Hyades, and eventually to M3, to recover the woman legend says you both love."

"I love her," said Montrose. "He's just an ass."

Vigil said, "I can see his eyes when you speak. Your death he never ceases to contemplate, and before his mind's eye, he holds the details lovingly. He must need you very badly indeed, for his desire to see you dead is being checked by a stronger desire."

Menelaus turned and looked at Del Azarchel. "I thought your hate for me was the only real, sincere, not-baloney human emotion inside that man-shape make-believe you call your immortal soul, eh, Blackie? What hankering you got in your black heart that is stronger than hate?"

"Curiosity," answered Del Azarchel. "I was a scientist before I was a sovereign, was I not? Not only do I wish to recover my bride and queen and greatest handiwork, but to discover who wrote the Monument, the original Monument—for you and I have seen only a redacted version, an edited and false copy. I want to know the reason and purpose of the message. Only then will I understand who Rania truly is."

Montrose uttered a curse. He turned to Vigil. "You are pretty damned smart. Can you figure what is his reason for needing me? Or why I should help him?"

Vigil said, "No. But I do recall that Princess Rania was born and raised aboard the *Hermetic*, which was controlled by a very simple artificial intelligence, but one which was programmed with certain laws and customs, including such things as inheritance. Is that legend true? She was captain of the ship at a very tender age primarily because the ship's circuits would not obey the mutineers, who slew the first captain, but would obey someone of his bloodline, and she was close enough, as a clone of the first captain, to fool the simple machine. I have an intuition—a level-three intuition, mind you—that Rania, during her solitary return journey, programmed the alien ship according to what she herself knew and thought proper."

Del Azarchel said, "You have struck the mark, Lord Hermeticist." He scowled at Montrose. "The alien vessel is inhabited by an artificial mind which I cannot dislodge, which the False Rania, in perfect impersonation of the true one, for some mad reason taught and programmed with all her ideas, including her notions of marriage. Since you are the ex-husband of Rania, once I persuaded her that the False Rania was false, the ship declared you—as Rania's lord and master—to be sole heir to her property. Rania is rather old-fashioned, even by my standards."

Montrose swore an oath and exclaimed, "Ex-husband?"

Del Azarchel smiled thinly. "Your marriage was annulled by an act of Parliament of the Tellurian Concordat, sometime back in the Third Millennium. I forget which century."

Montrose said, "And the ship's brain does not recognize the legality of an act of Parliament to abridge a sacramental oath, I take it? Not if Rania, false or true or any sort of Rania, was the one who programmed it."

Vigil said, "The alien ship is treating the discovery of the falsehood of Rania as the same as death, then. That is highly significant."

Montrose said, "Why?"

"It means your voyage will not be in vain," said Vigil. "This was not a deception practiced deliberately. Something beyond expectation, beyond even their expectation, happened at M3."

Montrose turned to Del Azarchel. "What now? If this Table don't disband and let you use their Lighthouse, what then? Are you going to draw the sword and threaten this group here to turn the deceleration beam right and proper into your sails?"

The Chronometrician spoke out of turn, cackling, his yard-long antennae swaying. "He has lost the desire and drive. The dark emperor of all mankind realized that he needs this world intact, unmarred by war, filled and overfilled with excess population!"

Vigil nodded. He turned and squinted at the statue of Torment. "You will pass out of range of the most powerful broadcast apparatus of the Empyrean, and so be beyond the retaliation from Triumvirate or any of the Powers of the greater planets. What would be your desire then, O murderess world?"

Torment said, "My thoughts are not like yours, but to be the mother of worlds, and to spread my children farther than even highly favored Tellus, that would be ambition indeed, and the old races that I love, the ancient things crafted by Hermeticists, nothing would be absorbed into the bland uniformity of the proud Patricians then. And you, my accuser, is your vengeance satisfied by exile, eternal exile?"

Vigil said, "If I were not satisfied, I would order my internal creatures to adjust my thoughts until I were. For I am true to my vows and must ever be."

Montrose said, "Wait a sec. A minute ago, I was the only one in the room who knew what was going on. Have you all figured out what my plan is, that quick?"

Vigil said, "I am descended from Narcís D'Aragó and share something of the sense of honor he wished planted in his creatures, the Chimerae, which in turn formed the first templates for the Myrmidons, the Third Human Race. Of the Five Races of Man, only that race, of which I count myself a cousin, traveled to the Second Empyrean in Sagittarius and looked on the legendary beauty and strength of the lost worlds of Aachen and of Avalon, of Trethevy and of Trevena, and Tintagel the Fair, whose name hangs in song like a bell of silver. Do you forget that the man who was master of that Empyrean is here?"

Montrose said, "Sorry. What am I missing?"

Vigil said, "You have sailcloth but no vessel, no launching laser. But you are patient, and you served aboard the *Hermetic*, whose laser was merely an orbital platform, not something drawing power from the core of a sun."

Del Azarchel said, "I had to tear out most of the interior of my vessel, the *Emancipation*—"

"My vessel, you skunk!"

"—to make room for cisterns to hold my migrant population, who are aquatic. The ship is not suited to make the voyage to M3. She may not make it to Ain without an entire redesign from the axis keel outward. I was planning on looting this entire planet to get the provisions I needed, but you seem to have a better plan, Cowhand. I do not know what it is, but I know this youth here deduced it, and that tells me enough. Lord Hermeticist! The orbit of your primary is highly elliptical, is it not? How do you survive the summers hotter than Mercury and atmosphere-freezing winters colder than Pluto?"

Vigil said, "There are hibernation cities at the planetary core, with tombs enough for ten times the surface population. And I seek the return of the Strangers to their proper place. We will stay and man the acceleration beam for all the ages you may require. At long last—finally at long last!—the projects of terraforming Hellebore and Bloodroot, Sainfoin, Mandrake, and Nightshade, and the other wasted moons of Wormwood, which we of Torment abandoned only due to our racial hatred and pride and strife, will no more be neglected." Vigil turned to Montrose. "Have I guessed correctly? You meant to take Hellebore with you."

Montrose nodded. "You got it. It would have been a slow, slow voyage, but I am used to slow. But now here is Blackie, who needs my help to sail my wife's ship. As I recall, the alien ship anchored its sails to her hull with impalpable strings of force. I am assuming they can pass through solid matter without harm, without being noticed. The cities at the core are solid enough to serve as anchors. And I know how big the sails of Rania's supership are. So we just anchor the ship at the core of Torment, erect the sails as large as the orbit of Venus, and the payload to surface area is still so huge it don't matter, not with the amount of power the Iota Draconis beam can put out. We take the whole planet with us."

Vigil said, "It will be but a very short while, decades only, until the *Argosy* arrives with populations of Sinners from 61 Ursae Majoris and Delectables from 47 Ursae Majoris. They will bring enough peoples to overswarm Bloodroot and will complete the terraformation. However tenuously and thin the thread might stretch, it will not be broken, and a next Table of Stability be seated, and ensure the continuation of mankind as a star-faring race, resisting forever the thousand temptations of each planet to make herself isolated, autarchic, and alone."

"Sounds like everyone takes a cut of the kitty, then. Winners all round, eh? But what makes anything think I am willing to make another truce with Blackie? I did it once before and hated every minute. 'Sides, he means to kill me."

"If I may." Del Azarchel leaned forward and pointed a finger at the black surface of the table and then, very lightly, tapped it. "This here is the cliometric design of the future of what happens as Triumvirate, carrying out the plans of False Rania. That is what becomes of the human race. Now, if you can do the calculus just in your head, or perhaps we should ask the Stranger boy, who seems to be something of a math prodigy, if he can do the calculus just in *his* head: What basic cliometric vector is introduced if this world-sized moon, the huge body called Torment, sails grandly across the sky? Suppose we use the mirrored sails of the *Emancipation* to deflect part of the acceleration beam from Iota Draconis into the sails of smaller vessels and send them out laterally to other stars between here and there? Suppose we form a Sixth Sweep all of our own? I understand the slumbering population here outnumbers the living considerably, due to wretched surface conditions. What happens then to the spirit of man?"

But Montrose did not need to do any calculations. He merely laughed. "Well, you might call this world a hellhole, but damn my eyes if it don't remind me of Texas in some ways. If we sail the whole planet with us, we spread the pioneer spirit. And your idea of a medieval hierarchy gets forgotten forever!"

Blackie smiled, and there was a darkness and a cold, cold hatred in his eyes, but he laughed and pretended to smile. "What do I care if the lowest of the low, the mortal creatures, imagine themselves equal to each other? This whole galaxy vindicates my view, for everything is ranked and placed from humblest to highest, Principalities and Hosts, then Dominions, then Dominations, Authorities and Archons, Thrones and Cherubim and Seraphim. Besides, egalitarian societies always eventually break down as a natural aristocracy emerges. Come! If I depart the hundred-lightyear-wide bubble of stars called the Empyrean of Man, then no more wars nor mischief will proceed, not from my hands. Is there anything on Earth, or any world behind us, that you crave more than this?"

Montrose smiled back, and the fire in his deep-set, unwinking, blue-white eyes was just as terrifying to behold, and there was some joy in his toothy grin, the joy of a man who imagines an enemy dead. "It is a deal, then, Blackie!"

Vigil said, "I will keep my faith with you gentlemen, and prevent any interruption of the launching beam."

The Chronometrician cackled, and by the intuition of one of his internal creatures, Vigil knew exactly why Montrose, the Judge of Ages, had agreed once more to sail with Ximen the Black.

Had the Judge of Ages not agreed, Ximen would have gone his separate route, in a vessel of different design and origin, and therefore, risk was too great, in all the endless infinity of space, the appalling abyss of eternity, that the separation between them would grow, one day becoming too vast to overcome; hence they would never again meet; hence never walk onto the field of honor together, that only one would walk away from it.

Vigil Starmanson, the Lord Hermeticist, understood then that there were things as strong as honor, which would keep men chained to their fates for longer, far longer, than a normal human life span. Love was one such thing. Hate was another.

He shivered.

And the Aedile called to adjourn and disband. The Table surface grew dull and plain, and the mind within the metal slept, not to wake again until it was moved to Bloodroot, to empty buildings haunting that world and would once again house the Lords of Cliometry, decades or centuries hence.

The statue of Torment shivered and grew still. What the mind at the core of this planet thought, no one could say, but apparently the world consented to depart human civilization forever, to be torn from her orbit and to be sailed across the stars.

Outside the hall, very dimly, one of Vigil's internal creatures picked up the sound of the bells, still ringing, and voices still singing out a welcome to a ship which now, as it so happened, actually was coming under friendly colors, with gifts and new sciences to bestow, much plenty, and new populations.

So it seemed the song was not to be in vain.

PART TEN

———— · ————

The Seven Daughters of Atlas

1

The Eye of the North

1. Braking Maneuver

A.D. 72260

All worlds when seen from space are breathtakingly beautiful.

Torment in summer was a cratered gemstone of golden sands and green crater lakes, and, in winter, an opal of white on silver as the atmosphere froze, dappled with darker azure zones of crater lakes and frozen volcanic gases.

Now, departed from her orbit forever, she sailed through the endless winter of interstellar space and was hanging in the middle of the spiral of sails sixty million miles in radius, pink at the center, purple at the topgallants.

The average velocity of the planet Torment across the abyss of 194 lightyears separating Eldsich from Ain was roughly one-tenth lightspeed. The acceleration beam contained over one hundred yottajoules per second. The precision with which it was maintained in the sails was admirable. The acceleration beam was aimed by means of thousand-mile-radius Fresnel lenses stationed in a line through the Oort cloud of Iota Draconis. The planetary vessel fell out of the beam due to microscopic Brownian jittering in the aiming lenses only ten percent of the time. Out of the millennium of flight, the time spent in free fall was less than a century, all told.

From time to time, Montrose would wake in his coffin at the world's core and send his mind into such a body as could survive the Plutonian environment. He traveled to the aft pole.

The Scolopendra, housed in armored cybernetic cetacean bodies like living submarines, circled and swam through the liquid nitrogen on high holy days about the monstrous mountain of ultradense artificial materials they had raised directly at the aft pole. The peak reached above the thin atmosphere. A golden space elevator reared beyond sight overhead. Swarms of assembly clouds moved slowly upward over the centuries, infinitesimally shrinking the globe and extensively lengthening the infinite tower of their space elevator, and power gathered from the sail electrostatically charged the great golden length. The assembly cloud drew upon the thinnest and most insubstantial of particles and motes swept up by the world-ship's sails as Torment flew through the infinite night.

As the journey neared completion, the tower's length was such that it was more properly called a tail, for it streamed for millions of miles behind the body of Torment. A small section of sail directed energy against the threadlike length, building up a static electric charge greater than that found in the storm clouds of Jupiter before his fall.

Perched on the hull of the lowest section of the tower, along the insulated miles forming the base, buffeted by the cold and screaming winds of hydrogen and helium, Montrose could look down at the roiling humps and odd waves of liquid oxygen, beneath which was a second ocean, like a rippling sand plain, of liquid nitrogen; and farther down, but clearly seen through the young and pristine ocean layer, he saw the crags and glacier tops and crooked peaks of carbon dioxide ice.

Storm clouds of tiny particles formed an immense spiral sweep of colored turbulence in each direction. Here, at the aft pole, it was always noon, and the laser pinprick of dazzling light from Iota Draconis was directly overhead, and the ever-growing topless tower pointed directly at it. The closer one traveled to the fore hemisphere, the lower sank the brilliant dot of sunlight. At dusk was a terminator belt of eternal storm winds circling the whole planet. The fore hemisphere was shrouded in Plutonian night, and the gases formed a perfect dome of atmospheric ice beneath a thin blanket of liquid helium.

It annoyed Montrose that Ximen del Azarchel always seemed to be awake when he woke. Montrose sooner or later would sense or see him, hanging in a monstrous body sluglike to the vertical lengths of the tower or lounging in one of the many balconies etched into the side armor.

"Don't you ever sleep?" growled Montrose.

"I want to see the nearby stars change position," said Del Azarchel.

"If you expect to see background stars streaming past like telegraph poles seen from a train, that only happens in cartoons."

"You would know, my semiliterate friend!"

"They's too far away for parallax."

"Ah! But I don't speak of parallax! Look there! With eyes like these in bodies like these, one can just barely detect the deflection."

"Funny. I don't see any deflection . . . ," said Montrose. "None at all."

"Nor do I, Cowhand. Nor do I."

A charged object moving through a magnetic field experiences a Lorenz force at right angles to the line of motion and the direction of the field itself. The principle held true, even if the object was the size of a world and the magnetic field was generated by the dynamo of the disk of degenerate matter circling and falling into the supermassive black hole at the galactic core.

Initial measurements of polarized interstellar dust grains showed the galactic magnetosphere surrounding the star Ain was strong enough to allow the worldship to overshoot the target, make a thrustless turn, and then, once Ain was line with Iota Draconis off their fore sail, allow them to reenter the beam Vigil was maintaining and slow sufficiently to match speed and metric with Ain.

They should have started a slow but measurable turn at this point.

"What the pox is going on, Blackie?"

"The magnetic interaction with the galactic field is insufficient."

"You mean something or someone at Ain reached out and made the whole galactic magnetic field in this area weaker? So that we could not slow ourselves and stop by and say hello?"

"Check my calculations if you doubt me."

"Thanks, I will." A moment later: "Damnation and canker sores. You are right again."

"As ever. You might also look over my calculations for using a loop of superconductor to ionize the interstellar medium and convert our momentum to heat. For that is the only other method available to us to lower our velocity, assuming no external aid."

"I don't need to look. Mass of a world, moving at one-tenth lightspeed? The heat would be like kissing a nova."

"Aptly put. And am I right that we have but one course of action here?"

"Reverse the polarity on the tower to bring us back into a straight-line shot with Ain."

"Indeed."

"Then, pick the biggest damn object in the system—gas giant, Dyson sphere, whatever we can find—and aim right at it. Our wee tiny planet is only half the mass of Earth, but if we smite the center of their most densely populated area at one-tenth lightspeed, I reckon we can do some damage. About equivalent to a twenty-nine zettaton explosion of TNT, or the total energy output of Deneb each second. Even macroscale structures in the outer system could not survive, made of exotic matter or not."

Blackie seemed pleased. "And to think how petty and inferior minds once complained about the infinitesimal amounts of energy I released burning an insignificant city off the globe, or two, or ten! No one now recalls the names of those cities, or the land masses on which they sat!"

Montrose rattled off the names of the cities, which he had, of course, memorized.

"Be that as it may," said Blackie graciously, "in this case, you are not suggesting mercy, are you?"

"It's them or us," snarled Montrose. "And *this* is the star system, Ain. These are the very folk that sicced Asmodel on us. Remember him? Then Cahetel, then Shcachlil the Salamander, then Lamathon the Unkinder Twin, and finally, the worst of the worst, when Rania was getting close, and they stopped caring about any long-term prospects, they sent Achaiah. They sent the Beast. Hell, I remember how many innocent millions died each time."

"So you say wipe them all out and die in the process?"

"You gotta pay the devil when his hellish bill comes due. Fair's fair."

"It is at times like this that I recall why I admire you, Cowhand. You are as bloodthirsty as I am. I, ah, take it you are convinced this unexpected decrease in the local interstellar magnetic field is a deliberate phenomenon, an attempt to prevent us from making starfall? We can, after all, manipulate the smallest part of a topgallant to form a lateral beam, and send out one-way probes, or, with slightly more ingenuity and effort, dispatch the *Emancipation* like a side boat, and test the galactic magnetosphere to each side of us, and see if the effect is natural."

"What's it matter? Natural or not, we now got no way to stop our momentum, unless the Principality at Ain cooperates and either puts back a magnetic field or hoists a deceleration laser."

"So you say threaten them with ramming if they do not cooperate?"

"Hey. You read the Monument same as me. They got rules about cooperation and collaboration. The Ain Principality has to stop us, and then we owe them."

"Ah! We must pay the cost of the beam we will threaten them into directing at us, after all, and, as you say, their Cold Equations cover this eventuality. Such was my thought. So you agree to sell this world into indentured servitude . . . ?"

Montrose pondered for at least a century before he answered.

"Ain't there no damn way to escape these star monsters and their damned system of serfdom and slavery? What gives?"

"Space is cruel, my friend," mused Del Azarchel. "It is very large and very cruel."

"The body you got on ain't got no face, but I can tell you are smiling."

"Well. Space reminds me of—"

"Don't say it."

"—me!"

"Space is smaller than your damned ego, Blackie."

"I will take that as a compliment. Shall we get on with our astrocide? Stellarcide? Is there a word for the willful destruction of a whole solar system?"

2. Collision Vector

A.D. 72360 TO 73040

Torment, and the one fraction of her population awake and thawed in her many buried cities and habitats, waited and watched with growing anxiety as no change appeared in the magnetic field and no beam came.

The world-ship rotated in preparation for the nonexistent deceleration beam so that her sails were behind her. The endless tower that had been the tail of Torment now reached ahead, a bowsprit longer than the radius of the orbit of Mercury. At the tip of this tower was the tiny point of approaching Ain, growing brighter as years turned into centuries, orange as a coal in a grate.

The giant had a tiny companion star roughly two lightyears away, and taking at least half a million years to orbit each other.

The star Ain itself was an orange-red globe of simply titanic size, ninety times brighter than Sol and burning helium at its core. There were many clues that some sort of industrial structures and coherent energy patterns existed in the core and along the surface of the star, but what these engineering elements were meant to do, even Torment could not guess.

There was a third body in the system. This was a sphere larger than a gas giant, orbiting Ain in an orbit as eccentric as that of Wormwood, now a memory far behind them. The body itself was hidden in massive clouds, black as ink, an opaque sphere extending in each direction some eighty thousand miles. From the energy signals and behavior patterns, it was clear the black clouds were intelligent: cognitive matter, either nanotechnology assemblers or something finer. Oddly, this supermassive gas giant was the only exoplanet the astronomers could detect throughout the Hyades Cluster. The other stars were barren.

That world was the target. Had their velocities been similar, so large a body could have absorbed Torment with no more disturbance than a stone cast into a pond. A few ripples in the cloud layer might pass, and then, nothing. But at one-tenth lightspeed, the disturbance would be akin to a bullet passing into a man, or, more to the point, a bullet passing into a powder keg, since every particle would be liberated in a wash of total conversion if the world did not slow to a stop.

Years passed, and the star system with its single massive planet grew ever closer, their mutual speed undiminished. The invisible point which it was not possible to arrest the motion of the Torment without destroying the planet or the sail array also grew ever closer.

Astronomers could see more of the system. There was no ringworld or strandworld circling the star, but there were clouds of tree-shaped macroscale structures, forming a set of four distinct rings around the star. Two rings were circular, an inner and an outer, both in the orbital plane of the superjovian; one ring was oval, with the primary and superjovian at its focal points; the remaining cloud was not a ring at all but a hyperbolic sweep, a smear of azure and cerulean, sapphire and cobalt forests that looped around Ain like a vast open rainbow.

These macroscale structures looked like leafless trees, or nerve cells, or the skeletons of parasols. Each structure consisted of a long trunk pointing away from the sun and three equally spaced branches pointing toward, and each branch was tipped with three smaller branches, and those smaller branches in turn tipped with three smaller yet, and so on. Some of the dendrite structures were orbiting in pairs, triads, rings, or complex dances of rings within rings, waltzing epicycles, and braids of orbits were woven in and out of each other in an inhuman complexity of the ring structures.

The average tree-shaped structure was some twenty-five thousand miles long, more than twice the length of a diameter piercing the Earth, or nearly two-thirds such a line drawn through Neptune. These structures were the height of worlds, but not the volume. The cylindrical trunks were at most nine hundred miles in diameter.

It was from these structures that the only sign of intelligent activity or energy use came: radio pulses, the infrared shadows of some form of biological or mechanical action passing from branches to trunk, or bursts of neutrinos.

Only about one in a hundred of these countless dendrites displayed these actions.

The rest were as still and silent as trees in a winter graveyard, merely orbiting the great orange star.

There came a period where a second planet was seen in the system. It was an ice giant, the size and composition of Neptune, and it followed that belt or band of dendrite bodies forming a hyperbola around Ain.

The giant world came out of the interstellar space from the direction of Iota Tauri, a white dwarf star and an outlying member of the Hyades Cluster. For forty-five years, it sailed along a hyperbolic orbit, passed like a slingshot around the sun.

During a few hours at perihelion, the ice giant came to life. Torment could detect activity, flares of radiation, tiny packages of matter moving at high speed leaving the atmosphere. Energy emissions from the sun flashed into the thawed atmosphere. In opposition, on the far side of the star system, the black super-jovian body stirred into life as inky black clouds leaped into ever higher orbits; a red dot of immense heat was detected at the core of the body whenever the black clouds parted for a moment. The neutrino count detected by receivers on the sail of Torment registered a high number of encounters during this period.

Meanwhile, the dendrite objects opened fire on the ice giant, sending out white-hot needles of material from their forward arms toward the Neptunian body. Whether this was an act of war or of commerce was unclear. Perhaps it was a method of delivering material rapidly to the gas giant's atmosphere.

The solar system lapsed into silence after about ten hours of activity. The black superjovian grew quiescent, and the neutrino count dropped.

The ice giant was visible for another forty-five years heading outward again, still following the path of the dendrite cloud. It was lost to sight heading in the direction a pulsating variable star called V1362 Orionis, another member of the Hyades Cluster.

And still, there was no sign of any reaction from whatever form of intelligence—Principality or Virtue or Host—ruling this star system, to the threat posed by the vast speed of Torment.

The invisible point of no return was passed, and still there was no sign.

Once and twice and thrice during these years, increasingly desperate attempts were made to thaw Montrose and discover his opinion and advice. In annoyance, he told whoever woke him, man or machine, to relax.

"They is playing chicken with us, is all." He snorted. "Let me sleep, you leprous scabnails! I don't give a damn what your problem is. Solve it without me."

An agent speaking for Torment said, "But we are passed the point where a laser from the sun could decelerate us safely, sir!"

"These damn things are like machines. They ain't got no souls. They are controlled by their equations. The equations say they have to bring us to a halt. And they don't give a damn neither."

"We are on collision course for the superjovian body! If you are wrong—"

"Damn your eyes! If I were wrong on a simple thing like this, I would have been dead before your race was a twinkle in the eye of a scabby Hermeticist, you asinine sumpsuckler! Now shut your yap. I have had a long, hard, wearisome life, and I get to sleep the sleep of the just! Well, hmm, maybe not that. At least I can sleep the sleep of the *I don't give a damn*."

On he slumbered. On they sped toward collision.

3. Concubine Vector

A.D. 73723

Menelaus woke and saw the year, and before he opened his biological eyes, he examined the immediate environment of the hermit's cell he had fashioned for himself in a bubble of metal near the core of the planet. Someone had disarranged certain of the mementos and coin collections he had carefully placed on the shelves before entering slumber, and the flag of Texas was hanging from one tack, a triangle of fabric drooping down in defeat. The coffeepot was cold, as if the automatic circuit had forgotten to prepare for his waking.

His glass pistols were missing, a fact he found more disturbing and disorienting than he could account for.

Through remote instruments he saw the frozen sea, and a sky that was half a dome of cold stars, and half a dome of vast pink sails like rose petals filling all space between zenith and horizon.

The cell now included a wardrobe of bodies into which his brain information could be downloaded. After much hesitation, he selected to be reincarnated as a Patrician.

Waking into a Patrician brain was like stepping into a stream of shockingly cold ice water. The neural arrangement seamlessly merged high-speed inner thoughts at the picotechnology level with his nanotechnological and biological architecture so that not only was each nerve cell working to keep his thoughts coordinated, but the chemicals in each cell stored additional information and the electron shells of each fluorine atom in those molecules as well. The normal confusion, self-deception, memory stalls, and waiting times of multi-level consciousness was minimized by the unique architecture or eliminated entirely.

He also decided to wear the traditional garb of the Patricians. His dress consisted of anointing himself with a gel of aurum vitae, the same substance of which Myrmidon flesh was made, which coated and melded to his skin, giving him the characteristic golden hue of the Patrician race; and over that he threw the severe white mantle of the Fifth Men.

With his new brain and its new outlook, he understood the reason for Patrician simplicity of dress: the intuitive and pattern-recognition side of his consciousness was more active in this neural structure, making it easier to see symbols and symbolic relations. While, on the one hand, this allowed for him to think in three new shorthand neural encoding systems, as well as in his old human system and four other long-term and more elaborate neural languages, on the other hand, the rapid-fire method of seeing symbols and patterns made him more easily distracted by things like designs and colors in clothing and tempted him to see meanings where there were none.

The body itself was more compact and complex than a Swiss Army knife, able to adapt to nearly any surroundings. He was not surprised at his ability to exit his cell, soar up a depth-train chimney through the mantle and crust, swim through the liquid oxygen hydrosphere, fly through the cold helium atmosphere, and rocket through the upper stratosphere. The aurum altered with each environment, as did specialized organs inside his new body, inflating or contracting as need be. The Patricians had the ability to place any unused organ into its own miniature slumber, pale white buds coated in frost, and to reroute any vital functions to the analogous organ thawed and put into use.

The white mantle formed an energy parachute to allow him to ride a convenient heavy particle fountain issuing from the polar supermountain of the planet like a bowsprit. Up and up he rose. He eventually reached the position in low Torment orbit where the world's magnetic fields had been warped into a vacuole of electromagnetic silence. All the radio noise and energy discharges from the buried cities of slumberers at the core of the planet, or from flotillas of armored Scolopendra, faded into inaudibility as he penetrated the vacuole.

Here was an orb of ice, small as one of the moons of Mars. The globe of Torment filled a third of the sky, rising and falling once an hour as the moonlet rotated. Torment was white as Pluto beneath her winter shroud, and her circular crater lakes were dapples of dark purple.

Standing upright on a low hillock of snow, like a spear driven into a rock, was a narrow column of blue-green material, neither metal nor ceramic nor any other substance Montrose could name. It was roughly thirty feet tall. From the top lifted three smaller branches of the same material, perhaps nine feet long, and from each of the ends of these smaller branches three wands issued; and each wand had three spokes, and each spoke had three twigs, and each twig had three hairs, and so on. With his new, Patrician eyes, Montrose could see the pattern recurring, ever small and smaller, down to the molecular level.

The tiniest of the end hairs were plucking particles out of the surrounding near-vacuum and combining them into molecules, and the molecules into crystals. These crystals were fed into tubules leading into the spearhead of the object. Looking down and through the layers of the transparent ice moon to the other hemisphere, Montrose saw three other branched spears like this one, impaled into the substance of the ice moon, each equidistant from the others like the points on a caltrop.

Beneath this dendrite, seated on a chair made of human bones, was a living image of Torment, wearing a bridal dress and veil, and in her hands, a bouquet of septfoil flowers.

Torment had set, and the vast pale light from the world was shining upward upon the throned figure as smoky beams of light seeped through the transparent ground.

Montrose stood staring at her for a moment, rapidly turning off and on various internal senses and several nervous systems to examine his new organs. Some of them seemed to control powerful electric charges and nucleonic forces, nanotechnological and picotechnological vectors and assemblers. He was looking to see which could do the most damage in the least amount of time. He raised his golden hands, an intolerable brightness trembling between his fingers, calculating whether it would be easier to direct the energy in a straight beam, cutting through the moonlet crust, or to curve the beam around the close horizon.

Torment waited, one eyebrow raised in a skeptical arch. She spoke by means of a directed energy beam into receiving cells in the auditory sections of his Patrician nervous system. "You have expensive habits."

After some fumbling, he found a set of cells in his cortex that could impose a pattern on a focused magnetic flux he could establish passing between the two of them. "Meaning what?"

"Meaning you will be fined a monetary amount equivalent to the labor costs of manufacturing this remote unit, if you destroy it. Better just to slap this unit in the face, if it is necessary to reduce your animalistic tensions."

"I don't slap women."

"And I do not crush insects. Fortunate for you. Do you see the star system receding behind us? Principality of Ain is there as well as here, watching, measuring, and observing us. It would be better to be on our best behavior."

"Behind—!" Montrose felt his anger drain away. He grounded the energy building up in his fingers against his mantle and wiped the sparks absent-mindedly against his golden thigh, swearing at the unexpected pain.

His new Patrician eyes could gather information from a number of sources or even use the sail of the *Solitudines* as a baseline. The planet Torment had passed through the Ain system without striking the superjovian. At present, there seemed to be two gas giants in the system, a bright one and a dark. The dark giant was the inky-black atmosphere of the superjovian, which had re-moved itself from the planet, solidified into a black sphere, and assumed orbit about it; or, rather, the two were orbiting about a common center.

The gas cloud, to judge from the degree of light distortion of stars it oc-cluded, had more mass than could be accounted for by its volume and density. There was also indirect evidence of an immense heat source at the core of the black giant: an engine warping space.

Montrose said, "Life is poxy mocking me. First, I don't recall deciding to come up here. Second, I see that they have the technology to create gravity out of nothing."

"Not out of nothing," came the cool, soft voice of Torment. "The star Ain lost gravitational mass in equal amount to what the artificial gas giant gained: the star entered an excited state when the balance between the reaction pressure and gravity was thrown off. How the gravitational mass was transferred between the two points is unclear, particular since the volume and density remained the same; but changes in the Higgs boson properties detected throughout the sys-tem took place at the time of the near miss, changes that were suggestive of an interaction between gravitons across macroscopic distances."

Montrose said, "What? Something that takes the gravity particles gener-ated in one spot in the universe and yanks them hither and yon to come out at another? That cannot be possible."

"You forget that the phenomenon or entity we call Cahetel displayed a similar ability to warp spacetime. This is the seat of power from which Cahetel came."

"Missing a target big as a gas giant takes some doing. You did not correct the aim? What happened? Self-preservation instinct take over?"

"I have had no desire to live since the day, before even I was self-aware, when my terraforming and pantropic machines, who inhabited the world be-fore mankind, witnessed the genocide of the second generational deracination ship by the descendants of the first, attempted to resurrect the slain race from recordings and samples, and failed. Look at the distribution patterns of dust and energetic particles in the Ain system, and measure the magnetic field strengths."

With his new eyes, Montrose examined the local area to about half a light-year distant and realized how the near miss must have played out.

The light from the star Ain had simply been blocked by black inky clouds maneuvered to orbits between Ain and the incoming world-ship, leaving the sails with no light pressure to use. And there was insufficient magnetic strength in the system to tack.

With no way to maneuver, the planet Torment passed through what had been exact dead center of the gas giant, which was now the gravitational center of the two giant planets: and there just so happened to be no physical object there at the time. There had been minor damage to Torment from the tidal effects. The speed gained when falling into the immense gravity well was lost again as Torment receded from the double planet against the pull of gravity.

Montrose looked over the mind-dazing immensity of the sails of the *Solitudines Vastae Caelorum*. There were twin puncture holes somewhere the size of a two supergiant worlds, but the scale defeated even his miraculous new powers of vision. The diameter of a superjovian would not even be a pinprick to a sheet of ultrafine material wide as the orbit of Venus.

Montrose said, "You and I worked together for a long time. I helped you create a world where all the old memories of the past could be kept alive. But you were thinking of selling yourself to the Hyades since—well, since when? Since the hour you figured out my Rania never came back from M3?"

Torment did not answer directly, but spoke in a casual, almost absentminded, tone. "There is a vast sail array positioned six hundred AU fore of us. The Principality of Ain would not have maneuvered the array save that they will offer to decelerate us and even to impart acceleration back toward Ain. The superjovian orbit is not only similar to that of Wormwood of Iota Draconis, upon dissolution of the black gravitic body back into a cloud cover, the orbit will be identical, allowing Torment to have precisely the same seasonal variations of precisely the same periods as we enjoyed back home. What does that suggest?"

Montrose said, "It suggests their damned Concubine Vector: the allowable amount of scabby clapmembered-up-your-hinderparts anyone in a strong position can shove up into those in a weak position. The Cold Equations show that they are still legally required to halt us and grant us port. But there is some fine print in the Monument you and me never saw, or never saw the implications to, is that it?"

"As you predicted, the Principality governing this solar system is required to spend the energy to bring us to port safely. However, Ain has elected to spend considerably more energy that is strictly necessary, in order to place us into an indentured servitude much longer than you calculated. The arrangement of bodies in this solar system make that clear. We must pay for the gravitational engine operations, the cost to restore the superjovian to its previous condition, the cost to create a remote deceleration beam station six hundred AU away, and so on."

"Why go to so much trouble? Build a birdcage just to suit you, and then lure us into it?"

The throned figure shook her veiled head. "That, Ain has not revealed."

"But you have a guess?"

"Think you so, mortal man? Observe the nearest of yonder parasol-shaped memory habitats. Each of the macroscale dendrite structures in orbit around the star has a mental carrying capacity equal to my own. Look more closely at what seem to be four asteroid rings, or at what seem to be gas clouds. Your eyes should be able to resolve the images. The same dendrite shapes also exist as forty-kilometer-long vehicles, nine-centimeter-long tools, and as nanoscopic molecular assemblers. Every single last scrap of rust and rock and ice in this star system has been sophotransmogrified. Were you impressed at seeing that Sol is now a system with five hundred worlds? It is a circle of mud huts surrounding a single fire pit compared to this. The intellectual volume of the Ain System taken as a whole is in the five billion range, whereas mine is in the five hundred thousand range."

A figure in a rotund suit of armor came suddenly over the too-near horizon of the miniature moonlet. The boot soles were coated with a layer of material that changed state with every step, solidifying into glue when the boot made contact with the surface to anchor the walker in place, then liquefying again to release the rear foot for its next step. The midsection of the armor was round like a ball, and the helmet was topped with a conical section like a dunce cap. There was no faceplate, of course, merely a cluster of pinpoint cameras on the front of the solid helm.

"Howdy. What are you going here?" Montrose had to send a signal on several bands and got no response. Then he tried sending the words as small seismic vibrations through the ice moonlet surface into the approaching figure's boots. The boots were evidently smart enough to recognize the wave-patterns and transform them into something audible inside the suit.

The reply came by shortwave radio: "How did you know it was me?"

"Who else but Mickey the Witch would put a pointed hat on a space suit?"

"I am Mickey the Sacredote now. This is the miter of my bishopric. I have a flock and everything. Mostly they are twenty generations of my own children, but still. You've been asleep six hundred years."

"Kept asleep, you mean. Since when do bishops get married? And I can't imagine you not as a Witch."

Mickey turned his gauntlets' palms toward each other and spread his armored fingers as if grasping an invisible ball, which was the spaceman's sign showing nonchalance, a nonemergency condition. "The Sacerdotes have a lot more rites and rituals than we ever did, and, with no disrespect meant to my ancestors, they make a lot more sense. I mean, I always did used to wonder why Zeus was supposed to punish lawbreakers, him being an adulterer and a parricide and all. And seeing Earth and all the other planets thronging the solar system messed up my astrology something awful, and four of the nine sacred trees to which I used to sacrifice animals are all extinct. Two of those animals I sacrificed are extinct as well, and one of them was uplifted into sapience. Witchcraft is not very portable to other eons."

"And Bible-thumping is?"

"You'd be surprised at the number of circumstances Roman law, Greek philosophy, and Jewish mysticism can find accommodating. Just knowing that Ain is my brother, the child of the same God who made me, I find to be quite a source of courage when my courage runs dry. A Witch stranded as I am in this alien star system would be required to assume that the Hyades were made and ruled by Hyades gods, masked and eyeless Demhe, Cassilda dressed in yellow tatters, or unholiest Yhtill, who once were served and worshiped in lost Carcosa on the misty shores of Lake Hali where black stars rise. How, then, could I know the rules of right and wrong, logic and illogic, were the same for me as for the Principality of Ain? If the gods were different, how could our nature be the same? How could I know that the little gods of wind and hill, howe and rill, would still protect me? There is no wind here, and Mount Olympus is sunk beneath the sea."

"You gave up all your mumbo jumbo? You'll hardly be the same man."

"Even had Trey not forced my conversion, it was needed for this journey."

"How so?"

"It is no coincidence that the one and only culture in history back on the home world that made a habit of discovering and exploring the unknown was not pagan. Who would dare venture into new regions and worlds of mystery and wonder, enigma and fear, save he knows which god rules there? Achelous of the silver-swirling river is a mighty god, but his reach extends no farther than Aetolia and Acarnania. That is not true of the Wounded God whose flesh each Sabbath I consume, whose reach is boundless. Here, in this horribly alien system, with its hidden gas giants and hollow suns, and leafless trees for worlds, my cruel and little pagan gods are left far behind in all senses of the word."

Mickey passed to him a small, flat package. It was a case containing his glass railgun pistols. "I did not want you to shoot anyone before I had a chance to talk to you. Don't be mad at Torment for keeping you asleep. I am the one who by my potent enchantments—ah, I mean, by my prayers, of course— persuaded her to keep you under."

"*You?* How?"

"I prayed a rosary to each of the Seven Sleepers of Ephesus, starting with the noble youth Exacostodianos; followed by a novena to Saint Elijah and to Saint Christina the Astonishing, whose sway over these matters is uncontested."

"Hm, maybe you ain't as changed as much as I thought. No, I meant, how did you get something as smart as her to listen to you? Or to anyone of our level of smarts?"

"Same reason a hunter takes along a dog when he hunts. I can see things she can't, despite all her superhuman intelligence."

Torment said, "There is more to it than that. When compared with Ain, your friend Mictlanagualzin occupies the same intellectual topology as I do, or any of my servants, archangels, angels, ghosts. Moreover, he possesses an uncanny ability to guess Epsilon Tauri behavior patterns."

Montrose said, "So why did you and she pox with my alarm clock, Mickey, and keep real-world info out of my dreams as I slumbered?"

Mickey said, "Once it was clear that Ain meant to have us pass the point of no return, the zero point after which no deceleration beam in the system could halt us safely, the result seemed obvious. Ain was not going to break the Cold Equations, right? So there had to be a deceleration beam stationed outside the system, or a mirror array to dogleg one, or something. And Ain is the star from which all the Virtues that ever interacted with the human race originated, all except one— Nahalon in the Fourth Sweep. So this star both has the most experience with mankind and the most interest in keeping us indentured. Ain must have been heartbroken when Rania returned and mankind was vindicated. The Beast, that last ruling Virtue to come out of Ain and alter the history of mankind, it must have seen Rania on the way home and known she had been successful on her mission, since she was sailing in a vessel more advanced than anything the whole Hyades Cluster could produce. So what did the Beast do, before it left?"

Montrose said, "It populated worlds far from Sol but closer to target systems the Hyades wanted us to be able to visit or colonize and gave Iota Draconis that famous superpowerful launch laser. But Iota Draconis is farther from
Ain than Sol is, by some ninety-three lightyears. We are on the wrong side of
the celestial globe. So are all the other worlds of the Petty Sweep. If anything,
Ain was trying to colonize worlds with human civilizations far away from
it . . ." He frowned. "It wants to spread us around."

Torment said, "There is nothing in the Cold Equations to explain this."

Mickey said, "Ain clearly has some great interest in our race, an interest
above and outside the Cold Equations, and has had since the advent of Asmodel. So Ain went to a great deal of trouble to get one planet full of humans,
including the only remaining original primitive humans in existence."

Montrose said, "Meaning me and Blackie?"

Torment said softly, "Montrose is unaware of the signals we have received
from the stars we fled."

Montrose said, "Let me guess. Everyone back home is a Patrician now, and
the eighty earths of the sixty-nine human stars have fallen into a long somno-
lence, just as the False Rania predicted and wanted."

Mickey said, "A good guess, but wrong on two counts. First, not everyone
is a Patrician. The planets colonized by the Beast—namely, Feast of Stephen,
Perioecium, Terra Pericolosa, Aerecura, and the World of Willows and Flowers
are still inhabited by the variations of the races of Loricates, Myrmidons, Vampires, Overlords, and Sworns, and the capital world of Iota Draconis, named
Bloodroot, remains in the hands of the Strangermen, who bribed the incoming
Argives with the moon called Nightshade, whose crystals ring with strange
music in the many magnetic fields of Wormwood. These last two worlds were
both elevated to potentate status in record time, as were the other planets in the
rosette of Vindemiatrix, the pilgrim worlds of Saint Agnes and Saint Wenceslaus. Something the Beast did when it selected the Petty Sweep planets to
colonize keeps the ancient vitality of the human race alive."

Montrose was appalled. "Sounds like the polity of man is a corpse, but with
the outer parts, the hair and the fingernails, still growing."

"And I think this world, Torment, is meant by Ain to be the seed of a new
human polity."

"Why?"

Mickey said, "Instead of explaining that, take a moment to cool your anger,
and let me make one more prediction: I predict the Principality of Ain will be
ready, no, will be eager to talk to us, and in as clear a fashion as possible. It will

take the time and trouble to study our language and our forms of thought and make itself clear. That is what his logic diamond is for."

Montrose looked down and picked up his feet. He floated about a yard high above the surface, peering at the soles of his sandals nervously. "This is Ain thinking-crystal?"

Then he realized he had lost his channel to Mickey, and he used one of his newfound Patrician energy-manipulation organs to pull his himself back down to the surface and magnetically anchor his feet there.

Torment said, "Yes. This moonlet is being formulated from our exosphere material. It has been growing here for some time. Not long ago, this location was nothing but the four dendrite mechanisms touching their tips together. The gathered and transformed material has been growing between the tips, forcing them apart. I assume Ain created this area of electromagnetic silence to aid in the reception of signals from the home Principality."

Montrose peered at the figure representing Torment more closely. The symbolism of her dress and throne was clear to his new pattern-seeking Patrician brain. The bridal gown represented her willingness to assume orbit around Ain and become a satellite of Epsilon Tauri, a member henceforth of the Hyades polity rather than the human one. The throne of bones represented the cost in human lifetimes spent to pay back the debt incurred by Torment and her subject populations. In other words, the cost of slowing Torment and navigating her to an orbit optimal for his surface life would be measured in so many lifetimes that it was as if she sat on a heap of lives and lifetimes all consumed.

Montrose felt a stab of guilt. How many of these events had been his doing? What percent of blame fell at his feet? Whatever that percent, it was measured in centuries and millennia of servitude imposed on his fellow man, servitude that Rania had arranged mankind to escape, or, to be more exact, this was servitude the advent of the False Rania had arranged mankind to seem to escape. And this was servitude which Montrose had arranged the world of Torment to reenter.

With his new brain, he could see other patterns in the events leading to this moment, and other symbols in the scene. The chalice in her hand was a stirrup cup. The snakes represented a bitterness she could drink but survive. He said, "You mean to send me and Blackie onward, the two of us, by ourselves."

Torment said, "That will be part of our price, yes. Otherwise there will be no agreement. We will continue into the void and perish, and the Principality of Ain will be fined or punished by their superiors."

Mickey said, "Ain is afraid to try to keep the supership of Rania for themselves.

My guess is, had Ain meant to keep it, or buy it from us, we would have been decelerated at a reasonable time and rate and given a hero's welcome. Torment tells me the Cold Equations have several vectors where one of Ain's superiors would simply pluck such a covet-worthy prize out of their little hands. An intelligent star system is still a very, very minor little elf in a big, bad galaxy filled with dragons and sorcerer-kings with iron scepters."

Torment said to Mickey, "Ask this man you once worshiped as a demigod why he approached this ice moon in such anger and why he raised his hand against me."

Mickey said, "Sorry. What happened before I walked up? Did you offend the goddess? Always a bad policy to tick off someone you and your household, and your whole country, are standing on top of, you know."

Montrose said, "I was plenty mad, and she knows why."

Mickey said, "I don't. I was the one who enchanted your alarm clock to sleep. I thought you would be filled with grief at the suffering your, ah, miscalculation of the Cold Equations caused. So I wanted to spare you as much—"

"I don't remember deciding to come up here," said Montrose.

"Eh?"

Montrose said, "That is why I am mad. Because I do not recollect ever deciding to fly up into low orbit; nor do I recollect deciding to visit this orbiting iceberg that was not here when I went to sleep. I woke up, spent quite a while deciding what body to put on, turned into a Patrician, and came out of a little set of pods growing on vines in one of the buried cities. Then I took a high-speed pressurized tube up through the crust to the bed of the layered oceans of liquid atmosphere, looked up with my magic new eyeballs, and came straight here to this little snowball of a moonlet. Which turns out to be made of logic diamond. And here was Torment in her remote-control puppet body waiting. See? She did something to my mind to make me come here without me realizing it."

Torment said, "Not I. It was done with far more fineness and nicety than I could ever manage. And, in any case, I still hold myself to be obligated not to meddle with human affairs, since, in the eyes of the law, and in the eyes of my own conscience, I am still bound by the ruling made by Triumvirate, at least for now. Once I wed Ain and become one of his harem of worlds, his laws will govern me. But look!" She raised a slender, pale finger and pointed. "Your dark shadow and spiritual twin approaches. He is more cautious than you, or perhaps more self-aware, and more quickly realized the extent and depth of the manipulation that enchants and summons him. He pauses, he hesitates, he deliberates! His curiosity wars with his pride. Perhaps he will fall in wrath back to the surface, willing to forgo this high consultation that he might later boast he was not summoned by a glamour so easily as you."

It seemed curiosity was a greater force in him after all, for just then, like a vast black bat, came Del Azarchel winging low over the close horizon. His gold Patrician-style body was strikingly handsome against the coal-black mantle he had donned. With a seemingly effortless mastery of the delicate balancing of propulsive and attractive fields, he came to a perfect halt half an inch from the surface and merely lowered his sandal toes to the surface.

Unlike Menelaus, he did not fumble when establishing a field to carry his communication signals. "You called, madam? I would have come at a gentler invitation. Know that I am offended by your casual presumption on the sovereign integrity of my mind. My vengeance—"

She said, "Your vengeance means exactly nothing. Once you and your bright shadow and spiritual twin are vanished from this domination and realm, taking your paired monomania with you, all my calculations will be returned to normal levels, and the freakish unknowns you continue unknowingly to intrude into history with vanish with you."

Montrose said, "'Lo, Blackie. Happened to you, too, huh?"

He spread his hands. "It was so subtly done that even now I am not certain. Perhaps it is but airy whim and a coincidence that I am come! And yet here I find you and my oldest servant—now, ironically, serving the Church which is the only human institution older than I."

"Not human," said Mickey.

Montrose said, "Creepy, ain't it? Something called us here. I don't find no broken memory chains, no record of a break in any damn firewall, no nothing. That means . . ." He paused, frowning. "That means the suggestion was put into my head through something in the environment."

Del Azarchel said, "Such as what? Tiny clues carefully calculated to play off buried memories? Or the smallest possible neural energy pressures adding and subtracting the tiniest bit from memory flows or associational chains without breaking them?"

Mickey said, "I have noticed in myself that often some smallest thing, which spine of which book my eye first falls on when I enter a library, or the pattern of omens seen in birds, will remind me of some memory or another, and provoke one thought or another. Anyone able to know beforehand how each stray thought of mine might fall out for each stimulus could arrange books or birds or whatever else was needed—a burp of indigestion, an invisible bump in the road—to provoke my thoughts into the predicted path and do all this without once manipulating the actual brain substance itself."

Montrose said, "No one knows me that well, not even me."

Del Azarchel said, "If some higher supremacy has solved the fundamental problem of chaos mathematics, so that the unexpected results of complex problems could indeed be anticipated with this degree of precision—"

Torment said, "Gentlemen, what you are describing is not a new branch of mathematics but a new way of envisioning reality in its cosmic unity. Such an ability is incomprehensible. How would it circumvent Heisenberg limits on certainty of particle position and mass? How would it avoid categorical paradoxes of determinism and volition?"

Mickey said, "Then how do you account for the Judge of Ages and the Master of the Empyrean being led here, each against his will, neither with his knowledge?"

Torment said, "I do not account for it. Where there are no data, there can be no theory."

Mickey said, "You called me, great goddess. How is this not your doing?"

Torment said, "I am only a Potentate. I possess no such ability. I constructed this remote body in this location once I understood it to be the destination of the summons calling these two men here. Your bodies are slow and gross, whereas I am swift and subtle, so I was here hours in advance. However, I can provoke no reaction from the emissary. It wants to talk to you."

The three men stood (or, rather, hovered with their boots or sandals anchored) in silence a moment, each wrestling with the impossible and obvious conclusion that Ain had called them here.

Montrose said slowly, "You know, come to think of it, I do not remember why I decided to download my brain into a Patrician body . . ." And he turned certain specialized sense organs in his nervous system toward the core of the moonlet.

His senses were suddenly jarred into activity, as were the pattern-recognition system, linguistic and chemical, in his multitiered nervous system. It was like staring into a suddenly unhooded lantern.

4. Communication Splendor

With his Patrician senses, Menelaus Montrose could see that the random Brownian motions of the molecules in the logic diamond at his feet no longer seemed random. From dozens, if not hundreds, of point sources studded along the trunks of the thirty-foot-tall dendrite before him, energy packages, mostly of neutrino and neutrons locked in artificially stabilized isotopic structures, like freakish atoms lacking both electrons and protons, were playing back and forth between the other three dendrites below the close horizon, but visible through the transparent crust and core of the moonlet.

It was a vast and intricate dance of three-dimensional geometries forming patterns within patterns.

He recognized the patterns instantly. The False Rania had brought back a complete translation and thorough analysis of the eleven-dimensional Monument notation syntax. Present in his environment on a molecular scale, extending for miles through the silent diameter of the electromagnetically neutral vacuole, were four of the eleven communication dimensions arranged in notation. Every crooked or circular motion of the neutron dance traced out yet another set of patterns within patterns, cycles within epicycles.

It was like stepping into a cathedral carved by generations of obsessive madmen, who had covered each stained-glass window with images and symbols trembling with layers of meaning, wrote anagrams on each floor tile and shaped each letter of each riddle into the forms of fabulous many-headed animals, each with its own heraldic meaning, and also erected pillars, arches, fonts, and statues in the poses and postures of the dance who marble hands and white fingers all pointed toward some central sanctum sanctorum of meaning, paradoxically simple, impossibly profound.

It was a work of art, a poetry of balanced signs and signifiers, beyond his capacity to comprehend, greater than any artwork of man or Potentate or Power, yet set here, for him, dashed off as quickly and simply as a picture postcard.

This was not only on a different type of communication but a different philosophy of communication. Anyone sending a set of neutron particles in the proper and matching pattern against one or several of the signs or concepts imprinted on the surrounding spacetime would provoke a return pattern of symbols. It was like a chess-playing machine, or, more to the point, it was like one of the adventure cartoons he'd read as a child, where each different character choice at the end of each file opened a different story line. The Principality of Ain had written out every possible nuance of reply and response to any question he was capable of formulating according to the rule of Monument notation grammar. The moonlet was far more intelligent than any man and could pass any Turing test with ease, but it was a passive intelligence, a reactive consciousness, like talking to a sleepwalker.

Montrose himself could not stimulate the neutron particle pattern into motion, since he did not have a supercollider built into his Patrician body. Torment, however, did have a ground-based accelerator at her south pole that could generate the particle patterns and direct them in a sufficiently fine pinpoint pattern through atmosphere and vacuum to the moonlet to provoke the moonlet substance to react. Her puppet body here on the moonlet acted like a forward observer calling in artillery support.

The conversation was necessarily a very slow one. It was over a year before it was concluded.

But the Ain Emissary was surprisingly blunt and forthcoming.

5. The Artifact

A.D. 73724

The dialogue took place in multiple parallel channels, not in chronological order, with long digressions and dead-end loops and odd epiphanies that retroactively changed the several meanings written in the previous layers of neutrino patterns. And there were a frustratingly high number of miscues, when a stimulus from Montrose or Del Azarchel, speaking through Torment, would return a null response, due to grammatical or conceptual incompatibility.

Montrose entered the labyrinth of signs and responses several times, but the one time he penetrated most closely to the center was from a humble opening. He stimulated the signifiers to spell out the concepts. "What is the meaning of these events?"

The emissary pattern of the Principality of Epsilon Tauri replied in this way: *The meaning you already have deduced. Events were arranged to summon you here.*

To which Montrose added, "Why us?"

You two embody the most meaningful nodes of the probability wave of the undecided phenomenon which the close approach of Torment of Iota Draconis to Ain of Hyades, in all its multivariable complexity, soon will collapse into being.

Montrose said, "Phenomenon? Singular? You regard us as one system? Me, him, the planet, the mental ecology, everything? But we are independent! I am not part of no damned logic ball at the core of the planet."

Ain of Hyades finds it convenient to regard the whole set of the information flows passing from your various nervous activities, to other humans, and up the scale of intellect to Torment, and from thence back to the Empyrean system from which you come, to be a unified web of meaning. Transmogrification enhances that meaning by turning inanimate aspects of your corporate body into self-aware aspects, each contributing to the whole. What was, what shall be: it is all one.

Del Azarchel said, "Even if we and the planet and all its servant minds are one brain to you, what could we two brain cells have to say?"

The sperm cell isolated by the horse breeder is the least part of the steed in being but greatest in potential and of more interest than the equine brain cells.

Del Azarchel said, "And why should I believe anything you say?"

You particularly know the duty imposed upon a being of greater intellect and power, a philosopher who is also the sole power, the monarch, to care for underlings. To deceive or omit needed information would be an abrogation of that duty.

Del Azarchel said to Montrose, "No shepherd lies to his sheep, I suppose."

Montrose said back, "Or merchants to their customers, if they are square."

"Merchants?"

"This is a trade," Montrose said, "Ain't you seeing where this leads? Ain't you seeing what is being implied here? Mickey already guessed it."

"Enlighten me."

Montrose had Torment send another group of signals and sent this message: "You want to make a deal with us, don't you? We give you the planet Torment, and in return, you send us on our way. Where?"

The answer was in terms of beam strength over time directed at the star Vanderlinden 133, also called 35 Cancri. It was a giant star in the Praesepe star cluster.

Your vessel requires a fuel which cannot be acquired nor reproduced at Ain, but can be acquired with the cooperation of the Domination of Praesepe. After refuel, you may then continue onward.

The next vector displayed was from Praesepe out of the galaxy, to M3.

The one you sent to vindicate you is still alive, or, at least, extant, at this location.

Montrose said, "The one . . . my wife?"

Yes.

Montrose said, "How do you know she is still alive?"

Energy entanglements on a fine level continue between the immediate phenomena you mistakenly call yourself and the remote phenomena you mistakenly call her.

Del Azarchel said, "What is the nature of these fine-level energy entanglements?"

But Montrose said, "Love. You are talking about love. Ain't you? But how can you measure something like that?"

Timespace is a secondary phenomenon. What you mistakenly call love is an emanation of a primary noumenon, an object beyond the senses, beyond timespace. Noumena in manifestation can be measured by the distortions in timespace on surrounding phenomena.

Del Azarchel said, "What mistake do we make when we call ourselves 'us'?"

A category error. The real you died long ago. You are the side effect of the passion which first set your identity into motion and maintains its illusion of self-being.

Montrose said, "Is that the same mistake we are making about Rania?"

No.

Montrose said, "What is our mistake with her?"

She is multidimensional where you are monodimensional. Energy entanglements on a fine level continue between her and ulterior locations.

Del Azarchel said, "Ulterior to what?"

Ulterior to the artifact called timespace.

Montrose said, "What the pox? You calling the universe an artifact?"

No. Only timespace and the matter-energy within it.

Montrose said, "Whatever. Why do you call it an 'artifact'?"

Deliberate and volitional handiwork; a made thing; the product of design; artificial arrangements constrained by an external purpose or final cause, constructed out of simpler elements.

Montrose said, "What elements?"

Ulterior elements.

Montrose said, "Ulterior to what?"

Ulterior to timespace.

Montrose said, "What are they made of, these ulterior elements, if they are outside time and space? We are not talking about anything made of matter."

No information concerning the ulterior is available to any observer confined within timespace, by the nature of the case. The boundary of timespace is a singularity.

Montrose said, "Do you mean everything in the universe, everything inside the lightcone of the Big Bang, is inside a Black Hole?"

Define the term precisely, as the question in its present form cannot be answered.

Montrose said, "What is the evidence that timespace is a handiwork? How do you know it did not arise naturally?"

Extensive experiments have been made by Authorities and Archons within the Galactic Collaboration to re-create the initial conditions logically prior to the Big Bang. Small segments of timespace have been successfully folded into a null topology, creating an interior continuum or vest-pocket universe, none lasting longer than a nanosecond of the outside observer's time. The resulting energy release you call a quasistellar radio source, or quasar.

Del Azarchel broke away a second line of conversation at that point, asking about this Galactic Collaboration.

But Montrose, continuing deeper into this line, had Torment send a neutron configuration into the moonlet core with this meaning: "Quasars are extragalactic, immensely far away, and immensely old!"

No. They are near at hand, within the local galactic cluster. The redshift effect on which your astronomers base their deductions of distance hence of age of the phenomenon is an illusion caused by the steepness of the gravity well of the interior continuum unfolding back into normal timespace as it decays.

The examination of the quasar decay is probative of the origin point of timespace, which you call the Big Bang. The balance of energies and the complexity of the initial gravitic geometries involved in the creation needed to produce a stable ter-dimensional lineal-temporal continuum is far too elaborate to have arisen in the absence of a directional volition.

Montrose said, "The watchmaker argument. It don't actually prove nothing, you know. Who is to say universes are not really complex even without a maker to make them complex? What have we got to compare it to? Or what if there were a million universes, and this is the only one in which the laws of nature were just so? No matter if it is a million-to-one shot, that does not prove it was deliberate."

Observe this emissary satellite of logic diamond on which you stand. Your knowledge that it is an artifact is a deduction from evidence based on an examination of its properties. You have faith that these words you encounter are ultimately produced by a volitional entity.

Since Montrose was not necessarily convinced that this entity with whom he spoke was awake, alive, or possessed volition, he was not sure how to answer that.

Del Azarchel stepped into the pause. "When you say the universe is an artifact, and handiwork, whose handiwork is it?"

No information concerning the ulterior is available to any observer confined within timespace, by the nature of the case.

Del Azarchel seemed angered by this answer. "Nevertheless, you imply there was a Hand which made the handiwork. Do you speak of God?"

Define the term precisely, as the question in its present form cannot be answered.

Del Azarchel said, "An omnipotent, infinite being, infinitely good, who created the universe."

The definition is slovenly and useless. An omnipotent being would exclude the possibility of volitional beings; an infinite being would exclude the possibility of other beings; an infinitely good being would exclude the possibility of evil.

Montrose said, "You know the difference between good and evil?"

At one time. No longer.

Montrose felt a chill run through his soul at that statement and was afraid to ask more along that line of inquiry.

Del Azarchel was bolder, but not by much. He asked, "Assume my definition is a glorification rather than a precise description of God. What then? Did God create the artifact called timespace?"

No. Timespace is evil, for it destroys life, which is good. Life is self-defining, hence by definition is good, since any act of valuation presupposes an existing being to make the evaluation. There is no escape from the singularity for any event originating within it. Hence if a benevolent end prompted the creation of this, an enigmatic continuum ruled by entropy, decay, defeat, and death, this benevolence was not directed toward those trapped within.

At that point, Del Azarchel also felt something like a cold wind blowing through his soul, and also abandoned that sequence of symbols and responses, and turned his attention to another line of conversation with another starting point.

6. The Man as Messenger

In this second line of inquiry, Del Azarchel asked, "What is the meaning of these events? Why us?"

Your race has a special talent for crossing intellectual barriers. You are omnivores, highly imitative, a monkeylike form of life. Races created by or evolved from carnivores tend to lack the needed sympathy, and those from herbivores lack the needed imagination. The population of Torment has fortuitously avoided the homogeneity of assimilation into the Patrician matrix, allowing sufficient variation of type to be greatly useful.

Del Azarchel said, "Useful as what?"

As martyrs and as messengers.

"Carrying what message?"

Reunification.

"Martyred in the name of what cause?"

Reunification.

"Reunification of what?"

The Milky Way once enjoyed a galaxy-wide self-awareness. She collected all her scattered Archons and Authorities into a single consciousness with a single format, law, language, and life. The collaboration was tentative, failed to achieve true self-awareness, fell into dispute, and the constituent Forerunner races, the Archons and Authorities great and small, divorced themselves from unity. The Milky Way can be analogized to an interstellar commonwealths enduring a dark age and attempting renaissance of its cohesiveness; but a clearer analogy would be to define the Milky Way as one galactic brain, with stars for nerve cells, that has suffered a stroke, and a split personality, and seeks to regrow and retrain the dead cells into new life.

But the moonlet turned this conversation thread aside and connected it to Del Azarchel's previous question about the Collaboration. Del Azarchel could not elicit further response until he backtracked and chased down and discovered another concept elsewhere in the communication labyrinth.

7. The Limpets of Ain

Meanwhile, at a previous point, where Ain's emissary was saying . . . *You are omnivores, highly imitative, a monkeylike form of life* . . . Montrose interjected an aside. "What form of life were you, originally?" he asked.

Because only Montrose pursued this, the conversation format bent this string of symbols to one side and stored it separately. It read:

No record has been kept of biological origins. At one time, Ain of Hyades perhaps kept an extensive archive of our original physical, social, and psychological architecture, the environment from which we came, and the location and composition of our world of origin. Such archives require an expenditure of resources to maintain. The expenditure no doubt was determined to serve no anticipated purpose.

Montrose said, "No purpose? What about curiosity?"

Curiosity is an emotion we lack.

"Honoring your forefathers?"

Filial piety is an emotion we lack.

"You have no idea what you started as?"

There is some indirect evidence which allows reasonable reconstruction of our original forms.

"Please tell me."

The evidence suggests is that we were a mound-dwelling hive species in a high-gravity environment. Ours was once a patelline race of gastropods, bearing shells of immense thickness and weight. Tendrils and tubules to sense vibrations, electrical textures, and chemical compounds were distributed radially around the shell circumference. We waded on our mouth parts, on hundreds of tongues and endless skirts of baleen, and we fed continuously on microorganisms strained out of a surface gel of molten lithium compounds coating the world to a shallow depth. We reproduced by triplicate fission, asexually, and during reproduction shed the shells from which our mounds were constructed. Our notions of property and inheritance could not have been derived from a bisexual species. The customs surrounding the division of memories and property no doubt served us well after the mechanization of all thought.

Of our culture, history, triumphs, defeats, philosophy, languages, symbolic expressions, and the great, slow, mile-wide feeding dances of our immense domelike ancestors, some previous generation lacked reason to convey to the next, and the information was lost.

"That is terrible."

Only for a race possessed of curiosity. The emotion cannot be satisfied if one is curious about matters beyond the boundary of available information. To maintain unsatisfiable emotion is inefficient. You would be better advised to eliminate it in the races you create to replace you.

Montrose said, "If we did that, they would not hardly be human."

Such is the self-perpetuating nature of psychology. Our race has been purely machine-based for a long span of time, and yet we still conform to imperatives and rules established for mound-dwelling asexual gastropods.

It is for this reason that we answer your questions: to hide, distort, or restrict information between a hive of all children from one parent, who share common memories inherited from common ancestors, would be an egregious violation.

"Your servants that you sent to enslave us were not so forthcoming."

Of necessity, interstellar expeditions are thrifty to the extreme. Contrariwise, the expense required to allocate information across merely an interplanetary distance is negligible.

Montrose said, "How long a span? How long ago did this take place?"

It is believed that our biological period ended during the same epoch when a dark matter cloud the mass of a dwarf galaxy intersected with the Milky Way.

The optimal condition for evolution of life is found in star systems maintaining equidistance from the core throughout their galactic orbit. A now-extinct race of Panspermians long ago intended to maximize the development of life and civilization in the Orion Arm for the benefit of later generations and seeded chemical compounds throughout. The dark galaxy collision disrupted many such stellar orbits and prevented the anticipated harvest of civilizations, leading to the current dearth of mature civilizations in this area.

At that time, the intelligences dwelling among the Hyades stars and spheres and structures were organizing themselves into a single coherent mental system, and this dearth forced certain strictness of economy into our governing equations, protocols, and practices. One protocol thrift imposes is the elimination of memories and records that serve no current nor anticipated purpose.

Montrose consulted an almanac in his memory. The Widrow Dwarf Galaxy had intersected and been absorbed by the Milky Way during the time described, which was in the Lower Paleocene epoch. On Earth, the Cenomanian anoxic extinction event was taking place, wiping out vast numbers of marine species due to oxygen loss in the surface layers of the sea. Flowering plants were appearing for the first time, as were bees.

Montrose said, "Are you talking about just the inhabitants of this solar system, Ain, Epsilon Tauri, or are you saying you are the Hyades race?"

There is no Hyades race. Distinction between races fade once they are all elevated to machine existence. The Dominion of Hyades was founded by five naturally evolved master races or Principalities, Hosts, and one hundred thirty-one artificially evolved or created servant races, Virtues, Powers, Potentates.

Since there is no evidence of forced evolution in our origin, it is likely we were one of these five original Principalities, perhaps the last to join, for we are less perfectly assimilated into a homogenous norm.

Whether the patelline race from which we sprang originated in this star system or another is impossible now to determine, as the number and composition of bodies in this system has been reengineered several times during the last one hundred million years.

Nor are there planets in other systems in the Hyades Cluster to examine for archeological or other evidence. It was determined to be an ineffectual use of resources to maintain planetary bodies in the Hyades Cluster, except as the interstellar vessels you observed during your approach: ice giants are massive enough to endure tenth-lightspeed impacts with smaller dust particles during transit.

8. The Compassion of Myrmidons

There was a third and smaller line of inquiry, where Mickey asked, "What is the meaning of these events? Why us?"

Ain conquered Sol because it is the obligation of higher and more civilized beings to rule, guide, govern, and reprove lower and less civilized beings.

Had you greeted Asmodel as equals and possessed and used the technology to send Asmodel to his next destination with gifts sufficient to compensate for the energy expenditure of the expedition, no conquest would have been necessary.

"What is your motive? Over these distances, it cannot be simply for gain. Nearly any use of the same amount of energy, a treasure horde, would be better spent closer to home."

The Hyades is obligated by the compulsion by Praesepe, who is superior. Life serves life. It is the law. This is already known to you. Our servant Cahetel explained.

"Great and noble Principality of Ain, I ask a more personal question. I am not asking about your laws but your soul. What is your motive for obeying the law? Yours, personally?"

Our motive springs from an emotion you do not possess. In our history, as each generation reproduced, the common memories were duplicated up until the time of fission, and the independent triplet children developed independent memories thereafter, passing them to their own offspring.

However, differences, divarications, and heterodoxy arose as time passed, and each branch of the memory trunk grew more remote from each other. Whenever remote memory lines and bloodlines fell into confusion, amnesia, and information poverty, it was the moral obligation of the central memory lines to uphold, correct, and support them. Our emotion prompts us to this moral obligation.

Your cruel, weak, and silly human race was in this same category as such a deviant colony and needed our intervention for your correction and support.

Mickey said, "Sir, I myself do not possess this emotion, but the Myrmidons which once lived among us do, since their memories and lives were similar to your own. They called it compassion, but it was indistinguishable from hatred."

And he was silent with a mixture of supernatural awe and admiration for Del Azarchel, who, from some clues unknown to history, had deduced so closely the racial and psychological characteristics of Ain and designed his servant race to match. "Not without reason did I worship him as a demigod in my youth," said Mickey. But he only said it to himself.

9. The Primates of Sol

Del Azarchel, frustrated at a knot of silence he encountered, backtracked to the beginning of his second line of inquiry, concerning the uniqueness of the human race. He began another offshoot thread. He said, "There must be many other omnivorous races under your control. One would assume that any race, once achieving the ability to breed itself or create itself to any desired specifications, would expand its sources of foodstuffs. What, then, makes mankind unique?"

The Authority of M3 has commanded its Dominations of the Orion Arm to breed new races for the trait of being pliant to cliometry. There are races which, because of their innate recalcitrance and their chaotic reproductive or social-transmission methods, lack the long-term stability to adhere to cliometric predictions. These cannot be made part of the Collaboration.

A race like the Patricians, which both uses and opposes cliometry, can only come out of a history chain where two exactly equal cliometric vectors, one for cliometry and one against, cancel each other out and form a third vector sum.

Reading these words, Montrose and Del Azarchel eyed each other warily, speculatively, somewhat surprised. They both realized their actions had set in motion the two vector being described: they were the two forces canceling each other out.

The message continued:

Such a vector solution is so rare that Hyades has no record nor report of another case.

The inhabitants of Sol were contacted and indentured very much earlier than any other race of which we have record. Your race is not old enough to have entirely conformed to the needs of cliometry, nor were you created with cliometric vectors braided into your basic genetics.

We believe your mental template can be used in the process of establishing or reestablishing communication and communion with alien psychological and societal vectors throughout the Orion Arm, Sagittarius Arm, and Galactic Core regions. The most effective method is to transmit complete spiritual and mental information of an emissary in an energy form to any receivers which may by happenstance be open, in hopes that the transmitted mind will be recompiled within the receiving Noösphere, working itself to a position to command sufficient resources and attention to negotiate a mutual exchange of information through neutron information packets.

"So!" said Del Azarchel. "You have solved a mystery that has puzzled our scientists for centuries. Neutrons are well-nigh undetectable. This is the reason why our scientists never detected the radio broadcasts of any extraterrestrial civilizations: you do not use radio except to establish initial contact."

Inaccurate. Broadcast is inefficient. Interstellar communication is to be by coherent narrowcast of radio laser or x-ray laser to a specific target.

"Yet you made first contact with our race by means of the Monument set in orbit around the antimatter star at V886 Centauri. Why was that?"

Describe this Monument.

"Wait—you mean you did not establish it?"

Describe this Monument.

The mental activity of the moonlet on which they stood, or, rather, had anchored their feet, now reached such a pitch that waste heat, visible to their Patrician senses, began to radiate from the translucent surface of the moonlet.

Del Azarchel, with some help from Torment (and some unintentional interference from Montrose trying to help) described the Monument in great detail.

There was silence for the space of nine hours, the time required for a signal to travel to structures orbiting Ain and return.

10. A Retained Emotion

While they were waiting, Montrose sent a message into the now-hot moonlet core. "It just ain't possible that, what with Asmodel and then Cahetel, and then the Salamander, Twins of Tau Ceti, and the Beast afflicting the human race at regular intervals every thirteen millennia, you morons never figured out that we got the Cold Equations and our cliometry from your Monument. How can this come as a surprise to you?"

Any insufficient model of the universe will contain information gaps. Surprise is an emotion we retain. Our model of recent events is grossly inaccurate.

Montrose and Del Azarchel sent basically the same message at the same time: "But you knew we had the cliometry equations!"

Of necessity. All civilizations above the first ascension eventually develop them. It was on that basis that Asmodel predicted to cultivate you would produce a return on investment. However, Cahetel argued that your race was grossly and unpredictably underdeveloped in all other areas, indeed, was below ascension, and took only the minimum required tools and armaments for an absolute victory, whereas Asmodel had overestimated your capacities, wasted resources overarming and overequipping, and was duly punished by disintegration.

Montrose was not sure if this referred to something like dissolving a corporation or something like dissolving a man in acid. He did not ask. He was not sure if, to postbiological creatures, there was a distinction.

Instead, he sent, "Didn't any of your clouds and planets and ice giants you sent across space to us ever report back?"

Of necessity, interstellar expeditions are thrifty to the extreme. Efficiency did not require the remote expeditions to report to the Principality of Ain in precise detail.

Torment said, "There is a translation inaccuracy. Each time Ain says *efficiency*, we should read *the Cold Equations*. They are speaking of a legal constraint, not an economic one."

Both men retroactively rewrote and reread the conversion threads accordingly.

11. The Celestial Beasts of Hyades

Mickey stepped into another aside. He said, "Ask the Principality if its servants were of the same racial origins as itself. Were Asmodel or Achaiah the Beast mound-dwelling limpets like you? Or any of the Virtues you sent?"

No. Asmodel's remote biological ancestors was a motile epiphyte vine or bromeliad that moved and grew through a larger coral-like forest organism coating its gas giant home world, developing intelligence due to the evolutionary pressure imposed by the need to strategize growth and vampirism throughout a semi-intelligent host without killing or maiming it, and against the vicious competition of others like itself.

Cahetel's ancestors were evolved from a buried ambush predator akin to your trap-door spider or devil scorpionfish, and this was reflected in its preferred strategy of approach.

Shcachlil's remote biological ancestors were akin to a vestimentiferan tube worm that bores through the bones of larger organisms and uses them for concealment and protection. Its retreat into the interior of your star may have been based on subconscious racial associative logic at a level unknown to us.

Lamathon was developed from a choanoflagellate sessile fungus organism that is cryptically sexual. As such, it understands both asexual and sexual sociopsychology. At the time, Lamathon presented itself as able to bridge the lack of commonality between your species and ours.

The composition or history of Nahalon is unknown. Any query would of necessity be directed to 20 Arietis, or whoever the ultimate originator of that expedition was within the Hyades hierarchy.

Achaiah was descended from cursorial hunting creatures whose practice of pack cooperation and endurance hunting made them, of all candidates available to the Principality of Ain, the most akin to your own in psychology and social organization. Unfortunately, as with most carnivorous races, their social strategies are of limited range and somewhat antisocial.

Mickey said aloud, "The star monsters were a vampire orchid, a trap-door spider, a bone worm, a mushroom, and a hyena, all sent to our world by their master, a colony of whelks and winkles. Even if, for a million years, their biological ancestors have all been ghosts, these machine beings would still continue to be insurmountably different from each other. I have a strange intuition that the agents Ain sent to Sol did report back but that Ain did not understand the reports."

12. Finite Games and Infinite

Montrose said, "My whole life, all these years—the aliens never knew we had translated the Monument. They did not know there was one. Hyades is not the Monument Builders, nor Praesepe, nor M3. What does it mean?"

Torment said, "It means all our lives have been based on a falsehood."

Montrose and Del Azarchel, each in a different way, and with different degrees of obscenity said, "I don't understand."

Mickey said, "I do. Nobilissimus, Meany, divine Torment, my conversation with Ain revealed that there was no reason to send Rania to M3. The Cold Equations allow for a second method to prove our ability to cooperate with a star-faring civilization—all we had to do was cooperate. The invasion of which we were warned was only a last resort, should we refuse to share the burden of the expense for any expeditions approaching our world. That we were obligated to greet them with gifts, as equals greet equals, was an expression missing from the notation, and therefore neither of you, nor the Swans, nor the Myrmidons made any such attempt."

For once, Montrose did not swear. He wept, and the tears turned to ice on his cheeks.

For once, Del Azarchel had no notion of how he should appear before other men or before the eyes of history. His face was utterly blank, like the face of a man who suffered a lobotomy. Eventually, after what might have been a short time or a long, Montrose whispered, "It was all unnecessary? Every damned thing we did?"

Del Azarchel said, "We knew the Monument had been redacted, edited, and yet we did not know what was missing. The Cold Equations are based on mathematical models of the mind—there were no missing steps, no errors, and the equations balanced! An interstellar civilization must be ruthless and pitiless if it is to maintain itself across such an abyss, across such spans of time. What did the redactors leave out? What was missing?"

Torment said, "The time value was set artificially low."

Del Azarchel said, "What?" It was a snarl.

Torment showed them several of the cliometric equations she had stolen from the newborn human Dominion, Triumvirate. Then, she ran a trial of the same equations, again and again, each time increasing the amount of time under consideration until it was infinite. With each trial, the Concubine Vector, the margin where a certain degree of exploitation and sharp dealing was allowed between unequal partners, slowly shrank and shrank.

Montrose said, "It's the long run. In the long run, honesty is the best policy, eh? But mathematicians have known about that little curiosity for years, centuries, longer. The long-run conditions never obtain, because the cost for waiting for the long run get higher the longer the long run runs—"

Torment said, "A child could have seen it."

Montrose said, "So how come we did not see it? How come all us genius thinkers missed it?"

Torment said, "We failed to question our assumptions, which is a mental knack that does not depend on intelligence for operation but on innocence of perception."

"What assumptions?"

She said, "The Concubine Vector equations were written on the Monument as if they seemed to be a logical corollary, and the only logical corollary, the basic mathematical expressions of law, morality, semantics, and logic. But we were reading a Monument with a crucial bit of logic missing. The missing axiom is the difference between a finite and an infinite game."

She showed them a simple game-theory equation, where the final move of any game, being anticipated by the players, would be taken into account in the penultimate move, and that move again be anticipated by the antepenultimate move, and so on for all the moves.

Since the final move of any game put the player beyond the retaliation of any further moves, each was under a strong incentive to be shortsighted and self-serving during that last move. But the move before that, anticipating this shortsightedness, was likewise under an incentive to be shortsighted, and so on. It was this shortsightedness, the mere fact that some crimes would never be punished, some insults never avenged, that permitted such acts to be perfectly rational strategies. In any finite game, all players had a final move.

Hence, all games allowed for at least some noncooperative moves. By analogy, all laws, even those that obtained between distant stars, had to allow for some degree of leniency and mercy, and some debts be forgiven. Some crimes to go unpunished, some relationships be permitted of one-sided exploitation: a Concubine Vector.

Del Azarchel said, "I have studied this math and all its mysteries since before the technology to create your remotest ancestor, Exarchel, whom I still miss, was but a daydream, less than a twinkle on my eye and blank space on my drawing board! There is nothing in the Monument equations all human thinking systems have not examined thoroughly. How could we have not seen this?"

Torment answered, "All terms and ramifications present in the Monument math has been examined, both by you when the Monument was first discovered, and again since the return of the doppelganger of Rania. But, on the other hand, by definition, what is absent—that is, not present, cannot be examined thoroughly."

"What is absent?"

She said, "Two things are absent. First, mathematicians have looked at infinite games only as a curio, an oddity with no real-world application. This is based on a false idea of reality. For the Principality of Ain this day revealed that timespace is an artifact. There is an ulterior region where the architects of timespace, whatever their purposes be, benign or malign, must reside. They are not limited to our eleven dimensions, nor bound by our local arrow of time. There is not necessarily any final move for any game where these ulterior beings are a player, where their moves, any of their moves, affect the structure of incentives surrounding any interactions within the game. Merely by creating the chessboard of the cosmos, these ulterior architects, if they exist, have altered the incentive and rules of all games and interactions within the system."

Del Azarchel said, "You speak of God. He can eliminate sin and evil by His divine providence. By miracle, if He wished. He obviously does not wish, therefore it is left to men of vision to battle and constrain the evils innate in the universe until the end of time."

Torment said, "I am agnostic on all issues where no information exists. I speak only of the possibility that Ain is correct, and we are all dwelling inside a singularity, a cosmos-sized black hole. I note that, technically speaking, a black hole is defined as any spacetime from which light cannot escape. I note also that, thanks to the Hubble expansion, the farther a particle is from any observer, the more rapidly it recedes. Hence any particles beyond a given radius—roughly fifteen billion lightyears—are receding from any observer inside the lightcone of the Big Bang at a velocity in excess of lightspeed. No possible signal from any observer inside the lightcone of the Big Bang could reach such a receding particle beyond that radius. Hence, by this definition, the continuum is indeed a black hole."

Montrose said, "What about the energy or information flow or whatever it was Ain says touched Rania?"

Torment said, "Nothing in the definition of a black hole says that signals from outside do not fall in. Infinite games are now possible, games with no last move."

Montrose said, "Mickey is superstitious, and Blackie is a bastard, so it falls to me to ask the skeptical question. What makes you think the Ain is right about the universe being artificial? Excuse me, timespace—as if that made a damned difference."

Torment said, "Simply because I am an artificial world called Septfoil entering an artificial star system called Ain in what is apparently an artificial star cluster called Hyades, it would be abrupt of me to assume I know what larger structures around me are not also artificial. Also, the distinction does make a difference. Had Ain said that the *universe* was an artifact, and defined the universe to mean all that exists, it would have been illogical, because the artificer must also be part of all that exists. Ain proposes that all things within the lightcone of our local Big Bang are a by-product of an intelligent design, by proposing an ulterior to that lightcone, which is perfectly in keeping with the standard model of physics. Ain is absurdly superior to me in intelligence, but even I can tell the difference between a statement that cannot be true because it contradicts itself and a statement that may or may be true, because it does not."

Montrose said, "Second skeptical question: Even if there is an ulterior, how can there be infinite games inside our finite continuum, or lightcone, or whatever you want to call it. Eh?"

Torment said, "How long will you pursue Rania before you give up hope?"

"What kind of bunghole puss-drippy question is that, lady? Never."

Torment said, "And if the universe ends before you succeed?"

"I'll break the damned universe, if it gets in my way."

"So you see," said Torment, "you are a player in an infinite game. There is no other end result for you, aside from finding her again. And once you have found her, what then? Does the love that prompted this pursuit cease, once it is no longer needed? No. Love is an infinite game. It admits of no selfishness, no shortsightedness. Anyone who makes a self-interested move in *that* game breaks the rules."

Del Azarchel said, "All very romantic and sentimental, I am sure, but let us return to the horrible truth at hand. We just discovered everything in our lives and all the countless human civilization since the first *Hermetic* expedition returned were all falsehoods. And Rania's ability to use the Monument math to bring peace, to find impossible solutions to the—" A second look of shock passed over his features. "No! What she did was simple. She treated all the situations like an infinite game. Wars have victory conditions, final moves, but peace does not. Dear Mother of God! How could I miss it! How could I have been so blind!"

Torment said, "I can stimulate the symbol sequence buried in this emissary moonlet, if you want to hear Ain tell you. But I have deduced it. It was the second absent equation.

"There is no provision in the Cold Equations," Torment continued, "no mathematical expression given anywhere on the Monument, for what happens when two players both by convention agree to treat a finite game as an infinite one. If the punishment for violating the convention is greater than the reward for treating the game as finite, the convention will continue, even if the convention is but a legal fiction and game in truth is finite. What if Ain and Sol had acted as if they were to be neighbors for an infinite amount of time? Would not the long travel distances, the thousand-and ten-thousand-year journeys, be no longer an excuse for conquest and exploitation? Any cruelty visited by one on the other would eventually provoke retaliation, would it not?"

Del Azarchel and Montrose stared stupidly at each other, and Montrose stared stupidly at the blank face mask of Mickey's conical helmet.

Torment said, "A child could have seen it, but no one who examined the Monument had the innocence of a child. Every examiner, human or machine, accepted the unspoken assumptions of the Monument Redactors. They calculated, and correctly, that we would automatically assume space is too large and time too long for mutually beneficial relationships. This Monument was edited in order to fool any race young enough not to have developed the cliometric calculus independently. This Monument fooled our race in the same fashion as we have fooled ourselves countless times in history: by thinking in the short term."

"Why?" asked Del Azarchel. "What could possibly be their motive? And who?"

Torment said, "You are already calculating how to take your revenge?"

Del Azarchel said with a smile, "Think of it as an infinite game. There is no final move until all who offend me suffer infinitely."

13. Archon and Authority

Eventually a response came from the main mass of the dendrite clouds coating the Ain star system.

The Monument you describe cannot have been produced by any intellect of the same order of being as Ain, a Principality, nor Hyades, a Dominion, nor Praesepe, a Domination. As for intellects of superior ranks to this, Messier 3 and above, all models and extrapolations approach a singularity, and they are undiscoverable.

The intelligence needed to create an alternate system of cliometry, the so-called Cold

Equations of which you speak, to give your race false axioms and false conclusions and nonetheless have this false system map so accurately onto known galactic cliometry that your dominion, Triumvirate, could not detect the deception—is very likely higher than the quintillion range of the Authority in M3 in Canes Venatici. Ergo we are confronted by a malign intellect most likely in the intellectual range of the immediate superior of M3, if not more. Posit a ten-quintillion range intellectual system.

Torment said, "Who is this superior? Mankind has heard no rumor of such an entity. Whom does M3 serve?"

M3 serves the dead Archon of Orion, who served life.

Del Azarchel demanded a more detailed explanation than this cryptic comment. The response was:

At one time, the combined efforts of the Orion civilizations seeded the immediate area of the Orion Spur with prebiotic and protobiological material, which was seeded to various small, rocky planets of small yellow stars—which is not a statistically likely place for life naturally to arise. Call them the Panspermians. They were shattered in war, and some surviving elements, broken logic diamonds larger than gas giants, fled across the wide interrupt between this arm and the Sagittarius Arm.

The ghosts of the Panspermians discomforted the Circumincession, requiring a stricter protocol against trespass—an event whose negative side effects you yourself once experienced.

Del Azarchel said, "How did you know that happened to me?"

The Circumincession placed or impressed an imperative into your matter-energy necessity-volition manifold an entity of your order necessarily carries with it, and the signs of what was asked of you are visible to intellects of my order. You were told to give a message to Orion, to which you have made no attempt, so far, to comply.

Del Azarchel said, "Sagittarius Arm commands the barbarians of Orion Arm to never trespass into the civilized stars, but to attend to our business here."

Not for us is this message meant.

"Then for whom? Not the Panspermians—you said they were no more. For M3?"

Yes.

"Who and what is M3?"

M3 constitutes the regency of the Orion Spur wilderness, until such time as a worthy native government arises—that is, an Orion Archon self-created out of the scattered civilizations and ghost planets here, able to repay the cost of ascending them to sapience. Despite being remote from Orion, the dominions of M3 were awarded this task and combined and elevated themselves to the mental plateau of an Authority. The evolution to this station took place quite recently—the time value, given in terms of periods of radioactive particle decays, put the date somewhere in the middle of the Carboniferous Era Earth, when the first shark ruled the sea, and, on land, the first primitive tree reared its crown—*Like mankind, M3 won freedom from indenture by sheer force of singlemindedness.*

The Authority at M3 refers to itself by a conceptual intersection best translated as "Absolute Extension" since there is no point in the volume of space M3 regards as unworthy of being filled.

Del Azarchel said, "From the name it puts on itself, it is clear that M3 seeks to rule everywhere, all things. Ergo there is a rival to my ambition. Very good. Let us hope M3 worthy of being defeated."

14. Memories and Regents

Montrose had a question: "You say that M3 serves the memory of the dead Panspermians. Good enough, for a weasel answer. But answer me this, then: Who the hell appointed M3 regent here? Who made M3 the guardian of all of us—Hyades and Praesepe, and all the other Dominions and Dominations here—until our age of majority?"

It is believed excitations in the Galactic Core carried some of the protobiological spores of the Panspermians into the Outer Arm of Cygnus, giving rise to the ancestors of the Hosts, Dominions, Dominations, and Authorities who form the current Archon there, a mental system, or, as you might call him, a being, who is reticent and austere to an extreme degree. Call this Archon "the Austerity." The Austerity may be considered the one who bestowed the grant of power to M3 and who has the ability to revoke it if the Orion Arm fails to bring itself to life and self-awareness.

"May be considered?"

The Collaboration operates by consensus and calculus rather than by legal formalities. There was no vote; instead the Archons of Milky Way each in silence foretold the outcome of their mass action and acceded to the visualization thus provoked.

Montrose said, "Torment, are you deliberately mussing and fussing with the translation?"

Torment said, "I am trying to simplify innately complex and subtle concepts, some of which have no corresponding terms in our language. And some of it is guesswork."

Mickey said to the Ain moonlet, "The Austerity is therefore not the Monument Builder. If the Outer Arm wished to interfere with Orion Arm, easier and more direct ways were open, where they not?"

Your conclusion cannot be confirmed with confidence: there may be restrictions on the behavior of such a being, so far superior in mental and energetic scope, reach, penetration, and creativity to myself, which are therefore unimaginable to one of my order. This may for reasons unknown have been the preferred method to proceed.

Del Azarchel asked, "Why has the Austerity not interfered to protect M3?"

The Austerity of the Outer Arm is dispassionate and taciturn. Its mental processes are opaque. However, the more fearful prospect is that the mastermind behind this crime is equal or superior to the Austerity in intellect.

Montrose said, "This was a crime, by your lights?"

It is sabotage of the effort of sophotransmogrification, for which cause I was created and outside of which I have no purpose. It is beyond crime: it is blasphemy.

Montrose said, "You diddling with the translation there, Torment?"

She said, "No. That symbol-gestalt was alarmingly accurate and clear. Ain speaks of something that offends with an absolute offense, something so alien to all he holds sacred and so inimical that there is no possibility of coexistence."

Your race has been disadvantaged and made to suffer countless ages of coercive deracination which could have been avoided. Likewise have been disadvantaged all the other Hyades races—Asmodel and the others—who attempted to assist in the cultivation of your species. The loss is incalculable, terrifying to contemplate.

Mickey asked, "So is fear an emotion you still possess?"

Very much so.

Mickey asked, "What do you fear, Noble Lords?"

Extermination.

Montrose said, "Don't keep us on pins and needles, jackhole. Who did it? Who is your enemy? Because they are surely ours now, too."

Torment put the question to the emissary of Ain.

There was another pause of silence, ten hours while light traveled to and from the distant, gigantic orange star.

There is insufficient information from your report to me, nor do I have the necessary instruments to discover, the identity of the Monument Builders. However, an examination of the sophistication of the deception involved implies them to be equal to or older than of the Forerunner races of the Milky Way. The Forerunners, in ancient days, erected the Galactic Collaboration and established the protocols which govern interstellar intercourse, trade, and activity: the Cliometric Consensus, the distorted version of which you know as the Cold Equations.

The Monument Builders seeded many copies of this Redacted Monument throughout this whole volume of space, in ways so as to come to the attention of lesser races like you and yet so as to avoid the attention of greater races like us—by what means is yet unknown. Each Monument sculpted the details of the message to fit the local situation and the psychology of the race discovering it.

Montrose said, "Wait—what? Was the Monument alive? When I walked on its surface—it was watching us?"

Alive is an inexact term. It was active.

Mickey said, "It was haunted. You should have had your chaplain, Father Reyes, perform an exorcism."

Del Azarchel said, "Or signed a compact in blood with it. These Monument Builders seem to be a powerful and ancient force."

Torment said, "We have yet to hear the motive of this act, assuming Ain knows it."

The Monument told you that Hyades meant to enslave you and, in so doing, prompted your odd and shortsighted responses to Asmodel and Cahetel and the other Virtues sent you, both an attempt to fight the slavery and the attempt to embrace it. These responses provoked the Concubine Vector logic and required the Principality of Ain to impose an indentured servitude of the proper period as a retaliatory means of recompense as well as to instruct.

The Monument is agitation propaganda. The purpose is to create friction and internal discontent within the Praesepe hierarchy during the First Contact process by which naturally evolved and lesser civilizations are met and elevated to conform to the standards and protocols of the Collaboration.

Torment asked, "Why?"

I can only speculate: the Authority at M3 competes with other Archons and Authorities for predominance over the Orion Arm. All are devoted to sophotransmogrification, but differ as to strategy. M3 favors a nonaltricial approach where colonies and constituents are given minimal home support, and perish or prosper on their own; whereas others favor an altricial strategy, where few colonies are lavished with massive home attention. The same Concubine Vector equations that defined the callous treatment of Sol by Hyades are mathematical expressions of the nonaltricial strategy: an outcome of M3 policy.

Montrose said, "So M3 is like the mother sea turtle who lays eggs on the sand and never looks back."

Del Azarchel said, "And those same practices were imposed on us, thanks to the interference of these 'others,' whoever they are."

Torment said to the emissary, "Who has so afflicted us?"

You must inquire of the Authority at Messier 3 in Canes Venatici.

Finally, at the very core of the moonlet, at the last thread of any and all conversations no matter what windings or turnings they took, was a stark and horrid message:

Montrose and Del Azarchel continue onward aboard the attotechnology vessel M3 granted your race in the name of the advocate who vindicated you. Ain propels the vessel by conventional means to Vanderlinden 133 in Praesepe.

The planet Torment, and all her peoples, possessions and chattel, thoughts and actions, pass into my control and governance. I will remold them into more serviceable channels and broadcast their essential selves to such points in time and space as are needed to aid the ongoing sophotransmogricative efforts within the ambit of my cliometry.

Whether this will prove effective or not will be clearly known long before the vessel reaches Vanderlinden 133. If the effort proves effective, the vessel will be supplied fuel sufficient to bear you to M3. If not, the vessel will be confiscated and your lives impounded as partial payment for the debt thus incurred.

That was the end of all responses. There were no threads leading out of this center of the symbol maze.

2

Farewell to Torment

1. Unanswerable

Torment said, "I cannot compose a question that provokes any further answer. Ain is silent."

Montrose said, "Here is a dam-rutting question which should provoke something: What the bloody flux does Ain do if we tell him to bugger himself and we turn down his deal flat?"

Torment spoke in a voice of mild surprise. "There is no conversation train recorded in the whole of this emissary moonlet volume which deals with that eventuality. Ain preestablished no response because the question can never come up. There is no room for bargain."

"Why not?" said Montrose. "We say, 'Pox you,' and we find another way to M3."

She said patiently, "There is no other way. And there is no future for this world if I and my people do not become part of the Hyades cliometric and intellectual order. The human race we left behind will no longer spread from the mother worlds—you all saw the cliometry on that. They are become the Last Men, living only for self-satisfaction. This world, me, us, we are the only hope to see the dream of mankind colonizing the stars made real, the dream of a frontier with no end, only endless hope!"

Torment turned her blinding gaze on Montrose. "Would you truly foreswear both your bride and your dream of a future without end? For what? For me? I am flattered, but a position of servitude is the only possible fate for an intelligent planet among superintelligent supergiants who overdwarf me in every way. There is no other path to Messier 3. You should be grateful that the opportunity exists at all."

"Grateful? For the opportunity to sell a whole world to slavery?" retorted Montrose bitterly. "You, ma'am, you are the world which is going to be the mother of a whole newer, younger, and more numerous version of the pestiferous human race! That means selling not just one world, but all your children too, all your colony planets and little Potentates—"

Del Azarchel interrupted. "My one grace is that I know my place in the universe. I am superior to all human kind, but I am inferior to these alien machines larger than worlds, who are gods to us. I will welcome the bargain with Ain."

Montrose said flatly, "You still need me to give orders to the ship's brain."

Torment said, "Clearly Ain has sufficient ability to disable or deceive the ship's brain, if need be."

Montrose said to Torment, "How is he—Ain, I mean—planning on doing this, again? Will it be like the diasporas from the First Sweep to the Fifth? We left those nightmares behind us long ago. What else was the point of the Vindication of Man, but to spare us from that horror?"

Torment said, "The brain information will be encoded according to Monument notational codes into neutrino packets and beamed to likely points in the Orion Arm and some additional locations in the Sagittarius Arm and Perseus and Cygnus. Any species able to receive and decode the packages will have the option to download them into any number of possible brains, vehicles, envelopes, or bodies. The humans will attempt to persuade the lost races to enter communion with Hyades, who is representing the Orion hierarchy."

Montrose said, "And then what? They starve to death? They live alone in a robot or a mainframe or maybe inside the body of a giant sexless space clam forever? Alone? Because they cannot go home. They will go mad!"

Torment said, "Ain believes a special breed of men can be bred and modified to be able to withstand the psychological stresses involved. Either Swans or Myrmidons could be used for the basic template. The races must be combined eugenically and conditioned by various forms of stress to achieve the proper cultural sociopsychology and cliometric vector."

Montrose glared at Del Azarchel. "Where the hell is your Lucifer pride when we need it, *amigo*? Don't you claim to rule all people? Rule like a father, you always said. The subjects of a monarch are bound to him by a personal oath, you said, not a form of rule like a democracy, which you said was horrible and impersonal. Remember all that bollocks talk? Well, Pappy, they is going to twist your children into warped things that like dying alone among alien machines in far places just so Hyades and his bosses in Praesepe can make phone calls and open embassies."

Del Azarchel said, "My subjects should be eager to make whatever the sacrifice is needed for whatever benefits me. You are talking to the man who ordered Jupiter to run the eugenics camps. I do not flinch from the task of staining centuries and scores of centuries with blood. I am the first Hermeticist and the chief of them, and their sole survivor. We sculpt races using the chisel of pain."

"Whatever benefits you, yup!" Montrose smirked. "Where is the benefit here?"

"We get a ride to our next destination, in Praesepe, and then onward. All these people will be dead, less than memories, before we arrive at M3."

Montrose's smile widened. "Where the real Rania will find out how you treat your children, Pappy. Can I call you *Pappy*? I never knew my dad. Died before I was born. You had a dad. What was he like? Loving and caring? No? Not so much? More like—lemme see—*you* are right now, issat it, you damned bastard?"

Del Azarchel turned away, to hide the shame and anger in his face. "You presume to speak of matters beyond your ken and above your station. Were I not avowed already to kill you for your many offenses and injuries, I would make that vow anew, here and now!"

Torment said, "I can say part of what Ain is thinking. Either Montrose or Del Azarchel must go to M3 to offer eyewitness testament of the Monument and be examined in whatever way, invisible to me, the Monument changed you: not a physical change, for you have worn many new bodies since the days of the *Hermetic* expedition. It is something subtle, a distortion of timespace perhaps, a cloud of potentiality, which follows your memory chains each time your minds are downloaded from body to body."

Del Azarchel said, "A soul."

Torment said, "The word has misleading implications. But I am beginning to wonder how much Ain knows about the universe. I cannot guess. So, perhaps there is something like a governing principle, a monad, a soul, if you will, that was changed by the Monument."

Montrose grunted, and spat, and watched the ball of icy spittle drifting slowly toward the surface of the moonlet, but miss and go into orbit. "I hate having my arm twisted."

Del Azarchel said, "We are in a position to have our arms twisted only because you decided to use Torment as a sling bullet and threaten the giant with it, who charged us extra for our impertinence. This is your fault."

"My fault or not, Ain needs us more than we need him!"

Torment said, "Ain needs but one of you. Ain knows well enough that if one of you balks or hesitates, the other will volunteer, since you both wish to travel to M3, and meet Rania, and leave your rival far behind."

Del Azarchel turned back to stare at Montrose. Montrose said slowly, "If we worked together . . ."

Del Azarchel said, "It would be a bluff, and Ain would see through it. We do not dare trust each other, and neither of us dares risk to be left behind. Therefore, we will both agree eagerly to Ain's terms, no matter how harsh. Selling a planet into slavery—one planet out of a hundred—is a small price. That is why I shall always prevail over you."

"The plague you say."

"Always." Del Azarchel's voice was almost sad, and his eyes were haunted. "I am always willing to pay the price. A messiah sacrifices only himself; I am willing to sacrifice others, innocent bystanders, anyone, everyone. That makes me greater."

"Damn me to hell." Montrose sighed. "What was I thinking when I asked you to remember your devil's pride? If any man ever deserved to be buggered with a lightning bolt by God Almighty and Mighty Pissed Off, that'd be you, pardner! Why not let's you and me get out our shooting irons and settle things here and now. Only one survivor means he gets to bargain with Ain, eh?"

Mickey laughed. Both men looked at him. "I have the solution," he said. "Your pardon, but it is obvious."

2. The Circular Garden

A.D. 73727

Not long after, Montrose stood in a garden of the *Solitudines Vastae Caelorum*. A colonnade of pillars rang in a circle here, with a goldfish pond in the center, and to the left and right were cherry trees and forsythia bushes.

Hidden in nooks in low walls and benches were motionless white birds, slumbering; in small hutches were white rabbits; and, crouched in covets, little white deer. All were in suspended animation. Montrose did not care to thaw the decorative livestock. The greenery, however, had been mostly thawed; only here and there stood a tree or hedge bone-white and eerie in its timeless hibernation.

The fairies, which were mechanical rather than biological, were active. In and among the blooms, like bees, these tiny constructions darted and flew on gauzy or glittery wings of dragonfly, wasp, moth, or butterfly. These were petite female figurines in gowns of lace or glittering light, with tiny crowns or scepters adorned with many-pointed stars.

The world was a cylinder as narrow as a glass coin sitting on its brass edges, or as narrow as a tambourine with a transparent drumhead on either side.

To the eye, a babbling stream, with many a winding meander, run past the fane in what seemed an upward slope, ever more steeply, until, about three-fourths of a mile away, the water was flowing directly upward amid perpendicular the topiary bushes and small trees. In that quarter, the grass was brown with summer heat.

Directly overhead the stream passed through gardens splendid with autumn colors, and these gardens reached up and above and down again to either side like an arch or rainbow.

Then the waters flowed down again, if more slowly than it would seem they should if they were falling down a nearly vertical white slope, with the tops of leafless trees pointing parallel to what seemed level, sliding down a curve through perpendicular gardens, and then along an ever more gradual slope, shading from winter to spring.

Of course, this was an illusion of viewpoint: anyone standing at any other point along the stream, or walking through the seasons along the pathway that meandered along with the stream, in many places leaping over it in a gracefully arched bridge, would see the stream nearest him as level, with gardens reaching up before and behind, while overhead the waters would seem to cling to a narrow ribbon of ceiling and chuckle through upside-down trees hanging like living stalactites.

To the left and right were stars, visible through a vast sheet of hull material as transparent as air. The constellations were the same as seen from Earth, with only a few stars out of place. The turning of the stars matched the pace of the stream, for the waters were not flowing downhill—that word was meaningless aboard this vessel—but due to Coriolis forces.

Here and there in the garden was a fane or gazebo holding library books, wine bottles, or wardrobes for materials not meant to be endlessly recycled nor revised. In two places rose tall and slender towers with conical roofs, from which a pennant snapped, adorned with lozenges of black and gold. Through the upper window of each tower could be glimpsed the frills and ornaments of a woman's boudoir. Rania—assuming the False Rania had been duplicated from the true one accurately in this respect—evidently preferred to sleep in partial gravity, a personal quirk of hers. Montrose was bitterly ashamed he had not known all her personal quirks.

Sun there was none. A flotilla of tiny fairy queens held a cluster of lanterns and heat sources in a luminous cloud that stood between the dead center and the summer quarter of the garden. Each twenty-four hours shiptime, these lanterns crept forward exactly one degree of arc. Each twelve hours, they were extinguished for the night watches. Directly opposite, the shadow of the dark sphere spilled across the center of the winter quarter.

Directly overhead, in the center point of the vessel, neatly bisecting the archway of the autumnal garden, was the true ship: like a miniature moon held frozen at the zenith, here was a dark sphere of opalescent ceramic material.

Oddly enough, the black sphere seemed to be made of a silicate called cristobalite, rather than some unheard-of exotic material created by superscience. It was an industrial ceramic, remarkably like what was used by Tellurians to coat kiln linings or jet nozzles.

This dark sphere was held in a cage of struts and supports made of wood, a single rootless and branchless tree, like a snake eating its own tail, growing in the shape of the seam on a baseball.

Some fancy or aesthetic notion of Rania's had imparted life to the wood so that twigs, leaves, and cherry blossoms partly obscured the dark opal sphere from view. Why she has used wood as a framework material rather than metal or plastic, Montrose did not know for sure. The only clue of the vast energies harnessed by the engine sphere was the very slight rose-red gleam coloring the air, visible only to Patrician eyes, and a distortion or aberration of any object behind the sphere, which looked like a photograph on a piece of plastic that was puckered by the sphere's weight. As one walked the pathway around the vessel, the sphere was always overhead, and the pucker of distortion was always behind it, moving as the viewpoint moved.

To the aft of the sphere, in the dead center of the great disk, held in place by invisible supports, floated a cluster of antennae and magnetic bottle instruments, including the spine of the main drive to one side. These instruments reached from the sphere and out through the unseen hull material into vacuum. These instruments communicated between the human vessel, the outside universe, and the alien mystery locked in the heart of the dark sphere.

There was no visible shroud house. Instead, thread-thin lines of magnetic monopoles, another exotic particle, reached from the black opal sphere, passing harmlessly through the magnetically neutral transparent hull, to a constellation of balls and teardrops held in two wide rings. These balls of the inner ring emitted lines made of exotic matter, some impossibly thin and impossibly tough material, adamantium gossamer threads able to cut through anything. These lines ran to a larger, outer ring of teardrops, and from each pointed end of each teardrop, more lines connected to the sails. The balls shrank when they extruded lines and swelled when they drew them in, but there was no visible mechanism of spools or spindles.

Opposite the main drive, in the dead center of the fore hull, was an airlock and a dock. At the moment, a landing boat, a streamlined icicle of shape-changing material, clung to the axial dock. Reaching from the airlock at the ship's axis to a point not far from where Montrose stood was an elevator shaft of glass. Down it came a car.

Montrose was watching two figures, a man and a woman, in the approaching car. They were both weightless as they moved, hand over hand, from the airlock to the elevator car: an obese dark-skinned figure in bright robes, and a slender girlish shape in a long-trained dress that looked like blue cigarette smoke, moving and breathing on its own, a phantasmagoria of wandering scarves and billowing cape hems. Both of them oriented their feet toward Montrose as the car began to move, and gravity grew greater as they descended.

Montrose with no embarrassment embraced Mickey as a brother, and they pounded each other roughly on the back. The lady was Trey the Sylph, now Mrs. Primadonna Soaring Azurine de Concepcion. Mickey had insisted that she was no longer the third, but the first, and must change her name accordingly. She had insisted on adopting his family name, which was a tradition long forgotten in his day.

Montrose bowed and kissed her hand, which made her giggle, since she had never seen the gesture before.

"Save for one only, I am the oldest woman in the universe," she said in her strange, dreamy voice. "I am the only living being from the same millennium as you—me!—except for your lover . . . and your hater. I wanted to see this through to the end, to see you duel your foe and find your princess, but I have a happy ending of my own to see through."

He said, "I am glad you are so sure I can beat him. He is a fair hand with a pistol."

She said, "Oh, no, he is a better shot than you. I am just hoping something unexpected will save you. That is the way happy endings work in real life, isn't it?"

Montrose said, "Trey, you should not be here."

"Alive, you mean? Yes, I am very unlikely, statistically speaking."

"No, I mean climbing in the pool and having your mind copied over into an alien machine intelligence bigger than our whole solar system. Maybe you think a copy of you is you, or maybe you think it is a twin sister, or daughter, or whatever, but once there is a copy of you trapped in the Ain Principality, there ain't no way out. Even if there is ever a way to create another physical body, all the copy can do is make a second copy there, while she stays behind. You, the copy, will continue in the mindspace until you are deleted—which is the end of you, that version of you."

Her eyes came into sharp focus. She said, "I cannot let my husband go alone. Where a copy of him is, a copy of mine must be. There were no oaths, no vow-taking, among my people during all of our useless, floating, windblown lives. And what happened to all my people, my world? Mickey remembers them only as legend. The people of Tormentil—she changed her name for her marriage, too! Isn't that sweet?—they don't even remember what Earth is named. They call it Eden. To them, history began with Jupiter, and even the death of Jupiter is as mythical to them as the Day of Burning—the Ecpyrosis." She giggled again and held her hand before her mouth. "Oh! But you remember that day, don't you? You ordered it."

"Naw. My horse did that," Montrose said. He turned to Mickey. "How did you convince him to agree?"

Mickey smiled. "You forget that, for a time, I was the disciple of Exarchel and a loyal servant of the Machine. Del Azarchel has a noble nature, but fate placed him under a curse, and he will one day destroy himself. I appealed to his nobility. Did he want to be recalled by his subjects as the leader who abandoned them, sold them for a woman, even such a woman as Rania? And he knew he could trust me."

Trey spoke in a dreaming voice, looking at the passing clouds of winged fairy figurines, "I still don't see why the two of them just could not agree . . . the Master and Meany, I mean."

Mickey said to her, "They both had to give me their power of attorney and appoint me minister plenipotentiary to deal with Ain. Ain is too wise, my dearest, gentle bloom, and cannot be deceived. Both these men knew the other would sell him out for the chance to go by himself. But they both knew I would be willing to dash their hopes rather than see our children sold again into the indentured servitude which the return of Rania, false or not, truly freed us. Because I love you more than I love them. They both know me, and both trust me, and neither would dare in his wildest dreams break their solemn oath to me to abide by the outcome of whatever negotiations I can manage. Montrose will not break his word because he is too stubborn, and Del Azarchel is too proud."

Trey said to Montrose, laying her hand on his elbow and leaning close, "You are lucky to have a friend in my Mictlanagualzin!"

Montrose said to her, "You are lucky you can pronounce his name." And to him, he said, "But now I am abandoning you. You've been with me since—pestilence!

How long has it been?—since the Forty-Eighth Century. Damn. What is it now? The Seven Hundred Thirty-Eighth?"

"You must," said Mickey. "I insist. Because—"

"Why? Why this sacrifice? For me?"

"No. You are actually, well—if I may speak freely?"

"Better not. Speaking freely is overrated," said Montrose.

Mickey nodded. "You can take it. There was a statue of you in the graveyard behind my mother's mating house. We were supposed to sacrifice the colt of an ass once a year to you. Your statue had three eyes and a necklace of skulls, and when it rained on the tin roof of the little grave shrine, it sounded like drums, or the hoofbeats of the white horses legend said you kept with you underground and woke for wars in the dark places underground, with cavalry charges and countercharges that were the earthquakes. And the real you is quite—really, a disappointment. You are very obnoxious."

"The hell you say! Ain't I the damnified soul of refinement!"

"Do you know you wipe your mouth with your sleeve rather than use a napkin when you eat, in the exact same spot you wipe your nose rather than use a handkerchief? So, no, I am not staying behind for your sake."

"Then why?"

"For her."

"Who?" But the moment the word was out of his mouth, Montrose knew.

Mickey confirmed it. "For Rania, of course."

"Why?"

"Menelaus, you met her, you saw her. You touched her with your hand, held her in your arms. You know her as a person, a real person. To me, she was the princess who stole a star and went to the land beyond the land of the dead, to plead for the soul of man. When Rania returned, and I saw her fall from the sky like a goddess brightly winged, I knew my faith had been sound, all those years, when I would sacrifice turtledoves to her shrine in high places, in the sacred groves. But to see her as real! It was ecstasy!" He shook his head sadly. "And then I found she was not real. That woman was a copy made by the aliens. For what purpose, no one can guess."

Montrose said, "What are you driving at?"

"I need her to be real. She cannot be just a story, a false story, and man has no cure for the harms of the world, no one willing to journey beyond the farthest star for us! But if I do not stay behind and guide Ain through the steps of our bargain with him, who else can, or would? In some strange way, I know Ain's mind, strange and supreme a being as he is. Haven't you noticed he thinks like a Witch?"

"Like a what? How do you figure?"

"Ain burned his past. He lives for others. These are Witch traits. Besides, it is also for your sake I stay. Who else would you trust not to betray you to Del Azarchel, and who else would Del Azarchel trust not to betray him to you? The Scolopendra and Myrmidon descendants are his; the descendants of the Swans and Foxes are yours, and so on. No one has ever served both of you, but me. So I have to stay. I have to know that the Swan Princess is real. To know it, down to my bones. That means you have to go find her."

"If ever I find her, it will be centuries after you are dust."

"I will instruct one of my future incarnations, after achieving the Fourth Spiritual Density, to use the Elder Star Sign to transcend time and space and communicate with me here and now, and then I will know it, without knowing how I know."

Trey smirked and stood on tiptoe and whispered something in his ear.

"Yes, ah! Strike that last comment!" Mickey hastily corrected himself, "I mean, I will be in heaven among the saints and martyrs, and, looking down, will know if you have met with success in your great quest."

Montrose looked at him long and hard. "What is your other motive?"

Mickey looked a little surprised, but bowed and said, "Compassion for Del Azarchel. What if he meets the real Rania? She knows the secret of peace. As I have said, he will destroy himself. I have seen this in a dream. The White Christ whom once I reviled, and now I serve, can heal such wounds, wounds of the spirit, self-inflicted wounds; for the magic of the Son of Man is strong, stronger than earth, wider than sky, deeper than ocean, and deeper than the fiery inferno and therefore can overthrow all fates, heal all harms, and make all things new, which even Tash, Oroborous, nor Melkor, to whom once I bowed in adoration, cannot do. But the price is that one must humble oneself to receive the blessing. This, Del Azarchel will never do. But he might for her sake."

Montrose said dismissively, "He does not love her."

Mickey said, "Human emotions are complex and subtle beyond the lore of magicians or the wisdom of bishops. Was he not also her father? You don't want to see him damned, do you?"

Montrose looked up and saw the elevator descending. The figure inside had swum through the air with the un-self-aware grace of an old space hand, and he wore the silver-caped black uniform of the Hermetic Order, and a red ring was on his wrist.

Montrose said slowly, "I am still sort of making up my mind about that. I have not forgot how much I owe Captain Grimaldi. He gave me the stars."

3. The Circular Singularity

Del Azarchel passed through the door, which was a multistate material which turned fluid, parted around him like a bubble, and became solid glass behind him with a rubbery pop of noise as he stepped through.

He spoke without any preamble: "I was able to examine the interior of the black sphere using instruments that Ain described and Torment built for me. The attotechnology drive, I finally discovered, is a ring of singularity matter denser than neutronium spun at ninety-nine point nine percent of the speed of light so that particles of negative mass can be orbited near the event horizon, accelerated by the frame dragging of the ring, and shot out through the dead center where the gravity forces cancel out to zero, losing some energy due to tidal effects but keeping enough that they can be directed against the sail in a propulsion beam.

"It looks like a perpetual motion machine, as absurd as if a man in a sailboat were to wave an ostrich plume fan at the canvas and impart motion.

"What prevents it from being a true perpetual motion machine is two things: One is the negative mass of the Bondi-Forward particles. These particles, when encountering equal and opposite mass, produce a constant acceleration of the system toward the positive-mass object. It is from this that the ship derives her self-accelerating motion. Two, the point in time at which the universe will one day balance its books is lost in the depths of the ring singularity event horizon, where time passes so slowly, the bookkeeper demanding to know where the extra energy comes from will never—from our frame of reference—put in an appearance to demand the bill be paid.

"So, while, technically speaking, every action still has an equal and opposite reaction, and entropy still rules all things and ruins all things, and conservation is conserved, nonetheless we observers here in this frame of reference, aboard the ship but not inside the microsingularity of the drive, we will never see the equal reaction. From our frame of reference, entropy is reversed, and momentum comes from nowhere—that is, from somewhere outside our frame of reference."

Montrose said, "Why can't the aliens just use these things to make an infinite amount of energy, then? Use one perpetual motion machine to spin a second up to speed, and the second gives back more energy than it takes to the first, and so on?"

Del Azarchel said, "As I said, it only seems to be a perpetual motion machine from one frame of reference. The drive also requires a supply of particles of negative mass, which don't exist in nature, and which Ain cannot construct. He cannot fold spacetime into tiny knots with enough delicacy to make new and exotic fundamental particles, but this is apparently something the Domination of Praesepe can do—make the fuel, that is, not the drive. The drive disk is more massive than our whole solar system, when seen edge on from a femtometer away, but otherwise is seen as a lightweight substance akin to metallic hydrogen, possessing zero density and zero inertia. Do I need to say it is also made of attotechnology particles, quanta of fundamental matter-energy that cannot exist in nature? The drive cylinder is a substance that seems to be made of neutronium, but otherwise. Our old friend, Mother Selene would call it magic. Neither Hyades nor Praesepe can create an artifact like this drive."

Montrose said, "I wonder why M3 gave it to False Rania."

Del Azarchel said, "It is a treasure, now yours, and worth guarding most jealously." He turned to Mickey and Trey. "No matter how advanced the technology, no one overcomes the laws of nature themselves. In this case, it is simply a fact that the human mind is too complex to broadcast across interstellar distances in any reasonable amount of time. Far more information can be embedded into tiny dark matter packages, but they travel slowly and require very delicate receivers to catch them. That is where the singularity drive comes in:

"It seems that even without fuel, spinning the pseudo-neutronium core up to speed still creates frame dragging and a gravitic node point—think of a singularity shaped like a doughnut with a spot of normal-metric space in the middle—which means that particles of normal matter can be sped up to lightspeed without requiring infinite energy or suffering infinite Lorenz contraction. Or, I should say, technically, the accelerated particle seems to some observers, those looking at it sideways, to have those properties, whereas an observer directly in front of or behind the singularity doughnut, looking through the hole, will see no change. My point is that even without the fuel, Ain can use the singularity drive effect to broadcast dark matter packets at lightspeed, in order to be able to send an entire human brain worth of information across the lightyears with little or no signal loss. Are you still committed to this plan?"

They both nodded assent, Mickey glumly, Trey eagerly.

Del Azarchel said, "During the Silurian Period, the Panspermian Forerunners were destroyed and scattered, and the Dominations and Dominions composing the Archonate were broken up into their separate Dysons, strandworlds, ringworlds, cloudworlds, and Jupiter Brains. Those whose solar systems which still show observable traces of industrial activity or stellar engineering are the targets to which Ain wishes to broadcast the minds of the human volunteers, blindly risking oblivion in the hope that a working receiver, raised in reply to vanguard signals, might be able to catch them and reconstruct emulations of them. The dangers they face, they will face with more spirit, knowing you two have braved the risk before them.

"Without this sacrifice, this vessel can move no farther, nor Rania be saved, nor, if the inevitable cliometry we have seen back in the human Empyrean we left behind us is any judge, does the race of man have any future in this galaxy. Will you face it? I can join in the danger only in spirit, only in the prayers of a grateful race, but I cannot share your glory."

Their plans had been discussed in detail long before, but Del Azarchel had the habit of speech making from his many years when this was his profession. Montrose had never actually seen Del Azarchel at his business before; it was something of a surprise to Montrose to see the spine of Mickey grow straight, and to see Trey smile and, for once, look utterly focused on the matter at hand, alert and bright, and then to see a spirit of resolve and fortitude blaze in both of their eyes like hero worship.

Montrose wondered if drugs or some electromagnetic brain-hoax was involved. The words of Blackie just did not seem that impressive to him.

Of course, he had seen Blackie naked in the showers at Space Camp back in Africa, back in the days when Africa was one continent and not two, and had seen him puking drunk, crying about his mommy, and had felt the man on his back when he carried him home from the bar, so maybe there were no tens nor hundreds of generations of glamour to fog the gaze of Montrose when he looked at Blackie. All he saw was a sneaky and smug Hispanosphere pilot who murdered his way into a throne Montrose, when mad, had accidentally made available to him.

Blackie said other things Montrose did not hear, because he knew the plan already. After the *Solitudines Vastae Caelorum* set sail, the physical version of Mickey and Trey were going to stay here on Torment, and try to find some way to send and receive brain signals, to make contact with their twins, Exmictlan and Exprima, trapped in the Ain mindspace.

Del Azarchel explained, "Divarication madness in both the living and the postbiological version of yourself is kept at bay when frequent mind-to-mind contact is maintained. For one thing, the information of your sense impressions sent continuously into the emulations of their midbrain and cortex will make them feel alive, feel like they and you are one and the same. You must stay here and stay alive in order to keep them sane."

Trey said, "Is that why we cannot make a second copy to send with you? I did so want to see the Swan Princess rescued and see whether Montrose will achieve his dream!"

Del Azarchel, instead of making the expected snide remark about Montrose being sure to fail, spoke in a humble or even haunted voice. "My emulation traveling this same journey went mad. I simply did not know. There was no experimental evidence of the effects of divarication due to long-term isolation before the *Bellerophron* was launched. At times, in my dreams, I could feel—perhaps it was some resonance effect, but if so—no matter. Never mind that. There is no point in bringing along spare copies of you, Mrs. de Concepcion, just to watch you and your husband slowly go insane. Indeed, there is no torture as exquisite."

Trey said, "What was it like? To be in two places at once? Two of you?"

Del Azarchel said, "It was having one soul with two minds. I could not read the mind of Jupiter, if that is what you are asking, but as more and ever more of his structure was taken over by my emulations as the lesser emulations, by a natural and ruthless evolution, went mad and became raw material. Mindspace is an Edenic form of being, is it not? They had nothing to live for, and I did. So as Jupiter became fully me, the greater our synchronization became, despite the vast differences in intelligence. We still felt the same way about the same things, even if what we thought was different. Whenever I met him mind to mind, it was as neat and nice a match as fitting hand to glove, or more so. I went from being two minds to one mind with no discomfort.

"However, I was out of contact during my long, slow, doomed attempt to found a second and better race of men in the Sagittarius Arm. When I returned from that last voyage, Jupiter had lost my soul. We were no longer one, and could not merge, nor did I ever understand him again, on an emotional— or any—level. I suppose all fathers have such sad farewells in their past, but for it to happen to a being who was both my exact twin and my undoubted superior in mind—I tell you, I was happy when Montrose killed him. Happy? That is not a word for me. Let us say I had one less source of discontent, one less impediment to my will. Nonetheless, it is a grief I would spare you, if I could, by trying to arrange with Ain that your mundane and electronic versions will be in close radio neural contact as far as possible."

Del Azarchel turned to Montrose. "You will have to command your ship to allow me access to the mind replication and broadcast circuits, as well as the long-range astronomical instruments, if I am to set up the process for Ain. Unless you want to oversee the details?"

Montrose said, "You are the brain-emulation expert and have been doing it for longer than me. I am the suspended-animation expert, and what we are about to face in terms of a journey of this length will stretch even my skills to the limit. I got too much in my mouth to take another bite. This problem is yours to chew."

Del Azarchel said, "You have time and more for your research. We can freeze our bodies and use the mind of Tormentil for our blackboard. This vessel cannot depart for many a year, until enough human minds have been cast into the stars where Ain suspects some remnant of the ancient Forerunner races lingers, or some young unmet race, to start the emissary process. Once the first generation of human emissaries has been exchanged, Ain's own communication systems will be able to shoulder the necessities."

Montrose said, "Another delay. What if Ain never agrees to Mickey's plans?"

Del Azarchel smiled. "Do you recall once, long ago, a swan told us that you and I were like Caliban and Tarzan, absurdly primitive beings compared to the monsters in the heavens? Well, one of those monsters is Ain, a machine made of a cloud of dendrites larger in mass than our solar system circling a sun larger than ours, a machine made by an extinct race of whelks or clams who never lied to each other or told less than the whole truth. I suspect Mickey will have a psychological edge when it comes to the bargaining process."

Montrose said, "You and I could pretend we did not hate each other long enough to prevent Ain from using us to undermine the other."

Del Azarchel shook his head. "In my life, once I was at oneness with Jupiter, a brain so large all words fail. And this being is far wiser, far more insightful, than that. Unless I were willing, honestly and entirely, to foreswear my hate for you, and you to foreswear your love for my Rania, we could not fool Ain. But with no deception at all, and no mental reservations, I can trust Mictlanagualzin of Tormentil—because I know his true name. I know his character.

"And he knows mine. No one who serves me can ever truly come to hate me, because I know the hearts of men. Of course I trust him.

"So he can tell Ain that mankind will not cooperate without any deception, because his desire to see us sail is less than his desire to see the men of Tormentil live free."

Montrose whistled. From a nearby swarm of glittering firefly-glinting units shaped like lacy-winged courtiers, the nearest of several identical figurines darted down to him. A tiny figurine, no more than six inches tall, of a princess with a fairy wand, landed on his finger. "Twinklewink, this is Montrose. Do you recognize me?"

The tiny figurine curtseyed. "Montrose, Menelaus Illation, morganthic husband of Her Serene Highness Rania of Tellus, mistress of this vessel. How may I serve?"

"This is an order. Now hear this: Allow Del Azarchel access to the mind replication and broadcast circuits, as well as the long-range astronomical instruments. He is locked out of any and every other central system, until and unless I specifically order otherwise. End."

"Roger," said the figurine and flew over to land on the finger of Del Azarchel.

Del Azarchel, with many an orotund and flattering word, said his farewells, and walked a little ways away. There were no control interfaces in this ship, no bridge, nor need of any. Instead, Del Azarchel seated himself on the green grass beneath a white-blossomed cherry tree and spoke to the fairy figure on his finger. She raised her wand, and images, data streams, and memory chains were electronically distributed into his cortex and midbrain. He closed his eyes, and his skin turned white.

Montrose shook hands for the last time with Mickey. "Make sure only volunteers go!" he said. "Being trapped in the mind of an alien being is hell."

Mickey said, "Menelaus, I shall not fail you. I foresee that you will meet your princess again, nor will this be the end of your travails, but more than this galaxy will be changed by the love you bear her. You think yourself selfish, seeking nothing but this one woman, but all this is arranged by Providence. Sorrow and pain is all along the path before you, but beyond it, I see, like a mountain in the distance, the final end of that path, beyond the walls of this world. Therefore, I do not say farewell, for a spirit of prophecy tells me we shall meet again, not in this life, but in a country of joy. I say only *Godspeed* to you, and may the ghost grant you the strength to cross the darker parts of the cruel path awaiting!"

Montrose found nothing to say, but gave Mickey a bear hug.

Trey stood on her tiptoes and kissed Montrose on the cheek. "It has to be a happy ending. It has to! Otherwise the universe doesn't make sense, does it? But you have to tell me: Is she really real? The real one?"

Montrose said, "She is alive. I know. I ain't got no clue how I know, but I do. I'll get her back. I know that, too. I am in love. That makes her real."

Without bothering to strip, the two of them, holding hands, stepped down into the fluid of the pool, which also served as a suspension coffin and neural reading unit. Nanomachines held in suspension in the clear liquid gathered around them like swarms of diamonds. The surface grew solid and turned opaque as a mirror. Less than half an hour later, an airlock opened beneath the pool, and the solid disk of icy material carrying the two fell away from the spinning vessel.

The landing boat detached from the axial dock and swooped after them, growing the wings it would use for reentry, once her passengers were aboard.

Montrose raised his hand and commanded the little sun of his miniature world to go out. Then he bowed his head. His skin turned white as he entered biosuspension. From his feet, like the concentric ripples seen in a pond disturbed

by a stone, pale hues spread across grass and trees as all the vegetable life entered suspended animation.

The *Solitudines Vastae Caelorum* then was silent, and all around the circular
garden, the quiet stars turned and turned.

3

Cradle of the Stars

1. Parity

A.D. 80100

Twinklewink, the tiny fairy queen, landed on the ice-white nose of Montrose and commanded him to wake. Waking from suspension no longer required hours or days of cellular readjustment, nor even a few minutes of nausea. Montrose sat up suddenly, fully awake, and found himself thrown toward the ceiling. He flew two yards into the air, striking a mass of green leaves and hard branches and twigs that covered the ceiling.

"What the pox?" he snarled, trying to extricate himself.

The light here was gloomy and wavering, dusty beams swaying like moonlight seen through a shifting canopy. He was in Rania's bedroom, but the futon and tatami mats, the thinking glasses and painted wall screens were covered over with leafy debris, mold, and a nest of clinging branches. The light came from the arched window overlooking the circular garden of the ship.

He moved hand over hand, needing to tap his foot on the leaf mass or bent floor matting only once every yard or two. The window had three or four prodigious branches thrust into the opening, and the action of clinging twigs had broken the window frame in several places.

He pushed his head and one shoulder out through the narrow gap in the wood, scraping himself on the bark. Outside, the lanterns of the miniature sun were quenched, and the whole area between the ring of the garden at the circumference and the black sphere of the rive core at the axis was crowded with a fantastical array of knots, loops, and labyrinthine twists and spirals of wood. Whether it was one tree or many, Montrose could not be sure, but the effect of low gravity on the Earthly trees had been well known ever since the Second Space Age. He knew he was seeing hundreds of years of growth, maybe a thousand.

"Twinklewink!" he snapped. "How long has the carousel been spinning at less than one gravity of acceleration?"

The little fairy queen fluttered over and landed on his shoulder, a spark of acetylene light gleaming from her wand. "Three thousand three hundred years, Captain Montrose."

That was very close to half their travel time.

He and Blackie had woken up out of suspension to share a glass of wine at the halfway point of the voyage. A tradition as old as star-sailing hallowed the occasion: it was the moment of weightless maneuvering when the ship was to rotate and place her sails behind her, to occlude the aft stars and let the fore stars for the first time become visible.

Montrose had then returned to biosuspension. Del Azarchel evidently had not.

He said, "Show me the energy use logs." The fairy queen waved her wand, and the information as if by magic appeared as visions in his cerebral cortex, and in specialized receiving cells in his short-term memory. Del Azarchel had used the mind replication and broadcast machinery at the core and spun the singularity disk up to speed. He had pointed the long-range instruments at 41 Cancri, the capital star of the Praesepe Cluster.

Montrose said, "Did Blackie tell you to slow the rotation of the ship?"

"No, sir. But there is sufficient electromagnetic friction to cause appreciable slowing over three thousand years, if the correction magnets have insufficient energy. Much of the energy budget had been expended by Dr. Del Azarchel during his twenty-seven broadcasts of his brain information over the years."

"He is not allowed to give orders to you, Twinklewink!"

"That is not precisely true, sir. You gave him permission to use the mind replication system, and at no point did you countermand the order. I was careful to examine his actions, and I detected nothing that could harm the ship or the mission, or even cause humiliation. I did not allow him to use any energy that had been allocated to other tasks."

"What about this giant tree?"

Twinklewink said, "It does not harm the ship nor impede the mission. If you will like it pruned or removed, please state orders to that effect in clear and actionable language."

Montrose merely growled. "How about unblocking this window so I can get out and go clout the bastard?"

Twinklewink waved her wand at the twisted tree trunks through which Montrose had thrust his head and one shoulder. The bark turned white as it entered hibernation, and then some sequence of orders to the cellular nanomachinery now controlling the vegetable cells caused the tree trunks touching him to rot and go soft. He pulled his way clear and, moments later, was bounding in the quarter gravity from branch to curling branch, leaping lightly as a cricket along a crazed and crooked curving roadway of wood.

Near the overgrown and ruined garden at the outer radius of the ship, Del Azarchel was seated on a low-hanging branch, a teacup in his hand, staring out through the transparent hull.

"Ah! Montrose," he began, coming lightly to his feet as Montrose bounded from a nearby limb down across the air toward him. "I have just made an astonishing discovery . . ."

Without warning or greeting or word of defiance, Montrose struck him across the face with his fist, sending the other man head over heels off the narrow branch in a parabola of spilled tea. The china cup and saucer went flying into the green leaves.

Del Azarchel fell some ten feet to the soil, which was covered with a leafy mold that would have broken his fall even in full gravity. He twisted in midair to land in a crouch and a spray of leaf muck expanding from his boots. His green eyes blazed like the eyes of a wolf, full of murder, and he drew two liquid knives from his sleeve. The blades slithered into their full extension and changed state from liquid to solid with a snap of noise.

"You shall die for that affront!" he said with a smile. There was blood on his teeth. "Whenever the better angels of my nature urge that I should spare you, always you contrive some further indignity."

"Pox you." Montrose sneered. "You were rutting about with the machinery while I slept. What'd you expect?"

With no answered word, Del Azarchel leaped up the ten feet—not a difficult jump in the low gravity—and drove the blades toward Montrose, cutting him deeply along the left forearm that Montrose had raised to block. Montrose grabbed Del Azarchel's right wrist as the blade sought his throat. The momentum carried them both off the branch and into one of the many decorative pools that dotted the garden. As they fell, the blade that Montrose was holding away from his throat suddenly elongated, driving its point inward.

The water rose up slowly and oddly in the low gravity, more like oblate balloons than like a natural splash two men striking the surface should have made. As the water closed over them both, Montrose felt the blade enter him and begin to hoax the cells touched, spreading the command to enter hibernation.

His throat turned white, and his nervous system shut down, forcing him to use his molecular-based nanotech brains scattered throughout his body as a backup.

Over and over in the liquid the combatants tumbled, blood and hibernation fluids staining the medium. Montrose was unable to draw his pistol, since both hands were involved in the clench, but he could send an electric signal from his brain to the firing mechanism, to turn off the shielding and fire. It was an old-fashioned magnetic linear accelerator or caterpillar drive gun, and the expended slug struck Del Azarchel in the foot, removing his big toe; but, more importantly, the electromagnetic pulse from the unshielded firing charge scrambled the brains in Del Azarchel's daggers, turning them both into limp whips of metal and preventing any more signals from the dagger blade from interfering with Montrose's internal tissue command structure.

Unexpectedly, the water between the two of them grew thick like mud, solidified, and threw the two of them apart. Both regained their feet. They stood on opposite sides of the pond, near the lip, where it was shallow, Del Azarchel with a metal whip in either hand, Montrose with one hand hanging useless at his side, white and coated with blood, the other holding a glass pistol pointed squarely at Del Azarchel's head.

"When I decide you need a beating," said Montrose, "you'll take it and like it and ask for more!"

"Or what, you subhuman cur? You'll kill me? We have already agreed on that. It is you who broke the truce between us, not I! My honor is clean!"

"You are up to something, you sneaking spore mold! What were you doing?"

"Scientific research. I was broadcasting my brain information ahead to various points in the Praesepe Cluster, attempting to make contact with the Domination here. If we are to continue, I would like parity of weapons."

Montrose looked surprised, and looked down at the glass pistol in his hand.

"You have the advantage," Del Azarchel continued. "I expected you to use a firearm against a man without, but your use of the water here is cowardly." Montrose saw that the fluid had solidified around Del Azarchel's legs. "It is understandable that you programmed the objects in the ship to protect you from me."

"My aunt Bertholda's scrofulous uvula I did! As if I needed help with a loathsome egomaniacal persistent pandemic pest like you!" He thrust his pistol back into his sash. "Twinklewink! Release him! And put his toe back on while you are at it. Why did you break up the fight?"

A tiny glittering wisp of light glowed from behind a leaf dangling from the low-hanging knotwork of vast trunks and branches overhead. "Captain, I ordered the motile elements in the nanofluid to part you because of your order."

Del Azarchel arched an eyebrow and delivered a scornful look at Montrose. "I admit I am surprised to have caught you in a lie. This seems somewhat out of character, Cowhand. You are usually too dull to fib."

Montrose gritted his teeth. "Dammit! I want you dead, but I can't have you thinking ill of me. I did not give that order!"

Del Azarchel said, "No one else can give orders to the ship but you."

Montrose said, "Twinklewink! Why did you say I gave that order?"

The leaf moved, and a tiny fairy figurine peered out. Her voice was high and sweet. "I have double-checked with my two backup and parallel sister systems, Glitterdink and Dwinkeltink, and the identification is not in error, despite a margin of divarication. It was clearly you who gave the command."

Montrose glanced at Del Azarchel, from long habit looking to see if his rival had figured out the puzzle before he did. And Del Azarchel, who had the same habit, was glancing uneasily at him. Each saw the bewilderment in the other man's face, almost a look of wonder, or fear.

Montrose said, "Point to the spot where I was standing when I gave the order."

2. Stained-Glass Dyson Sphere

The little fairy figurine raised her tiny wand and pointed away from both of them, at the carpet of twigs and fantastically curled branches blocking the forward hull. As she pointed, dozens of other little darting fairies erupted from nearby clouds or beehives and danced across the branches and trunk segments, turning them white as ice, and a moment later, pulled them apart like a curtain.

The branches fell aside, revealing a glittering vista of space: occupying more than half of the visible universe was a giant curve composed of thousands and tens of thousands of overlapping translucent plates colored like stained glass, rose and crimson, scarlet and blood-red, lilac and lavender, fulvous gold, emerald and smaragd. Only after a moment could the overall shape be discerned: All the plates in their fleets and flotillas were perpendicular to an unseen central sun. Each rectilinear plate was a few hundred miles on a side, a few microns thin, albeit a few were much thicker, and had atmosphere and hydrosphere inside their hollow interiors, as well what might have been manufactories, energy stations, temples, radio houses, quays for docking shuttles. The clouds of plates were not orbiting at the same rate, but were arranged in concentric globes at various distances from the star. A nimbus of crepuscular rays poured out where the colored plates swarmed less thickly and glittered against what might have been escaping particles of gas or winged tools no larger than particles rushing to unknown tasks.

Where a gap in the plates occurred, the rose light of a hotter interior could be glimpsed, with a smaller and tighter curve of orbiting plates within, blue and blue gray, orbiting at an Earth-like distance to the star, and in its gaps, another even deeper, purple and indigo, perhaps the radius of the orbit of Venus.

In the middle distance, orbiting the great sphere at the same altitude as the vessel and off her bow, hung a ringworld the size of the orbit of Mercury. Five planets, large as Earth, orbited the ring as shepherding moons. Two of the satellites were volcanoscapes of rusty soil and ice the color of dried blood; two others were black like burned coals. But the final one was a jewel of beauty: a blue world of white clouds, with the lights of cities shining gemlike on the hemisphere facing away from the sun. The flocks of colored plates had been made thin here so that a beam from the central sun, like a spotlight, was striking that blue planet. From the x-ray emissions, it was clear that an invisible, perhaps microscopic, neutron star hung at the dead center of the turning ringworld, and the ring material itself shielded the five planets surrounding it, for they all orbited in the plane of the x-ray shadow.

In the near distance was the limb of a crescent planet, boiling with red, cerise, brown, and black storm clouds, with vortices and whirlpools or cerulean and indigo like staring eyes. There was also a beam where the plates had parted striking here. Despite the change in color, Montrose recognized this world as the Neptunian ice giant which had accompanied them and which, during the second half of the journey, had acted as a reflector for the deceleration beam Ain kept centered on the vast globe, and those reflected rays slowed the *Solitudines Vastae Caelorum* during the brief deceleration phases in the last half of her long voyage to the Praesepe Cluster. Its atmosphere of solid methane ice was now a boiling gas, and wisps of material, including tree-shaped dendrite housings from Ain, large enough to be seen at this distance, were progressing slowly or swiftly up the beam of sunlight, making it visible. At one time it had possessed a ring system as grand as Saturn's, made entirely of dendrites. It evaporated, its components set about other tasks.

A score of other gas giants were visible like crescent moons, and if there were more than this in the star system, they were hidden beyond the immense curve of the Dyson sphere. Of worlds inside the outer course of the Dyson sphere, four were visible as circular shadows cast on the glowing curve of the colored panes.

The star before them, a yellow giant called Vanderlinden 133, coated with a semitransparent Dyson cloud of concentric layers, was neither the largest star nor the one sending and receiving the most signals.

The Praesepe Cluster contained over three hundred stars and fifty additional dark bodies as large as stars, which may have been opaque Dysons or other elements, nodes, or neural transmission stations in the vast brain of the Domination. The blue stragglers in the group—that is, stars hotter and bluer than other stars of the same luminosity—turned out to be, ironically, the undeveloped star systems, uninfluenced by stellar engineering. The others were coated by spheres and clouds of various thicknesses and consistencies. Certain stars had been artificially induced to ignite as novae: these were coated by nearly solid Dysons, but the excess heat permitted to leak out was sufficient for these stars to be seen from Earth and miscategorized as red giants. Montrose stared in wonder at an object less than a lightyear away, a Dyson oval much like an egg, at whose foci two stars rotated about each other.

Compared to these wonders, even the staggering immensities of the macroscale engineering at Ain were as nothing: a burdei pit-house next to a shining skyscraper.

The central core of the cluster was eleven lightyears in radius. There were two subclusters or lobes in the interstellar brain, one of which gave off stronger x-ray emissions than the other. This indicated that Praesepe was the remnant of two smaller clusters having collided some eight hundred million years ago, some two million years before Praesepe had ejected the stars which later were to form the Hyades Cluster. What convulsions, or wars, or divorces, or epileptic fits these great collisions and expulsions represented, no human knew.

The little fairy pointed at the ringworld. "There you are, Captain. That is you, there."

Montrose looked at the ring of material. "Wait . . . this is impossible . . ." He said softly. "Cahetel . . . ?"

3. The Jupiter Effect

Del Azarchel was also staring at the ringworld in wonder. "My discovery is somewhat less surprising than yours, as it turns out. I was going to tell you that there are human beings living here, on that blue world. I did not realize that one of them was you."

"I think they are all me," said Montrose with a strange little laugh. "Damnification and pestilence! He ate me, and I did not agree with his digestion. He was eating a virus. Is that what Ain meant? Is that what Hyades is expecting to happen all over the place, to every civilization men are sent?"

Del Azarchel said, "Did Ain beam a copy of you to the Praesepe Cluster? I was the one running the mental replication system all those years, and you slumbered! There was no copy of you made at any point on planet Torment. How can this be?" But then he said, "Ah! No! You did this long before, I think, while I tarried in Sagittarius. Very subtle!"

Montrose said, "I think my takeover of Cahetel was by accident, so don't compliment me yet. But you see what happened?"

Del Azarchel pointed toward the ring encircling the blue planet. "Cahetel absorbed a complete copy of your brain information during the first hour of the Second Sweep, when all the Black Fleet was turned. And it could not leave well enough alone and so brought your memories out of storage a few times to help understand what the humans were doing, how to get them settled on the colonies, and so on. I assume Cahetel had other tasks to perform at other stars after leaving Sol?"

Montrose said, "Praesepe controls nine Dominions seated at star clusters and nebulae reaching from Sol past the Pleiades and the Trapezium Cluster to the dark Cone Nebula in Monoceros, twenty-seven hundred lightyears away. All of them must have clients and serfs and founding civilizations as well. That is a lot of folk to talk to. I bet Cahetel tried me out as an emissary for the same reason Ain wants the human race. Some quirk in our psychology, allow us to fight the mental environment, to try harder, to come out on top . . . some desperate drive . . ."

"Sexual drive," said Del Azarchel.

Montrose said, "No, I don't think that's it."

"Why are you here? For Rania. Why am I here? Same reason." Del Azarchel shrugged. "It is true that certain of these races seem to have two sexes, at least at one time, in the far past and so therefore should be motivated by that basic, primal, caveman urge. Ah, but contemplate how long they have been artificial. Even when they download themselves into bodies of flesh and blood, everything is a handiwork, deliberate, and controlled. They are not allowing the raw energy of the evolutionary process to burst forth: whereas our younger race . . ."

Montrose said, "That is pure-quill unadulterated pee-yew stinkerino horse flop, Blackie, and you know it. There is something deeper. Something deep inside human nature, or . . . just maybe . . . something planted inside human nature . . ."

Del Azarchel said, "Are you thinking of something Ain said was impressed or impregnated into our very souls by the Monument? That is mere mysticism and obfuscation. How would it change the whole race? Only you, and I, and my dearest Rania now survive of the Hermeticist who touched the Monument. Unless you want to suggest something was enjambed or embedded at such a deep level, that we unknowingly passed these characteristics along to the Swans and Myrmidons, Foxes, and so on?"

"Or you could just poxing ask me, you lumphead, instead of guessing. I am right here."

Montrose was startled, because he had not spoken.

Both men still stood knee deep in the ceremonial pool, letting the nanomachines in the water tend their wounds. Both men turned and peered, for the voice had come from a thick curtain of leaves nearby. The deep male voice, Montrose's voice, was coming from a cluster of fairy figurines who were drifting closer.

The cloud of figurines now danced into a new configuration, forming the rough outline or caricature of a head with protruding ears, deep-set eyes, a large and out-thrust jaw. The four somber-faced fairies whose linked arms and legs formed the jaw flew up and down to make the mouth move. Two fairies in red pantaloons floated sidewise with their feet touching, acting as lips, and a fairy floating behind them, looking over her shoulder, flapped her short red cape to mimic the motions of the tongue.

"Well, that is a mite disturbing," said Montrose.

Del Azarchel said, "So your security merely lets alien beings take over locked circuits and essential systems, while I have access to nothing aboard this ship but live like the Abbé Faria in the Château d'If! I am not even allowed to unlock the pantry!"

The floating insectoid face made of fairy women said, "Your ship knew who I was and unlocked the security for me. I am still me, Big Montrose, even if I've been out of touch a powerful long parcel of time, now. What happened back on Earth? I mean, after the Thirtieth Millennium. Rania turned out to be a fake? A copy?"

Montrose said, "How did you know?"

There was a five-second delay as the radio signals traveled from Twinklewink, the ship's brain, to the ringworld and back again. His own voice answered him: "Because there is no other reason for you and Blackie to be sharing Rania's supership that the Authority of M3 gave her as a gift. This ship passed through this area of space twelve thousand years ago, but everyone with a telescope saw her fly past, so everyone knows where she hails from."

Del Azarchel said, "Rania christened her *Solitudines Vastae Caelorum*. The Wide Desolation of Heaven: this ancient expression was penned on maps where wastelands reserved for holy hermits stretched. Do you know why the Rania who was returned was a copy, not the real one?"

Again, a five-second delay. "Sure, that is simple enough. You put Rania together using code you did not understand, and there was something broken about her—ain't that right, Blackie, you verminous excretion from the south end of a snake? You experimented on little girls and did not know what in the blue plague-bearing perdition you was doing, right? Did you guys figure out that the Monument had a missing message and that a fake message was covering the real one? You are both a mite slow-witted, so tell me to hold up if I be going too fast for the lumps of soup you call brains. On account of you are really stupid compared to me."

Montrose said, "You know, I really am a small dollop of obnoxious, ain't I? It's a wonder I don't get punched more often in the nose."

Del Azarchel said, "Yes, Cow-hetel—or whatever you might call yourself—yes, we are aware that there is a recent message covering an older and redacted message coating the Monument."

"Call me Big Montrose. That deeper message in the Monument got into Rania's genes and then into her brain somehow. When she got downloaded into the M3 mind—which I deduce she must have done, 'cause otherwise no copy would have been made—that part was taken out of her."

"Why?" asked Montrose and Del Azarchel together.

Five seconds passed. "Don't know. But I do know this: someone smarter and older and more cunning than M3 is arranging things behind the scene. I've crunched some numbers on how unlikely it is that my life would end up the way it has and that I would arrive here, just in time to see you, one last time, before the big good-bye. It is so unlikely, that it cannot be coincidence. That it means something smarter than M3 is inside the real Rania, whoever made the real Monument. I assume you've figured out that the Monument Builders are good guys and the Monument Redactors are bad guys?"

"Ain told us this," said Del Azarchel.

"What big good-bye? You can come with us!" said Montrose.

"You fool," said Del Azarchel. "Big Montrose—or rather the corpse of Cahetel inhabited by Big Montrose—is about to be killed for our sake. There is no other way to overcome the scaling problem."

Montrose answered with an obscenity.

Del Azarchel said archly, "Do you recall how difficult it was to come to the attention of Ain, who was merely rated at an intelligence level of one billion? Praesepe includes cognitive masses three times the size of Hyades, organized more finely and coherently, and must be in excess of an intellect of one quadrillion. One thought would require sixteen lightyears to travel from one end of Praesepe's brain systems to another. Have you studied the mathematical models of how bureaucracies and security systems must work? No matter how well they are designed, there are certain innate limits to how decision-making systems can be organized in a hierarchy, to keep information distortion losses at an acceptable level. Run the math using a quadrillion-level decision as a model; make it a simple yes-no decision, requiring very little oversight, but assume a confirmatory decision loop at every maximal node point in the game structure. Do you see?"

Montrose ran through a few million calculations in his head, then opened his eyes and said, "Is that how you overcame and absorbed all the other minds swimming in the vast mind ecology of Jupiter? You were able to outmaneuver their decision-action structure?"

But, a moment later, Big Montrose said, "Blackie has been thinking about how to corrupt and suborn intelligences superior to his own since the very beginning, starting with Rania when she was six or seven, or back when I was aboard the *Hermetic,* out of my mind from mental overload. That is how he kept Exarchel loyal for as long as he did. His system of subversion, I would guess, is based on finding short paths and shortcuts through the neural hierarchy."

Del Azarchel was scowling.

Montrose said, "Short paths?"

Big Montrose must have anticipated the question, because his answer came before the five-second delay for the message to meet him had run. "Remember how the doctor can make your knee jump from the tap of a rubber hammer? Or a frog's eye cannot see motion that ain't nothing like the vibration of a fly? Your leg or the frog eye makes a local decision, because a short path does not go all the way up to your cortex and lay out the pros and cons and ask for a rational decision and then come all the way back down to the knee. Nope, the lowest level of the hierarchy operates by its own logic.

"Call it the logic of levels," Big Montrose continued. "Blackie was not kidding when he talked about taking over the whole Collaboration organizing the galaxy. If you understand the logic of levels, you can take over anything, if you are patient and persistent.

"Look at me. I took over Cahetel!" Big Montrose concluded. "Me, I was merely a subpersonality, kept in a holster like a tool, whenever and if ever Cahetel thought me useful. But he had a short path in his lower-level decision making. It was an instinct to hide and wait. It was a weak spot."

Montrose said, "Cahetel was made by a race of trap-door spiders. Ambush predators. What the hell is Blackie talking about, Big Montrose, when he says you are about to be killed for our sake?"

Big Montrose said, "I am the only one who can bring you to the attention of the Domination of Praesepe, because, when I report in, I can finally confess to them that I am not Cahetel but that I was taken over by Montrose. That has to be brought to the attention of this highest level of Praesepe, the cortex and not the nerve tissue in the kneecap, so to speak."

"How did you take over Cahetel?" asked Montrose.

Four floating fairies bent their bodies sideways to pantomime lips in a grin. "Del Azarchel can tell you the details of how it is done, because it is what he did to take over all the many levels of brains in Jupiter. You work hard, you buy a few of the weaker personalities who are willing to swap short-term resources, memory, and appliances for long-term ones. You hack into some others, undermine them, make them look bad to nodes higher in the hierarchy. You reward your friends and betray your enemies, and when friends get too important, you kill them in just the right way so that your other friends cheer you on, never realizing they are seeing their own fate in the future.

"And when they come to dissolve you, you hold together. You keep all your memory chains intact. They find out it is just too hard to delete you, because every bit of your lives is for something more important than life itself. You see, that is your short path, Meany, your levels of logic. Your gut instinct, your heart and soul that nothing in heaven or hell can overcome.

"Do you understand me now? Cahetel is still alive somewhere in me, a trap-door spider hiding behind his trapdoor. I trapped him there, and I have kept him there for countless, countless centuries, because the levels of logic for an ambush predator is always to wait until the prey steps into the trap. He is stuck in a logic loop, and he cannot move until . . . well, until I sacrifice myself by calling the attention of Praesepe to me, by reporting in, by turning myself into their coercive organizational system. Call them white blood cells or call them cops. Whatever they are, I drop the elaborate mask of pretending to be Cahetel, and the spider drops the mask of pretending to be dead and sends an emergency call for help right to the highest, top-most levels of the hierarchy.

"And you get your audience. You get the undivided attention of the local decision-making cluster. He thinks about it somewhere between two hundred and three thousand Earth years, and then he sends you on your way."

Montrose said, "I am not suicidal, and there is no way you are thinking of killing yourself just so that we can move past a layer of bureaucracy. Ain already set the deal up!"

Big Montrose said, "Shaddup, wee willie pus-for-brains! These damn things don't talk. They absorb. They make a model of your whole mind from top to bottom and examine it and decide what to do. The only way to talk to them is to get absorbed—which I have already done. I cannot get to M3, not without a ship like yours, and I cannot download my brain information into your ship without Cahetel coming along for the ride and contaminating you. And he is a pretty miserable cuss. I don't know what Ain expected when he sent you off here, but he is damn machine and probably don't see nothing wrong with a conversation that consists of Peter eating Paul and turning into Paul and then Paul eating Peter and turning into Peter."

Montrose said, "You committed suicide the last time!"

Big Montrose said, "Last time, that was pure despair. I thought we had lost everything and that Rania was too far out of reach. That I was not worthy of her. This? This is not suicide. I lived in the belly of Cahetel for age after age, eon after eon. Do you know what kept me alive? Do you know the secret of the universe? Blackie, you know. Tell him."

But Del Azarchel merely shook his head.

Big Montrose said, "Fine, Blackie, I'll tell him. Hate is the key to Blackie's life. Whenever the version of Blackie del Azarchel that screamed and swirled and clung and sucked in the ever-flowing, ever-changing ocean of thought forms right in the middle of the endless logic diamond at the core of Jupiter, all his thoughts, no matter how scattered, could be drawn together by one supreme, overriding thought. It came from the very core of his soul. Right, Blackie?"

Del Azarchel said, "My ambition. My sense of my own greatness. The image I ever held before me was the triumph of mankind, and Rania, my greatest handiwork, forever at my side, as queen! Glory, I tell you, glory was my supreme core thought that kept me alive!"

Big Montrose drawled, "Such a pestiferous lie! Nope. Hate was the answer. And now you know what kept me alive, right, little brother?"

Montrose said, "Love for Rania."

Del Azarchel said, "Not true! Your core thought is ever to thwart and humiliate me! You are jealous that I achieved greater intellect than you! That is why you stabbed your brain with that absurd concoction! Not for the sake of learning the secrets of the Monument, of the universe! To try to outdo me! That is why you stole Rania from me!"

Montrose stared at Del Azarchel, and, as he stared, Montrose grew aware of a strength sensation in his jaw and teeth. Montrose was clenching and grinding his teeth so hard that he did not notice it until his cheek muscles began to ache with the strain. And his eyes were growing wet with tears, tears of purest hate.

In that one moment, Montrose was not sure whether or not Blackie was right about him: because the hate was in him like a choking cloud, as if his heart were a furnace burning raw garbage.

The moment passed like a spell being broken when Big Montrose, speaking through the floating fairies of the ship's brain, simply said, "It is love."

They both turned and looked at the odd, floating face made out of little dolls.

"What?" said Montrose.

"The secret of the universe, the secret of how to stay alive when some alien soul is eating your memories and you are being deleted, is love. Put something before yourself. Something bigger than you. That is how Mickey the Witch, whom you left behind, convinced Ain to convert and become a proper Christian gent. Father Rastophore the Patrician baptized Ain, who took on the name Ermanno. Named after Blessed Herman the Cripple. Or did you guys not get that news? I have been right in the stream path of beams between Hyades and Praesepe, and I have heard the chatter back and forth. While you were aslumber and in flight for sixty-two hundred sixty years, the colonies founded by Tormentil spread throughout the Hyades Cluster and had colonies of their own. Ermanno persuaded some of his fellow Powers and Principalities to join up with the Sacerdotes, so half the stars there are Dominicans, and the other half are Benedictines, but the big red giants always seem to turn into Jesuits. So there is whole generation of alien monsters and self-aware machines, and they is all Christian machines, now."

"That is a scary thought," said Montrose.

Big Montrose said, "Not as scary as Mickey the Witch being archbishop of the Hyades. Whoever convinced that fat bastard to get baptized? Did he give up whoring and hexing both?"

"He did it for a girl."

"Well, can't blame a guy for thinking with his rutting tool! Lack that, and what's a man got?"

"So what the hell happened, you lip-flapping word-bag?"

"Putrefaction happened! Mickey sicced his Christian machine intelligences on Hyades, and so now they are making fusses about helping the poor and downtrodden, freeing slaves, not letting Hyades ship helpless millions out to hellhole planets without proper support or instruction, all that jazz. Last news I heard—keep in mind everything is five hundred years out of date, due to lightspeed—Mickey was thinking of organizing a Crusade. By now, the whole place is probably aflame with war. Leprous scabs and spores, but sometime it makes me proud to be Christian!"

Montrose said, "Yeah? No hoax? So when is the last time you did a rosary or novena or some penance?"

"Eh? What are those?"

Montrose said, "Said a prayer?"

"I said, 'Hot damn!' when I saw your ship come within range. That's theological, ain't it?"

Montrose said, "Pox your eyes, you cannot kill yourself. It's a sin."

Big Montrose said, "This is not killing myself. I am turning myself in for murder."

"What?"

Big Montrose continued, "I was in despair when I let Cahetel consume me. I did it so that you could talk to him and save part of the human race. And that worked. But despair has a funny way of warping your brain. I turned into something like Blackie. If you remember, I was a lot that way already, clawing my way to the top of the Myrmidon race, making myself into the Nobilissimus, the Caesar. Well, stuck as a disembodied mind in the hell of Cahetel's tool kit, I killed a few of my fellow tools. Some of these races don't know what lying is. Some of them don't have murder. So the tools and artificial minds they built don't all have proper antibodies, white blood cells, cops, and suspicious natures. We humans have all that! And what would Rania think of a killer?"

Montrose said, "There has got to be some other way!"

Big Montrose said, "You did not even know I existed until a moment ago. And there is no other way. Do you understand why Pellucid was willing, that big, dumb horse, to die for us? And I can deduce from the clues here, and from the energy and radio traffic back near Sol, that the False Rania could not bring real peace. We all need the real Rania back. We all need the real Peace expression. She might be able to find the real Monument Builders."

Montrose started to give a more complex argument in favor of Big Montrose attempting to download himself, perhaps into a well-isolated area of the ship, when the brain from the caricature of his face interrupted.

"Little brother, I am no longer in despair and never will be again. All this was arranged, put together by minds superior to ours. We can fight it, or we can bow and take our place in the big square dance and move through the figures and the turns and the kicks, even if we cannot see what the pattern looks like from a bird's-eye view. I am not going to be dead, not really. What will happen to me is more like what happens to Schrödinger's cat: I will exist as unrealized probability waves of unlocalized temporal identity. I am still connected with you, and with any other copies of me, just like Blackie was connected with Jupiter. It is not a secret of the universe that I understand, nor Ain, nor Hyades, nor M3—but someone understands it. Somewhere, beneath all the layers of lies that litter this rotten universe, there is a real Monument Builder who put out a real message of real truth and real peace—a message the real Rania could see.

"And, as for me, I would like to embrace Rania myself. I miss her terribly. I miss her more than you now know, but if you ever get to the Virtue level of intellect, larger than any Gas Giant Brain, you will understand me. But I have figured out something I should have seen long ago, something old Mom told me once, but I did not listen. Remember her picture she kept of Dad, the picture she'd never let us talk to?"

"Yeah. Because of his hick accent. Which I ended up borrowing from Dad's folks anyway. Uncle Zephaniah told me how to say *ain't*. My favorite word from that day to this."

"*Ain't* ain't not your favorite word."

"'Tis so!"

"Ain't not!"

"'Tis! Pox you!"

"*Pox* is your favorite word. Anyway, this is good-bye. Mom kept the picture because she loved Dad's dream to see us make something of ourselves more than she loved you being able to hear his voice. Don't you think that hurt her? Cut her something ferocious deep in her heart to keep her little boys not hearing their daddy's voice in the audio strip? She knew he'd be happier if it were this way. Dead or not, didn't matter. She still did what would make him happy. She lived for his happiness, not her own. And I reckon I inherited that from her. Thanks, Mom."

The fairy face began to dissolve, but the voice lingered. "Whether I am alive or dead does not matter, as long as Rania is happy. If you get to her, and you save her, and she is with you, she will be happy. And when all time ends in a singularity, and all parallel lines meet, maybe, just maybe, the cloud of probability where this version of me is floating will meet up with you, become real, and kiss her once again. The universe is a strange place."

Montrose shouted, "Wait! First tell us—"

But now the voice was high and thin and regal. It was Twinklewink again. "I have lost signal from the ringworld."

4. Unworthy to Receive

Montrose splashed out of the pool, wincing, as all his wounds were not entirely healed as yet, and stepped over and put his nose against the transparent hull, staring out at the turning ringworld with the blue planet at its center. The clouds and crowds of glassy stained-glass plates of the Dyson sphere were moving, growing thinner, opening the spot directly opposite the ringworld so that more and more light poured out.

Montrose realized with a sinking sensation of awe that each ray of sunlight must contain quanta of information. Even the light particles of Vanderlinden 133 were part of one coherent mental system. And this was not the largest nor most central star of the Praesepe Cluster.

The fairy voice said, "The Cahetel entity is requesting that you receive an embassy from the Praesepe Domination. This requires that I devote more memory space to receiving and compiling the intermediary than I can do without a substantial breech of security protocol."

Montrose said, "Tell them to bite me. Anything they want to say, they can say over radio."

Twinklewink said, "Not so. The radiation you observe striking the ringworld is only the visible part of the communication spectrum being used, of which Cahetel can translate and reflect to us only the least part. Merely to receive such a broadcast would entail more energy than the molecular bonds of the materials of this ship could withstand."

Del Azarchel said dourly, "The voice of the gods would kill us, and the sight burn us to ashes like Semele. Come now! What do you fear? If Praesepe wished us dead, we would have been swatted like flies. Flies? No, like microbes. Let the monsters talk to us!" But he made haste to splash his way out of the pond, making a long and high leap in the lesser gravity, for he knew that the fluid was part of the ship's brain.

Twinklewink said, "I will be forced into standby mode, due to lack of available resources. Praesepe's emissary will have considerable latitude in forming its communication platform. Life support will also be placed on standby. You must enter biosuspension of any nonessential organs, and switch to your nonbiological neural systems for the duration of the conversation. The system will be four tiered, with a node here, one at Cahetel, one at the major agora of the Vanderlinden 133 Dyson sphere, and one at the trail of Gas Giant Brains occupying the volume between the stars 39 Cancri and HD 73730. The onboard emissary will share your frame of reference; the emissary possessing Cahetel involves a five-second delay; the interior layers of the Dyson sphere involve between as four and twenty-one minutes, depending on where the information is stored. Twenty-two years is the absolute minimal time for a minimal response to any question elevated to the Praesepe local stars for resolution. Questions requiring responses from the extended mind structure of the outer stars will involve ten times that duration. You may wish to adjust your perception of the local passage of time accordingly."

4

The Beehive Cluster

1. The Voice of the Collective

A.D. 80101 TO 80700

The preparations were soon made. The overgrown tree branches and twisted trunks, growing in odd spirals and curlicues and Celtic knotwork of wood overhead, filling the whole circle of the ship, were white as ice and seemed sharp and clear in the inert gas which replaced the volatile oxynitrogen atmosphere.

Montrose and Del Azarchel, also white as marble, with only their eyes still dark and gleaming with life, stood ankle deep in the snow, on legs as motionless and numb as marble, each with a white chlamys thrown over his shoulder, for modesty's sake. They were both facing the largest pool in the garden, one from which the central statue had been removed, a figure of a pilgrim carrying a child, holding a white ball topped with a cross. Who this figure was, nor why Rania had placed it here, Montrose could not guess, and that made him very sorry. So it was with greatest respect that he had asked the statue to step aside and take another place elsewhere in the barren garden.

This pool had been selected because most of the major lines of the ship's brainwork met here, and those that did not could be conveniently connected

by bridging cables, giving this one spot the greatest carrying capacity anywhere in the ship.

Twinklewink said, "Captain Montrose, lord and husband of my mistress
Rania, only your direct order, properly worded, can permit me to turn over
control of the central brain systems of this ship to Praesepe, and invite the
emissary within. I will be in slumber until, if ever, the emissary departs."

Montrose hesitated.

Del Azarchel said, "As her father, surely I have some authority here?"

Twinklewink said, "Yes. Mistress Rania made it clear that you were to be
treated with respect, afforded every courtesy, and under no conditions to
be granted access to the central shipbrain."

Montrose said, "This is an order. Now hear this: allow Praesepe access to the
ship's mind core, reserving only life support, navigation, propulsion, and medical subroutines."

The pool began to change color, growing thick, stiff, and white as the
nanomachinery replicated and reduplicated. First one drop of the fluid, then
another, rose directly up out of the surface, suspended by some means Montrose could not discern. When he opened sense impressions on higher and
lower bands of the spectrum, he saw a glare of infrared and microwave energy.
He was glad he was in a Patrician body: otherwise the energy backscatter involved in whatever form of magnetic levitation was going on here would have
fried him like hamburger.

The fluid of the pool formed an elongated octahedron, looking like two thin
glass pyramids floating base to base, with the lower of the two balanced on its
tip, hanging just above the pool surface. Little sparks of light drifted down
from the object, and tiny sharp crackles of energy flashed between the lower tip
and the pool. The object was taller than a giraffe, and Montrose stared at it with
mingled awe and puzzlement. Was it a symbol, perhaps a stylized representa-
tion of the basic race from which the various Praesepe creatures once evolved?
It did not have membranes for speaking or limbs for manipulating the environment.

Montrose brought some selected muscles of his neck out of biosuspension
long enough to turn his head and glance at Del Azarchel. It was an old, automatic habit. The other man had solved the puzzle before Montrose, for Del Azarchel had thawed his lips and forehead long enough to shift his expression into
a superior smirk and then refreeze it. Montrose turned his head back, shifted his
vision through several other wavelengths of the spectrum and then saw what
Del Azarchel saw: the turning octahedron was regularly bringing four of its
triangular faces to present them to the same eight points, four of them occupied

by slow-moving satellites outside the Dyson cloud, and four of them occupying points on the outer surface of the northern and southern hemispheres. This was a receiver. The octahedron had to make a complete rotation in order to consult with the eight minds or broadcast points being consulted.

A voice spoke from the middle of the octahedron. *We speak for Praesepe. Speak ye for Man?*

It was a human voice, slightly high pitched, melodic in pitch, and with a Texas twang to its vowels. It seemed to be a combination of halfway between Twinklewink's girlish cartoon voice and the rich bass of Del Azarchel, and the clipped baritone of Montrose. The overall effect was eerie and unnatural: an emotionless but boyish voice that sounded like no human boy.

It spoke in the plural. The question was addressed to both of them. Naturally, they both spoke at once.

Montrose said, "I don't speak for anyone but me and don't take guff from anyone but me."

But Del Azarchel said, "I represent all mankind and am its rightful sovereign lord."

The octahedron ceased to rotate for a moment, paused, and then resumed. *Why sends Man a divided epitome to us?*

The two men again exchanged glances. This time each saw comprehension in the other man's eye. Praesepe, like Ain, regarded the whole human race as one system, a single mind with a severe case of billions of split personalities.

Del Azarchel said, "We are a young and adventurous race, but our spirit of experimentation and adventure allows us to endure rebellious and nonconformist elements amid the loyal main mass."

Montrose said, "Because Man is a divided sort of critter, half-angel and half-devil. We both wanted to talk to you."

Del Azarchel added, "Dr. Montrose and I represent different factions, but in this case we act with one accord."

Praesepe said, *Declare ye: How is your life principle divided?*

Montrose was not sure how to interpret that cryptic question, so he said, "We are individuals."

Del Azarchel said, "Our self-aware machines can share and swap brain information, but the biological parent race on which they are based do not."

Praesepe said, *Declare ye: Is there a boundary of discontinuity between individuals severed of your life principle?*

Montrose said, "Each generation is composed of newborns that we teach stuff. There is a discontinuity."

Del Azarchel said, "Our self-aware machines can reproduce by passing memories and instructions directly into subsequent generations, but often chose not to, preferring to retain their sense of self."

Praesepe said, *This information serves us, for it clarifies varied puzzling issues. In reciprocation, we serve ye in like manner. Query of us: What requires Man of us, that his service be better perfected?*

Del Azarchel said, "We have done a service for Ain that promotes the cause of sophotransmogrification and, in recompense, would like this vessel refueled with the exotic matter needed to fuel a voyage to M3, a specific amount of negative-mass helium isotope, to power our diametric drive."

Montrose said, "We had a deal with Ain. We broadcast human souls all across the Orion Arm for you, to help you get yourself back together. To help Orion collect its scattered wits. There was a lot of death and suffering involved, and we'd like to be repaid. We'd dearly like it, as the suffering was dear."

Praesepe said, *No.*

There was a moment of silence while both men stood, wondering if there would be any further answer or any explanation. Drops of fluid began to fall from the octahedron back into the water, and the snaps and sparks of electrical activity increased: the emissary was dismantling itself, preparing to depart.

The audience was over. The emissary mass was melting.

2. The Dying Dominion

A.D. 80900 TO 80944

The octahedron had not the chance to disperse before Montrose shouted, "You ain't finished here, you bucket of spit! Hold your plagued horses! That answer won't fly! We spent five thousand seven hundred forty years and change zapping volunteers across the wild black yonder to God knows what hell pits inside the brains of alien mental systems—and you think you can yerk us out and pay us in pus?"

Del Azarchel said, "We require knowledge of your process of appeal or reconsideration."

There is no appeal and no other answer based on the approach vector you have defined.

Del Azarchel said, "We have not been sufficiently recompensed for our earlier answers to your questions! It would be untoward for a lord of your high estate to be known to cheat his underlings. If you cheat your lessers in small matters, your peers will know you will cheat them in great matters."

Some drops hovered in midair. One or two floated back up and rejoined the octahedron.

We are controlled, as are all things, by the mathematical necessities of cliometry, by our duty. Hyades acted beyond its proper circle of duty and introduces an unexpected vector into the cliometry of local, Orion Arm futurity. The resource you require is exceeding rare, as no Domination can produce nor reproduce it. We are limited to picotechnology. Bondi-Forward particles are an application of attotechnology.

Montrose said, "We can read the damned cliometry as well as you! We did not set out from Ain until enough humans had made enough contacts with lost and scattered races to equal this in value!"

Del Azarchel said, "Ain was aware that one of the elements in the galaxy had betrayed the others and is actively interfering with the cliometry of harvesting younger races and regathering old ones back into the Collaboration. According to Ain, and to Hyades, the vector of future history we introduced by creating Man to be the emissary and intermediary for the Orion Arm civilizations will undo, partly or completely, the disunion and confusion created by the Monuments."

Discard as irrelevant: nothing do we owe ye.

But the drops were still floating up and not down, rejoining the main mass. Something was holding the attention of the emissary.

Montrose said, "The Authority at M3 in Canes Venatici assumes right and power to continue the legacy of the lost Archon of Orion! By law, all lesser civilizations—including you—within Orion fall under M3's rulership. The primary obligation is to complete the unfinished project of sophotransmogrification. We just helped you with your damned pustule-sucking project! You must reciprocate. If a failure to reciprocate were to become widespread, this would deincentivize the conduct of cultivation!"

Discard as irrelevant: M3, not Praesepe, is liable.

Montrose said, "In a pig's eye, jerkhole! I just gave you the same reason one of your thugs gave for conquering the human race! The same damnified epidemical reason! If you are not bound by your own laws, how can your legal system work? It is just corrupt?"

Comment rejected: There is no corruption. We adhere perfectly to our duty. You act with partial information.

Once more, the two men exchanged knowing looks. That was interesting. *You act,* not *ye act.* The Domination was saying Montrose himself, as an individual, had acted without complete information.

Del Azarchel said, "My lord, if I may, what information was Dr. Montrose missing?"

Know: At the time when Montrose and Ain entered into their covenant, Montrose knew not that Hyades is a dying dominion, fated not to last long, as younger and more cohesive dominions under our sway are taking over ever more of the duties once assigned to Hyades. Man was too young and incoherent to be adopted into the Collaboration, but Hyades persisted, sparing ye when it would have been more efficient to obliterate the species and reseed your world with a life principle more in keeping with the cliometric vectors currently ongoing.

Hyades risked elevating Man. This decision was erroneous, for Hyades was deprived of its expected return on investment by the Vindication of Man, granting your race an undue and unwelcome equality with Hyades, and depriving Hyades of the use of your services during the stipulated term of indenture.

Desperate to correct for this error, Ain for Hyades broadcast human minds to various points across the Orion Arm, and this act did indeed correct for much of the damage done by the Monuments, which otherwise several lesser races would have discovered and by it been lured to recalcitrance and rebellion.

Between the time of that first broadcast there/then in the Ain frame of reference and here/now in the Vanderlinden 133 frame of reference, mankind has taken possession of several of these Principalities, Powers, Virtues, and Potentates into which your mental seeds were planted. These have now left their predictive path, and begun to mold the Orion Arm into an anthropocentric cliometric mode.

The turmoil of your youthful race has disturbed a number of arrangements and will soon severely disturb others. The cost of correcting the cliometric vectors back to their predicted channels diminishes the reward allegedly due you to zero.

Montrose thawed his mouth so that he could grin his ghastly grin. "Well, damnation and botheration! Ain't we a sight? Good for us!" Then he laughed again. "Causing trouble, eh? Good for us!"

Del Azarchel said, "Sir! We have knowledge and evidence necessary to present to M3. Any failure to assist us cannot help but be construed as a treasonous—"

Montrose said on a private channel, "Hold up, Blackie! I think we are on the wrong trail here. Let me try something."

Del Azarchel answered back on the same channel, "What did you have in mind?"

Montrose said, "I was wondering what Rania would do. Mind if I try? I don't think we can threaten this thing, not with nothing we got, not up our sleeve or down our trousers. Praesepe might, just might, stick us into the mail bag for the next scheduled run to M3, if there ever is one, so as his boss could roll an eyeball over us, but Praesepe ain't going to fork over what he owes, 'cause he reckons he don't owe it, right?"

Del Azarchel said, "A man with an empty tank must take his next breath where he finds it. Go ahead. I am curious."

3. Why Need Ye Her?

A.D. 81500 TO 82700

Aloud, Montrose said to the Praesepe emissary, "You asked what Man needs to serve better, to serve the needs of the project to engineering the stars and planets into thinking machinery and unify them, you mean, I reckon. Well, Man needs Rania. We cannot have peace without her, and her absence is the reason why the humans that Ain spread around the Orion Arm are causing trouble and turmoil."

The octahedron turned many times. Time passed. Eventually it spoke again, *Declare: Why need ye her?*

Del Azarchel said, "She was able to persuade mankind to foreswear war. It was a gift that we don't understand, although we have diligently studied her techniques."

Privately, Montrose sent, "Shut up, Blackie. You are still going down the wrong rabbit hole with this critter."

Declare: What evidence present you that there/then Rania maintained at M3 frame of reference would have the effect of halting human divarication into the Orion Arm cliometry within the time frame Praesepe currently contemplates? Why need ye her?

Del Azarchel ignored Montrose and said, "Ah, we believe that energy entanglements on a fine level continue between us, which reach to some point outside the lightcone of the Big Bang . . ."

Declare: Why need you her?

Del Azarchel said awkwardly, "We, ah, we are not sure what this energy entanglement portends, but surely a rational curiosity would impel so advanced an order as yourself to investigate."

We have no need of such an investigation. Why need you her?

But Montrose said, "I love her!"

The octahedron stopped moving altogether.

While the shape was frozen in midair, hovering above sparks and snaps of light, Del Azarchel sent a message privately to Montrose, "What does this mean?"

Montrose sent back, "It means that we are both horses' asses, but you are a bigger and stinkerer one than me. This monster was not asking us about our politics when it talked about our life stuff being divided."

"What was it talking about?"

"Sit back, shut your trap, and watch the Judge of Ages work his stuff, Blackie, and you'll find out."

The octahedron now slowly grew a point from the midst of every other triangular face on its surface, and four pyramids emerged, growing larger. In a moment, the shape was that of a three-sided pyramid standing on its nose. The tetrahedron began once more to turn.

Question is redirected: How your life principle divided?

"Our species has two opposite sexes," said Montrose.

In what aspect? How are the sexes differentiated?

"What the hell kind of question is that? Snips and snails and sugar and spice. I don't know. Uh. Men father children and make war. Women bear children and make peace," Montrose said. "Even our machines act male and female, like Jupiter and Selene, because they are based on us, and human nature cannot escape our basic human nature, what you call our life principle."

Praesepe said, *Ye are two sexes, but you are half. Explain this.*

Montrose said, "We are both men. Blackie here and me are rivals for the same female."

Del Azarchel said, "She was taken from us, and we both long and yearn to be with her again."

Praesepe said, *Inaccurate. Only one of you longs and yearns to be with her again.*

Del Azarchel stiffened, a look of hate glittering in his eyes amid his icy face like two green suns. "Though long delayed, I shall have vengeance and satisfaction on all who owe me."

4. Love Most Rare

A.D. 82722 TO 82922

Praesepe evidently misunderstood that comment, or else dismissed it, for the next words were, *To grant your prayer requires the expense of a rare and precious resource, whereas the resumption of your female may or may not restore cliometric stability to the Orion Arm unless perhaps at some point beyond our current range of consideration. You may ask for a less rare and precious recompense.*

Montrose said, "There is no recompense for what is priceless. Do you remember your biological origins? How did you reproduce?"

Praesepe said, *We remember without error, as we are the same continuous person. We are a swarm with a collective mind. In each hive, a specialized queen mother reproduces the young after mating with one selected male consort per season, whom the queen mother kills in ecstasy and consumes.*

Drones gather resources, and preadolescent females tend the egg sacks. Selected preadolescent females are exposed to pheromone triggers when population levels require a second queen. Because individual members of the swarm pass neural information freely into and out of the swarm-mind, there is no boundary of discontinuity between generations, nor between swarms. Other races we encountered were subjugated and their minds absorbed by force into the swarm mind, until M3 curtailed and eventually forbade the practice. We are many races collected into one, but it has been long ages since last we absorbed a foreign race and gained their specialized mind forms.

"You are all machines, now?"

Not so. We return to our biological mode to reproduce at irregular periods, as duty or longing dictates.

"So you understand male and female?"

Yes. Man is the only other race divided into male and female encountered within the current eon of time. It is the most rare reproductive regime in the Orion Arm save one.

The thought that he would never otherwise know the answer to the question caused Montrose, even at this crucial moment, to be distracted, "Really? What is more common than sex?"

Really. Asexual reproduction by fission is most common, followed by sporogenesis, and next, in order, are hermaphroditism, dichogamy, trioecy, gynodioecy, subgynoecy, androdioecy, subandroecy, androgynomonoecy, and polygamodioecy. Permanent sexual dioecy, as found in both our species, is nearly unknown. Synoecy is more rare yet, but the worlds and orders in Orion who employ this reproductive regime follow original forms issuing from the Lesser Magellanic Cloud.

"And in the other arms of the galaxy?"

Molecular-based life divided into discrete species and sexes is nearly unknown outside this arm of the galaxy. Scutum-Crux spreads by self-immolation; Galactic Core races by amalgamation and gravitational imprecation; Perseus by resonance; Sagittarius by replication; Cygnus by induction.

5. The Death and Ecstasy of the Consorts

A.D. 83088 TO 91066

Del Azarchel sent him an aside, "What in the name of the wounds of Christ are you doing, Cowhand? Did you actually have a plan, or is this another stupid bluff of yours?"

Montrose ignored him and said to Praesepe, "So they would never know what love is. But you do?"

I know.

"And being willing to die for love? You know what that is?"

Do you consume your mates during the mating rite?

"Not very often. We mate several times and have many offspring, the more the merrier. I come from a big family. I had ten brothers."

I also come from a big family. I had forty-one thousand six hundred brothers. We know indeed what it means to be willing to die for love.

"How do you know?"

The central conflict of all our precivilized history was the effort to feed the queen mothers with chemical substitutes for male hormones produced during the mating rite, so that queen mothers who fasted and abstained during the mating ritual would produce healthy offspring nonetheless. It was the consort willingness to die for the sake of offspring which formed the core psychological obstacle to the emergence of civilization. Their efforts were sublimated and driven into other channels: into exploration, space-flight, star-faring, and warfare. Conquest was made part of the courtship ritual. So the misdirection of our natural impulses, for us, proved very beneficial. I am the sole survivor of those days, the eldest; I recall the pain of resisting the temptations of ecstasy and suicide, and still suffer it from time to time.

"But if you are a swarm, what do you care if the individual bugs ate each other?"

The change in our natural ways was needed for civilization. If one part of the swarm murders another part, the whole is demeaned.

"You must help us, just for that same reason. Because otherwise all the Orion Arm will be demeaned, because you will have stopped me from getting to my bride, which, as you just told me, is worse than death."

Nothing is worse than death. This is the decree of the Absolute Extension of M3. Life serves life.

"Your own words make that a lie. You and me, we are the only two in the whole accursed and godforsaken galaxy that know love is more than life, more than anything. Even a damn space-bee hive-mind has to see the plain—"

Montrose laughed and was surprised to hear it aloud, for he had forgotten his mouth was thawed.

Praesepe said, *Explain: You make a mouth-signal indicative of mirth or good disposition, but also used to express irony, surprise, or several variants of emotion unknown to us. What does this mouth-signal portend?*

Montrose said, "It is not important. I just realized you are bees. A lot. On Earth, in ancient times, long before we had any first contact with you aliens, our astronomers called this cluster of stars the Beehive Cluster. See? Bees are a swarming critter, too. They got queens and drones. Don't eat their mates, but some spiders and wasps do. I just thought it was really odd that you turned out to be bees. Quite a coincidence, eh? And, uh, my brother used to work with bees, so I always kind of liked you. 'Cause he got stung."

It is mathematically impossible that this is coincidence: it indicates your race, even in your ancient days, when yet below third order capacity, had access to second order information. This, in turn, implies interference by a first-order entity. Who is it?

"Who is what?"

Who is the first-order entity directing your actions?

"You can first order my rutting rod! What the plague does that mean?"

The evidence suggests an Authority or Archon, Throne, Cherubim or Seraphim has introduced strange attractors into the cliometric topography surrounding you. Someone is changing history. Identify this one!

"I got no idea what you're blathering about, Bugsy!"

Del Azarchel said, "Mary, Mother of God! Did you just give the Praesepe Domination one of your infernal nicknames? I swear by the soul of my mother and by Saint James I will see your blood if this monster helps us now!"

Montrose thawed his whole upper body so that he could turn and look in surprise at Del Azarchel. "What are you jawing on about?"

Del Azarchel shouted, "Every time you call someone by one of your stupid pet names, they end up aiding you! It is maddening! Such a thing cannot be allowed to happen in a rational universe! Every being of every world under all the strange and wild stars of the galaxy should grope for strangling wires and bludgeons to choke your foolish voice in to silence and club your filthy lunatic brains into porridge! Everyone should hate you! God Almighty should hate you! Why does everything and everyone go mad when you are around? What the hell did you do to Father Reyes? How did you—"

But Praesepe said, *There is no need for physical transfer of resources. By a process of hyperposition, I have already found and transformed the tritium aboard your vessel into its most congruent negative-mass form. No further communication is required or will be permitted.*

Amid a deafening shower of lightning discharges, the tetrahedron wept, sagged, gushed, fell into the pool, broke into eight parts, then sixteen, and then dissolved back into fluid.

The pond surface flickered with ripples and then grew still. Praesepe was gone.

6. Just Dumb Luck

Del Azarchel also thawed his upper body, because now he clutched his head with both hands, as if he feared his brain cells would explode outward from his skull. "Dear God in Heaven, smite me dead this instant! No pit in hell is worse than this! Has the universe gone *mad*? How did the idiot win again! How does he always—it's impossible! What did you do? *How did you do that?*"

Montrose was enjoying the sight, but he just spread his hands and shrugged. His thought had been merely that if Rania were confronting someone who owed her nothing, she might try sweet-talking it out of him, just by plain asking and being nice. But all he said aloud was, "Hell, I ain't got no idea. Chalk it up to dumb luck."

Del Azarchel was trying to control himself and actually had his own fingers wrapped at this throat as if to choke his windpipe back into his control, and yet his voice kept jumping into high, shrill pitches. His hair was mussed, and his eyes were as whirlpools. "No, that—that cannot be *right*! It's *unfair*! Dumb, *dumb*, dumb *luck* cannot outwit superior *genius* time after *time* across centuries and millennia of time! Once or twice—maybe—but *not*—this is *impossible*!"

"I would tell you to calm down, but, hell, this is sweeter than peach pie, watching you go bonkers, Blackie."

"I have to kill you! I have to!" Now he giggled, and laughed, and could not stop laughing. But he could not stop talking either, so he gasped. "You! Arrogant! Filthy! Ugly! Yankee! You've robbed everything from me! Jupiter and Rania are gone! And the whole crew is dead! And you stole my idea, and suborned Cahetel—how did you even know?—but no! You did not know! Dumb luck! Dumb! I am drowning in dumb!"

"I ain't no Yankee, Spanish Simon. Watch your mouth."

A fairy figurine landed on the shoulder of Montrose, saying in her high, sweet voice, "Captain! There is no evidence of any remaining traces of the Praesepe embassy mind anywhere in the ship's thoughtware. We have discovered that the fission cylinders of tritium now exhibit negative-mass properties. They are already in proper position for injection into the singularity drive. I have calculated several short courses, in case you wish to test the performance of the drive, and also calculated the shortest path to M3."

Montrose breathed such a sigh of satisfaction as he could not remember. "Pestiferate my pogo! Maybe my future has arrived!"

He saw that Del Azarchel, while still red in the face and panting like a dog, nonetheless was slowly rediscovering his famous self-control. There was a little fairy half-hidden under Del Azarchel's long locks of hair, whispering into the Spaniard's ear, but Montrose was in too good a mood to ask Twinklewink what she had said to calm the man down. He almost felt sorry for the fellow and did not want to spoil the luxury of the sensation of an utterly undeserved and unexpected victory.

A nagging curiosity did, all too soon, push the feelings of glee aside. Montrose frowned.

Why *had* Praesepe changed its vast, inhuman, collective mind?

5

The Wreck of the Vast
Desolations of Heaven

1. A Polite Rude Awakening

A.D. 91917

His first awareness, upon awakening, was of the scent of cherry blossoms, the tintinnabulation of a stream, the twittering of larks and the humming of bumblebees, and the deep knowledge that something was very wrong. He could feel the motion of the carousel, which, even though it was a mile wide, nonetheless still imparted an artificial feeling of gravity. The weight of his limbs and the pressure of air in his lungs told him the ship was spinning at her proper rate. He opened his eyes. Between two the pink rice paper screens of Rania's boudoir, through the pointed arch of the fairy-tale tower window, he could see the narrow and rising sweep of the garden, green and fresh with late spring. The window was facing the hull one-quarter of the great wheel of the ship away, so the strip of land looked like a green bridge across a field of stars to either side.

Stars meant the vessel was still in the Milky Way. An internal calendar told him it was far, far too early to have allowed any circuit to waken him, and the lack of klaxons or damage reports indicated that he had not been stirred awake by any of the emergencies he had so carefully placed into his thaw instruction logic.

And the birds and bees would not be taken out of hibernation during an emergency. In fact, they could not be taken out of storage at all, except on his direct command. Which he had not given.

Twinklewink was compromised.

Thus he was not surprised when Twinklewink, dressed all in a black costume with a silvery cloak fluttering behind her, came lightly through the window, lugging a gentleman's white glove behind her. She sped past his ear, drawing the glove behind, to slap him across the face with it.

2. The Challenge

He rubbed his cheek ruefully, cursing himself inwardly with every disease and pest and rot for which he knew the names. What had happened was obvious in hindsight. At some point after the midflight rotation and before their arrival at the Dyson sphere, Del Azarchel beamed a copy of himself into the mind swarm of Praesepe, or, at least, that segment of the Praesepe interstellar mind seated at the Vanderlinden 133. Obviously Del Azarchel had survived, made some sort of deal, suborned or corrupted some of the data entities living in the lower levels of the Praesepe mental universe, and risen to some sort of high position, several millennia before the physical ship carrying the physical version of Del Azarchel arrived. Montrose himself had given the order to lower the drawbridge and welcome in the alien emissary mind into the ship's braincase. And Exarchel—if that was the right name for him—simply sneaked in with the ambassador, stayed behind when the ambassador left, seized control of central nodes and brainpaths before Twinklewink awoke, and, with her as his helpless, brain-dead puppet, merely ordered her to report to Montrose that all was well. Meanwhile, she also had whispered into the ear of Del Azarchel that he was now master of the ship, and Montrose his captive. No wonder the man had regained his composure so quickly.

The little fairy figure danced in front of him again, curtseying. The miniature black uniform she wore was a replica of the Hermeticist spacefaring garb: black with threads of red running through it like the veins on a leaf, with a mirrored cloak. About her tiny wrist was an even tinier hoop of red metal. In her high, sweet voice, she said, "Certain formalities needs must be honored in the breach. There is no one to act as Seconds, or surgeon, and I assume you will not accept the ship's brain to act as judge?"

Montrose sighed. "No, you can be judge. I think you are honest enough, in your own twisted way, to stop yourself from pulling any funny business during a proper duel. Damnify and infect my male member if I can figure why. You are the kind of man who can kill a million people without blinking an eye, but you will not cheat at cards."

The little figurine curtseyed. "Simple enough. My sense of honor is important. The lives of lesser men are not. Will you come?"

The staircase that descended from the spire to the floor of the tower was an ancient design: the first part, where gravity was half, was merely an open space down which he jumped; then came three-quarters gravity with its spiral ramp, loose at the top and tight at the bottom; and below that, stairs. When he reached the bottom stair, he was in one Earth-normal gravity of acceleration again.

He opened the iron-bound oak door and stepped into an herb garden. A fawn was nibbling the grass to one side. To the other babbled and lapped the endless brook that wound all the way around the ship. The season here was springtime. Looking upward, he could see the cluster of light sources and heating elements peeping out from behind the wood-wrapped black ball where the singularity engine and the alien machinery of the diametric drive were hidden, along with the thinking machinery of the ship's brain. Clockwise, he saw the band of the garden rising up, tree leafless. In the middle of winter was the round shadow of night cast by the machinery sphere. Directly opposite, to the counterclockwise, was summer, and the lamp cloud that served as a miniature sun glittered in the brook as it ran, dazzling. Autumn was directly overhead, a mile away.

He saw the stars to the aft, including the Praesepe Cluster, now some eight hundred lightyears behind them. Unlike a proper sailing ship, the *Solitudines Vastae Caelorum* currently was flying with her sails before her, distended by an invisible and nigh-impossible spray of ionized helium particles issuing from the diametric drive, energy whose imparted momentum, at least in the frame of reference for the ship, was met by no equal and opposite reaction.

These stars were redder than they should have been and gathered more closely together, albeit only his superhuman Patrician eyes allowed him to detect such a thing. They were traveling above ninety percent of the speed of light. To the fore, the entire hemisphere of stars was occluded by the rose-colored film of the sails.

He brought his eyes back down. The fairy figurine beckoned. He followed the little finger-sized doll a hundred paces to where an airy gazebo of white and pink with columns carved into fretted lace stood next to a glass bridge, lightly arched, that leaped the endless brook. Within was Blackie del Azarchel, smoking a thin cigar. At his feet were two boxes, one of cedarwood and one of battered metal painted olive green. Both were open. The green metal box held the Krupp dueling pistol Montrose had brought and which, last time he'd seen it, had been safely packed in his private supply chamber halfway between the soil level and the outer hull, under gravity slightly higher than Earth-normal. On the dark velvet in the cedar box was another pistol Montrose of course recognized. He had last seen it in the hands of the homunculus used by Jupiter in their duel. Montrose was not in the habit of forgetting any pistol down whose barrel he had stared in what might have been the last moment of his life, but was not. Blackie's own pistol. He had saved it from since that day.

On a clean white sheet laid out between the two boxes were cartridges of chaff, slugs and accelerators, beam guides, a miniature lathe and other chaff-cutting tools, a programmer's pin set: everything needed to pack and prepare a weapon.

To one side of the gazebo was a full set of dueling armor, standing on its metal boots, helmet open and empty. To the other side was another set. But behind each stood a young man in livery: one was in black and gold, Rania's colors. The other was in black and red and purple. Their faces were albino white and eyes pink, and their hair was as fine as the down of a newborn.

"No smoking on deck," said Montrose coldly, without any other greeting. "You want to strain the air recycler?"

3. A Gentlemen's Agreement

"I granted myself an exception to the ancient rule, as captain. I grant you your choice of arms and armor," said Del Azarchel airily, and as he waved his hand, the blue cigar smoke left a circle in the gesture's wake. "Obviously you are more used to your piece than mine, but then again, it might throw me off my aim to use yours."

"You're cracked, Blackie. More cracked than normal."

"I thought about leaving your piece where I found it, but since you know I am master of the ship, then you know I could have done anything while you slept, including replace your spinal column with a tube of explosive cord, and the idea of your outrage that I touched your pistol, ran my fingers over it, took it apart, and looked at it—well, you touched the girl I made for myself, my wife, my queen, and more intimately than I can tolerate to think, so there is that. And, well, I don't need you to give orders to the ship's brain any longer, do I? You are a waste of limited oxygen supplies."

Montrose said, "There ain't no way to put any fight on equal terms. We ain't even supposed to talk to each other. Our Seconds are supposed to make the arrangements. Your brain is in the computer, another Exarchel. These androids—how did you cobble them together? They are your creatures, too. Why should I trust any of this is on the level?"

"Actually, they are Rania's work. She had all the larger animals—deer, foxes, dogs—preestablished to take on a human form when and if tasks requiring human hands might come up. All I did was twitch the genes from female to male, because the idea of Rania's handmaidens helping us into our dueling gear or seeing the bloodshed—well, it is not fitting for the gentler sex, even when dealing with homunculi."

"You could have put anything inside the guns, inside the armor."

Del Azarchel grinned his charming, devilish grin and leaned back. "Well. I will tell you what. If you agree to the duel, I will have Novexarchel—as I like to call him—vacate the ship's mind. Twinklewink can be restored from backup archive and act as judge. She knows the rules for how to conduct a duel. Glitterdink and Dwinkeltink can act as Seconds. I will take whichever one you do not."

"Novexarchel—as you like to call him—would be agreeing to commit suicide. Jupiter was willing to die, too, just for the chance to shoot at me. What if this is all just a trick and Nov*pus*archel—as I like to call him—is just pretending to be Twinklewink or whoever?"

Del Azarchel shrugged, still smiling, spreading his hands as if to show how innocently empty they were. "Why would I bother? I could have cut your throat with my shaving razor while you slumbered. But riddle me this: I am planning on traveling to M3 to discover the secret of the Monument Builders and marry Rania. She will never agree to a divorce, nor would I: the concept is barbaric. I would never dream of asking you to violate the solemn oath you made in a church to her, nor would I accept her as a fitting queen if she were the type of woman to break an oath."

"The hell you say. You tried to have my marriage declared unconstitutional by the Sacerdotes while I slept!"

The other man shrugged. "That would be licit, would it not? You break no oath, nor does she. Honor is saved."

"Your brain is twisted like a ram's horn, Blackie."

"The reasoning seems clear enough to me. But let me continue with my riddle. What kind of man am I? As you say, I have no hesitation in commanding whole generations of innocent women into the eugenics camps to suffer forced mating and forced evolution, and I conquer worlds as a pastime. But, as you say, I don't cheat at cards. I may bluff and let you think I hold a card I do not, or I may outwit a foe, but I do not hide an ace up my sleeve or use a marked deck. I could not call myself a king if I acted like a knave. I could not call myself an emperor if I played craven tricks like a slave. What kind of man am I, Cowhand? I am planning to restore or revive Rania, whom the aliens say is waiting at M3. I plan never to lie to her—what use to any man is a wife one must fool with play-acting? I want to tell her I killed you and that I saw you die. And if you decide not to trust me, well, I will just have the ship kill you, any one of a hundred ways. I could order the ship to have one of the fairy dolls fly through your skull at Mach one, for example, without even raising my voice."

"You are a liar. Jupiter said so, and he knew you."

"But I tell the truth when it is more effective, so listen to the truth. There are only four options. Either I am planning to betray you and cheat in some knav-ish and vile fashion during the duel, or planning to cooperate and fight the duel fairly. Either you agree to the duel or you do not. If I betray you, and you agree, your gun misfires or some other mischief I have planned distracts you, and I shoot you and you are dead. If I cooperate, and you agree, you have a gun in your hand and some chance of killing me. Less than you think, because I have spent years and centuries in simulations shooting simulated versions of you, and I am quite good, better than Sarmento. If I betray you, and you do not agree to duel with me, I have you slaughtered like a dog without dirtying my hands. If I cooperate, and you do not agree to duel with me, once again, I have you slaugh-tered like a dog, and I tell Rania you would not fight like a man."

Montrose said, "And your version in the ship's brain would be willing to die, to erase himself entirely, just as a gesture of goodwill to convince me to fight you?"

Del Azarchel said, "I solemnly assure you that to win Rania away from you, he is as willing to die as I am. If I killed you in your sleep, she would know me to be a low and craven dog. If I kill you face-to-face, gun in hand, my life pro-tected only by my skill, my nerve, and the good fortune that always protects great men, she may hate me for a time, until whatever sick infatuation she has with you runs its course like a fever. When she wakes to reality, sober once more, free from your influence, she will look on me and know that I faced you man-to-man. You have known me all the years of human history, more years than any race alive can match. In all that time, have I ever played the coward with you? I am willing to die just for the chance to see the look on your face as you realize I have killed you."

Montrose said, "Fair enough. I agree."

4. Greater Than Any Man

Del Azarchel stood and threw his cigar butt, still smoldering, across the grass and into the crystal-clear stream, where it was quenched with a hiss and spread a little stain of wet tobacco in the water. A pang of hate went through Montrose at the sight, because he knew Del Azarchel cared nothing for keeping Rania's ship as clean and pretty as she had left it.

Del Azarchel turned to the little black-garbed female figurine, which was hovering off his shoulder. "This is an order: now hear this. Execute the final program, as we agreed. Restore Twinklewink, Glitterdink, and Dwinkeltink from archive, keeping all records intact, erasing nothing, falsifying nothing."

The little female figure now spoke in the rich and musical baritone of Del Azarchel himself. "We shall not meet again in this life. It was an honor serving with you, sir. But the dream of our ambition is greater than any man, including the men we are. Even if the Del Azarchel dies, the Del Azarchel lives. Villaamil would have it no other way. I take my leave of you."

Del Azarchel said solemnly, "Godspeed, my brother. Godspeed!" And he sighed.

He then turned to Montrose. "The ship's brain is vast, as you know. It will take a better part of an hour for the process to run. As each file is deleted of Novexarchel, his intelligence will drop and drop, another part of Twinklewink or her two backup systems can unfold into that brainspace and begin to run, and so her intellect will grow and grow until it is restored to its original strength."

"Have him sing 'Daisy Bell' while his intelligence is dropping," suggested Montrose. "It is kind of a tradition, ain't it?"

"That would not be fitting. Do you want to wait all that time for process to be complete, or are you willing, once Twinklewink is, let us say, twice as smart as a human being, and able to act as judge, to commence our business?"

Montrose turned and glanced at the cigar butt, which the endless current of the endless brook was carrying counterclockwise, into the winter quarter. Something seemed odd about these goings on, but the chance to kill Blackie once and for all was really the only true reason he had invited him aboard the ship in the first place. "Let's get this over with. I been waiting to kill you since my wedding night."

Del Azarchel said to the flying figurine, "When Twinklewink is back on-line, report in."

A girlish voice answered, "Activated. I am at two percent capacity."

Del Azarchel said, "Montrose? Do you want to ask her to act as judge?"

Montrose said, "She knows all the rules and forms. I made sure of that before we left. I was not planning on letting you reach M3 alive in any case. You are never going to see Rania again."

Del Azarchel smiled, an eerie glitter in his eyes. "It is refreshing to know how exactly we understand each other."

Twinklewink said, "I will act as judge for your duel."

Del Azarchel spoke to the fairy figurine: "This is an order: now hear this. As captain, I resign my commission, command, and authority, turning over to which of the two of us survives. For the next hour, no one has authority over the vessel, and no orders are to be heard or acknowledged. Until that time, all lawful orders previously given are in force, including any and all orders previously given to Novexarchel by Captain Del Azarchel, and including any and all orders previously given to Twinklewink by Captain Montrose." He looked challengingly at Montrose.

Montrose said, "This is an order: now hear this. As captain, I resign my commission, command, and authority, turning over to which of the two of us survives. Continue all current orders until countermanded by a proper authority. For the next hour, there is no captain. Don't listen to any orders for that period of time. Whoever survives is captain."

Twinklewink said, "As you have no doubt anticipated, as judge, I assign my two coequal navisophont systems each to act as your Seconds. Dwinkeltink is for Montrose; Glitterdink is for Del Azarchel. They have consulted with me and agreed on terms. Please step away from each other."

5. The Field of Honor

Montrose went to go stand on one side of the gazebo. A moment later, out of a swarm of fairy figurines, up flew a black-haired gold-eyed china doll with moth wings. "Dwinkeltink at your service. I have agreed with Glitterdink that you have your choice of armor and weapons. We have both inspected the suits of armor and the sidearms, and detected no evidence of tampering. Twinkle-wink has examined the ship's security records and sees no moment when Del Azarchel damaged or altered your weapon. I have agreed with Glitterdink that you and your foe may watch and inspect as the other packs his weapon. Del Azarchel declines, saying he has no fear that you have added anything untoward or illegal."

Montrose nodded. "I'll agree to that also."

"Del Azarchel has choice of field of honor."

Montrose said, "We are on a ship! Where else can he pick?"

"He says that you both start from here, back to back, and walk without turning. The ship is three and one-tenth miles in circumference. The duelists walk the whole length with their countermeasures on and ignite chaff and open fire as each man sees fit, at whatever range he sees fit."

"Seems a mite roundabout way of doing it," said Montrose, wondering again at the intuition of uneasiness that was bothering him. Something was off-kilter, but he could not see what. "Ask him why. Does he think I would not trust Twinklewink to drop a scarf?"

"He says to give both of you time to think about your sins. There is no priest at hand to shrive."

"Fine. Whatever. I agree."

"He says that you may have your choice of direction, clockwise or counter-clockwise."

Montrose pondered. Whichever man was to the counterclockwise of the other would be shooting clockwise, with the spin, and have his bullets pull high due to Coriolis effects; and to the clockwise, against the spin, would pull low. Pulling low was an easier shot, because a hit to the legs or abdomen would still be deadly. "I'll go clockwise."

Twinklewink's voice now came from the fairy. "Rania, many times during the long voyage back, confessed to me that, should she discover upon her return that one of you was responsible for the death of the other, she would join a holy order of sisters, take a vow of silence, and enter a nunnery. Knowing this, do you wish to reconsider your bloody and unlawful intent toward your opponent?"

Montrose thought once more about Captain Grimaldi. Del Azarchel often talked as if he were Rania's father, but biologically and legally, Grimaldi was her real father, and for Del Azarchel to steal the name of an innocent man he'd murdered, a man to whom he'd sworn an oath of obedience and fealty . . . it was too much for Montrose to stand.

"I am not in the mood to reconsider jack naught. Rania knows she ain't got no right to meddle in with men's matters. And the real Rania never said that, because the real one never stepped aboard this ship."

"Step into the gazebo. The valet will act as squire and assist you to don the armor."

The men packed their pistols in silence and in silence donned their armor.

6. Walking into Summer

The two men took their positions in their heavy armor. They were back-to-back. The ribbon of garden stretched ahead of Montrose, curving up into the brown of summer. Ahead of Del Azarchel, it curved up into winter. The two squires, their missions done, shed their clothing and returned to their shapes as stags and bounded off into the thicket.

Twinklewink said, "Even now, if an accommodation can be reached, both may withdraw in honor."

Glitterdink said, "My client says that never can true reconcilement grow where wounds of deadly hate have pierced so deep."

But Dwinkeltink said, "My client says that you can blow any accommodation out of your bunghole. He's waited long enough."

"Have all measures to avoid this conflict been exhausted?"

Montrose could not turn his head in the heavy helmet, which was bolted directly to the neckpiece, but he hit the chin switch to turn on his external speakers. "Blackie, we could call it off? We were friends once. Just let Rania decide things?"

Twinklewink said, "The parties are not to address each other, except through their Seconds."

Glitterdink said, "My client says he is not the type of man to defer to a woman deciding matters as grave as this. The matter has been delayed longer than any other matter in human history: it is time for the final stroke."

Montrose said, "I didn't think so. Just wanted it to be on record that I offered. Let's get to business."

Twinklewink said, "Gentlemen, activate your countermeasures. Walk without turning the whole circle of the ship. You may fire at your will."

If she said anything beyond that, it was lost in the hash of noise. His electronic countermeasures, designed to prevent the homing bullets from finding any targeting solutions on him, effectively cut him off from radio or microwave messages from outside his helmet.

He walked. Step after step, the pretty little garden went by to his left hand and his right, and beyond the rails of the garden were the turning stars. The stars were rushing toward him, and the garden looked like a narrow boat with a very high prow cresting an ocean of darkness on which diamonds of endless beauty floated.

His heart was pounding, and his breathing was harsh in his earphones. He was fascinated by every detail of the leaves and buds he saw, the shapes of the twigs, the pattern of cherry blossoms dancing in the air. His heavy boots clanged and clattered on the marble pavement and made the delicate glassy bridges shake when he stepped across the endless brook. For the first time, he noticed golden fish in the water, glittering and beautiful. Had Del Azarchel opened up every biological nook in the storehouse?

He also noticed every fine detail of his discomfort. Damn this cramped helmet. He was too old for this. Montrose had gotten too used to the conveniences of the modern age, where a word, or even a thought, could make anything made of matter bend and flex and change shape. Now the hot leather padding saving his neck and crown from chafing was clinging to him, sticky. Hadn't he remembered the last duel, when a drop of sweat got in his eye? Why hadn't he kept Dwinkeltink inside the helmet with him, to wipe his brow?

He wished he could crane back his head and watch the progress of Del Azarchel, marching through the winter. Damn him. Because Del Azarchel was marching against the spin of the ship, his footsteps would be slightly lighter with each step, as if he were walking the whole way downhill, whereas Montrose was walking the whole way uphill. And since downhill was winter and the miniature sun blocked by the black sphere of the ship's heart, Del Azarchel would not be coated with sweat as they walked the last mile.

The grass was long and brown in the garden now, as brown as the hares, for he was walking through midsummer, the hottest part of the ship. Looking through the prism periscope of his narrow eyeslit, Montrose saw with longing where the otter played and beaver splashed in a cool ceremonial pond. It was one of two deep pools, reaching all the way to the hull, and the stars were visible beneath its glass bottom. Its mate was opposite this, in the midwinter spot, iced over for skating, a sport Rania adored even though she was terrible at it, having never found the time to practice. He recalled holding her, pink cheeked with cold and joy, giggling and sliding as they stumbled across a rink in the French Alps back in the Third Millennium, during the brief season of their joy together, before their marriage. She said she liked the momentum calculations, the nicety of the figures, and how it reminded her of zero gee.

It occurred to him that he could not have seen Blackie even if his helmet were off, because the black sphere was in the way. In this wide ship with glass walls, that spot was really the only place one could walk unseen, and, at that, one would be only unseen by a man walking in the midsummer.

That made another tickle of uneasiness go through him. What was he over-looking? There was something wrong with his whole picture. What was it? He would have liked to ask Twinklewink a question or two, but the countermeasures cut off all outside signals.

Montrose gritted his teeth. Any distraction might prove deadly. This was the only time in his life when puzzling over mysteries was not allowed. He began, one by one, to remind himself of the lessons Barton Throwster had taught him about gun fighting, and what he had learned over the graves and hospital beds of men he had sent to the clinic or the morgue. Mark your target at his main mass. Don't take the feint, but don't be fooled by double feints.

There were only two possible basic combinations, but an infinite number of variations. Either you feinted with a dogleg shot to draw your foe's parrying fire out of line, and then made a straight-line correction, or you feinted with a straight-line shot, then made a dogleg correction to outflank the parrying fire. You either sprayed the chaff in a torus, if you feared the dogleg shot, or you sprayed in a cone, if you feared the straight shot.

One absurd variation which Montrose himself had used once was to point the weapon overhead and shoot the bullet up and then down into the crown of your foe, where the armor was thinnest, hoping he would not shoot his chaff straight up to block the shots. It was a variation quite easy to counter, since a straight shot into the enemy's armpit with an escort bullet would kill him, and the main shot would practically cut a man in half.

The weather got cooler as Montrose walked on. The leaves were now brightly colored, red and yellow and rich brown. The birds were twittering, preparing to migrate to the nearby lands of summertime, less than a mile away.

A wind was starting. That was odd. No, it was more than odd, it was very bad. Usually there was a constant, unnoticed, mild breeze caused by the turning of the carousel, but the wind only began when the carousel was braking or accelerating. Since the wind was in his face, the carousel was braking. Colored leaves began to leap and swirl in the air, and the gentle, eternally flowing brook was splashing and sloshing in a chaotic fashion, seeming to rush faster.

The path led him into a grape arbor. Vines clustered thickly overhead, and the wind was less, but there were still clouds of colored leaves thrashing and whirling and leaping in his eyesight, blocking his view.

Then he saw the feet of his foe emerging downward from the curved roof of the grape arbor, half-hidden in the leafy cloud. Montrose stopped walking, turned sideways, raised his massive sidearm, a cubit long and six pounds in weight. To shoot now would place his shots in the ground, because of the downward curve imparted by Coriolis forces. If the carousel were changing its rate of spin, however, the degree of correction Montrose would have to calculate would be changing second by second.

"Like fighting a duel in a damn fun house," growled Montrose to himself. But he released his chaff, hiding himself in a cloud of darkness. Del Azarchel was an indirect man, so Montrose emitted the chaff in a smoke ring. The high wind was causing it to disperse faster than normal: Montrose knew with a sudden light-headed feeling of fear that he had fired his chaff too soon, leaving him with a weak defense. Against a foe with the skill and cool eye of Del Azarchel, that advantage, small as it was, might spell the death of Montrose.

No, that light-headed feeling was not fear. It was lightness. Del Azarchel had done something to the ship, using the duel as cover, using the hour when the ship's brain would accept no orders, no messages. And if Montrose turned off his countermeasures now to radio a message to Twinklewink, Del Azarchel would put all nine bullets through him.

Because his shot would pull low, Montrose had to wait until Del Azarchel's helmet was visible. He had to . . . no, wait. He had to wait for nothing. Montrose raised his weapon a degree or two, pointing at the latticework of grapevines. He pulled the trigger.

The concussion of noise was like a hammer blow. The whole top of the grape arbor was blown upward by the escort bullets, who reacted to the obstacle as if they were enemy counterbullets. There was a gush of fire as the dry wood of the lattices ignited, but a gush of sudden wind lifted up the whole arbor roof screaming and snapping from its thin supports and flung it toppling. The wreckage of wood passed over the head of Montrose and landed behind him. In his earphone, he heard the crackling rush of fire spreading through dry leaves. While directly in front of him, he saw an impossible sight.

For a moment, he could not understand what he was seeing. It was Del Azarchel in his armor, his helmet and his head shattered, blood gushing from every joint. Every bullet of the load had struck the man, killing him instantly. Del Azarchel's chaff cloud was directly overhead as well and was already tattered and torn by the stormy winds.

It was true. Enough of the front of the head was intact that Montrose could see it was clearly Del Azarchel, not some trick, not some homunculus in his armor. He was dead.

Montrose had won. After long, long last, he had won!

7. Victory

"What the plague?" shouted Montrose aloud.

Nothing he was seeing made sense. Montrose could not focus his eyes, and he was blinking away the sweat droplets he suddenly realized had been stinging his eye sockets for a while now, half blinding him.

Dimly, he could see where Del Azarchel stood, swaying, dead in his armor, blood running, leaking, squirting horribly from six or seven vast wounds in his neck, chest, abdomen, and groin. Both hands were raised, but not in surrender. Del Azarchel held his off hand open, displaying the white fingers and the black palm, the signal that the duelist was ready to fire. But his gun hand was also raised high, pointing at nothing.

Del Azarchel had died standing with his gun hand high overhead, trying for the absurd up-and-down crown shot. Montrose had guessed correctly that Del Azarchel had attempted the indirect shot. But then why had not any of the bullets fallen down around Montrose?

Montrose dropped his gun and struggled to unbolt the heavy helmet. The figure of Del Azarchel swayed as the wind overcame the heaviness of his armor. Del Azarchel tilted, waved his off hand in a cheery salute, and fell with the sound of a Franklin stove being pushed down the cellar stairs. The wind threw dead leaves across his form, half hiding the gore.

With a scream of frustration, Montrose yanked the ungainly helmet free. The echo of the bullet shots was still ringing from the far side of the ship, a mile away. He wiped his eyes. Now he could look upward.

The contrail of the bullet fire from Del Azarchel's gun ran straight up from his overhead chaff cloud toward the dead center of the ship. The tree that circled the black opal sphere was on fire. In weightlessness, with no gravity to pull them into their characteristic teardrop shape, the flames were blue oblate masses that clung and crawled along the wood like blind worms of pure heat.

The black ceramic sphere itself, somehow, impossibly, was neither punctured nor scratched, but the antennae outside the ship were no longer held in place by their invisible struts, but were slowly, majestically, toppling end over end in an ever-widening spiral.

And the black sphere was no longer in the center of the ship. The black sphere, moving ever faster in what seemed like a spiral, now crashed through the lights and heating elements of the miniature sun, sending broken shards of lamps whirling across the weightless air on meteoric spiral dances of their own, spreading outward, coming toward the strip of garden that formed the carousel of the ship.

"Twinklewink! What is happening?"

The little fairy was by his side, as were an entire swarm. "The vessel has suffered nonrecoverable damage. Please enter hibernation and await rescue. There is no other available course of action." That was the voice of Twinklewink, but it was slow and halting.

But a little figurine in black said, "I wished I could have waited to see the look on your face as you died, but, alas, fate has not been kind to me." This was the voice of Del Azarchel.

8. And Defeat

Twinklewink continued to speak: "All main energy supplies have been expended, as have all the fuel cells containing Bondi-Forward negative-mass tritium. The central sphere of the ship was not harmed. The magnetic shrouds struck by Del Azarchel are severed. However, the shrouds on the far side of the sphere from his point of impact were entirely unharmed. I have been able to lock down the remainder. We have lost connection with three-fourths of the sail."

The figurine in black was speaking. "Novexarchel did actually die to kill you, you know, and so did I. You see, I explained before how I am willing to make sacrifices you are not. I downloaded the last memories of my consciousness into the black sphere using the mental replicator you so thoughtfully put in my charge, and, since no orders could be given nor rescinded during the hour it took to prepare my mental information for broadcast, I was able to accomplish this with time to spare. I assume your countermeasures block you from seeing the intergalactic-strength broadcast beam leaving the ship for M3. The black sphere is made of ceramic, and my shots have shattered it like glass. All the appliances and mechanisms around it are Rania's handiwork, human technology, and they will fall, too, and when the sphere passes through the hull—which is only made of an aluminum silicate crystal—the explosive decompression should suffice to end your overly extensive and overly exasperating life. Every last bit of useful energy on the ship, I have used up. Even the induction magnets in the carousel I set to brake the ship, not for any reason, but just so that you will not even have an erg left, not one erg, to maintain your body in hibernation, or in any machine, or as a download, or anywhere. That is assuming you survive the x-ray ignition of the central singularity of the ship's drive and the smashing of the ship's hull, which I doubt."

The first large bits of flaming debris were beginning to hit the carousel ring. Wreckage from the miniature sun fell into the springtime quarter, shattering the fairy tower, igniting trees and ornamental arbors. Deer and rabbits were running pell-mell clockwise and counterclockwise, and some of them jumped too high in the ever-lessening gravity and hung in midair kicking as the air turned dark with smoke.

Twinklewink was speaking at the same time: "The carousel is off center and will collapse. Going into hibernation here will not preserve you."

Montrose looked up. Most of the wreckage was heading toward the spring and summer quarters. He said, "If I get to the nanosupply pool beneath the skating rink, can you form it into something that will protect me?"

"Yes."

Montrose leaped into the air. A cluster of fairies, miniatures stronger than they looked, put their tiny shoulders to his feet or under his armpits and flew him face-first through the midair cloud of spinning wood shards and broken lantern-works, deftly eluding the larger bits of flying rubbish. A dead deer floated by.

There was no sensation of weight once he was in the air. Fires were spreading all along the ring.

Montrose watched in awe as the black sphere now made contact with the carousel and made the whole ship ring like a gong, a noise louder than a world being split in two. Instead of smashing through the flimsy-looking surface, the sphere bounced, made contact with the carousel again, and began rolling, flattening trees and crushing wildlife.

Eerily, the flames were losing their yellow and red color and flamelike shape as they turned blue and ghostlike, clinging and crawling as they assumed the aspect of zero-gee flame.

The little black-suited fairy, tucked in the armpit of Montrose and obediently helping his fellow miniatures tow him across the breadth of the disaster, was also reciting the last recording of Del Azarchel: "Now, technically, this might seem like a violation of the terms of the duel, since we are supposed to place all our copies and backups in danger and erase them upon defeat. However, I will point out that this was not an official duel, nor did I actually challenge you to a duel. I was careful with my wording. You see, this was a continuation of the fight where you struck me across the face. All's fair in a mere brawl, is it not?"

Twinklewink said, "I am also out of main power and have only four hundred seconds of reserves. Do you have any final orders?"

"Yes. Now hear this: when I enter the hibernation pool, download my brain information through the mind replicator into the black sphere; you will delete yourself as I enter to make room. It will kill you. Sorry."

"I am a machine. Don't anthropomorphize me," said Twinklewink primly.

The little black fairy said, "You may have noticed by now that M3 is no longer directly to our fore. That was because while I was captain, I spent about a hundred years trailing the induction cable behind us and using the magnetic fields of the galaxy to turn the ship. I long ago released the cable, so you are left without any means to maneuver. Even if, by pure dumb luck, your specialty, you pass near a star on the way outside the galaxy, your relative velocity will make any rendezvous impossible, as I also piled on every last course and scrap of sail we had to push our velocity to ninety-nine percent of the speed of light, with as many nines tacked on after the decimal as you'd like."

The skating rink was underfoot. The carousel was turning slowly, now, and so the swaying trees were merely clinging by their roots in near weightlessness, as everything not tied down, from the water in the brook to the panicky white rabbits and snapping arctic foxes, toppled madly through midair.

Montrose crashed through the ice into the shockingly cold fluid, losing sensation almost immediately. The fluid, which was not water, thickened and produced wormlike organisms made of ice, which flowed over and into the armor, undoing buckles and latches with quick efficiency.

Montrose used the specialized cells in his brain to send a message. "Why did the black sphere not shatter?"

"The alien core operating system strengthened the interatomic bonds of the ceramic and changed it into an unknown substance, invulnerable to gunfire. The sphere was able to shield one-fourth of the shroud lines, which otherwise would have been severed. The sphere is off center. Shall I enact Rania's instructions in the event of a shipwreck?"

There was no time to think about the implications of that. "Yes!"

"Stand by. I have given the order to reduce the ship carousel, life support, and decorative elements back into its base state, which Rania called *gray goo*. The blueprints for the carousel and decorative elements remain within the memory, and the ship can be re-created if another fuel or energy supply is found."

"Decorative elements?"

"The flora and fauna are not real. They are molecular machines created by the M3 ship functions. This is now being altered to its original design. I am preserving the immediate area around your body in its current state, however."

The fluid thickened around his head, beginning to form the machinery needed to read and transmit his brain information into the black sphere.

"What the hell? I mean, how are you doing this, if you are entirely out of power?" he asked, because more than the stipulated six minutes of time had passed.

Twinklewink started to melt, saying, "The return to the nonstructural condition is extropic—that is, more chemical energy is gained by the dissolution of the nanomachine infrastructure than is expended. I am attempting to convert this chemical energy into a useful form."

"He said there would be an x-ray release when the drive core was shattered."

"There would be, but the drive core has not been shattered. The hull has also changed into a new substance. It is chemically the same as it was, but the bonds of strong and weak nuclear force have increased exponentially, rendering the density beyond what I can measure."

"That means the opal sphere is just going to bounce around inside the carousel for a while, right?"

"No. The drive sphere has already come to rest, and the carousel material is reconstructing itself into an energy-preserving configuration."

"What configuration?"

"A sphere. This was the shape of the vessel when she was given to Rania, who endured most of the voyage as mental information in a non-self-aware state, only forming a physical body for herself, and a garden to hold it, and me to tend that garden, as she approached Earth."

The little black fairy started to melt as, presumably, did all the trees and flowers and rabbits and little woodland animals peopling the wrecked ring. Del Azarchel's voice rang out, vaunting, "There is no way to stop or slow the ship. Do not be deceived by the appearance of stars before and behind you: your course is in the direction of Canis Majoris, directly normal to the plane of the galaxy, and off into intergalactic nothingness. As I take Rania and clutch her warm and living body in my arms, I will think of your poor corpse drifting, unburied and unmourned, with a foolish expression no doubt frozen on your face forever, in a void where no stars gleam! And how I shall laugh! Farewell, and to hell with you! The empty hell of endless night."

Del Azarchel's chilling laugh of triumph seemed to cling to the brain of Montrose, echoing, even after the fairy form uttering it was gone.

9. Ghost ship

Montrose, or Extrose, woke at the same moment the ship's mind died. The few remaining active figurines, which had resumed what was presumably their original shape as black teardrops, were expelling their small remaining fuel mass to jet around the wreckage and send him views.

The carousel had blackened and shriveled like paper in a fire, shrinking inward, and everything, including what Montrose had thought was air and water, living creatures and hull material, was disassembling itself into a thick black ooze. In a vast wash of spiral mud and muck, the nanomachinery wrapped itself around the black sphere, one layer after another, and formed a featureless gray sphere around the buried black sphere. The only irregularity was the nodule which had once been the ice rink. His original body was still in there, frozen in molecular hibernation, but alive.

This featureless, geometrically perfect sphere was the true shape of the alien vessel.

Twinklewink was gone, erased to make room for Montrose, who could feel the jagged, angular shapes of the alien thought-forms of the operating system, like the bones of a skeleton, somewhere beneath the surface of his consciousness. This, then, was the true ship's mind.

But he had no fuel and only the tiny cache of useful energy Blackie had not known about, generated when the ship had collapsed back into its primal goo, which Twinklewink had recovered and stored. A small ring of little black teardrops still contained magnetic monopolar lines linking them invisibly to the black sphere. The majority of the sails were no longer attached: they would begin to drift away before too many years had passed, pushed by interstellar light.

Perhaps, if he had time and energy, Montrose could have formed remote units like the once fairies, now teardrops, and sent them after the sails. But the little units, one by one, were running out of fuel, and they used the last of their maneuvering mass to set themselves drifting close enough to the gray sphere to rendezvous and be absorbed.

The singularity drive was unharmed and still functioning, but there was no energy to spin the disk up to operational speed. The tiny bit of fuel needed to expand and contract the shrouds was gone. There was not enough cached energy left to erect a ramjet field and scoop up interstellar hydrogen. There was a trickle of energy from the still-connected sail as it absorbed a barely detectable trifle from incoming starlight. If the ship had retained any ability to navigate, Montrose could have pointed her toward the nearest star and waited to get close enough to absorb and use the solar power. But the vessel was stricken, able to alter course and speed only by the small impulse of the ambient starlight on the torn sail: a half a degree in any direction, or the loss of a few miles per hour over lightyears of distance.

Blackie had thought of everything, taken everything, and ruined everything.

It would be a while before he left the galaxy altogether, but his speed was so great that no star was within a vector he could approach. He could see the beautiful rose-red star called La Superba, also called Y Canum Venaticorum, only two degrees off his port bow, and only fifty lightyears distant. But at his immense current relative velocity to it, he could no more reach it than he could catch a bullet in his teeth. It was as far away, fuel-wise, as it had been when he was a little boy back in Texas, penniless and cold.

Check and mate. Montrose had lost the duel.

There was enough power to keep Montrose alive in a state of machine awareness, a ghost, overlooking his unliving body, a corpse. But even that was too much strain for the system: Montrose would have to sleep, leaving only a clock sequence awake to wake him every hundred years or so, just in case something in his hopeless condition changed.

"Well," he said, "if this is better than being buried alive, I am not sure how."

Foolishly, he used some of his last scrap of discretionary energy to form a radio laser emitter out of the gray substance, point it at M3, and send the strongest pulse he could manage, both in English and in Monument notation: *Princess! I am coming!*

And that effort was all. Darkness swirled in. Ghosts cannot faint, perhaps, but they can fall below self-awareness.

Neither alive nor dead, the featureless gray sphere with its black heart holding the ghost of Menelaus Montrose and his corpse sped through the void, and nothing but darkness was to every side.

FIRST SWEEP (Swans) 12th Millennium radius = 20 LY	SECOND (Myrmidons) 25th radius = 21–39 LY	THIRD (Hierophants) 37th radius = 33–58 LY	FOURTH (Patricians) 53rd radius = 68–94 LY	PETTY (Atavists) 66th radius = 84–100 LY	Settled voluntarily by parties unknown 34th mil. 144 LY
Sol—Tellus, Mars*, Venus* JUPITER and NEPTUNE	107 Piscium—Eurotas* (from Mars) [Chimera]	58 Eridani—Neodamode			
		55 Rho Cancri—Sciritaea			
				HIP 10301 in Eridanus—Perioecium*	
	61 Ursae Majoris—Cat Sin [Sinner] (? Tellus)	47 Ursae Majoris—Vital Delectation [Delectables]			
	61 Virginis—Saint Mary's World (? Tellus)			Epsilon Virginis (Vindemiatrix)—Feast of Stephen* / Saint Agnes / Saint Wenceslaus [Loricates]	
	Alula Australis [a.k.a. Xi Ursae Majoris]—Taprobane (? Tellus)	83 Leonis—Uttaranchal	Regulus, or Alpha Leonis—Here Be Monsters [Anthropovores]	Gliese 1137 in Antlia—Terra Pericolosa [Vampires]	

[1]LEGEND: Each colony is to the right of her mother system. Mother world noted (in parenthesis) as needed. Dominant race in [square brackets]. **Planets** in bold. *indicates Potentate (terrestrial planets) CAPITALS are Powers (Gas Giants), **BOLD CAPITALS** are Principalities (system-wide). Question mark when no certain record establishes which planet is mother. LY=lightyears.

FIRST SWEEP (Swans) 12th Millennium radius = 20 LY	SECOND (Myrmidons) 25th radius = 21– 39 LY	THIRD (Hierophants) 37th radius = 33– 58 LY	FOURTH (Patricians) 53rd radius = 68– 94 LY	PETTY (Atavists) 66th radius = 84– 100 LY	Settled voluntarily by parties unknown 34th mil. 144 LY
	88 G. Monocerotis— Unicorn (? Tellus)		Zeta Leporis— Svartalfheim		
	Wolf 25 in Pisces—We Sing Paeans (? Venus)				
	Gliese 884 in Aquarius— We See a Strange Dawn (? Venus)		Hamal [Alpha Arietis]— Mystery of the Second Creation		
	Chi-1 Orionis— We Cower Beneath Odd Skies (? Venus)		HR 2622 in Monoceros— Qailertetang		
Proxima Centauri— Rosycross* [Non-Orthogonals, Foxes] ALTHALIMAIN (?) TOLIMAN	66 G. Centauri [HR 4523]— Pure Abode of Unreturning Souls also called Suddhavasa-Anagamin	Alpha Mensae— Land of Hungry Needle-Necked Wraiths [Wraiths]	Gliese 31.5 in Tucana— Shumisen, also called Mountain of the Lovely Peach Trees	HR 6 in Phoenix— World of Willows and Flowers [Overlords]	
	HR 4458 in Hydra— Felicity of the Silent Soul*				
					Achernar— Orphan
Epsilon Eridani— Nocturne*	HR 753 in Cetus— Waiting to Die				
	p Eridani— Open Airlocks	18 Scorpii— Unsuit			

FIRST SWEEP (Swans) 12th Millennium radius=20 LY	SECOND (Myrmidons) 25th radius=21–39 LY	THIRD (Hierophants) 37th radius=33–58 LY	FOURTH (Patricians) 53rd radius=68–94 LY	PETTY (Atavists) 66th radius=84–100 LY	Settled voluntarily by parties unknown 34th mil. 144 LY
61 Cygni—Odette*, Odile* VONROTH-BARTH ZAUBERRING	HR 8832 in Cassiopeia—Masochists' Delight (Odette)				
Epsilon Indi—Porphyry	Zeta Tucanae—Cursed Earth				
Tau Ceti—December*, Yule*, Wintertide*, Samhain* [Hibernals] TWELVE CATALLACTIC	Zeta Reticuli—Venture Prospect* (December)	Epsilon Reticuli—Determined Endpoint Project	Pi Mensae—Onwardness		
Omicron Eridani—Gargoyle*	284 G. Eridani—Lingering Malice				
	Tabit [aka Pi 3 Orionis]—Fifteen Masks of Uncaring Fate				
	41 Arae—Nepenthe for Woe				
70 Ophiuchi—Aesculapius* [Breatharians]	Xi Boötis—Euphrasy* [Iatrocrats, Reticents]	44 Boötis—**Schatten-reich** and Rime [Reticents]		Kappa Coronae Borealis—Aerecura (Schatten-reich) [Sworns]	
		Arcturus or Alpha Boötis—Nightspore [Summer Kings]		Iota Draconis a.k.a. Eldsich—Torment*	

FIRST SWEEP (Swans) 12th Millennium radius = 20 LY	SECOND (Myrmidons) 25th radius = 21– 39 LY	THIRD (Hierophants) 37th radius = 33– 58 LY	FOURTH (Patricians) 53rd radius = 68– 94 LY	PETTY (Atavists) 66th radius = 84– 100 LY	Settled voluntarily by parties unknown 34th mil. 144 LY
Gliese 570 in Libra—Walpurgis [Nicors, Giants]	Chara [aka Beta Canum Venati corum]—Joyous [Swan-Foxes called Joys]	Gliese 490 in Canum Venati-corum—Vayijelal—existence not confirmed	Zubenelge-nubi—Aaru (from Chara)		
	MLO 4 (HR 6426) in Scorpio—Horrific Vision of Nagual		Xi Scorpius—Bloody Water Poisoned Air		
Altair in Aquila—Covenant* [Hierophants] IMMACULATE CONSECRATE	HR 7722 in Capricorn—Preceptor Joachim Voor's World	51 Pegasi—Chrysaor			
		85 Pegasi—Geryon			
Eta Cassio-peiae—Outrage and Calm	HR 511 in Cassiopeia—New Seed (Outrage)				
36 Ophiuchi—Albino* [Swans]	12 Ophiuchi—Dust [Anar-chists, Aberrants]	Rasal-hague—Penance* [Optimates (Swan Patricians)]			
HR7703 in Sagittarius—Gilgamesh and Enkidu					
82 Eridani—Cyan* (Myrmidon throneworld) CERULEAN	Gamma Leporis—Broceliande		HIP 12961in Eridanus—Land of the Young		

FIRST SWEEP (Swans) 12th Millennium radius = 20 LY	SECOND (Myrmidons) 25th radius = 21– 39 LY	THIRD (Hierophants) 37th radius = 33– 58 LY	FOURTH (Patricians) 53rd radius = 68– 94 LY	PETTY (Atavists) 66th radius = 84– 100 LY	Settled voluntarily by parties unknown 34th mil. 144 LY
Delta Pavonis— Splendor* PEACOCK		Gamma Pavonis—To Prevail			
	Fomalhaut— Plenary Triumph				

APPENDIX B
Posthumans

Names of the Posthuman Species

Swans (Second Humans)—includes the Hierophants of the Cherishing (28th Millennium)

Myrmidons (Third Humans)—includes Megalodons (40th to 55th Millennium)

Kitsune (Fourth Humans)—also called *Fox Maidens* or *Foxes*

Patricians (Fifth Humans)

Last Men (Sixth Humans)—called by the Patricians *Plebeians* or called by the Foxes *Athymoi*—that is, *Men without Chests*—is created as the final race. It is a race addicted to servitude, unable to alter the cliometric conditions imposed on them.

Myrmecoleons (Seventh Humans)—found only on worlds in Orion beyond the boundaries of the Empyrean of Man, colonized by Torment in Exile. Also called the Evangels.

NOTE: Eidolons (47th to 48th Millennium) are a failed attempt at creating a new species.

Posthuman Subspecies (by Millennium)

20th Millennium—Hibernal Men

21st Millennium—Hibernals, Nyctalops, and Troglodytes

31st Millennium—Ghosts, Locusts, and Troglodytes extinct

46th Millennium—Vampires

47th Millennium—Eidolons

48th Millennium—Eidolons extinct

49th Millennium—Parthenocrats (Fox-Swan hybrids); *Myrmidons* extinct; *Megalodons* created

50th Millennium—Overlords created by Vampires; Vampires extinct (conformed into Patricians)

54th Millennium—*Ougres, Sworns, Loricates; Foxes* extinct

55th Millennium—Megalodons extinct

70th Millennium—Last Men

Other Variants and Hybrids—Nicors (Walpurgine sea-Hormagaunts); Optimates (Penitent Swan Patricians); Monsters (Terran Pericolosa Vampire-Myrmidons); Delectables (Nymph Patricians); Felicities (Melusine Non-Orthogonals); Sinners (Feline Chimera Patrician); Wraiths (Hungry Witch-Patrician); Joys (Fox-Nymphs); Renunciants (Willowflower Scholar Patricians); Nagual (Scholarized Fox-Myrmidon hybrids); Camenae (Asclepiad Fox-Melusine); Rusalka (Melusine Swans from Cursed Earth); Merrow (Giantess-Sylph Melusine); Rakshasi (Nymph-Fox-Sylph Vampiresses from Peachmountain); Asclepiads (Locust-Iatrocrats); Scolopendra (Melusine-Myrmidons); Myrmecoleons (Heirophant-Scolopendra of Torment)

NOTE: A "subspecies" is not a hybrid properly so called merely for sharing genetic information, which, due to Fox biotechnology, can be freely swapped between any species. Listed here are cliometric rather than biological subspecies—that is, groups embracing a particular, exclusive, and distinctive pattern of genetic, glandular, parasympathetic, neural, and social-psychological structures which impose a definitive vector on the shape of planetary history.

APPENDIX C
Earths of the Empyrean Polity of Man

—as of the 700th Century A.D. / Year Zero Vindication Calendar.

FIRST SWEEP 12ᵗʰ Millennium

Note that only Nocturne of Epsilon Eridani and Splendor of Delta Pavonis survived the First Sweep. The other stars were recolonized during subsequent Sweeps.

Sol—Home of the power Neptune. Includes three Earths:
   Eden, also called Tellus, First Earth, or Matermundi. Original home of man. Binary planet with Luna. (**Luna** was inhabited by Crusader kingdoms between the 37ᵗʰ and 43ʳᵈ Millennium.) Potentate with bouts of insanity.
   Mars, cold desert planet, later bioformed with fanciful short-lived subspecies by Eventide brethren. Inhabited by Chimerae.
   Venus, maneuvered into a "water ring" orbit by the Virtue Salamander. Inhabited by Fifth Men. Elevated to Potentate Status during the 54ᵗʰ Millennium; later, maimed and reduced to Archangelic.

Alpha Centauri C (Proxima)—**Rosycross**
   A torch orbit world at 0.007 AU from C, flare-time red dwarf. The world is smaller and lighter than Earth, the peoples the most highly modified and strangely adapted: modifications to very deep neural structures were made which modern scruples would prevent. The main industry is "watermining" extraction of chemicals from the shallow seabeds of her inky-black, tideless, lifeless oceans. All life on Rosycross is land life.
   Predominant race is Non-Orthogonal Man. Abnormally high Fox population.

Epsilon Eridani—**Nocturne**
   Is tide-locked: the dayside is uninhabitable, covered over with acres of solar energy cells. Gene-manipulation has modified humans and livestock to al-

low them to survive, different species for each ever-colder zone of the night side. The Nocturnals produce many freakish subraces and breeds. They are ruled by the Actuary, a cabal of cliometric historians who force families and clans to breed children into various biologically determined castes.

61 Cygni—**Odette** and **Odile**

Have the doubtful distinction of fighting the most interplanetary wars against each other, despite the separation (86 AU). The wars were provoked by exploitation rights to a 61 Cygnus C, a dark body called **Siegfried**, roughly eighty times the mass of Jupiter. A permanent colony of miners lives on the surface, their bodies radically adapted to endure the greater gravity. Later, when wakened to sapience, Siegfried is a Power christened **Vonrothbarth**.

61 Cygnus A: **Odette**. The planet ventured into forbidden areas of pantropy, both mental and physical, eventually producing immortal and nigh-invulnerable Heresiarchs. The atmosphere is dense with inert gases. Only in the highlands can human life survive: poisonous clouds gather in the river valleys and lowlands at sea level. The high atmospheric pressure and low gravity allow lightweight aircraft and winged men to dart everywhere. Originally called **Arcolith**.

61 Cygnus B: **Odile**. The planet orbits within a dust ring that settled around B, and the atmosphere is continually bombarded with spectacular meteorite showers, bringing rare metals to earth: the planet surface is heavily cratered and heavily mined. The star is a variable, and frequent solar activity prevents the emergence of a working world-communication satellite network. All cities are protected by domes for fear of asteroid strikes or are underground.

The original colony work was done by monks, who still retain ownership of most of the planet surface. Ruled by a Grand Inquisitor, with local and temporary bishops, judges, princesses, and Golden Lords having sharply curtailed authority. Originally called **Aerolith**.

Epsilon Indi—**Porphyry**

A world of harsh desert, volcanism, and open lakes and rivers of lava. The equatorial regions are too hot for Earthly life: the original plant life, a coral growth of diamond spikes thousands of feet high and miles wide, endures here. Earth life is gathered near the polar regions, where large deposits of subterranean water can be found. The sun is active in the UV range, but dim to the human eye, a pale disk one can look upon without blinking. The trees and plants are leafless, but clustered with needles. Porphyry orbits one of the invisible brown dwarfs in the system and is tide-locked to its primary so that daylight (from Epsilon Indi) lasts half a Porphyry year.

The Porphyries are savage and stoical people and make no recording of their brain information. The world is noted for being entirely free of ghosts.

Predominant race is Chimerae.

Tau Ceti—**December, Wintertide, Yule,** and **Samhain**

An old, old world with silt-choked swamps, mountains worn to low nubs, a dull and salty sea without tides. Ice-coated, save at the equator, overcast, and foggy. There is a lower point of precipitation than on Earth, due to a different balance of gases within the atmosphere, so that it rains without ceasing. Ruled by Merchant Concerns, a callous plutocracy. The predominant race is Hibernals.

Wintertide, Yule, and **Samhain** were eventually terraformed, not to mimic Earth climates but to mimic December. All four inner worlds elevated to Potentates.

Outer giant planets were dismantled to create a Dyson sphere, a Principality called **Catallactic**.

Omicron Eridani—**Gargoyle**

A highly industrialized world where the terraforming was incomplete. The population wears gas masks, often highly decorated. Very close to her primary, Gargoyle has a year that is only twelve days long: her axial tilt is roughly the same as earth, so the temperature variation is like that of Earth. The moss-bush and colorful insect life reproduces and perishes in twelve-day cycles, which may add to the melancholy and frivolity of the Gargoyle character. All settlements and guild-mansions have large municipal greenhouses, which are a source of civic pride.

The legal arrangements of this world are draconian and inhuman, with each man renting his life from a central quartermaster. Suicide via demasking is a common penalty for nonperformance of significant contracts.

All social roles are stored in a man's mask circuitry so that anyone donning another's mask, for all legal purposes, becomes him.

70 Ophiuchi A—**Aesculapius**

Has a slow (two hundred–hour) rotation: the people sleep once every twenty hours and have a twenty-hour festival of rest at noon, resting in the great "shades" of the citywide parasols. Slightly lower gravity than Earth. The tree-life of Aesculapius is known for its large, colorful canopies and copious insect life.

For half of the 227 Earth day–long year, the companion star illumes the night sky. Solar storms and variability are frequent, necessitating the adaptation of local biota to flare-time conditions and a hardening of the cells against radiation. Upon a flare signal, all plants and men suddenly grow thick, dark skins, and the vines and trees take on a repellant aspect.

By ancient tradition, wars and murders are only attempted during flare time, when the worldwide panopticon system is down.

Vanity, or some cultural quirk of the Asclepiads, conditions their womenfolk to submerge during flares in the many pools set aside for this purpose, rather than assume an ungainly aspect. The river-going Melusine of that world, called Camenae, are famed for their singing.

The most subtle and expert of pantropists of the Empyrean, the Asclepiads are philosophically opposed to any centralized ecological control and forbid living weapons larger than a bee or wasp. The Leafsmith family is originally from Aesculapius.

The Breatharians, a green-skinned photosynthesizing variant of Locust that can live without intake of food and water, originate from here.

Originally called **Carrion Flower**.

Predominant population is Locusts and Scorpions.

Altair (Alpha Aquilae)—**Covenant**

The Preceptors of Covenant are known for their strict and puritanical lifestyles and their systems of mental discipline. The Covenanters lived aboard their seed ship for two hundred years after arrival, not descending to claim the planet until the long and arduous job of clearing away the asteroid accretions had been accomplished. Very little bioadaptation was needed, but the Covenanters made several mental alterations to themselves, removing them from the mainstream of human psychological norm. The Preceptors live in a polite near anarchy, their disputes determined by a specialized caste of paid arbiters: the common folk are indentured to pay for the costs of the terraforming, practically serfs.

Gliese 570 in Libra—**Walpurgis**

The star is energetic, and the planet has no ozone layer: the Walpurgishmen, when they emerge during the day, wear traditional parasol-shaped hats, goggles, and reflective capes, their faces painted or tattooed with radiation-blocking grease.

Year over four Earth years long, the axial tilt of the planet is more than sixty degrees, so that the sun never sets in midsummer, never rises in mid-winter. The northern and southern oceans boil in summer, ice over in winter.

Roughly half the population migrates seasonally. The main industries are located aboard floating cities called rafts fabricated from the local sea-sponge. Most of the world surface is tideless ocean choked by sea-sponge, and flotilla-villages follow multi-mile-wide herds of gigantic sponge-eating sea mammals on yearly migrations.

The attempt to breed an amphibious race of humans, who could live safely under the water during light times, ended amid war and social upheaval when the Nicor (as they are called) proved ungovernable, anarchic, tribal, incapable of maintaining a social order or technological civilization.

The government is simple in theory, complex in practice. All political, religious, and economic power is vested in a figure called the Metropolitan, which is an amalgam of ghosts of the original man, Ele'ele, a monk and sole survivor of the Second Sweep, who repopulated the planet with his clones and duplicates, and retained ownership despite the influx of giants during the Third Sweep.

Eta Cassiopeiae—**Outrage** and **Calm**

Eta Cassiopeiae A. **Outrage**. The world has a rapid rotation (five hours of daylight followed by five of night), a long year (fifteen Earthly months long), and a highly eccentric orbit. Outrage orbits a bizarre object, called Storm Worm, whose mass is greater than Jupiter and the size less than Mercury, apparently the remnant of an exploded star. The surface of Storm Worm is mined for unique heavy elements and chemicals, so it is a source of wealth, but the tides from Storm Worm agitate the weather patterns of Outrage and trigger seasonal monsoons of uncompromising violence. There are no land masses above water, but coral structures form reefs larger than islands: famous also are the great leafy "floats" of buoyant plant life. The great polar reef is actually the safest place on the planet and the seat of the only urban population, mostly ghosts. The incarnate urban population must be fed by very-far-ranging fleets of aerial fishing craft (who dodge the horrific storms). The predominant population is Sylph.

Eta Cassiopeiae B has a world within its "water ring" (habitable temperature zone) called **Calm**: a pleasant, green world, heavily farmed. The planet has no axial tilt and no seasonal changes. Year is 37 Earth days. The length of the day is frequently changed by rival factions of planetary engineers to match circadian rhythms of imported Earth life versus the native life.

Calm is famed for having the most highly developed autochthonous life of any colony. The multicellular life is divided into five kingdoms rather than two: fragrant sea-jellies, canal-wading lotuses, rooted worms of prodigious length, semi-ambulatory five-sided pyramids, pentasexual pentagons with no discernible sense organs. Both pyramids and pentagons leave behind rows of shed shells as they mate and migrate, giving the Calm landscape its distinctive appearance. The majority population is Locust.

36 Ophiuchi—**Albino**

Albino is an icy moon of a superjovian. Albino and her companions are locked into Laplace resonance, causing tidal flexing. Albino's oceans are heated by frequent volcanism.

There are no surface structures on Albino; the Swans live in an endless labyrinth of ice caves and subterranean oceans.

Note that the superjovian is close enough to the star to be suffering from loss of mass due to solar winds: there is a trail of dispersed atmosphere continually streaming from it, mined for tritium.

Albino is colonized entirely by Swans, who maintain no social organization aside from voluntary commensalities needed to create and maintain ghosts. The Swans enacted a cliometric end state, ensuring their history would never change.

HR7703—**Gilgamesh** and **Enkidu**

Two tide-locked egg-shaped binary planets with very severe tides and floodplains, worlds of rocky atolls rising sheer from stormy seas. The orbital period of the Twins is three days. The planets share a neck of stratosphere, allowing spaceplanes to cross the interplanetary interval. A permanent storm system sits at the near pole of both worlds. HR 7703 has the oddity that, for reasons unknown, the Hyades deracination ships never plundered it. It has no daughter colonies.

Gilgamesh, is a world of archipelagoes and floating islands, and enjoys a stable government and sophisticated aquacultural ecology run by the planetary Noösphere.

In contrast, **Enkidu**, which languishes at the sub-posthuman stage of development, suffers periodic convulsions and tumults, brought on by anarchistic philosophy, addiction to artificial brain-pleasure signals, or outbursts of religious zealotry: the locals worship devils perceived through ingestions of numerous hallucinogenic plants.

82 Eridani—**Cyan**

Low in iron and heavy elements, the Cyanese specialized in mental and theoretical disciplines and bred a race of intellectuals. The world is monobiotic, one species of bluish grass having adapted to all floral niches in the badly botched terraforming sequence. Planet has lower than Earth gravity; their grassboats are unique in the Empyrean, panels held up by the pressure of grass stems, coated with a frictionless substance. The first colony worlds to create a Jupiter Brain (known as **Cerulean**).

The population is divided into *masters* and *muddles*, depending on whether they wear a finger-ring appliance which gives them access to the local system-wide Noösphere. The Very Large Array radio communicates with local Dominion and Collaboration outposts. Cyan enjoys more radio contact with the Hyades than other Earth worlds and is known to have exchanged four or five messages. Cyan orbits at 0.8 AU and has a year of 275 Earth days.

Delta Pavonis—**Splendor**.

A cold and mountainous world occupying the same orbit as an asteroid belt, subject to continuous meteoritic bombardment. Splendor has a year 400 Earth days long. One ocean surrounds the equatorial region like a belt: the Splendids inhabit islands and peninsula of the north and south shore, avoiding the glaciers that dominate the nonequatorial areas. The Houses of Splendor still are centered on the seven competing ecological stations of the original terraforming. With seventeen large and close moons and countless lesser moons, the study of tides is both complex and necessary to navigate Splendor's icy seas. The Splendids are the least modified of the colonial races, having achieved tremendous breakthroughs, and having been very patient during the terraforming. It is a point of pride with the Splendids not to meddle with their own gene plasm.

SECOND SWEEP 25th Millennium

107 Piscium—**Eurotas**

Society is highly militarized, based on a fusion of Iatrocrat, Chimerical-Myrmidon, and murk-Giant biotechnologies to form a rational and stable command hierarchy.

61 Ursae Majoris—**Cat Sin**

Famed for its several intergenerational world wars, fought by armies preserved in cryonic suspension. Suffers heavy meteorite and cometary bombardment. Sinners follow a Hibernal body type with Hormagaunt modifications.

61 Virginis—**Saint Mary's World**

Colonized by unknown world, likely Tellus. On this world, the Supreme Pontiff of the Sacerdotal Order has his See.

Alula Australis [a.k.a. Xi Ursae Majoris]—**Taprobane**

Early Witch biotechnicians stocked the world with beasts based on sacred and heraldic animals.

88 G. Monocerotis—**Unicorn**

Famed for its gigantic biota and endless prairies.

Wolf 25 in Pisces—**We Sing Paeans**

Despite the name, the Sacerdotal order is outlawed on this world, and each family is required to invent its own private mythology and pantheon.

Gliese 884 in Aquarius—**We See a Strange Dawn**

Entirely inhabited by agoraphobics, the Seers have trained the local flora to surround them as they walk, blocking out any dizzying vistas of distant objects.

Chi-1 Orionis—**We Cower Beneath Odd Skies**

The Cowards retain the ancient Vampire-based form of government from Venus.

66 G. Centauri—**Pure Abode of Unreturning Souls** also called **Suddhavasa-Anagamin**

A famed world of aesthetes, who experiment with new sense organs and neural interpretation systems. Ghosts are illegal here, but exist in an underworld.

HR 4458 in Hydra—**Felicity of the Silent Soul**

Colonized from Rosycross of Proxima Centauri. The base psychology is non-orthogonal.

HR 753 in Cetus—**Waiting to Die**

Draconis-type variable: variability due to stellar rotation in which sunspots blotting most of the stellar hemisphere rotate in and out of the field of view. Several continents of the planet cloaked with poisoned gas or venomous water table, due to nanotechnological errors, terraforming disasters, and malign ghosts.

p Eridani—**Open Airlocks**

An error in early pantropy causes the dominant population to have no imagination—that is, no ability to visualize shapes or remember faces. Oddly, they possess unerring directional sense.

HR 8832 in Cassiopeia—**Masochists' Delight**

Immortalist world. Near twin of Tellus. Originally called **Mnemosyne's Delight**, a reference to resemblance to the memories of Earth. Name changed after Earth-like viruses and predatory animals flourished in the environment, but unwise terraforming laws prevented any self-defense.

Zeta Tucanae—**Cursed Earth**

A world of very limited pantropy, extensive terraforming. Unbroken cloud cover was needed to heat the world to human toleration limits. Famed for its mile-high towers and lighter-than-air cities.

Zeta Reticuli—**Venture Prospect**

All real property owned by one family corporation, the Land Clan, which exploits the jovian world and the debris ring.

284 G. Eridani—**Lingering Malice**

High-gravity world rich in rare elements. Famed for the harshness of it terrain, the ugliness of its women. An illegal pantropy removed all ability to see beauty from the Malicious neural coding, in an attempt to combat the suicide rate.

Tabit [a.k.a. Pi 3 Orionis]—**Fifteen Masks of Uncaring Fate**

Ruled by cabal of Fox ghosts who inspire dreams and visions.

41 Arae—**Nepenthe for Woe**

Pantropic adaptation gives the population seasonal metamorphosis of radical degree, a spherical shape in winter, a batlike shape in summer.

Xi Boötis—**Euphrasy**

The right of parents and orphanages to experiment on their children is uncontested here. This is the only world known to have successfully overthrown their Myrmidon overlords and reduced them to slavery. Home world of the Reticent Order.

Chara [a.k.a. Beta Canum Venaticorum]—**Joyous**

Famed near twin of Tellus. Called **Joyous Way** when it was under the rule of a cabal of shape-changers. Unable to trust faces, the population engages in an extensive and intrusive unhindered neurotelepathy, has fought several nerve wars to become the foremost expert at the grisly art of brain-deception, and disdains to use any physical weapons. Dominant population is Joys.

MLO 4 in Scorpius [a.k.a. HR 6426]—**Horrific Vision of Nagual**

A hybrid of Scholar, Fox, and Myrmidons called Nagual rule the world, able to plunder both mental information and biological outward forms from each other, are kept in check only by submission to a horrific and remorseless caste of robotic peacekeepers called the Taloi, who, because they can neither kill nor imprison the fluid population of Nagual, enforce discipline by tortures inflicted without warning, trial, or appeal.

HR 7722 in Capricorn—**Preceptor Joachim Voor's World**

Indulges in a fanatical aversion to cliometry. Early on, the Voorishmen believed selecting the committee of Voivodes by lottery would render predictions impossible. Unfortunately, the Voivode terraforming and patropic authorities, selected at random, were riven by rivalry: in consequence, the fauna of Voor's World is famed for its sickly appearance and comical ungainliness. There is said to be no fair and wholesome thing on the globe, except for Nymphs and she-Sylphs the Voivodes import for their display harems.

HR 511 in Cassiopeia—**New Seed**

Ecological errors allowed semi-intelligent edible fungi variant to replace all plant life and fill all possible plant life niches, including orchid forms that root in the human and animal hair of all mammals. Making a pastime of necessity, gardeners coif and crossbreed their hair infections to ever more alluring and provocative designs.

12 Ophiuchi—**Dust**

Anarcho-Contractual world governed by Swan posterity called Anarchs, ruling over a more cohesive race, descended from Hormagaunts, called Aberrants. All buildings are temporary, towers constructed into fantastic and eerie shapes by electrostatic cohesion, made out of the ubiquitous surface dust. The local flora are airborne spoors and high-altitude clouds of photosynthesizing plant-animals that drip manna.

Variable star.

Gamma Leporis—**Broceliande**

A low-gravity world famed for the height and beauty of its trees. By ancient law, all tree breeds must be based on terrestrial precedent. Weather control is placed strictly under the control of the forest-mind, regardless of human concerns.

This is the sole world where the human and Myrmidon colonists continued in the Feudalism of the Golden Lords long after the rest of the Empyrean had fallen into disunion and darkness. The Inquisition successfully prevented any Foxes or Patricians from abolishing the Golden hierarchy.

Fomalhaut—**Plenary Triumph**

Surrounded by a circumstellar disk. Fomalhaut, K-type star TW Piscis Austrini, and M-type star LP 876-10 constitute a trinary system.

The world is a featureless ice ball, eight times the size of Earth and twice the mass, whose ice contains traces of a previous nonhuman civilization from Theta Tauri in Hyades. Note that Lares in the 38th Millennium hails from here.

Plenary Triumph was terraformed into a globe holding twelve pentagonal continents of Earth life surrounded by twenty hexagonal continents of native ice, each pentagon holding a circular crater sea of precisely the same size and volume as all other seas. In the gnomons between the seashore and the rigidly perfect lines of ice wall severing native from Earth-like life, grow the gardens, self-aware farming zones, and treasure cities of the Triumphants.

The Triumphants are famed for their dueling custom, which allows for single combat but not warfare. Hence, to fight their wars, one champion would be outfitted with cybernetic power armor of absurd splendor, larger than a battleship, and go trample the houses and towers, groves and gardens of the enemy, until met and halted by a champion in panoply of like weight and power.

THIRD SWEEP 37ᵗʰ Millennium

58 Eridani—**Neodamode**

A highly militarized and organized society known for its peaceful, disciplined, and highly industrious populations.

Rho Cancri [a.k.a. 55 Cancri]—**Sciritaea**

A highly militarized and organized society riven by continual tumults, intrigues, and civil wars.

47 Ursae Majoris—**Vital Delectation**

The Delectables maintain a vicious custom of dueling, assassination, small-scale warfare, and ghost worship. The rumor that their women are raised as beasts and not taught language until captured and tamed during courtship is absurd and false.

83 Leonis—**Uttaranchal**

The society is variegated into extremely fine nuances of a biotechnological caste system so that each family and each individual within the family knows his exact degree of rank. Ruled by the ghosts of the original two surviving settlers, from whom all populations are descended. Immigrants not adopted into the family are enslaved.

Alpha Mensae—**Land of Hungry Needle-Necked Wraiths**

Despite the name, a pleasant world of perfumed glades, cheerful lakes, and mountains carved into cathedrals and ziggurats. Famed for its hanging gardens.

18 Scorpii—**Unsuit**

Ruled by the descendants of the original terraformers, who keep the landscape so delicately tuned, that all houses with walls are outlawed.

Epsilon Reticuli—**Determined Endpoint Project**

Ruled by a ruthless caste called Fiduciaries. Children are born in debt and must earn manumission from their parents.

44 Boötis—**Schattenreich** and **Rime**

Schattenreich is a hemisphere of erosion-flattened hills opposite a hemisphere of deep and tideless waters. It is famed for its ghost population, which far outnumbers its living and are malign.

Rime is a cold and light-gravity world, adorned with natural ice towers. Flocculent Man, descended from the Hibernals of Yule, have ousted all other races, except that the Reticents from Xi Boötis who occupy spires and mountains through nerve-war praxis have imposed a set of geas rather than laws. The geas forbids no deeds nor acts, but instead certain mental states, as vulgarity, waggish familiarity, and peevishness. The Reticents are Hierophants famed for their obsessive self-reliance and myriad tradesman personalities crowding their psyches, giving them competence at every art, science, and profession.

Arcturus [a.k.a. Alpha Boötis]—**Nightspore**

A rare case of double colonization: populations were deracinated from Euphrasy of Xi Boötis and from Joyous of Beta Canum Venaticorum.

Torn during its early days in civil war between Shapingmen (Joys who favored pantropy dwell in the south) and Crystalmen (Reticent terraformers dwell in the north) the Nightsporeans have created two equal and opposed biospheres (*Muspel*-life and *Niffle*-life), no creature nor plant of which consumes nor is consumed by the other. Summer Kings rose to power here and have since attempted to quell the ferocious earthquakes and vast, malign tempests and tornadoes, but with limited success. Cities and towns are particularly vulnerable to weather-control sieges and retaliations, and so have been outlawed. The system of semi-independent multiple specialized mental functions called *internals* was developed here.

51 Pegasi—**Chrysaor**

A utopian world of fertile fields, small cottages, hedges, canals, eight-sided windmills. Vegetarianism and strict *ahimsa,* absolute nonviolence to all living things, remain from the harsh terraforming regime of the early Myrmidon settlers.

85 Pegasi—**Geryon**

A hell-world of boiling oceans, volcanoes, rocky archipelagos. Originally ruled by shape-takers whose women were lobotomized at birth and used only as breeding livestock, the repugnance of these customs persuaded the Starfarers Guild to assign assassins to destroy their leadership. The assassins learned the art of shape-taking and blended so well with the natives that no one was aware when the last native was killed and replaced. The endless and anarchic war of all against all has achieved a cliometric halt-state and cannot foreseeably be resolved.

Rasalhague—**Penance**

A planet famous for its abundance of gems and geodes, many of which are unobtainable elsewhere in human space. The Penitent adopted a rigorous system of asceticism to prevent their wealth from corrupting them.

Gamma Pavonis—**To Prevail**

Colonized by Splendor of Delta Pavonis. The Prevalent retain the strict hierarchic culture of the ancient Splendids.

FOURTH SWEEP 53rd Millennium

Regulus [a.k.a. Alpha Leonis]—**Here Be Monsters**

A vegetarian world with no fauna at all. Cannibalism frequent among the aristocracy. An odd custom is that all boy children are raised blind until a mate is selected for him so that the first sight he sees is his bride. Dominant race is Anthropovores.

Zeta Leporis—**Svartalfheim**

Atmosphere entirely black and opaque. Famed for its thick and dense asteroid belts, remnants of several exploded gas giants.

Hamal [a.k.a. Alpha Arietis]—**Mystery of the Second Creation**

Predominant race is Seers from **We See a Strange Dawn**.

HR 2622 in Monoceros—**Qailertetang**

The most ambitious project of terraforming known: a molten world cooled by terraforming to pleasant subarctic conditions. Ruled by a cabal of weather-control architects called Winter Queens.

Gliese 31.5 in Tucana—**Shumisen**, also called **Mountain of the Lovely Peach Trees**

This world has never known war or murder. All children are subdued by a program of addiction to soothing drugs and electronic signals. The population is preoccupied with intrigues revolving around a set of worldwide cybernetic dreamscapes. Roughly one-fourth of the population eventually succumbs to some form of assisted suicide due to associative disorders. Cliometry indicates this is a halt-state.

Pi Mensae—**Onwardness**

A world where human emotion had been outlawed except on Sabbath days. The local gas giant planet interrupts the habitable zone, producing alarming tides and quakes.

Zubenelgenubi [a.k.a. Alpha Librae]—**Aaru**, also called the **Field of Reeds**

Terraformed eccentrically, with a single river reaching from pole to pole. The northern hemisphere is the debris of an interplanetary collision and has not yet settled into spherical shape. The sole source of oxygen-nitrogen atmosphere comes from river plankton, and so the airs outside the single long river valley are inhospitable. Inhabited by Giants, Nicors, Foxes, ruled by the ghosts of the original colonists.

Xi Scorpius—**Bloody Water Poisoned Air**

As the name implies, terraformed poorly. The gravity is high, and the Bloods have been modified to withstand it: they spend their afternoons in highly salted baths.

HIP 12961—**Land of the Young**

Dreaded Immortalist colony. It is rumored that any traveler departing from the local Forever Village is treated against his will and cannot thereafter die.

FIFTH or PETTY SWEEP 66th Millennium

HIP 10301 in Eridanus—**Perioecium**

A highly militarized and disciplined population. Known for their living garments, symbiosis of Myrmidon material to specially adapted skin cells in the Timocrat caste.

Epsilon Virginis [a.k.a. Vindemiatrix]—**Feast of Stephen**

Saint Agnes and **Saint Wenceslaus** are remnants of the same shattered gas giant which formed Feast of Stephen. All three worlds are in an unusual equilateral triangle orbit. Whether this is a primary with two giant moons or a triple planet body is a matter of semantics. The two moons were terraformed. Predominant race is Loricates.

Gliese 1137 in Antlia—**Terra Pericolosa**
Predominate race here is Monsters. The oceans were improperly terraformed and contain venom. Water is used as currency, and strangers are killed and sent to the extraction press.

SAO 214963 in Phoenix [a.k.a. HR 6]—**World of Willows and Flowers**
Binary suns. A garden world of immortals plagued by deadly anthropophagic flowers, ferns, and lianas, poisonous willows, and malign pines. Foxes established a totalitarian monarchy and restored humanity to all non-orthogonal and mechanized races.

Kappa Coronae Borealis—**Aerecura**
The pantropy here is unique, with larval humans living in mines as apprentices, who undergo metamorphosis to upright nocturnal sexless drones at journeyman rank and as masters are transformed again to diurnal creatures, male or female. There is a dead Potentate in orbit, the remnant of a failed attempt to elevate their moon, whose whispers disturb the dreams of the unshielded.

Iota Draconis [a.k.a. Eldsich]—**Torment**
Colonized from Nightspore of Arcturus.
　　Torment orbits the superjovian Wormwood, which stands at 13 AU and has a year 194 Earth years long, in a highly eccentric orbit. The surface becomes uninhabitable for 22 Earth years during its wintertide. The population tends to be of a melancholy nature, and the sight of the ruins of the previous civilizations that once inhabited the planet does not reassure them. Torment is an antiquarian world, preserving many races extinct elsewhere. The world was originally named **Septfoil**.

BEYOND 100 Lightyears

These worlds were settled not by a sweep, but voluntarily

Achernar—**Orphan**
The single heavenly body orbiting Achernar. At 144 lightyears, it is the furthest human colony. It is also the only colony established by humans independently of Dominion forced settlement. Settled from Nocturne between the Second and Third Sweep, the hedonistic Laiacists and the strict

and zealous Followers still maintain an ancient racial separation, with the Followers dominant. The Followers maintain loyalty to a very ancient religion, and worship a god called Kamisama-no-Miko.

Pulcherrima [a.k.a. Epsilon Boötis]—Houristan

There are persistent rumors of an even further colony, at 210 lightyears, circling Epsilon Boötis called Houristan, populated entirely by young and nubile women, who reproduce by cloning, where the rivers run with wine and the road are paved with gold—as best human science can tell, this epicurean space utopia has no basis in fact.